*The Silken Cage*

# The Silken Cage

## SOPHIE DANSON

Black Lace novels are sexual fantasies.
In real life, make sure you practise safe sex.

First published in 1994 by
Black Lace
332 Ladbroke Grove
London
W10 5AH

Typeset by TW Typesetting, Plymouth, Devon
Printed and bound in Great Britain by
Cox & Wyman Ltd, Reading, Berks

ISBN 0 352 32928 9

# Chapter One

'*A*nd Tony ...'

The young man with the golden-brown hair turned on his heel, his expression at once roguish and questioning.

'Yes?'

'If I don't get a draft of that third chapter by the end of next week, you're for the high jump. No second chances – understood?'

Tony grinned, his open face full of the unthinking confidence of one who has not yet encountered failure, his lean, eager body a testimony to the unfailing biological optimism of youth.

'You'll have it by next Thursday, I promise. You know me, Maria – if need be I'll stay up all night.'

I bet you will, thought Maria to herself as Tony Fitzhardinge swaggered off across the quadrangle, his hands thrust deep into the pockets of his well-cut trousers. Her lips twitched into a reluctant smile as she appraised the clean, muscular lines of his athletic body; wholesome but distinctly appetising in his crisp cricket whites.

How many pretty innocents had surrendered to the lure of that firm young body after a romantic afternoon on the river and a cheap dinner at the Varsity Restaurant? How many more had fallen for that easy-going charm, never once suspecting the razor-sharp intelligence behind the permanent smile? Stay up all night? Maria didn't doubt it for one second. What she did doubt was that he'd be working on his thesis.

Maria hadn't succumbed to Tony's charm – at least not yet – though he had tried every trick in the book to win her over: flowers, champagne, even the invitation to spend a long weekend at his politician father's country house in Oxfordshire. She had to admire his perseverance. If he spent half as much time and effort researching his PhD thesis as he did on trying to get her into bed, he'd be heading for academic distinction, not the threat of being sent down in disgrace.

Reaching the other side of First Court, Tony disappeared through the ancient archway which led to the porter's lodge and a short passageway opening out onto the busy Cambridge thoroughfare beyond. Even in May, King's Parade would be crowded with gaggles of foreign tourists, their eyes glinting with a manic determination to photograph absolutely everything – whether they knew what it was or not.

Unquestioning ignorance annoyed Maria Treharne more than anything else. A lecturer in philosophy and women's studies at St Alcuin's College, Cambridge for the past three years, her naturally combative nature had brought her into conflict with the College and University authorities on numerous occasions.

The trouble was, the Academic Board was still packed with stuffed shirts who ought to have retired years ago. No doubt some of them would be delighted to see the back of her too – but Maria Treharne had never had any intention of leaving. From the moment she'd first walked through the door of the Master's office, she had set her sights on a Fellowship, and now, after three years of hard work, that goal was at last in sight. In its six-hundred-year history, St Alcuin's had had only four women Fellows, and Maria was determined to be the fifth.

She walked across the narrow, enclosed stone bridge that led from First Court to King's Court. Looking out through windows in the ornate stonework, she could see the river glittering below, sunlit and inviting. A punt slid under the bridge and she recognised a party of post-grads from Fitzwilliam; two strong, massively-built rugby players and their petite, giggly girlfriends.

'No, Gavin, don't! You'll push me in!' The blonde girl was perched precariously at the back of the punt, ineffectually jabbing the punt-pole into the greyish, swirling water. The darker-haired of the lads was kneeling up on the floor of the punt, stroking a hand up her leg as she fought to keep her balance. Maria noticed that the girl's skirt was wet and sticking to her, revealing the outline of bare, slim thighs.

'Don't worry, I've got hold of you. You're quite safe with me.' His hand slid a little higher up the girl's thigh, and Maria imagined it making contact with the damp, cotton-covered mound of her sex, smoothing over the fabric, eager fingers feeling for an entrance to the burning heart of her desire. He was holding the girl quite tightly now, one hand supporting her at the waist whilst the other disappeared up underneath her skirt. 'There – that feels better, doesn't it? Why don't you just relax and let me . . ?'

The punt slid away downriver into the golden haze of the afternoon, and Maria gave a nostalgic sigh as she walked on. Life was so much simpler when you were a student. For a start, you didn't have people like David Armstrong-Baker to contend with. Armstrong-Baker was Chairman of the Appointments Board, and the champion of all pains in the arse. At the end of the day, it all came down to the fact that he just didn't like women – except in bed – and of course this had led to tension between him and Maria ever since she'd arrived at St Alcuin's from unfashionable Liverpool. What's more, after her spirited performance on television the other evening, things weren't going to get any easier.

The invitation to take part in the late-night youth programme *Now!* had come as something of a surprise to Maria. It seemed they were doing a special on alternative religion in Britain, and needed someone from the fringe, as they put it. Never a shrinking violet, Maria had been quite happy to go on and chat about her long involvement with Wicca, and all in all, she felt it had gone rather well. The problem was she'd got a little carried away and said more than she'd meant to – so Armstrong-Baker was bound to have a few well-chosen words to say to her on the subject.

Maria reached the doorway to her staircase, and scanned the name-board to see who was at home. At least that creep Terry Kestelman wasn't around, so there was no risk of a farrago of double-entendres from him. Flicking across her own marker from 'out' to 'in', she climbed the spiral staircase to the second floor, where she had her set of rooms.

Before she had even reached the landing she saw Anthea standing outside her room, scribbling something on a scrap of paper. When she saw Maria she screwed up the paper and dropped it on the floor.

'At last! I thought you'd never show up. I've been waiting ages.'

'What's up?' demanded Maria breathlessly, struggling up the last few stairs. The sooner she got her Fellowship the better – they'd have to give her a half-decent set of rooms on the ground floor then.

Arms folded, Anthea regarded her with a look of amazement.

'You're a cool customer, Maria Treharne.'

Maria fiddled in her pocket for the room key and jabbed it into the lock.

'I'm not with you.'

'That TV programme on Wednesday night! You went a bit far, didn't you? Don't tell me you haven't heard what Armstrong-Baker's saying? It's all round College.'

Maria pushed open the door and they went inside, closing the door behind them. She dropped her pile of books into the cavernous depths of a tatty old armchair, then flopped down onto the sofa.

'Go on, surprise me.'

4

'Samantha only heard him telling the Chaplain he thought it was "extremely inappropriate", one of St Alcuin's lecturers going on TV and talking openly about paganism.'

Maria shook her head.

'Oh, come on. He's been telling people I'm "inappropriate" ever since I got here.' She laughed drily. 'I mean – a young female lecturer from a red-brick university, and a practising pagan at that: it's not quite the done thing, is it?'

Anthea plumped herself down on the sofa beside Maria.

'Anyway, the last I heard he was saying he wanted to see you about it – there's probably one of his famous memos in your pigeonhole by now.'

'He can write all the memos he likes, but he knows I'm not going to shut up just to please him.'

'So you don't think he's serious, then?'

'Of course he's serious, but there's damn-all he can do about it. And you'll never believe this – the Master's wife rang me up this morning, to tell me how much she and the Master had enjoyed the programme! "Most enlightening and forward-thinking", that's what she said.'

Anthea's concerned expression relaxed a fraction, and she leaned towards Maria, her voice hushed with excitement.

'You certainly opened my eyes,' she remarked. 'And as for all that stuff you said about ritual sex . . . I mean, I know it's none of my business, but do you really *do* all that stuff . . ?'

Maria laughed.

'Yes, of course I do. We all do – occasionally. It's part of the Wicca religion we follow, but it's not something that happens very often, we just use it to empower specially important rituals. Sex is the most potent source of magical energy, you know – it helps put us more closely in touch with the Mother-goddess.'

Anthea sprawled back on the sofa, her long thin legs stretched out and her head thrown back. Her face wore a child's expression of mischievous wonder.

'I bet you enjoy it, though,' she said.

'Sometimes, sometimes not.' Maria's smile was serenely unruffled. 'Anyway, enjoying it is hardly the point. It's the end result that really matters.'

Anthea chuckled.

'So it's not as good as with Jonathan, then?'

Maria sighed. Little shivers ran over her skin like an ice-cool mountain stream as she thought of him: his strong hands; his slim, muscular hips; the taste of his sweat on her tongue as she kissed her way down his belly towards the blossoming stalk of his manhood. She would be seeing him again tonight, and together they would play all the wicked, blissful little games she so loved to play. Already she imagined that she could feel his touch on her as his fingers let down the knot of her long, chestnut hair; as his lips pressed softly into the smooth sweep of her neck.

In her mind's eye they were already together. Jonathan Gresham's supple young fingers were slip-sliding over her flesh, warm and slippery with bath-oil, and swiftly finding the secret entrance to the heart of her pleasure. She smiled as she gave Anthea her honest reply:

'*Nothing*'s as good as that.'

The presence of the Earth-spirit was all around Anthony Pendorran. He could feel it bubbling up inside him, like molten lava in a volcano, as it always did when something very special and significant was about to happen. He let the feeling possess him; for time was short, and there were questions which must be answered. Questions of life and death.

He stood atop Brackwater Tor, with the old house behind him and, before him in the far distance, the long, grey line where turbulent sea met tumbling sky at the margin of the north Cornish moors. Between and below lay the village of Lynmoor: a few narrow roads crisscrossing, then fading out into a straggling collection of cottages, flung like a stray handful of pebbles across the valley floor.

There was a savage chill in the May breeze that cut across the moors, chasing away the last of the clouds and blowing Pendorran's long, dark hair away from his face, throwing his strong features into relief. Pendorran was a striking man, tall and slim, with raven-black hair and eyes that gleamed a wild sea-grey against the skin of his wind-tanned face. His aquiline profile and bright eyes gave him the appearance of some aristocratic bird of prey; beautiful but with a dangerous beauty.

With the silver-tipped toe of his boot, he described a small circle in the dirt, then knelt at its centre. He shut his eyes and raised them to the sun, so that its light glowed a warm blood-crimson through his closed eyelids as he made his supplication.

Today the power was swift to answer him. Already he could feel it humming and vibrating in his head, spreading down to fill his whole body, summoning and centring every ounce of his spiritual energy, until at last the power began to awaken his desire.

Eyes still closed, he let his right hand move to the front of his tight black leather trousers. It rested there, unmoving, for a few moments, and as his fingers met smooth leather, and the rougher inner surface of his trousers rubbed deliciously on the bare skin of his phallus, he savoured the harmony of flesh on leather and leather on flesh.

Pleasure was beginning to enter his mind and body, but pleasure was not his goal. As Pendorran unzipped his trousers and slid in his hand to cup the full globes of his testicles, a picture began to form in his head; the intriguing portrait of a woman with long, dark-red hair, a woman filled with pride and defiance. He sent out his spirit to her, trying to make contact; but her soul still seemed to be resisting him, denying the power he sensed within and around her.

Yet he knew she must be the one. He had seen and felt her strength. There could be none other but she.

Slowly he began to touch himself, stroking the swollen shaft of his penis until it ached for release. He was calling out to her in the silence of his thoughts, willing her to come to him. In his mind he could see her very clearly now. She was walking towards him, barefoot on the grass, her green-brown eyes filled with a questioning apprehension as they met his gaze, and her long, burnished hair fluttering and dancing about her face as the wind caught it.

As she came closer he saw that she was naked under the gauzy, many-coloured wrap she was holding about her. He glimpsed the full swell of her breasts beneath, bobbing and quivering as she moved, and the creamy whiteness of her flesh as she stepped forward, letting the thin veil slide away, revealing the long, smooth sweep of her thigh. Trembling, he felt the scorch and burn of desire as he had never felt it before; his mouth was dry with arousal and his cock-tip slippery-wet between his fingers.

Now she was only a breath away – so close that he knew he had only to reach out and touch her. And how he wanted to touch her, longed to know how it would feel to have her skin against his fingertips, against his swollen manhood. The fingers of his right hand were still curled about his shaft, working it with long, smooth strokes; but he stretched out his left hand and instantly felt the warm silkiness of the woman's bare arm.

As Pendorran watched her, entranced, she smiled at him; suddenly opening her arms very wide so that the filmy wrap fluttered open, offering him the sacrament of her nakedness. She did not speak, but he could read the doubt and the desire in her beautiful eyes.

He soared with her into the embrace of his dream; a vision now grown so real that the mundane reality of the earth beneath him no longer even existed. She was yielding to him at last, and he was smoothing a blood-warm, scented oil over her breasts, her nipples as hard as hot iron beneath the palm of his hand. The power was so strong today, the spirit-joining so complete, that he could breathe in the sweet flower-scent of her skin, feel the oil slide under his fingertips as he smoothed it down over her breasts and belly and flanks.

8

Her arms enfolded him and she sank to the cloud-soft earth, drawing him down on top of her so that they were belly to belly, mouth to mouth. He kissed her, and her breath tasted of cinnamon and honeysuckle, spicy and sweet. His tongue toyed with hers, and in the unfettered time and space of his dream their bodies writhed and rolled on soft grass, quite oblivious to the inclement wind cutting across Lynmoor from the distant sea.

The wanting burned within Pendorran like an insatiable thirst. He felt himself beginning to melt into her, longing to drown in her desire, as the tip of his manhood darted unerringly to the heart of her sex and slipped between those twin, silky thighs.

Flower-soft, she had opened to him at last, the last traces of her resistance ebbing away; and it seemed to Pendorran that he and she had together transcended the material dimension. He no longer possessed any separate, individual identity, any bond with the reality that surrounded him; for he had entered her world. Their existences were one, their life-forces melded into a single whole in which only the most exquisite, irresistible pleasure belonged. His mind was filled with the scent of honeysuckle, his senses overwhelmed almost to the point of pain. And still he saw those clear, green-brown eyes, gazing into the deepest heart of him, pleading with him for understanding.

Together their spirits danced towards ecstasy, and as his fingers summoned up his climax, Pendorran once again felt the awesome power of the Earth-spirit tear and burn through him; a mighty force that shook him and left him frail and trembling, his thoughts filled with the single word written in flame across his soul:

Maria.

# Chapter Two

*P*atsy Polgarrow put her arms round her lover's neck and felt a surge of indignation as he tensed and pulled away.

'It ain't no use, Patsy,' said Geraint dully. 'You won't get round me like that. Why don't you just pack up an' go home? I'm no use to you like this.'

Patsy sighed. She was used to Geraint's fluctuating moods, but this episode of gloom was lasting longer than she'd bargained for. On this sun-filled May morning, it felt like a crime to be depressed. She tried a different approach.

'It's a lovely mornin', don't you think? Summer's comin', you can feel it in the air. We could go out onto the moors like we used to – you remember, don't you? To our special place, where no one can see what we get up to . . .'

'Go away and leave me alone,' said Geraint flatly. 'I told you, I ain't in the mood.'

'You just think you ain't, 'cos you're a bit down,' soothed Patsy.

She sat down on the floor at the foot of Geraint's chair, her legs curled up underneath her, and gazed up at him, silently pleading with him to look at her, to want her. With the top two buttons of her casual shirt unfastened and the neckline artfully arranged, he had only to glance down for an unrivalled view of her large, unfettered breasts; but today he seemed scarcely to notice that she was there.

This was a source of annoyance and frustration to Patsy. The sun was shining, the sap was rising, and Patsy Polgarrow couldn't help but feel the hunger-cravings within her getting stronger, every time she looked at her lover.

Fit and muscular, with weather-tanned skin that seemed to glow with health, Geraint was the only man Patsy had ever truly wanted. Oh, she'd had a few others – mainly just to spite Geraint when he strayed a little too far from her bed – but it was Geraint she'd always wanted, and she had no intention of letting anyone else steal him from her.

They'd been inseparable since they were kids, and secretly Patsy had always known Geraint was hers for keeps. She might get mad at him sometimes, but really it didn't matter who else he bedded, who else he ran with for a while – in the end he'd always come back to her, because only Patsy Polgarrow knew him intimately enough to give him everything he wanted. On top of that she was a better than average-looking girl, well-nigh insatiable sexually, and not nearly as stupid as Geraint might imagine she was. All in all, Patsy liked to think there wasn't anything he needed that she couldn't supply in ample quantities.

Not easily daunted, she snuggled her body between Geraint's parted thighs, resting her hand on his jeans-clad knee, but he scarcely responded to the advance.

'What's the matter, sweetheart?' she asked. 'Someone been gettin' at you, have they?'

She slid her nimble fingers very lightly up the well-muscled inner surface of his thigh, stopping an inch or two short of the generous swell that always made her dizzy with excitement just to look at it. Whenever she thought of the fat pink serpent slumbering between Geraint's thighs, Patsy knew that she would forgive him anything – even his habitual infidelities.

11

The whole village of Lynmoor knew about Patsy and Geraint, and had long since stopped asking questions about their strange relationship. So what if Geraint liked to think he had a *droit de seigneur* over every woman and girl in Lynmoor? So what if he and Patsy spent half their time having passionate sex, and the other half throwing plates at each other? Whose business was it if Patsy chose to let him get away with any and every indiscretion? It might seem like a peculiar arrangement to some, but it had always worked for them. The only trouble was, it didn't seem to be working very well at the moment.

Mind you, Patsy had a shrewd idea of what was wrong. These last few weeks, Geraint had been uncomfortably short of work, money, and girls. His father – a local farmer – had rented out several of his bigger fields, and consequently only needed Geraint to help out two days a week. In the rural communities of north Cornwall, work was hard to come by at the best of times, even with the summer coming up. Only the most determined and enterprising tourists ever made it as far as Lynmoor, and there was precious little for them when they got there. The nearest middle-sized town was a good fifty miles away. Geraint was taking it all very badly – these last few days, he'd spent most of his time slumped in a battered old armchair, staring into empty space.

'You don't want to worry,' purred Patsy, in her most seductive voice. 'You've got me.'

She rested her blonde head on his knee, and this time he did not tense. Encouraged, Patsy let her skilful fingers toy once again with the inner surface of his thigh, and at last she felt him relax just a little – very reluctantly at first, then with an almost inaudible growl of real pleasure, as she set about planting a trail of little kisses all over his denim-clad thighs.

A little thrill of triumph quivered through her as she felt his hand stray from his lap to her shoulder, toying with tendrils of curly, bottle-blonde hair that had escaped from her pony-tail. She reached up and slipped off the blue satin scrunchie, so that her tousled curls came tumbling down in bright disarray. Geraint's hand dived into the thick mass of her hair, gently but eagerly twisting it around his fingers, savouring its springy texture.

On a whim, she took hold of his other hand and guided it to her lips. Heart pounding, she began kissing it, running her tongue-tip over the palm then taking each finger in turn into the warm cavern of her mouth. With a truly sensual enjoyment, she amused herself by winding her long, versatile tongue around his index finger as though it were a miniature penis.

Her inventiveness proved a great success, and she felt a little shudder of response as the full force of the mingled sensations hit Geraint, once again irresistible in their power. Inwardly she smiled; this, at least, never failed. She'd seen it once in a film and taken very careful notes. Geraint just loved to have his fingers sucked – perhaps because it reminded him of just how good Patsy was at sucking cocks.

He murmured appreciatively as Patsy aimed his index finger between her lips and slid it into her mouth, making it disappear right down to the knuckle.

'You've got the devil in those lips, Patsy Polgarrow.'

She did not reply, but sucked and licked him more assiduously, sliding her free hand up the inside of Geraint's thigh until the fingertips were just brushing the deliciously hard swelling in his pants. As she watched, it seemed to her that the sleeping serpent awoke and began to uncoil, pushing its lively head against the inside of Geraint's work-worn jeans, eager to escape from its constricting prison.

Too long the passive partner, Geraint withdrew his hand from Patsy's lips and seized her soft, welcoming body in his strong arms, drawing her up until she was leaning over him, then crushing her lips against his. His tongue forced its way between her lips and darted into her mouth – it was a serpent's tongue, quick and strong

13

and so, so lascivious. The violence of his kiss took her breath away, and she felt her head reel with a wonderfully intoxicating dizziness. Instantly she remembered why it was that, no matter what he did, she always forgave Geraint all his transgressions. How could you not forgive a man who made you feel as good as this?

Stretched taut between her thighs, the gusset of Patsy's panties was moist with her own fragrant juices – juices that were instantly replenished and renewed as Geraint reached up and fumbled with the front of the old torn cotton shirt she was wearing.

'How the hell do I get into this?' he muttered, fiddling and pulling at the buttons. 'Anyone'd think you were tryin' to put me off.' Then, giving up the struggle and hungry to enjoy the delights within, he simply took hold of the front of the shirt and ripped it open, tearing off the buttons and exposing the irresistibly voluptuous, deliciously bare breasts within. 'Oh my God, Patsy, how come you do this to me every damn time . . ?'

His words were a groan of intense need; the expression of an impetuous hunger that demanded to be satisfied. Anything Geraint might lack in skill as a lover, he more than made up for in enthusiasm. And Patsy adored him for his combination of roughness and gentleness; the eagerness that reminded her of a lusty young animal.

Geraint took hold of Patsy in his strong arms, and hauled her onto his lap, so that she was kneeling astride him, her soft, bare breasts bobbing free on her chest and her thighs spread wide apart. He pressed his face against her warm flesh and began licking her breasts, beginning at the top of her throat and working his way down in crazy circles and drunken spirals that wound their way ever-closer to the throbbing buds of her nipples.

As his lips closed about her right nipple, she threw back her head in a groan of extreme pleasure; it was almost too intense to bear. And this delicious torment would not be the last of it, not by any means. Now that

14

she had roused the full force of Geraint's dormant lust, she must take the consequences. As if answering her thoughts, his bear's-paw hand slipped down her flank and ruched up the hem of her denim skirt. He slid it up over her bare, brown legs to reveal the prominent swelling of her Mount of Venus, made more protuberant still by her sex-swollen pussy-lips, their flesh plump with longing.

The wisps of tawny curl that escaped from the sides of her pink cotton panties were surely enough to convince any other man that Patsy was no natural-born blonde, but Geraint wanted to explore the hypothesis a little further, and he rummaged in the hip-pocket of his jeans for his penknife, expertly flicking open the blade between finger and thumb.

Patsy's eyes widened in slight alarm as he lowered the penknife and positioned its tip between her outspread thighs.

'Geraint! What do you think you're . . ?'

A second later she felt its cold blade touch the skin of her upper thigh as he slit through first one side of her panties, then the other. Then he pulled the useless scrap of pink cotton out from between her thighs and pressed it to his face, deeply inhaling the overpowering fragrance of her quim-juice, heady and utterly intoxicating.

Letting the screwed-up ball of cotton fall onto the floor, he pulled Patsy closer to him and kissed her again, her hardened nipples pressing again and again against the rough fabric of his denim shirt. When he let her escape from the kiss she was gasping for breath, but he had no intention of giving her any time to compose herself. That would only spoil the fun. And Patsy was just as keen as he was not to let the moment pass – he knew her every bit as well as she knew him. When all was said and done, and you left love well and truly out of it, they fucked well together.

Patsy – reluctant to take on quite such a passive role – found herself overwhelmed by sensations as Geraint's probing finger explored the outer margins of her brown-fringed love-lips with lewd satisfaction. She wasn't often given to fanciful imaginings, but as he teased and tormented her maiden-curls, she almost thought she could see swirling patterns of colour in her head – colours as bright and as vivid as the raging, pulsing desire she felt inside. All at once, garrulous Patsy, who was always being told to shut up, found herself inarticulate and overwhelmed. Nothing but meaningless sounds of pleasure escaped from her lips:

'Oh, oh, oh . . .'

Geraint slipped his finger between Patsy's pouting vulval lips, suddenly finding that he had tapped a reservoir of sweet honeydew that made his cock strain once more for release from its cruel imprisonment.

'Unzip me, Patsy love,' he gasped, as his finger sought out the tiny, diamond-hard love-button he knew so well, and began exerting a rough, but well-judged, pressure on it. Patsy moaned and writhed in his grasp, so overcome by her own need that she was barely conscious of his request. In exasperation, Geraint grabbed hold of her hand and placed it on his zipper, forcing her to take hold of the tag and slide it down.

Suddenly aware of what she was doing, Patsy looked down through the mist of her desire and saw the pinkness of male flesh appear as the zipper slid downwards, exposing Geraint's stiff, bare cock. He quite often chose not to wear underpants – he always said how he loved the feeling of tight denim against his bare flesh. And now Patsy had the delight of seeing that beautiful, spitting serpent emerging from its prison, its single eye glistening with a diamond-drop of venom as it surveyed its victim, preparing to strike.

The upward-curving spike of Geraint's manhood seemed to beckon to her, and her fingers moved from the zipper at the arc of smooth pink flesh, emerging from a nest of dark-brown curls. As her fingers closed around his cock, Geraint gave a shuddering groan and frigged Patsy harder so that she sobbed with the helpless fear of her pleasure, so overwhelming and so close.

16

Patsy tried thinking cold, unexciting, unsexy thoughts to make the feeling go away. She didn't want to come now, not yet. She wanted to make it last much longer, it would be better then. But the heat was in her and Geraint's finger on her love-button was inexorable and pitiless.

She squirmed from side to side, trying to evade his merciless caresses. But Geraint didn't want her to escape, and his other hand was over hers now, making her wank him. Her captive fingers moved rapidly up and down his shaft so that his foreskin slipped back and forth over his cock-head. With each stroke his strong hand forced her to rub him harder and faster, exerting greater pressure on her burgeoning bud and making her dance faster too. She was jiggling her body to and fro on his rough fingertip, bringing herself off; though she wanted to stop, just for a moment, to make it last . . .

Orgasm crashed over her, drowning her in wave after wave of brutal, neon-bright ecstasy that left her weak and trembling.

'Geraint, please . . . wait. I need to . . .'

But Geraint was offering her no respite. She had begun the game and now he was hungry for his own gratification. Besides, he knew that was what she wanted too; he could see the hunger in her eyes. One orgasm was never enough for Patsy Polgarrow. Even before the last spasms of her pleasure had died away, he put his hands about her waist and lifted her onto his upraised prick, sliding her down onto him with a delicious violence that made her cry out for more.

The old armchair creaked and groaned under their combined weight as Patsy used her strong thighs to raise herself a few delicious inches, then pump back down, ramming the skin-tight sheath of her sex-lips down over his prick, her wetness anointing him like some sacred unguent that both soothed and tormented. He craned his head forward and took her nipple into his mouth, sucking on it like a greedy child as she struggled to control the second wave of pleasure that threatened to engulf them both. The second; and the third . . .

Much, much later, in the golden aftermath of their coupling, Patsy lay on Geraint's lap, his arm around her shoulders, his fingers toying with the still-sensitive crest of her nipple.

'Better now?' she murmured.

He chuckled.

'You know all the best medicines, don't you, Patsy? Reckon a man don't need work if he's got a girl like you.'

She snuggled close, flattered and happy.

'Anyhow,' she said, 'I reckon there's goin' to be more work on Lynmoor, just you wait an' see.'

'Says who?'

'Says in the local paper, don't it? Some . . . what d'you call it . . . consortium wants to build a great big leisure complex, right slap bang in the middle of Lynmoor. Big conference centre for the business types, swimmin' pool, the lot.'

Geraint sat up and took notice.

'No kiddin'?'

'They want to start buildin' as soon as they can, so they're bound to want big strong men like you, ain't they?'

'S'pose they just might, at that,' conceded Geraint, reflectively. Today was looking up.

'Who knows?' added Patsy, curling her fingers about Geraint's still-hard shaft. 'Maybe someone will even buy the old house on Brackwater Tor.'

Geraint laughed.

'That old place! Now you really are joking. Nobody in their right mind would want to live in Brackwater Hall.'

Maria emptied the contents of her make-up bag onto the dressing-table with a clatter. She rummaged impatiently for a lipstick in exactly the right shade of red – passionate but not too tarty. She didn't want Jonathan to think she was easy . . . just very, very keen.

She pulled back her long, wavy hair and secured it with clips, carefully patting on foundation with a damp

18

sponge. In term-time she generally didn't have the time or the inclination to take this much trouble over her appearance, but -- marking or no marking -- Jonathan was worth it. They'd only been seeing each other for a few weeks, and yet she felt she already knew him intimately; she understood all the little love-buttons that had to be pressed to make him purr with pleasure. It wasn't like her to get serious about a guy, but Maria was beginning to think she could quite easily get serious about Jonathan Gresham. The fact that he was playing just a little hard to get only served to make the pursuit all the more delicious.

Beside her, on the dressing-table, stood a small incense burner filled with aromatic oil of bergamot, a tiny spirit lamp warming the oil so that its rich, spicy vapours were released into the room, creating an ambience of luxurious sensuality. Maria's knowledge of Wicca lore had taught her to respect the power of the essential oils she used in her rituals. Each perfume held its own inner magic, the secret power to heal, or soothe, or excite; uniting the body and the spirit in a natural harmony.

She fought to stop her hand trembling as she ran a thin line of dark brown eyeliner along her eyelid. A perfectly sensible, experienced, independent woman of twenty-eight shouldn't be nervous about seeing a man. It was ridiculous. But she couldn't stop thinking about the party tonight, living every moment in her imagination, picturing how it would be when she caught sight of Jonathan and he greeted her with the 400-carat smile that made her go weak at the knees. Maybe she was expecting too much, hoping for something that wasn't going to happen? They hadn't made a firm arrangement to meet, it was true, but he had made a point of telling her that he'd be there. He wanted her. She was *sure* he wanted her. Please . . .

Of course, it was still very early days. In fact it was only three weeks and four days since they'd met, that rainy evening at Petra Kovinsky's dinner party.

19

By nine-thirty the place was already crowded to the doors; evidently news of the American's largesse had got all round Cambridge, and the gatecrashers outnumbered the invited guests. Showing her invitation to an uninterested doorman, Maria pushed her way through the crowd, catching incongruous snippets of conversation as she wriggled between the closely-packed bodies.

'My God, Melissa, you should have seen it – bloody terrible, it was.'

'. . . and if she thinks she's going to get a First just because I bedded her a couple of times . . .'

'I need a drink. Get me another drink, Julio.'

Relieved to find a tiny gap in the swirling mob, Maria seized a well-filled glass from a passing waiter's tray. She scanned the room – no sign of Jonathan, but then it was early. Half-hearted disco music was pouring out of a speaker above her head, but there was hardly room to breathe, let alone dance, even if she'd felt like it. And what was the point of dancing on her own?

Something brushed her backside with a lewd deliberateness, jolting her out of her reverie, and she turned round sharply. A familiar voice sent her spirits plummeting.

'Well, well – fancy seeing you here. Bet you came just because you heard I was going to be here, eh? Am I right?'

Maria's heart sank at the sight of Terry Kestelman, his round face beetroot-red with alcohol-induced hilarity.

'Piss off, Terry,' Maria enunciated, very clearly and precisely, projecting her voice above the disco beat.

Terry protested his injured innocence.

'Is that any way to greet a very old and very dear friend?'

'You may be very old, Terry, but you're definitely not my friend.'

Terry ignored this rebuff, and squeezed a little closer, using the teeming crowds as an excuse for a degree of intimacy which Maria found frankly revolting.

'Lovely dress, Maria. Really shows off your assets, it does. Lovely.'

She intercepted his hand in mid-air, fending off the clumsy grope with the sort of weary irritation usually reserved for bluebottles.

'I told you, piss off. I'm waiting for somebody.'

'I know.'

'What do you mean, you know?'

Terry's face split into a filthy grin.

'I know about your little tryst with our friend Jonathan. Very touching. Well-endowed, is he?'

'What?' Maria stared at him in disbelief.

'You want to give me a try sometime, Maria.' He leered and pushed his face into hers. 'You know what they say about men with big noses.'

With difficulty, Maria avoided laughing in his face. Rumour had it that big-nosed Terry Kestelman had a dick like a microdot – but she was in no hurry to find out if the rumour was true. She took a step back, found herself pressed up against the wall, and spat out her exasperation:

'And you know what they say about men who poke their big noses in where they're not wanted,' she snapped, doing her best to ignore him as she nodded a perfunctory greeting to a couple she knew from Grantchester. She fervently hoped they didn't think she was with Terry.

'I just thought you'd want to know about your precious Jonathan, that's all,' sniffed Terry, his shapeless body still disconcertingly close.

'Know what?'

'I saw him this afternoon, and he asked me to tell you he'd wait for you outside.'

'Is he there now?'

'Dunno – he might not be here yet. Now do I get my reward?'

Maria stared back at him stonily, refusing to rise to the bait. All she wanted to do was get to Jonathan. Her body ached for him, her mind sang for the sheer exhilaration of knowing he was out there in the hazy blue of the dusk, waiting for her. All this wasted time . . .

25

She tried to step forward, but Terry stood his ground.

'Look, Terry . . .'

The perennial optimist, Terry reached out a pudgy hand and squeezed a handful of flesh.

'That really is a nice dress, Maria, makes your tits look bigger.'

'Thank you for sharing that with me, Terry. Now will you please let me pass?'

Terry observed her through narrowed eyelids, lizard-like.

'A girl like you, Maria, a girl who wants to get on. A girl like you needs all the friends she can get. Remember, I've just been elected to the Appointments Board. How about a kiss?'

'For God's sake, Terry, will you get out of my fucking way?' Her impatience exploding into rage, she gave him a mighty shove and he tottered backwards a few steps, his expression of lewd infatuation changing to one of surprise.

Pushing her way through the crowds of freeloaders, she headed towards the bar where Marco was busily washing glasses. His eyes followed her with a connoisseur's interest which his staid wife Hannah would certainly not have appreciated; taking in the creamy swell of her breasts, the roundness of her backside, firm and appetising in its second skin of dark-green velvet – so tight that it clearly delineated the deep crease between her buttocks, so short that it offered occasional, tantalising glimpses of her stocking-tops as she walked.

More than one hand seemed to brush deliberately against her backside, her belly and her breasts as she pushed through the throng. It was an exhilarating feeling, as though the whole world wanted to make love to her tonight. That thought alone renewed the familiar sensation of warm wetness between her thighs, the deep-down ache of longing that centred on the rosebud of her clitoris then spread out in long, languid waves through her entire body, making her mouth dry with anticipation, stiffening her nipples into shameless pleasure-crests of need.

She was a sensual woman, a woman with needs. And she was certainly not oblivious to the approving glances. Another time, another place, and she might have abandoned herself to the mischievously sexy little thoughts coursing through her brain. That guy over there, the one with the soft brown eyes and the tight, tight jeans – she could really go for him. And he was looking at her as if to say 'just make the first move and I'll follow'.

But no. Another time, maybe; another place . . .

She turned away, her overheated brain and body in need of fresh air, and pushed open the side door that led to the secluded little garden where Marco's customers sipped their chilled Lambrusco on warm days. The summer visitors loved the garden, particularly as it sloped down to the riverbank, offering great photo-opportunities for the dedicated tourist in search of the ultimate holiday snap. Once a year, regular as clockwork, the *Cambridge Evening News* would report that one of them – the worse for wear after a litre of Marco's house red – had overbalanced and taken an unscheduled swim in the none-too-pristine waters.

As Maria stepped outside, a rush of cool air hit her, and she began shivering, unaccustomed to the relative chill after the sweaty heat of the party. A capricious breeze played across her bare skin, tugging little tendrils of chestnut hair from the securing pins. She looked around her. There didn't seem to be any sign of Jonathan. By now the dusk had faded to a deep royal blue, and it was difficult to make out anything more than dark, looming shapes in the gloom, with the occasional sparkle of white light from the river sliding by at the bottom of the garden. She tried to focus her eyes, peering into the darkening distance, and wishing Marco would switch on the outside lights.

'Jonathan?' she whispered into the semi-darkness. 'Are you there?'

Something rustled in the bushes and she wheeled round, pulling her jacket more tightly round her shoulders. Doubts began to crowd in on her. She wouldn't put it past Terry Kestelman to have been lying to her.

'If that's you, stop playing games!'

She did not hear the footsteps coming towards her across the soft, springy grass, and the sudden embrace made her jump half out of her skin. Strong arms, bare but summer-warm, wrapped themselves tightly around her waist, and suddenly he was behind her, planting passionate kisses on her bare neck.

'Maria! I thought you were never coming.'

'Jon . . .' His name escaped from her lips like a soft sigh of release. It felt so blissful to be in his arms again. Her body needed him, craved its fix of the delicious sensations that only he knew how to coax from her tired, hungry flesh.

'I hope I didn't frighten you,' said Jonathan, pulling her gently round so that she was facing him. Even though her eyes had become more accustomed to the waning light, his face was no more than a silhouette.

'Of course not!' she retorted, recovering some of her composure. 'But why the cloak and dagger stuff?'

Jonathan laughed, his huge hands surprisingly gentle as they smoothed and kneaded the plump swell of her backside. She murmured her satisfaction, and pressed a little closer to him, soothed and excited by the familiar presence of his burgeoning desire which felt hard and impatient against her belly. She fancied that she could feel the energy-pulse of his need, throbbing through to his cock-tip with a quickening beat; or was it just the pounding of her own heart, the surging of the blood as it raced to swell her pouting love-lips?

'I hate parties, don't you?' he remarked, casually running his finger-tip down the crease between Maria's buttocks.

'But I thought . . .'

'Too hot, too noisy, and too many damn people,' he continued, his voice softly suggestive. 'Yes, far too many people. I thought we might have our own little party – just you and me out here, with no one else to disturb us.'

He kissed her again, this time full on the lips, and Maria's head swam; she felt drunk with appetite for him, delirious with excitement, like a teenage virgin with a desperate crush on her teacher. There was nothing mystical or spiritual about her feelings for Jonathan Gresham, she admitted to herself with a start: this was a celebration of gloriously intense physical lust. And perhaps that made it all the better.

She put her hands round his neck and returned his kiss with enthusiasm.

'So where are we going – your place or mine?'

'Neither.' He slid his hands between their bodies, and ran the flat of his thumbs over Maria's nipples, rubbery and erect beneath their slinky velvet covering. 'It's a beautiful night, the stars are coming out . . . Don't you just love making love in the great outdoors?'

'What – here?' Maria was at once thrilled and alarmed, but Jonathan seemed to have no interest in her doubts. He just carried on talking as though she hadn't spoken.

'Yes, of course you do, Maria. I saw you on that TV programme the other night – hell, half of Cambridge did. And when you started going on about having ritual sex in the open air, well, it sort of got me thinking. Made me pretty horny too. Just feel if you don't believe me.'

He took hold of Maria's hand and laid it firmly on the long, slanting baton of his swollen cock.

'That's all for you, Maria – I get hard just *thinking* about you. Have you any idea what you do to me, you . . . you little witch? And when you start talking dirty . . .'

Maria giggled. She didn't need Marco's free wine to get her drunk. This whole, crazy situation was going to her head.

'Listen, Jonathan, I'd love to, really I would, but . . .'

'But what, pumpkin?' He was pinching her nipples between finger and thumb now, his touch lewd and unforgiving.

'But having ritual sex with my coven in a deserted forest isn't quite the same as having it off with you in Marco's garden! I mean, I know it's dark out here, but what if someone comes out and sees us?'

'Who said we were going to make love in Marco's garden?' retorted Jonathan, seizing her by the hand. 'I've got a much better idea. Just come with me.'

He led her down the garden with impatient haste, Maria half-stumbling as she tripped on tree-roots and divots of grass in the darkness. Above them, a blue-black, velvety sky announced the supremacy of night. The all-encloaking darkness wound itself around them like a cape, secret and caressing and intimate.

Jonathan guided her past the piled-up plastic tables and chairs towards the glittering ribbon of the river. Moored at the foot of three concrete steps was a rowing-boat.

'Go on – get in,' urged Jonathan.

'But – but that's Marco's boat,' protested Maria.

'He won't miss it for one night.'

'Well, I suppose not . . .' Reluctantly, Maria had to admit to herself that the idea was intriguing; appealing even. 'But where are we going?'

'Wait and see.'

Jonathan stepped down into the boat then reached up to guide her in. Despairing of ever managing it, with her tight skirt and impractical heels, Maria slipped off her shoes and dropped them into the boat; then hitched up her already thigh-high skirt, revealing the lacy tops of her stockings. She couldn't see Jonathan's expression but she could imagine it as he helped her down into the boat and his hand slipped from her hip to the ruched-up velvet, garnishing the bare flesh of her upper thigh. And if his hand were to slip just a little higher up, thought Maria, what else would he discover?

The boat wobbled alarmingly as she got in, and she put her arms round Jonathan to steady herself. He seemed in no hurry to let go. On the contrary, he tightened his grip and she delighted in the contrast between the heat of his hand on her backside and the cool of the night air, brushing lightly and teasingly across her bared thighs. How more delicious still it felt to have that self-same cool air licking between her parted thighs, kissing and caressing the red-gold curls that veiled the naked secret of her pussy-lips.

In the flickering lights from the wine-bar, Maria made out the beautifully-sculpted lines of Jonathan's classically-handsome face, and the smooth waves of his blond hair as he bent to possess her with his kiss. Shouts and laughter rose above the distant thumping of disco music, but Maria had ears only for the hoarse whisper of Jonathan's breathing, the seductive purr of his voice.

'Maria, just feel what you do to me . . .'

His cock was hot and hard against the palm of her hand, and instinctively she curled her fingers about the turgid flesh, still tantalisingly covered by his cotton trousers. It would be so easy just to slide down the zipper and slip in her hand. She eased her fingers upwards to take hold of the little metal tag, but Jonathan caught her hand, raised it to his lips and kissed it.

'Plenty of time for that later. We have all night, remember. Just you, and me, and this great big night.'

Their embrace seemed to last for mere seconds, and then his hands left her and she felt bereft. With infinite gentleness, Jonathan helped her to sit on the little bench-seat which spanned the stern of the boat, then sat down himself, facing her.

The moon was up now and glimmers of pale, silvery light reflected white off the rippling surface of the river, illuminating Jonathan's face and torso as he slipped the mooring rope and began rowing the boat slowly downstream. He looked like a classical sculpture brought to life by the magic of the moonlight, Maria thought to herself dreamily as she watched him, wanting him more and more by the minute.

They were alone on the river, and as they rowed further and further away from Marco's, a thick, soft blanket of quietness seemed to slide further over them, blotting out the sights and sounds of the outside world. The predominant sound now was the regular plash, plash of the oars as they dipped in and out of the water, producing little showers of sparkling drops as they emerged, to

31

plunge in once more. Maria trailed her hand over the side, enjoying the sensual caress of the cold swirling water on her bare skin.

'There's a bottle of champagne under the seat,' announced Jonathan, with studied casualness. 'Bollinger – I remember you saying it was your favourite. Why don't you open it?'

Maria reached under the seat and her fingers closed about the neck of a cool bottle, wedged into an ice bucket. Jonathan really had thought of everything.

'There's a blanket there too, if you're cold,' observed Jonathan, a tinge of humour in his voice. 'But I can think of lots of other ways of keeping warm.'

It was funny, thought Maria as she unscrewed the little wire cage from the champagne; she had completely forgotten how cold she'd felt. Here, in an open boat with Jonathan and a bottle of rather good champagne, she felt as though she had entered a dream-world where such mundane considerations as feeling cold just didn't apply.

'I'm fine,' she said, her voice quavering slightly with an excitement she could scarcely conceal. 'It's quite warm really.'

'Good,' purred Jonathan. She could tell from the warm tone of his voice that he was smiling. 'Then why don't you take off your jacket? I bet your bare skin looks beautiful in the moonlight.'

She slipped off the jacket and let it fall to the bottom of the boat. It felt like shedding a skin – abandoning the last vestiges of her reluctance, too. Her body was in control now, and her body wanted to go anywhere and everywhere that tonight's adventure took them.

With a sudden rush and a pop, the cork shot out of the neck of the bottle, showering Maria and Jonathan and the boat with a fine, bubbling spray of champagne. It trickled everywhere: in her hair, down the front of her borrowed dress – whatever would Anthea say? – down her bare thighs and into the secret garden already moist with its own sweet honeydew of desire.

32

In the moonlight, Maria saw that Jonathan's eyes were fixed on her, seemingly transfixed by the wet fabric moulding itself to her skin, and the glistening film of cold champagne, still running in slow trickles down into the deep valley of her cleavage. A wicked impulse overtaking her, she raised the bottle to her lips and poured champagne into her mouth, deliberately ensuring that some escaped, to run in rivulets down the front of her dress.

Suddenly Jonathan shipped the oars and slid down the boat until he was right in front of her. The boat swayed on the slow-rippling water, but Maria no longer cared about the danger of falling in. She was lightheaded with a desire she had fought to control all day. She didn't want to go on fighting any longer.

Jonathan took hold of the champagne bottle and she let go of it willingly, wondering what he intended to do next. She wasn't disappointed. He lifted it to his lips and drank deeply, and the moonlight seemed to caress his bare throat as he swallowed down the cold liquid. Then he raised the bottle and emptied its remaining contents all over Maria's dress, so that the fabric – already damp – became a dripping-wet second skin that moulded itself to her body with an unforgiving zeal.

'Jonathan!' she gasped, the icy coldness suddenly working its way through to her skin. It tingled, excited, and teased her nipples into shameless crests that pushed against the wet fabric as though demanding release.

He pulled her towards him and the heat from his body oozed into her across the tight wet fabric. As he darted kisses on her throat, her lips, her eyes, her cheeks, his hands slipped behind her and unfastened the emerald green bow which held her hair, sliding out the glass-headed pins one by one.

'You look so much more beautiful like this,' he breathed into her ear as her hair came tumbling down over her shoulders in an abundance of dark-red waves. 'So natural and so . . . sexual.' His fingers ran through her hair, winding and unwinding its long, thick tendrils as he kissed her again and again.

33

And then Maria felt his hand on her neck, undoing the top button of her dress, and sliding the zipper down with tantalising, unbearable slowness. As the fabric peeled away from her skin, she felt liberated; she longed to tear off her remaining clothes and offer herself to her lover, naked and hungry.

He slipped the dress down over her shoulders with an urgency which betrayed the need within him; and she heard him gasp with pleasure as her breasts bobbed free of the imprisoning fabric, their flesh ivory-white and almost translucent in the moonlight. Seconds later he was stroking and kneading them, and with a curious detachment, she heard herself moaning and whimpering for the sheer, unadulterated pleasure of his touch.

She reached out to unfasten the buttons of his shirt, and was pleased to find that he no longer made any effort to prevent her. Button by button she unfastened the shirt, following the downward progression with a trail of little kisses. His scent filled her – an irresistible blend of sweat and champagne and cologne – and a rush of juice filled the well-spring of her sex, making her pant for him. Frenziedly now, she wrestled with his belt buckle; she was beyond giving a damn whether or not the boat capsized and threw them both into the chilly river water.

At last the buckle yielded, and the top button of his trousers with it. A moment later, she had succeeded in sliding down his zip and at last her fingers made contact with hot, throbbing flesh.

His prick was even more beautiful than she remembered it: large and thick with a smooth upward curve which ended in a juicy plum of a glans; and at the base of his shaft, two golden fruits that held all the abundant seed of his longing. The touch was electric, and she sensed that he felt it too, for he shuddered as her fingers encircled his flesh, stroking it with a butterfly gentleness which must surely torment more effectively than it satisfied.

'I've got to have you,' he gasped.

She made no move to resist him as he slid her body down until she was lying at the bottom of the boat, her bare back on the rough boards; and he was pulling the dress down over her hips and thighs, revealing the shameless secret of her nakedness.

'My little witch. You know exactly what to do to drive me wild, don't you? I just can't resist you, and you know I can't.' He knelt between her parted thighs and she shivered – no longer with cold – as his thumbs insinuated themselves between her pussy-lips, parting them for the delicious onslaught which she knew must surely come.

His tongue sent electric shocks through her entire body as its tip searched out the pleasure-centre of her sex with an uncanny accuracy. Pleasure made her delirious, taking away all sense of time and space. Beneath them the boat swayed gently, long, lazy waves lapping against the painted wood as they drifted slowly downriver. Opening her eyes, Maria gazed up at the night sky. The stars seemed to be dancing in the velvet blackness, the moon slipping in and out of focus as approaching ecstasy robbed her of all her senses save that of touch. And Jonathan's touch was so, so exquisite . . .

A flood of clear, honeysweet liquid gushed out of Maria's sex as Jonathan's fingertip toyed with the entrance to her eager womanhood. She felt her flesh contracting involuntarily, as though trying to suck him into her, to fill the desperate void of hunger that only he could fill. And he answered her need, slipping his finger further and further into her until it was knuckle-deep, the tip just touching her cervix.

A voice was whispering: 'Want you, want you, want you,' and with a start, Maria recognised it as her own. It seemed alien and far away, a long, long way from the burning, searing heart of her desire that cried out to be fucked, fucked, fucked . . .

Jonathan's finger slid in and out of her with a rhythmic, silky smoothness that drove her crazy. Her pussy tightened around him, trying to hold him, drive him deeper inside her, but each time he slid out of her grasp, only to return with yet more tormenting caresses. And all the time, his tongue was flicking its own teasing caresses across the head of her super-sensitive love-bud.

On the very brink of orgasm, he withdrew from her, leaving her half-maddened with frustrated lust.

'Jonathan!' she pleaded. 'Don't leave me like this. I'm burning for you.'

'Want me?' he demanded, kneeling over her. His wavy, golden hair, touched by the moonlight, seemed like a halo about his shadowy face. Here, adrift with her on the waters of her wild and unquenchable desire, Jonathan Gresham had become the angel – and the demon – of lust.

'Yes, *yes*!'

'Ah, but what do you want me to do?' teased Jonathan. His fingers brushed lightly across Maria's bare belly, pulling lightly at her reddish curls but stopping agonisingly short of her burning clitoris. 'I want to hear you say it.'

'Take me!' cried Maria, not caring if anybody heard her. 'I want you to give it to me – *now*.'

'Never let it be said that I disappoint a lady,' replied Jonathan. 'And especially not one with the prettiest, tightest, sweetest pussy I've ever tasted.'

Another time, another place, and Maria might have resented his arrogance; but here and now, all she wanted was his beautiful body on top of hers; his enchantingly hard dick filling up the emptiness between her strong and hungry thighs.

She opened up to him like a flower, and he entered her in a single, smooth stroke that seemed to go on forever. Her love-juice was in full flow now, flowing strong and deep like the river upon which they were drifting, carried away on a tide of mutual lust.

The pleasure was too intense and too violent to last: a hunger so desperate demanded the swiftest satisfaction. And Jonathan, too, was beyond the point of self-control. Maria felt his thrusts become faster and deeper; she heard his breathing grow hoarse and shallow, and knew that their crisis must come soon. Her body responded to his, her clitoris sending wave upon wave of pleasure rippling and shuddering through her body as they coupled in the darkness.

And as they slid on down the river, Maria abandoned herself to the full force of her need, opening herself to the pure delight of that first, breathtaking orgasm.

For after all, why fight it? Didn't they have the whole night ahead of them?

'Morning, Dr Treharne.'

'Good morning, Alfred. Any mail for me?'

The duty porter at St Alcuin's hardly gave Maria a second glance as she walked into the front lodge just before eight o'clock in the morning; but his quick eye hadn't missed a thing. Under the loose raincoat draped over her shoulders, her clothes were quite distinctly crumpled, and her hair looked dishevelled too. Not that it was his place to judge or disapprove. Alfred had seen a lot worse in thirty years at St Alcuin's man and boy, and besides, he rather liked Dr Treharne. There was a spark of life about her that the college sorely needed.

'Just these three, Dr T. Lovely morning, isn't it?'

Maria's face lit up with a smile that made Alfred wish he were twenty years younger.

'The best, Alfred. The best.'

She pocketed the letters and strolled across First Court. At this time of year, the limbo-land between the end of lectures and the mass exodus homeward for the Long Vac, the college was distinctly quiet, erupting into only occasional outbursts of hysterical jollity when the strain of Part II Tripos exams got too much for the third-year students. Maria was glad all that was behind her; glad, too, that this year she had little involvement with exam marking, as most of the students she was supervising were post-graduates in the first year of their research studies.

Gladder still that she had a magnificent young stud

like Jonathan Gresham to keep her from getting too bored.

The smile was still playing about her lips when she reached the bottom of her staircase. That had been one hell of a night; making love in an open boat under the stars, drinking far too much champagne, making love again . . .

They hadn't made any firm plans for their next meeting, but then that was how they both wanted it. Or at least, that was what Maria kept telling herself. Like it or not, that guy Jonathan was getting under her skin, and she couldn't help wondering when and where and how they would make love again. But she hated being dependent on any man, so perhaps it was safer that they kept some small distance between them.

Still thinking of Jonathan, she unlocked the door of her flat, stepped inside and threw Jonathan's old raincoat onto the sofa. Walking through into the bedroom, she took one look at Anthea's best dress – a matted wreck of damp green velvet – and made a mental note to flee on the next banana-boat to South America. What on earth would Anthea say when she saw the damage? Even the best dry cleaner in town would have difficulty restoring this to its former glory.

She peeled off what remained of the dress, slung on a towelling robe and went back through the sitting-room to get herself a much-needed drink. A drink, a shower, then a few hours in bed before the dreaded departmental meeting: that was what she needed.

As she slumped on the sofa with her drink, Maria remembered the mail she'd collected from the porter's lodge, and she rummaged in the pocket of Jonathan's raincoat for the three crumpled envelopes.

End of term Buttery bill – that could wait. She didn't even open it, dreading how many bottles of college claret she and her inebriate friends had put on the slate since the beginning of term. The second envelope contained a curt note from Armstrong-Baker, summoning her to his office at 2 pm prompt. But the Cornish postmark on the third envelope puzzled her: did she know anybody in Cornwall? She didn't recollect ever having been there, let alone having friends there.

Curious, she slit open the envelope and unfolded the sheet of thick, headed paper.

Myint and Calloway
5 Fort Row
LYNMOOR

23 May 19XX

Dr M Treharne
c/o St Alcuin's College
CAMBRIDGE

Dear Dr Treharne

**ESTATE OF THE LATE MISS CLARA MEGAWNE**

My partner and I have been attempting to contact you for several months, but until your recent television appearance we were unable to locate your current whereabouts.

Could you please contact me at your earliest convenience? It is most important that I talk to you in connection with the estate of your late aunt, Miss Clara Megawne. As you may know, the estate comprises a large sum of money, together with several acres of land and the ownership of a substantial local property, Brackwater Hall.

I look forward to hearing from you.

Yours sincerely

**Theodore Myint**

Maria stared at the letter in her lap, utterly mystified. No matter how many times she read it, it still didn't make sense. The thing was, not only had she never heard of Lynmoor, or Brackwater Hall, she didn't have an aunt – and certainly not an aunt called Clara Megawne.

# Chapter Three

'It's nothing like I'd imagined it,' commented Allardyce as he surveyed the vast sweep of moorland before him.

'Ah, but that's the beauty of it, don't you think?' replied Leon Duvitski, leaning with his elbow on the roof of the sleek red car. Although only of average height and build, he was an attractive man, in a brooding, Slavic way. There was something in the steady gaze of his dark eyes that compelled attention.

'What exactly are you driving at?'

Duvitski picked up the thread again, genuinely enthused by his subject.

'OK, so Lynmoor isn't what you'd been expecting, but it's a thousand times better. And every time I come up here, the place seems subtly different. There's always something new. The punters will love it. Besides . . .' He scratched his chin thoughtfully. 'It's so different that no-one else will even have considered it.'

Allardyce scanned the distant horizon and the blue pencil-line of the far-off ocean. His eyes met with craggy heathland, a valley with a huddle of cottages and farms, and further off on the higher ground, an untidy muddle of old cars, vans and tents, grouped around what looked like an old stone circle. A thin column of dirty grey smoke was winding up into the sky from a makeshift camp-fire. He nodded towards it.

'Is that it – the New Age settlement you were telling me about?'

'That's right.'

'Bloody awful mess,' grunted Allardyce. 'They'll have to go, of course. Can't have them littering up the place once the development's up and running. Nothing but troublemakers, the lot of 'em.'

His archetypically English features tensed with irritation. Charles Allardyce, head of CA Developments, was not about to let a bunch of drop-outs and petty criminals spoil his plans for the most spectacular business and leisure park in the whole of Western Europe. Allardyce always, but *always*, got what he wanted: money, loyalty, success, beautiful women. Whatever he wanted, he simply took. It was surprising how many women – and for that matter, men – found his ruthlessness attractive, and each new success energised his sexual appetite like an electrical charge, giving him a massive hard-on that only more and better sex could satisfy. He would take that, too.

'They'll go,' promised Duvitski, rubbing finger and thumb together. 'Money talks to a man like Carolan.'

'Carolan?'

'That's what he calls himself, but I'm pretty sure the name's phoney – just like the rest of him. He's their self-appointed leader – an arrogant little sod, but he has a certain raw charisma. Fancies himself as a bit of a magician, too. With all his mumbo-jumbo he's got those hippies eating out of his hand; they'll do anything he tells them.'

Allardyce permitted himself the hint of a grim smile.

'And this Mr Carolan . . . You think he'll do anything we tell him – for a price?'

'That's how I see it, yes. But it's an avenue we've hardly begun to explore.'

'Explore it. And when you've done your homework, bring him to me. I think our Mr Carolan and I should have a cosy little chat.'

The sun re-emerged from behind a fluffy white cloud, bathing the fresh greens and browns of the moor in honey-coloured light. Allardyce drew in breath sharply. He hadn't reckoned on the wild beauty of this place. Even he – by no means a sensitive or romantic man – was drawn to its ever-changing face, caressed by a breeze that seemed to whisper to him seductively of money, fame and sex.

Duvitski's voice broke his reverie.

'Shall we get back to the village now? I've been staying at the pub there – the Duke of Gloucester. Very hospitable. There's this really tasty local girl I spent a couple of nights with . . .'

Allardyce raised his hand to stem the flow.

'Yeah, yeah. Just a minute. I'm thinking.'

Turning his head to the right, Allardyce focused on the craggy swell of a dark, rocky mass behind them, emerging like some mad, organic growth from the body of the high moorland. Atop it, framed against the sunlit sky, stood the black, rather formless shape of a building. He jabbed his finger towards the shape.

'What's that?'

Duvitski followed his pointing finger and screwed up his eyes against the painful brightness of the sky. He consulted his map.

'Oh, that? That's Brackwater Tor. The building you can see on top of it is Brackwater Hall. It's ages old.'

'It's perfect,' said Allardyce, his voice low with excitement.

'Perfect . . ?'

'Can't you see? It's right in the middle of the land we're proposing to buy and develop. If we buy up those farms to the west, and get control of the land where the New Age travellers are camping, it'll form an almost perfect circle around the tor, and we'll own everything between here and Barncastle. I have to have that house, Leon. Ducasse has been bleating on about wanting the right site for his hotel and conference centre – and believe me, that's the one.' He flashed a glance at Duvitski. 'Who lives there?'

43

Duvitski consulted his notes.

'Er ... nobody. As far as I can tell, it's empty. Has been for a couple of years. It's pretty run-down, by all accounts.'

'Excellent.' Allardyce's eyes narrowed as plans formed in his mind. Blood seemed to be pumping faster through his veins, exciting and arousing him. His hand strayed momentarily to the front of his pants, swollen by the bulge of his hardening cock. Nothing gave him so much pleasure as success – and even now he could taste it on his lips, on the lips of Duvitski's pretty barmaid as she knelt to suck his cock. He snapped his fingers. 'Who is the owner now? Quickly.'

Again, Duvitski consulted the notes his PA had prepared for him.

'The Hall used to belong to a Miss Clara Megawne – some batty old woman who'd lived there for years. She died a couple of years ago, with no heirs. Seems the estate's being handled by the local solicitor in Lynmoor, a guy named Theodore Myint. Oh – and the last I heard, he thought he might have found a beneficiary of the will . . .'

'Good, good, good. Well, whoever it is, they're hardly likely to want to live in an old heap like that, are they?' observed Allardyce, getting into Duvitski's car and opening the sun-roof. He wanted to feel the slight chill of the morning air tearing into his lungs. 'We'll offer them a fair price. Not too generous of course, but fair.'

Duvitski got into the car and switched on the engine. 'Where to now?'

Allardyce settled himself back in his seat.

'The Duke of Gloucester, of course. I want you to introduce me to this pretty little barmaid you've been having so much fun with.'

Maria hated teaching at the History Faculty. A sixties' monstrosity in glass, steel and red brick. It felt freezing for ten months of the year and roasting hot in July and August. It also gave Maria the creeps – for no good reason other than that it felt spiritually as well as physically cold.

Lectures were theoretically over for the summer term, but for the postgraduates who had no examinations to take, academic life would carry on for a few more weeks. As a favour to Dave Kenroy, who was heavily involved with exam invigilation, Maria had reluctantly agreed to take a seminar on medieval history. And so, in a concrete box of a room on the sixth floor, Maria had spent all morning trying to concentrate as a series of students read out their seminar papers on the suppression of heresy in fourteenth-century Languedoc.

As if it wasn't bad enough having to take on someone else's lecturing commitment, there was still this nagging question of the message from Theodore Myint. She still had his letter in his pocket. She'd meant to throw it away; she'd even crumpled it up and thrown it into the wastepaper basket, but had retrieved it almost instantly, somehow afraid to dismiss it from her life with such finality.

As the days passed, the dilemma had eased a little. The longer she left it without acting on the letter, the further away the whole thing seemed. Maybe if she just ignored it, it would go away. After all, it was obviously a mistake. She hadn't got, and never had had, an Aunt Clara. In any case, what the hell did a woman like Maria Treharne want with some godforsaken rathole in the middle of nowhere? She was surprised at how much the very thought disturbed her.

This morning though, Lynmoor was a very long way from her thoughts. The desire for sex filled her mind and body, driving into her thoughts again and again no matter how hard she fought it. The heightened sensuality which she possessed along with her latent psychic abilities could be a curse as well as a blessing.

Every time she lifted her eyes from the page in front of her, her gaze met Jonathan's. Wicked and sly, his eyes seemed to twinkle with a lascivious merriment. He did not need to speak; his eyes told her everything he wanted to say. He wanted to take her, enjoy her, pleasure her as he had done that night in the boat on the river. Maria wasn't by any means a shy woman, but she had to fight hard not to blush, not to betray the feelings of sexual excitement that thrilled through her every time she looked into those wicked eyes. Even when she turned her face away from him, she could still see his eyes and imagine those lips forming the words she longed to hear . . .

I want you. I want you now, Maria Treharne.

The more she tried to ignore her sexual feelings, the more intense they seemed to get. By the time it was Jonathan's turn to read out his seminar paper, Maria could feel a distinct pulse of pleasure between her thighs. It was like a tiny heartbeat, making her clitoris quiver with an anticipation which, try as she might, she could not quell. The lower half of her body was hidden from view by the desk and she squeezed her thighs together surreptitiously, sincerely hoping that none of the dozen or so students would notice her confusion, or the slight quickening of her breath as her body surrendered to the unstoppable advance of her desire.

She heard her own voice tremble slightly as she spoke.

'That was an excellent factual account, Shona, but a little thin on analysis. Perhaps you and Gary could exchange papers later? Now, Jonathan – I believe you've prepared something for us?' She consulted the clock on the wall and saw that it was almost twelve o'clock already. 'Mind you, we're running rather short of time . . .'

Jonathan got up from his seat and she saw – as if for the first time – how tall he was; how kissably soft the blond hair that refused to be tamed and kept slipping in wavy locks over his forehead. Her eyes travelled downwards over his strong torso, his slim hips and flat belly, taut with well-trained muscle. She imagined how he must look in full rowing kit, his powerful frame bending over the oars as he set the stroke for his college eight.

In her imagination she could almost taste the sprink-

46

ling of sweat over his tanned arms and back; smell the sour, savage fragrance of his body as she stripped off his rowing vest and shorts, to reveal the bounty of his young nakedness beneath. And when she had had that first pleasure, she would amuse herself by running her tongue over his shoulders and back and chest, toying mercilessly with his nipples before pursuing her odyssey of discovery. Maria's tongue pressed against the roof of her mouth as she swallowed, picturing herself tasting and lapping at the sweat where it had collected in hollows and rivulets on his gorgeous young body.

At last, when he was desperate with lust and crying out for her, she would show him a little mercy. Her lips would close about the swollen stalk of his penis, and she would hear him moan to her softly as she kissed his weariness away, her matchless skill bringing him slowly to the summit of unbearable pleasure . . .

'Maria?'

At the sound of Jonathan's voice, she snapped out of her trance and looked around. Several pairs of eyes were on her, lips curling into suppressed smiles. How long had she been like that? Did they know, had they guessed? She was sure they must have. And Jonathan was still bending over her; she could smell his unique scent, the spice of his desire driving her crazy with need for him.

'Oh, sorry – I was miles away,' stuttered Maria.

'You wanted to see my paper,' said Jonathan, laying it down on the desk in front of her and opening it at the first page. 'I spent a lot of time on it. I hope you find it *interesting*.'

Something in the tone of his voice made her glance down at the desk, and as soon as she saw what he had written she felt a ripple of guilty excitement, deep in her belly. The words swam before her eyes:

"I don't give a damn about this seminar, but I want you, Maria. I want your sex. And this afternoon I'm going to have it. You'd like that, wouldn't you? I know exactly what you like. You like to feel me rubbing and licking you . . ."

47

There were pages and pages of it, close-packed handwriting that had absolutely nothing to do with Albigensian heretics in the medieval mountain village of Montaillou. Maria's grip on the desk tightened, her head reeling with the anticipatory thrill of wicked, wicked pleasure. With an effort, she summoned up a smile of regret and handed the paper back to Jonathan.

'I didn't realise it was so long, Jonathan. As you can see, we don't have much time left, and I do want to make sure your work gets *all* the time and attention it deserves.' She was sure he had caught the sub-text of her words. His eyes were gleaming with a shared understanding of the pleasures they would shortly be enjoying together. Maria got up from the desk and put her books into her briefcase. 'We'll go through the rest of your papers next week. In the meantime, I'll just remind those of you who are my personal students to see me next week and arrange supervision times for next term.'

Luckily, most of the students couldn't wait to get out of the chilly lecture room, and didn't spare Maria so much as a second glance as she hung back, ostensibly sorting through the papers in her briefcase, whilst really waiting for Jonathan.

As soon as the last student had closed the door behind her, Jonathan took the briefcase from her and dropped it on the floor; then he put his arms round her and treated her to a golden smile.

'At last! I thought that was never going to end.'

Maria wriggled in his grasp, ineffectually pushing him away but already longing for a tighter, more intimate embrace.

'Jonathan – someone might see.'

'So what if they do? Do you really care?'

She could find no reply to give him. Oh, but she cared all right. She cared desperately about the way his right hand was rubbing her backside, his lips darting little kisses all down her throat and into the deep V of her open-necked shirt. She cared about the desperate ache of sensual need, deep in her belly; the throb of passionate hunger that only he could satisfy.

'Come with me.' He took her by the hand and led her towards the door.

'Where are we going?'

He grinned, and she felt herself melt in the insistent heat of his lust.

'Relax. You ask far too many questions.'

Out on the empty landing he took her in his arms again, this time pressing her back against the chilly concrete wall. The chatter of the departing students receded gradually into the distance, as they hurried down the stairs, leaving nothing but an echoing silence. At last they were alone.

Jonathan's lips possessed her hungrily, and she let herself yield to his kiss with a sigh of satisfaction. She had been waiting all morning for the touch of those lips, the taste and feel of that long, pink tongue, moving slowly and sinuously in the wetness of her mouth. It seemed to last a long time, the kiss becoming as natural a part of her existence as breathing; and when at last he pulled away he left her gasping for more. But Maria's pleasure was tinged with a vague anxiety as his hand strayed to her leg, pushing up the hem of her skirt.

'No, we shouldn't, Jonathan – not here. There are other classes in the building, someone might come out and see us . . .'

'See what? We're just having a little fun.'

'But what if . . .' Jonathan's impetuosity was infectious, and she knew her resolve was unlikely to survive another onslaught. Jonathan's fingers were snaking stealthily up the inside of her bare thigh, towards the wisp of cotton veiling her pubic mound.

'Not afraid, are you? Surely not *you*, Maria . . .' There was a slight darkening of his tone that Maria could hardly fail to notice, and she knew that he was daring her, as one child dares another to some immense and joyful wickedness. Maria Treharne had never in her life refused to respond to a challenge.

'Oh course I'm not,' replied Maria as scornfully as she could, her initial instinct for caution losing out to the insidious pleasure-impulse that began between her parted thighs and sent aftershocks pounding through her brain. She couldn't help wondering what Armstrong-Baker would say if he could see her here, his little pink-rimmed, piggy eyes contracting to points of malevolent blackness in his stodgy face. She tried another tack. 'But maybe somewhere else, somewhere a bit quieter? I mean, this is hardly romantic, is it?'

Glancing around, Jonathan took in the litter-strewn tiled floor, the broken window patched with a sheet of hardboard, the dismal and echoing stairwell. He smiled.

'It's absolutely perfect. Anywhere's perfect if I get to have you, Maria.'

'Really, I think we should wait,' she protested feebly, suddenly feeling quite frail in Jonathan's determined grasp. She wasn't even sure that she believed what she was saying, and Jonathan evidently didn't think much of her protests.

'I thought you wanted me, Maria.'

'Yes, of course I do . . .'

'End of argument.'

There was no escape; not from Jonathan, not from her own desire. Her back was pressed up against the wall, and her lover's arms formed a cage around her, a force field of sensual need. She told herself that she wanted to close her legs, but Jonathan's fingertips were caressing the smooth, bare skin with such exquisite gentleness that she could not summon the strength to resist him. Almost without realising what she was doing she was offering herself to the caress, her feet sliding a little further apart on the smooth tiled floor in an instinctive welcome.

'It's pointless fighting me, Maria. You're hot for me. I can see it in your eyes.'

Jonathan's words sounded like a purr of satisfaction in Maria's ear. She wanted to be annoyed with him, to tell him that he shouldn't flatter himself, that it wasn't true – but of course, it was, every last word of it. Desire had been bubbling inside her all morning, and now, with Jonathan's fingers moving almost imperceptibly towards the epicentre of that desire, she knew he had as good as won. Never over-endowed with modesty, Jonathan knew it too.

Suddenly, two floors above, a door opened and Maria's heart fluttered with panic. There were voices up there, footsteps crossing the landing to the stairs. She tensed and held her breath, her body seemingly frozen in time as Jonathan ignored the danger, planting kiss after kiss on the soft curve of her neck.

A sigh of relief shuddered out of her as the footsteps moved away, heading upwards to the ninth floor. For the moment, the danger was past. But for how long? How long before a party of wide-eyed foreign exchange students emerged from the lecture rooms on the floor above, only to find one of their more colourful lecturers *in flagrante delicto* with a postgrad? Jonathan didn't allow her the time to think about what might happen. He murmured softly to her as he bent to kiss the crest of her braless nipple, hard and prominent as a hazelnut beneath her thin summer blouse.

'I've waited ages for this, Maria. Too long.' His lips fastened over her nipple and she felt the moist heat of his breath through the flimsy silk, then the nip of his teeth as they bit gently but hungrily into the rubbery flesh of the teat. 'If you don't want me to lust after you, you shouldn't flaunt these wonderful breasts.'

He flicked his tongue over the very tip of her nipple, and she gave a tiny, whispering sob of longing.

'Oh. Jonathan, oh . . .'

'It's bad to deprive yourself of pleasure, Maria, didn't they ever teach you that? It makes you tense. Wouldn't you like me to massage that tension away?'

The fingers of his right hand slid abruptly upwards, making contact with the dampening gusset of Maria's white cotton panties. Instantly, Jonathan released her nipple from his mouth, professing disappointment.

'Panties, Maria? You surprise me. I mean, we didn't

bother with such formalities the other night,' he remarked. 'Don't you remember?'

Of course she remembered. Remembered how it had felt to sense Jonathan's sunburst of sexual excitement as his fingers enjoyed their first touch of her dew-spangled pubis, naked as nature intended.

'You'll just have to find a way round them, won't you?' she teased, beginning to enjoy the game now. 'I don't see why I should make everything easy for you.'

'I could always strip them off you, I suppose,' teased Jonathan, tucking his fingers under the elastic of her panties. 'But then again, maybe I don't need to. There are other ways.'

'Such as?'

'Such as this.'

Quick as lightning, Jonathan pulled Maria's floaty skirt up to the waist, baring her body from the belly down. Then he slid aside the gusset of her panties and let his index finger plunge straight up into the warm, wet depths of Maria's sex. As he had anticipated, it was succulent with juice, running with rivulets of her own sweet honeydew.

At this deliciously brutal violation, Maria felt shiver after shiver of pleasure press through her hypersensitive body. Every nerve-ending cried out for Jonathan's touch, and the tight lips of her swollen pussy closed about Jonathan's finger as though they were reluctant ever to let him go. Instinctively she ground her hips against his, forcing forward her pelvis so that Jonathan's wriggling, tormenting finger plunged deeper still into her womanhood. He stooped a little to penetrate her more deeply; a second finger following, and then a third, until at last his whole hand had forced its way into her, filling her up, stretching her yearning flesh to the point where pleasure was so intense that it threatened to become pain.

Though she tried hard to keep silent, Maria could not suppress little ohs and ahs and moans as Jonathan's fingers twisted and turned inside the tight wet tunnel of her sex. His fingers sought out her G-spot, and she sighed with the strange pleasure of this new caress, the curious excitement as his curled fist pressed upwards, pushing hard against her.

The coldness of the smooth painted wall behind her back contrasted sharply with the burning hunger of her sex. In that moment, Maria wished that every bit of her lover could have been inside her; his whole being, stretching and thrusting and tearing the pleasure from her. And still he made no attempt to touch the fiery bud of her clitoris, now incandescent and throbbing with unsatisfied need.

'Touch me,' she pleaded in a hoarse whisper, trying to grind her pubis against the hard bulge of his penis, still trapped inside his pants. Maria despised herself for her weakness; she had not wanted to beg, but the need was becoming desperate. She could imagine the taste of his cock on her tongue, and the thought made her madder than ever for his caresses. 'Touch me there.' She took hold of his left hand and pushed it determinedly between her thighs, to the pleasure-centre between the plump petals of her love-lips. 'There. Please.'

'You want me to frig you?'

'Yes, yes! Make me come.'

He hesitated, as though he sensed the intensity of her need and wanted to make her wait a little longer. The torment was almost unbearable.

'This way?'

His fingertip grazed the hood of Maria's clitoris, as quickly and as lightly as a butterfly; but even so, the touch was like an electric shock to Maria – too sudden, too intense. Taking his finger from her pulsing bud, she raised it to her lips and moistened it with her saliva. Jonathan's eyes closed and he let out a sigh of pure pleasure as her lips closed round his finger, covering it with a warm wetness that was so very reminiscent of her sex.

That done, she guided his finger back towards her clitoris. The moistness of her saliva made the brutal

53

pleasure of his caresses a little easier to bear, but inside her vagina Jonathan's fingers continued to tease and torment her, searching relentlessly for the G-spot that would drive her to the edge of madness and beyond. Slowly and triumphantly, he sank to his knees on the grubby tiled floor, pressing his face against the fragrant tangle of her maidenhair, and beginning to drink ...

The sound of chairs scraping across a floor signalled the end of a lecture somewhere in the building; but it was difficult to locate the source of the sound, more difficult still to care. The first wave of panic quickly dulled into a throb of anxiety which merged with the pulsing of Maria's clitoris, and became no more than another aspect of her desire. The danger of discovery might be all around them, but here and now, sexual satisfaction was all that mattered.

In the throes of her passion she moved slightly, her back sliding a few inches along the cold, smooth wall that was such a contrast to Jonathan's hot and hungry body. Her hands stroked his soft blond hair, kneaded the muscles of his shoulders, toyed with the tiny short hairs on the back of his neck that he so loved her to run her fingers over and over. She heard him moaning softly as he kissed her mount of Venus, his warm, moist breath condensing on her reddish pubic curls like the crystal-clear dewdrops of her own love-juice.

But her own need for satisfaction overrode her desire to pleasure Jonathan. He was teasing and tormenting her, doing his utmost to delay her orgasm – perhaps even prevent it altogether, so that for the rest of the day he could keep her in a permanent state of hungry frustration, longing only for the moment when he would give in to his own hunger, and deign to thrust his cock into her welcoming haven.

Maria would not wait for Jonathan's selfish mercy; she wanted pleasure – now. Lifting her hands from Jonathan's blond head, she touched the protuberant crests of her nipples, erect and pressing hard against the inside of her blouse. Little damp circles around the right areola showed where Jonathan's lips had kissed her desire aflame, his breath moistening the fabric as he licked and bit at the flesh underneath. With a lascivious satisfaction, she let her fingers follow their instincts, pinching and rolling the hard buttons of flesh between finger and thumb, so that an electric current of mad, desperate pleasure coursed and crackled through her veins, awakening every nerve in her already sensitive body.

The whole game could not have lasted more than minutes, and yet it seemed to Maria that she had always been here, on this bleak open staircase, with Jonathan. In the insane rush towards the pleasure-grail, she could remember no time when she had not been standing here, with Jonathan's curled fist filling her up and his fingers and tongue exciting her swollen clitoris to ever-greater need.

With a shuddering cry that escaped from between her clenched teeth, Maria at last reached the summit of her pleasure and felt herself falling, swirling, tossed like a little white feather caught in the eye of a raging storm, helpless and without direction. Her psychic sensibilities served to heighten the orgasm, as they did all pleasure and all pain, raising both to a fearful intensity. In her deaf-blind pleasure, she hardly noticed the hot flood of syrupy juice that forced its way out between her pussy-lips, to be lapped up by Jonathan's eager tongue.

Eyes closed and floating in a world of pure pleasure, she might have remained in a trance for many minutes, had she not felt Jonathan move abruptly away, his fingers withdrawing from her with a cruel suddenness. Her eyes flickering open, she saw Jonathan gazing upwards, an expression of alarm on his face. He seemed unaware of her, totally absorbed in whatever it was that had caught his attention. Curious, she followed his gaze, but saw nothing.

'What's the matter, Jon?' She touched his arm and he turned round, suddenly aware of her presence once more.

'I'm sorry, Maria. But I saw someone – up there,

watching us. I don't know who it was, he was gone too quickly, but . . .'

'But what?'

'It looked a bit like Terry Kestelman.'

Maria felt a succession of contradictory emotions pass through her: alarm, amusement, anxiety, complacency. In her current state of post-coital goodwill, it was hard to feel real panic.

'I expect it wasn't him at all – just some student,' she said, drawing Jonathan closer to her and pressing her lips against his. The taste of her pussy was still strong on them, and she took great delight in licking her juices from his face. 'I don't suppose he saw anything much, anyway.' Mentally she was crossing fingers and hoping to goodness she was right.

'I'm sure you're right', Jonathan agreed, putting his arms round Maria's waist and giving her backside a squeeze. Maria wondered, not for the first time, how such a physically strong young man could combine that strength with a touch every bit as gentle as a woman's. The combination was both subtle and very, very attractive.

He ran his finger down the furrow between her breasts, pressing on the fabric of her blouse so that it tightened across her nipples, stimulating them into greater hardness. 'And so – what's your answer to my invitation?'

'What invitation?'

'The lunch invitation I'm giving you now.'

Maria thought about playing hard to get, then discarded the idea as ludicrous. What was there for Jonathan to get that he hadn't already had – several times? She smiled and nodded. Heck, lunch with Jonathan Gresham was a whole lot more fun than camping out on some Cornish moor. What did she need with Theodore Myint and this phantom Aunt Clara? She'd had a bad, crazy, weird feeling about that letter ever since the moment it had arrived. Now, as Jonathan kissed her and let his hand brush across her breast, she made her decision. She would tell Mr Myint that she simply wasn't interested.

She returned Jonathan's kiss with a playful enthusiasm. This was a beautiful day, a beautiful city; and here she was with a beautiful young man offering the promise of even more beautiful sex.

'Sounds good to me.'

'Terrific,' grinned Jonathan, his face transformed from boyish enthusiasm to lecherous joy in a split second. 'Because I don't know about you, Maria, but I'm really looking forward to dessert.'

Facing the warm wind that blew across the moors, Anthony Pendorran stood alone on Brackwater Tor. He could feel its anger and its pain beating and pulsing beneath his feet. He knew that he must make something happen, but up to now his plans were not working out at all as he had planned.

From where he stood, he could survey almost the whole of Lynmoor, from the dark, scrubby high moorland to the relative lushness of the valley where the village lay. In the distance beyond the encampment on Hilltop Tor, he could see the wild Atlantic coast where his own house stood, proud and defiant on the wave-lashed cliffs.

Unconsciously he clenched his fists, very tightly; the whitening knuckles a barometer of the tension within him. His striking face was also pale and tense, his lips a thin red line of distaste as he looked out over the beauty that might soon become a wasteland.

Modern man had brought devastation to Lynmoor, with his money and his plans and his promises of 'new developments'. Now there was talk of new houses, new roads, new people: people who had no understanding of, or interest in, Lynmoor, beyond the profits they could make from it. To Pendorran, it seemed that this ancient and profoundly sacred place was under siege from all the evils of the modern world. Someone must save it from rape and sacrilege. Pendorran must save it.

He felt the bitterness of bile rise to his throat as he looked across the valley to Hilltop Tor, and the stone circle where Carolan and his followers had pitched their camp. Carolan. The very name filled Pendorran with a violence that he had sought to shun. Carolan was a smiling charlatan, poisoning the Mother-spirit's soul with his fakery. And as for the 'New Age village' he had built? To Pendorran it seemed nothing more than an ugly, profane jumble of broken-down vehicles and grubby tents, soiling the beauty of the place, littering his ancestors' graves with the trash of their tawdry existence.

Behind him, the old Hall seemed to embrace his anger, silently echoing the blackness of his mood in its dark and looming silhouette. He turned to look at the overgrown hedges, the peeling paintwork, the herb garden that had been left to run to seed. As he turned, the afternoon sunlight caught the silver belt-buckle that he always wore, and a cold white light flashed from the raven's crystal eye.

Pendorran would not, could not, abandon this place to the developers and their subtle, creeping corruption.

He would *make* the Mistress come.


Anthea stood in the open doorway of Maria's college flat, watching her in a bemused silence that lasted for several minutes before she announced her presence.

'Maria . . ?'

Maria turned around. To Anthea, her hazel eyes seemed brighter than usual, her pale face slightly flushed.

'Are you OK?'

Maria nodded.

'Yes, yes, of course I am.' She carried on throwing clothes into a suitcase, in a more or less random way. 'Was there something you wanted?'

Anthea came into the room, closing the door quietly behind her.

'Nothing special, just a chat. Jonathan said I'd find you here. He also said you'd started acting strangely.'

Maria laughed – a little nervously, thought Anthea, but maybe she was imagining it. There certainly seemed to be something a little jumpy about Maria today.

'What's strange about taking a little trip? Jonathan's just annoyed because he didn't manage to talk me into bed this afternoon.'

She recalled the scene at Fitz's restaurant with slight embarrassment: his hand on her knee as they sat in a cosy corner, his face filling with petulant disbelief as she told him that no, she wouldn't be coming back to his place this afternoon, because she had something more important to do. More important than Jonathan? She still couldn't believe she'd said that. But the decision was made now, and she was going.

'A little trip? But Maria, end of term's still two weeks away. What's going on?'

'It's OK. I got special dispensation from the Master – family reasons, you know.'

'I can't believe I'm hearing this, Maria. This morning you were telling me how hot you were for Jonathan, and how you couldn't wait to spend the whole summer screwing the life out of his delicious young body. Now you're telling me you're going off on a wild goose chase to Cornwall! What the hell changed your mind?'

Maria finished folding up the blouse she was holding and laid it in the suitcase with hands that trembled almost imperceptibly – or was Anthea imagining that, as well? Without turning round, she replied in a voice that was quieter and flatter than it ought to have been.

'I really don't know. Crazy, isn't it?'

Anthea put her arm round Maria's shoulders.

'Then unchange it. Stay here – we'll have a great summer. You've got your Fellowship to look forward to, and there's Jonathan, and ... well ... looks like I may have a rather hunky new boyfriend, too.'

To Anthea's surprise, Maria showed no interest, but carried on packing, squeezing rolled-up bras and panties and bits of jewellery into the crammed corners of the suitcase. When she had finished, she closed the lid and pressed down on it with all her weight, until it clicked shut. The sound held a note of finality.

Anthea obviously wasn't getting through to her friend. She changed tack.

'How long are you going for?'

'I don't know – a few days, a couple of weeks, maybe longer. Just until I get something sorted out.'

'So when are you leaving?'

'First thing tomorrow morning. The car's packed up so I'll have to take the train and get a bus from Truro.'

'Then at least let me be here to say goodbye.'

Maria smiled, and curled her hand around Anthea's. They'd always been so close; they'd told each other everything. Why couldn't she explain what was happening to her now? Maybe because she couldn't explain it to herself. She squeezed Anthea's hand.

'Of course. I'd like that.'

As Anthea walked back down the rickety wooden staircase towards First Court, questions tumbled over and over in her mind. The promise of a legacy was tempting, of course it was; but Maria had been so very certain that Cornwall was a bad idea, something to be avoided at all costs. It was rare indeed for her to ignore her instincts. So what could have changed her mind? And what could be so good that it lured Maria away from a sultry summer of love with Jonathan Gresham?

'Just relax and let me . . . Lie back and enjoy it.'

Terry Kestelman needed no further persuasion. Hell, he was a fair-minded man. Give him what he wanted, and he was willing to do a deal. That was fair, wasn't it? All he'd wanted from Maria Treharne was a little friendly co-operation, but the bitch was too snooty by far.

Well, well, so be it. He didn't need that tramp Maria to give him what he needed. And Dr Kirin Johanssen might not be as well-qualified academically as her rival, but when it came to inter-departmental relations, Kirin was up with the all-time greats.

Kirin smiled to herself as she unzipped Terry's none-too-impressive dick from his white cotton underpants. Unlike Maria Treharne, Kirin Johanssen was more than willing to employ a little give and take if it got her where she wanted to be. And now that Maria was off to some far-flung corner of Cornwall, she was in with her best-ever chance.

Her white-blonde hair fell like a bridal veil over her laughing face as she bent to take Kestelman's cock between her lips. In a strange way, she was enjoying herself. The taste of Terry Kestelman's hardening dick was the taste of power.

Terry gave a groan of satisfaction as Kirin's cool fingers slipped inside his pants and cradled the burning globes of his balls. It wasn't just the physical pleasure that made him almost climax on the spot: it was the satisfaction of knowing that Kirin Johanssen might just give Maria Treharne the fright she deserved.

# Chapter Four

Grace Harmer drank the rest of the orange juice and threw the plastic cup out of the car window. It bounced off over the tufted grass, and down the slope into an old field drain. Below and beyond was a breathtaking view over Lynmoor; a riot of greens and browns and blue, blue sky. But Grace had seen it all before, and she was bored to tears with it. Allardyce was right: this place would be one hell of a lot better with a shopping mall and a few nightclubs.

Stifling a yawn, she turned to Benedict Green.

'Duvitski's wasting our talents on this one.'

'Give it time, Grace. Give it time.' He spat out a tasteless ball of chewing gum, and flicked it neatly into the ashtray.

Grace looked him up and down with growing annoyance. Four days they'd spent up here, watching Brackwater Hall to see if anyone came to the old house. What had they seen? Nothing. Myint's information about the girl from Cambridge must have been wrong.

Four whole days up here with Benedict Green, who had no conversation, no interests, not even any sex appeal that she could discern. It wasn't that he was badlooking, well not really. There was a certain roguish charm about the unruly curls of his sandy hair, the glint of those chocolate-brown eyes. But boring! Tell me about it, thought Grace, rubbing her forehead with the back of her hand.

'It's getting stuffy in here,' she observed. 'Couldn't we get a bit of fresh air?'

'I suppose if you really want we could take another look round the outside of the Hall,' replied Benedict doubtfully. 'But we'll need to be careful no one notices us.'

'Up here? Nobody comes up here, you know that.'

With a sigh, Grace opened the car door, got out and stretched. At least out here she wasn't forced into quite such uncomfortable proximity to the gum-chewing Benedict, with his smelly shirt and unshaven chin.

'Come on,' she announced decisively. 'I'm taking a look. You can stay here if you want.'

To her disappointment, Benedict chose to trail after her like a lost spaniel, unwilling to be left behind. It was just like taking your younger brother to a party; he was more of an annoyance than a help.

The old Hall was picturesque, but a bit of a mess. The ground floor was barely visible through the overgrown front garden, and a reddish-brown creeper had rioted all over the stone so that in places the upstairs windows were partially obscured. One or two of the tiny leaded panes seemed to be cracked, and the white paint on the ornamental weatherboards was worn and peeling.

It was a pity really, mused Grace. You could make something of a place like this. Still, once the developers got their hands on the place, they'd transform it. Grace simply didn't understand how the locals could be so ignorant and ungrateful as to oppose Allardyce's plans to drag the place into the twentieth century.

They slipped through one of the side gates, its rusted hinges squeaking in protest as they passed with difficulty into the mad tangle of what had once been an Elizabethan knot-garden. The fragrance of chamomile and thyme hung heavy on the warm air, making Grace's head swim rather pleasantly. Even after so many long months and years of neglect, there was still a discernibly sensual elegance about Brackwater Hall.

She reached out and touched a frail, floating spur of greenery, twisting the fronds around her hand, then crushing the small leaves between her fingers. On a whim, she plucked a small sprig from the bush and slipped it into the buttonhole of her jacket. Sweet muskiness rose from the crushed leaves, an evocative scent that lingered on the sun-warmed air, and brought a smile of recognition to her face. It was an almost perfect distillation of the sweet aroma of sex.

Despite its isolation – or maybe because of it – this would be a great place to bring Jorge. She couldn't help thinking how much her wild Basque lover would like it here, how much *she* would like it when he stripped her roughly and took her on a carpet of scented leaves and flowers.

If she closed her eyes, she could just picture his powerful torso, the old knife-scar on his shoulder, so white against the deep tan of his chest and back. She could taste him, too: the coarse, full-bodied red-wine on his breath, the misting of sweat on his chest and belly, the irresistible potency of his cock, left deliberately un- washed because Jorge knew how it excited his prim little English girl to taste the leavings of his other women.

How many other women did Jorge have? One, ten, a hundred? Grace knew only that she would never know for sure, and that certainty in itself excited her. It swel- led her clitoris to know that her lover was an untamed animal of a man, who came to her after he had satisfied the first urgencies of his lust with other women. But always, always he came back to Grace; and always there was more than enough left for her.

Yes, here would be a wonderful place; in this neglect- ed garden, with no one to see them. She had always wanted to do it with him in the open air. Already she could imagine Jorge's delight as he threw her down on the ground and his magnificent rod of a cock parted her love-lips with a single stroke, his very indifference to her enjoyment a source of intense excitement.

She sighed as she turned to see Benedict forcing his way through the straggling undergrowth onto the old stone-flagged pathway that meandered through the grounds, forming a rough circle around the Hall. Benedict, alas, was not Jorge. Not by a long way. Jorge might have his faults, but at least he was not boring. She caught up with Benedict quickly, half-enjoying the way the springy twigs and branches caught against her as she pushed past them, their bony fingers lavishing rough, whiplash caresses on her thighs and backside.

'This place gives me the creeps,' muttered Benedict, disentangling threads of his trousers from a bramble thorn.

'Yeah? In a funny way, I like it. Sort of.'

Grace looked across what had once been a carefully-manicured lawn, towards the amiable jumble of Brackwater Hall. Her feelings towards the place were somewhat ambivalent, but there was no denying the simple, childlike pleasure of entering this secret world where nature thrived, untamed. It was like being in a kids' adventure story.

How long had the Hall been here? No one seemed to know. As far back as you cared to go, there were records of the house, in one form or another. Of course, over the centuries it had grown and changed, but still its weatherbeaten face gazed out over Lynmoor, silent and knowing.

Grace and Benedict walked side by side along the flagstones, half-obscured in places by lush, green cushions of moss and yellow-grey scabs of lichen.

'Mind you, I don't know what Allardyce thinks we're supposed to be looking for,' remarked Grace, somewhat belatedly. 'It's obvious there's nobody here.'

Benedict shrugged.

'So it's a wild goose chase. What's it to us? Allardyce pays us by the hour, remember.' He rubbed his hands together. 'I've just booked three weeks in the Seychelles.'

Grace knew the route through the grounds by heart

now. The path skirted the house and ran through a brick arch that had once held a wooden gate. The gate led into a formal walled garden that was now a hotch-potch of overgrown herbaceous borders, weeds and shrubs which together encroached on a central rectangular pond, now covered with an impenetrable sheet of greenish-black weed. Grace wrinkled her nose. The water underneath looked stagnant and brackish, and it smelt terrible. According to the locals, the pond was filled from an underground spring which had long ago supplied the Hall with drinking water; but it certainly didn't look very drinkable now. Brackwater Hall, indeed.

They crossed to the other side of the walled garden, the dilapidated gate yielding on its one rusty hinge. Beyond was a small, scrubby plot that Grace assumed must have been the kitchen garden, back in the days when Brackwater Hall was an elegant country residence. Now the asparagus beds were clogged with couchgrass, and strawberry runners covered the feathery heads of a few stunted carrots.

The back of the house was an even odder mixture of the pretty and the bizarre than the front: a hotch-potch of styles, patched up with different shades of grey stone where the tribulations of the centuries had robbed it of a stanchion here, a windowsill there. She glanced at the house, not really looking, but something caught her eye. She stopped in her tracks, tugging at Benedict's shirt. He turned round.

'What's up? Have you spotted something?'

'I don't remember that. Do you recognise it?'

'What?'

'That door.'

A few yards to the left of the conservatory, the stonework bulged out into an almost perfect three-quarter circle, forming a rather picturesque turret. Set deep into the stone was a small, red-painted door; a simple construction of wooden planks, with a bronze handle and hinges. There was really nothing terribly remarkable about it, nothing at all. Except . . .

'I remember looking at that turret yesterday, and it was just smooth stone. That door wasn't there before, I swear it wasn't.'

Benedict laughed.

'Sure it wasn't. And there are fairies at the bottom of the garden.'

Grace turned on him, irritated.

'I tell you, it wasn't. Surely I'd have noticed if it was – the rest of the house is painted white. And just look at it, it's as fresh as if it was painted yesterday.'

Even Benedict had to admit there was something a little strange about the door. He trudged towards it across the neglected soil. Close up, it was as unremarkable as ever, but it nagged at him. He reached out a finger and ran it over the paintwork, inspecting his fingertip with suspicion. Whereas the rest of the house was covered in a thin film of grime, the red door was completely clean.

'So someone's been up here,' he hazarded.

'How could they have been?' retorted Grace. 'We've been keeping watch on this place for four days and nights. No one could have got in without our noticing.'

Benedict shook his head.

'So what's your explanation? The damn thing just appeared from nowhere?'

'No, of course not.' Grace seized the door handle, then hesitated.

'It'll be locked,' observed Benedict flatly. 'All the doors in this place are locked – we tried them all, remember?'

On impulse, Grace gave the handle a quick twist. Smooth as silk, it turned, and the latch lifted with a quiet click. A triumphant smile lit up her face.

'I knew it! Coming in?'

'I guess.'

Grace went first, stepping into a short passageway which had no discernible windows, and yet was bathed in a dusky golden light, like the glow from a setting autumnal sun. She caught her breath as Benedict closed the door behind them.

'Don't want anyone knowing we're in here,' he pointed out. Grace noticed how the honey-coloured light flattered him, casting soft shadows on the regular features that she had always thought of as bland and slightly boring.

The walls of the passageway were bare stone. The floor was made from the same stone, but worn into smooth indentations by the feet of centuries. In front of them hung a curtain of dark red, heavy material that obscured the rest of the passageway, giving no clue as to what lay beyond. But, as Grace reached out to touch it, it seemed to her that the fabric moved slightly, as though caught by the wind.

She pulled back the curtain, and saw that beyond stood a staircase, with carved banisters above bare, wooden treads. Perhaps a dozen stairs led up to a small landing, where the stairs changed direction and led further on, out of sight. The anticipation of discovery flooded into her like the waters of a crystal-clear ocean, making her feel alive for the first time in days. Alive and excited.

'Come on,' she urged, placing her foot on the first step. The banister felt warm and reassuring to the touch, like the hand of a friend.

'You think we should go up there?' There was a note of doubt in Benedict's voice. 'Why don't we just . . .'

'Come *on*.' In her eagerness, Grace had completely forgotten her resolution to give Benedict a hard time. She felt like an adolescent again; an adventurous and slightly wicked adolescent, doing what she shouldn't do in a place where she wasn't supposed to be. She took Benedict by the hand and they climbed the stairs together, silent now except for the sound of their footsteps on the bare treads, and the low, whispering harmonies of their breathing.

Three narrow, arched windows lined the first landing. Grace felt sure she had not noticed any windows quite like that from the outside of the Hall, but evidently she was more unobservant than she had thought. The painted glass set into the deep-cut stone surround had all the irregularities of extreme age; Grace paused to touch one of the panes, and felt the swirling ridges under her fingertips.

Yet the colours remained vibrant, casting pools of red and blue and green and yellow on the age-darkened wood of the staircase. Colours within pictures that were not pictures; that seemed at first to be one thing, and then changed as she looked at them. A face, a tree, a star; changing, shifting images that made no sense and yet drew the eye with an unrelenting fascination. A woman, a man, the joy of naked, unbridled coupling in a cascade of jewel-bright colours . . .

Drawing away her gaze with difficulty, Grace turned to Benedict. In the shifting colours from the windows, he seemed suddenly very different, not at all the same Benedict Green who chewed gum and shaved only when he felt like it. He seemed different, and much more attractive somehow. She had the strangest impulse to touch him . . .

Her fingers made contact with his face, and a little shiver of electricity seemed to run from her fingertips into his body, answering her need with his own. Benedict's chocolate-brown eyes locked on to hers, and for a few seconds they were spinning together in a vortex of multi-coloured light, a dream-world of the senses in which their bodies met and melded, to the rhythm of pure pleasure.

In the pleasure-dream they were no longer individuals, but a single, sensual whole. Together they moved like silent swimmers in a rainbow of light; sight and touch blending like the notes of an unheard symphony.

With a gasp Grace tore herself free of the whirlpool of desire. As her fingers left his skin, she saw Benedict's eyes close as though in sudden pain. And in that moment it was over, and the craziness had left her. Had Benedict shared the strange hallucination? Grace felt sure that he had. And yet it seemed quite unbelievable. They were just two ordinary people standing on a staircase. A man and a woman. A woman whose body still throbbed with the embers of her sudden and inexplicable need.

They turned away from the windows and climbed three more flights of stairs. They did not speak. There were no words to describe what they had seen and felt – or had they just imagined it?

At last they came to a door – a simple, red-painted door like the one they had entered by. It seemed the most natural thing in the world to turn the handle and step inside.

'It's ...'

Lost for words, Benedict stood in the centre of the circular attic room, his face a picture of delighted astonishment. Grace understood exactly how he felt. This room was like nothing she had ever seen before, and yet she accepted it without question. She did not question how a room that had been closed up for over two years might contain not a trace of dust ...

'Do you suppose the rest of the house is like this?' Grace heard herself speaking, but it sounded like someone else's voice, very far away. 'Look at all that gold, the silver ...'

'There's something about this place,' murmured Benedict. 'Something I can't quite understand.'

The room was large for an attic, and a curious combination of the opulent and the spartan. Solid gold and silver trinkets lay on a polished walnut table, which in turn stood on bare boards. Twin oil lamps, carved in the figures of naked women, stood at the head and foot of an elegant couch, upholstered in softest red velvet.

Scarlet. Scarlet, the colour of passion, the colour of sex.

There were mirrors everywhere. The whole room was filled with mirrors. Silver frames, gilt frames, brass and gilt and papier mâché frames. The light spilling in through the tiny windows caught each in turn, filling the room with light.

Standing in the centre of the room with Benedict,

70

Grace looked slowly round and caught the multiple reflections of a young man and a young woman. They
were standing very close together, their hands almost
touching, and their eyes full of a desire they did not
have the guile to conceal. She tried to turn away, but
everywhere her eyes met with the same truth. Her heart
began to beat faster. She was unsure if this was what she
wanted, if she dared give in to the instinct that was
burning in her belly.

Her mind reeling, she fought to control the rising tide
that was not quite fear, not quite desire. Benedict's face
was slightly turned away from her. She saw how beautifully the light seemed to favour him, how soft were the
sandy-brown curls on the back of his neck, how strong
the curve of those shoulders.

'Benedict . . ?'

He turned to look at her, and she was lost. She no
longer saw him as the colleague she disdained, the man
she had for so long disregarded.

'You're a very beautiful woman, Grace. I never noticed it before – God knows, I don't understand how –
but you are. The most beautiful woman I've ever set
eyes on.'

Grace trembled at the light touch of his hand on hers.

'I want you, Grace.'

As she looked deep into his eyes, all memory of what
he and she had been faded away, leaving only the image
of purest desire. In that moment, Benedict became the
most attractive man in the world, her one and only
lover, the embodiment of her deepest desires.

Still she fought the impulse, some faraway voice telling her no, when all she wanted to do was say yes.

'It's crazy, Benedict. You know that it's crazy, it makes
no sense.'

'I want you. I want you now.'

His hand smoothed the back of her collar-length red-
blonde hair, and she responded to the touch instinctively, as a cat responds to its master's caress. A low murmur of pleasure escaped from her lips.

71

Slowly, gently, he slipped off her jacket and let it fall to the ground. Underneath, she was wearing a sleeveless t-shirt and short cotton skirt; her feet were bare in low-heeled sandals. So scantily clad, she was, oh, such easy prey for her hungry lover.

As he undressed her, he kissed away her fears, kindling her passion with a skill she had never imagined he could possess. His lips were cool and gentle, yet they seemed to spark fire from her flesh, burning where they touched, making her nipples and her clitoris throb with an intensity that had ceased to frighten her.

His hands roamed over her backside, his fingers deftly releasing the button at the side of her skirt and sliding down the zipper with a soft hiss. The skirt itself, normally tight about her hips, slipped easily down over her thighs and onto the polished wooden floor.

The t-shirt he slid up over her head, revealing the lace-clad swell of her bosom. The friction of her nipples against the hard lacy fabric was almost painful, they were so aroused; and Grace gave a little sigh of release as he unfastened her bra and slid it slowly from her breasts.

It felt good to be naked in this place, naked with her hardened nipples rubbing against Benedict's shirt-front. His warmth oozed into her through the thin fabric, the tang of his sweat an aphrodisiac she knew she would never tire of. He put his hands on her hips and drew her very close as he kissed her face – her cheeks, her lips, her brow, her closed eyelids – and she growled with pleasure as the secret hardness of his dick pressed against her pubis, awakening still more thoughts of the pleasure that she must and would have with him.

Her mind was a kaleidoscope of vibrant colours; some as cool as the touch of Benedict's fingers on the swell of her backside; others as hot as the passion that burned in the inferno of her sex. And when she closed her eyes, she saw the same image that she had seen before: a man and a woman naked, their bodies locked as they entered the vortex of desire.

Grace purred with delight, grinding her sex-moistened pubis against the agreeable roughness of Benedict's zip. The little metal teeth were stretched taut across the bulge of his cock, making them stand out so that they bit gently into her flesh, tangling oh so prettily with the wiry curls of her pubic hair. Eyes still closed, she clutched at her lover's back, urging him to force himself harder against her, rubbing herself up and down the long, hard ridge of his cock, so that her pussy-lips opened and anointed him with a fragrant smearing of her love-juice. She was ready for him now. More than ready.

Benedict was right. There was something about this place – something that made you feel raw and sexy and soft and yielding, all at the same time. But even as the thought entered her mind it was gone, to be replaced once again by the hot red glow of burning hunger. There was no time now to ask questions of why or how; no need, and no desire, to break the warm and sensual spell which held them so effortlessly in its thrall. It was as if someone, something, did not want them to think; only to fuck.

They kissed, and Grace parted her lips to take Benedict's eager tongue into her mouth. It seemed immense, a battering-ram of flesh that mimicked the hard thrust of a penis; arrogant in its strength. It wanted to possess her, and she yielded to it joyfully, loving the way the muscular tongue-tip pushed deep into her mouth, then retreated to invite her own tongue to enter the warm, wet cavern between Benedict's parted lips.

Grace felt herself growing mad with desire, all self-control ebbing away fast as Benedict's lewd and knowing fingers traced the forbidden furrow between her buttocks, seeking out and tormenting the tight amber rose of her arse. She shivered with delicious shame. Even with Jorge she had not enjoyed such pleasure. And he had never taken the time to play with her so intimately, so knowingly. Jorge's imperative was always to get his dick between his woman's pussy-lips. Well-endowed

73

and never short of sexual partners, he took it for granted that she would enjoy the experience.

His right hand between Grace's buttocks, Benedict's finger moved slowly downwards, the sharpness of his nail making her gasp as he teased the sensitive membrane of her perineum; then, just as she was longing for him to go further, to be more extreme, it moved still further downwards, diving suddenly into her dripping-wet womanhood.

'Yes, yes, yes,' she heard herself moaning. She clutched convulsively at Benedict's backside, as though trying to mimic the movements of his fingers with her own. Her song was a mantra of need, an invocation to ever more intense pleasure; and Benedict responded to it, thrusting his finger in and out of her, winding it in a circular motion so that it stretched and tormented the walls of her vagina, making them ooze still more with her fragrant honeydew.

Suddenly he reached between their bodies with his left hand and felt for the tag on his zipper. It yielded easily, almost with relief, as though grateful to be released from the pressure of his bursting cock.

He pulled slightly away from Grace, and took hold of her hand. Her eyes followed greedily as he placed it on the front of his pants, and her fingers explored what lay within. Inside his jeans, Benedict's silk boxers were damp with the oozings of his own arousal. Her fingers pushed impatiently through the vent and closed around the hot shaft of his prick. A sigh of pleasure trembled through him at her touch, and she could feel a pulse throbbing beneath her fingers; the pulse of his desire.

Grace felt dizzy with expectation, her head filled with the swirling coloured lights and images of passion. She felt as though, like the windows, she too was made of stained glass, and the fierce glare of sexual need was burning through her, like a painted prism.

Benedict unfastened his shirt, peeled it off and let it fall to the floor. His skin was the palest golden colour, and when Grace ran her tongue over his small, erect

74

nipples, they tasted salty, like the clear blue ocean lapping against a tropical beach.

His jeans and underpants followed, and as they stood naked in each other's arms, the truth of Grace's daydream flooded back to her. Like the figures in the dream, they were blending; their bodies so tightly clasped together that they were one entity, one passion.

Benedict's voice was barely a whisper, but she heard it clearly above the rushing of blood in her head, the frantic pounding of her heart.

'I want to have you, Grace. I *must* have you.'

The words sent shivers of delicious excitement through Grace's body, like a trickle of melting ice on a sunbather's skin.

'Take me now. I want it so much . . .'

His arms closed about her again, lifting her up, carrying her across the room to the couch. As she looked up at the ceiling it seemed to be slowly spinning, and she almost fancied she could hear the faint strains of distant music. But that was crazy – as crazy as the fact that she was about to make love with Benedict Green.

He laid her down on the couch, her skin very white against the scarlet of the soft velvet cushions, her pale red-blonde hair forming a halo about her face. She looked up at him and he smiled. His cock was an arching bow of flesh, its clubbed head slick with moisture; and she longed to lick it off, to taste its spiciness on her tongue. Her swollen clitoris throbbed and ached with the thought of it; the thought of that smooth, hard cock sliding into the wet haven between her thighs.

'Touch me,' she breathed.

Already she was painfully close to orgasm. All it would take was the lightest touch of a fingertip, the flick of a playful tongue across the head of her love-bud. But Benedict had other plans for her.

His hands smoothed and stroked her breasts and belly, paying special attention to the nipples before moving slowly and tantalisingly down over her belly. He was as aroused as Grace; she could hear his breathing, quick and shallow, filled with the anticipation of ecstasy. But he was playing with her, toying with her need, building it up by denying her the one thing she craved: the touch of his fingers on her clitoris.

He smoothed the skin of her belly and thighs with infinite delicacy, and she groaned and writhed in pleasure which was all the more piquant because it was blended with intense longing. Her inner thighs were wet with the juices from her pussy, her love-lips pouting and swollen with need. For a brief moment he brushed the damp curls of her maidenhair, and she arched her back, certain that he would release her from her agony. But his fingers moved away again, arousing and tormenting as they soothed and caressed.

Little by little, she rolled onto her side and then her belly, submitting to the tyranny of Benedict's skilful caresses. As he massaged her buttocks, her pubis rubbed up and down slightly on the soft covering of the couch, and her love-lips parted a fraction, releasing a trickle of clear, sweet fluid onto the red velvet.

Benedict's hands felt strong and resolute on the soft swell of her backside, his fingers taking hold of her flesh in handfuls and prising her buttocks slowly apart. When she felt his tongue probing the furrow between her arse-cheeks, she squealed with pleasure. The warm wet tongue-tip was moistening her flesh with saliva as it flicked across the secret rosebud of her anus.

He slid up her body to kiss the bare nape of her neck, and his cock-tip danced its desire against the flesh of her lower back. Inarticulate in her excitement, Grace could only sigh and moan her need, praying that Benedict would understand.

He did. With a deliberate slowness, he pulled apart her bum-cheeks and placed the tip of his swollen penis against the puckered kiss of her anus. Her whole body tensed as she felt him prepare to enter her, some vestigial instinct still afraid for the loss of this one last virginity.

But his first thrust astonished her in its savagery; the

secret gate of her intimacy was torn open with delicious brutality. Tears of pain and pleasure flooded her eyes as he thrust a second time, this time entering her like a burning sword, his manhood filling her so tightly that she felt she could not take much more.

Slowly they began to move together, discovering their own ways to pleasure, exploring the forbidden as an adolescent explores her own body, with a lascivious innocence. And as Benedict thrust deep into her again and again, Grace felt her pussy-lips opening, parting to allow the stalk of her clitoris to be caressed by the scarlet cushions on which she lay.

Fierce sunlight flashed through dozens of tiny windowpanes, casting many-coloured shadows on the floor, the ceiling, the couch, where two lovers writhed, impervious to anything but their own passion.

Soon all was silence in the attic room, save for the staccato harmony of the lovers' breathing and the rhythmic squeak of the old couch beneath them as they coupled.

And a soft click as the door closed behind them, shutting out the outside world.

In his office on the fourth floor of the CA Building, Leon Duvitski contemplated the distance between his ideal world and the realities of working for Charles Allardyce.

Not that there was any real discrepancy in their opinions; quite the reverse. From the first time they'd met, Duvitski had believed implicitly in Allardyce's plans. But Allardyce was an ambitious and impatient man; he did not always fully comprehend the difficulties involved in turning his dreams into reality.

Take Lynmoor, for example. Duvitski stood over the table-top scale model of the Lynmoor Development, and told himself that a few ignorant villagers and stubborn archaeologists were not going to stand in the way of progress.

It was unfortunate, of course, that the proposed new road would go straight through the middle of an ancient stone circle and Bronze Age burial ground, but the Consortium had made a perfectly reasonable offer to move the stones to a more suitable location, on the other side of Lynmoor. They'd form a nice tourist feature there, too, and CA Developments had even drawn up plans for a visitor centre and family picnic area. What more could you do for these people? You couldn't expect progress to be halted by a few tatty old stones – half of which were broken anyway. But still people grumbled.

Then there was the question of Brackwater Hall. Allardyce had set his heart on it, and Duvitski had to admit that it was the ideal site for the luxury hotel complex. Using the old Hall as a starting-point, they could build on a series of modern extensions, and Ducasse would have a field-day creating a deluxe hotel that the people of Lynmoor could be proud of. The only snag was finding someone they could buy the Hall from. Myint's scant information had suggested that a woman from Cambridge might be coming up to claim it as an inheritance, but – to judge from Grace and Benedict's silence over the last few days – she hadn't turned up yet.

And what if she did turn up, and then decided that she didn't want to sell? It was a possibility they ought to consider, though Duvitski couldn't imagine anyone in their right mind wanting to live in a crumbling old heap like Brackwater Hall. Compulsory purchase orders left such a nasty taste in the mouth, and CA Developments could do without the bad publicity.

The door of the office opened and Janis, his PA, shimmied into the room.

'You look good today, Janis,' he observed, taking in the swell of two pert bosoms, tightly encased in a short black suit which managed to be both sophisticated and tarty at the same time.

She returned his schoolboy leer with a self-confident smile.

'I always look good,' she replied. 'At least, that's what you always say.' Happy to have put him in his place, she produced a manila folder and placed it neatly on his desk. The knowing way she bent over his desk, showing several inches of firm thigh, drove Duvitski wild; and she knew it.

'The file you wanted,' she announced, then turned to go. 'And if there's anything else you want . . .'

'Well . . .' began Duvitski. He could think of at least one thing he wouldn't mind having, right now.

'I'll be in a private meeting with Mr Allardyce.'

With another of her come-hither-but-don't-touch-me smiles, she was gone. Duvitski sat down at his desk and tried to apply his brain to the matter in hand. Lynmoor. And to be more precise, opposition to the development plans. What CA Developments needed was an ally.

He looked down at the cover of the file, and opened it. Inside was a police photograph of a bearded young man with a black eye. The picture was labelled: '203497 Benjamin Tarrant.'

Benjamin Tarrant – also known as Carolan.

It was late afternoon when Maria got off the bus in Lynmoor, tired but relieved. It was an unseasonably hot afternoon for early June, with air so still that not even a blade of grass moved, but Maria found it not in the least bit oppressive. She raised her closed eyelids to the sun and basked like a lizard in the heat. If this was what it was usually like in Lynmoor, perhaps she was going to like it here after all.

To her surprise, she realised that she was already liking the place more than she'd expected. It had none of the pretty-prettiness she'd seen in Cotswold villages, or the dreary flatness of the fens. Here the countryside seemed carved from the earth with a true passion; deep valleys and rugged moorland, a whole rainbow of greens and browns beneath an ever-changing, ever-moving sky. Behind and above the village, a few heavy white clouds hung over the high ground. They cast dark shadows on what looked rather like a gypsy encampment, clustered round what was surely an ancient stone circle. She must visit the site and find out more about it.

She had always been fascinated by this part of the British Isles; its mysterious history, unique language and connection with paganism and goddess-worship. Her paternal grandfather had been born in Cornwall but detested the place, moving north at the age of fourteen, never to return. Since then, the family had had no connection with Cornwall – so it seemed odder than ever to Maria that she should have had a Cornishwoman as an aunt. Still, when she saw Theodore Myint in the morning, he would doubtless be able to clear up the mystery.

As she cast her eyes to the moorland above the other side of the valley, a rocky tor on the horizon drew her gaze and her heart quickened. The far-distant, irregular shape of a house stood silhouetted against the blue sky, still darker and more mysterious than the ground upon which it stood. She had studied the map; she was certain she couldn't be mistaken. Surely that must be Brackwater Hall.

Picking up her bags, she made her way across the road to the Duke of Gloucester, where she had reserved a room for the night. Perhaps tomorrow, if the house was habitable, she would spend the night at Brackwater Hall. The thought gave her an unexpected thrill of anticipation. If nothing else, this was turning out to be an adventure.

A rather hunky young man, blond with twinkling blue eyes, greeted her on the threshold of the inn. He had the hard physique and tanned skin of a man who is used to working out of doors in all weathers. Their eyes met and Maria could hardly fail to respond to his amiable grin.

'Ain't seen you around before,' he observed, blocking the doorway so that she would have to put down her bags and talk to him. 'New, are you?'

'I'm a visitor.'

'That so?' The young man took a swig of beer from the bottle he was holding, and Maria found herself looking at him with interest only slightly tinged with annoyance. He set down the empty beer bottle on the windowsill. 'Then what you need is someone to show you round.'

'Maybe.' There was a certain raw charm about the young rogue, an innocent sensuality imperfectly masked by his veneer of cocky self-assurance. 'We'll have to see.'

'Buy you a drink, can I?'

'Later, perhaps. I'm very tired.'

Maria picked up her bags.

'Can I just get inside? Please?'

Regretfully, the young man stepped aside and she pushed past, only too aware of the way he rubbed himself against her as she squeezed through the narrow doorway. The sensation was not entirely unpleasant.

'Just you remember,' the young man called after her. 'You want showin' round, or anythin', you just ask for Geraint Morgan. Ain't no one knows this place like I do.'

Anthea loved parties, and these post-exam bashes were always the best. It was a pity Maria wasn't here to enjoy this one too. She still couldn't understand what had got into Maria's head, wanting to go off like that on what would inevitably turn out to be a fool's errand. It all sounded rather suspicious to her. People didn't go round leaving their houses to complete strangers. There was bound to be a catch.

But Anthea had neither the time nor the energy to think too much about Maria's whims. Not when Tony was catering so beautifully for her own.

Anthea was under no illusions about Tony Fitzhardinge. She knew all about his reputation, and about the fact that he'd been pursuing Maria for a good six months. She also suspected that he had only taken a carnal interest in her to try and make Maria jealous – not that there was much chance of that. But Anthea had no intention of becoming just another in Tony's long line of victims – used and disposed of as easily as an old Kleenex. She had him where she wanted him and she knew exactly what she was doing. Or at least, she hoped she did.

81

'Let me, Anthea.' Tony's voice was insistent as a small boy's in a sweetshop. 'I locked the bathroom door. No-one will see us.'

He tried to put his hand on her breast, but she caught it before it made contact, and lifted it away.

'I told you – not till later.' She smiled teasingly at him and made sure he got a really good look down the front of her dress as she touched up her make-up in the mirror. The sounds of frantic partying rose up from the room downstairs.

'But you haven't let me touch you all evening,' protested Tony.

'That was the whole idea, remember? No touching until much later. Until I say.'

Tony gave a suppressed groan of frustration. Anthea looked at him and felt a rather pleasing mixture of conflicting impulses. He looked so crestfallen and sulky that she wanted to laugh, cry, tear off her clothes, suck his poor, neglected prick, and let him do all the things he longed to do to her. But a bargain was a bargain, and a game was a game. If Tony could play games, so could she.

The sex-game had been Anthea's idea in the beginning, but Tony had loved it. She'd read about it in a cheap American novel. The heroine – a rich, sophisticated older woman – had wanted to tantalise her young stud of a lover, and revive his flagging interest. So she had put on her sexiest, slinkiest underwear in front of him, slowly and seductively, whilst he watched, positively drooling for her. Then her stockings, her dress, her jewellery . . . At which point they went off together, to a party.

It was an ingenious game, but it had only one rule. That rule was inviolable. The heroine's lover must not try to touch her at any time until he was given permission to do so. And it worked. By the time they got back from the party, four hours later, they were both at the exploding point of frustration, and had the best sex of their lives.

Yes, it had seemed like a wonderful idea to Tony at the beginning, watching his brand-new lover dress herself up in satin and lace, just for him, but once he'd realised that Anthea was going to play it strictly by the rules, he began to get edgy and insistent. Here in the bathroom, he'd cornered her at last; and he didn't intend taking no for an answer.

'Don't you want me any more?' He edged a bit closer to Anthea and tried putting his arm round her waist. He could see the outline of her tight satin bra through the light, clingy fabric of her party dress.

Anthea eased away with a suppressed smile. She was enjoying this.

'Of course I do.'

'Then let's do it. Here, now. You don't even need to undress. Just take off your panties and let me . . .'

'Uh-huh.' She shook her head.

'Look, you needn't worry. No one will disturb us, not in here.' He rested his hand lightly on her arm, though what he really wanted to do was grab her firm, juicy arse and rip her panties down. She'd really got him going. Insolent, imperious, gorgeous little minx . . .

Behind her cool outer veneer, Anthea was desperately tempted. It would be fun to let him have her, here in their host's opulent bathroom. Maybe they could even do it in the sunken bath; or she could bend over that little shell-shaped sink with the gold-plated taps, and let him ram into her from behind. The gusset of her panties was sodden with excitement at the very thought – but then that was the whole idea of the game, wasn't it? She giggled.

'You know what they say.'

'What?'

'Abstinence makes the heart grow fonder.'

'For pity's sake, Anthea, you're such a prick-tease!'

'I know. Isn't it wonderful? Don't you just love it?'

'This is slowly killing me, I hope you realise that.' Tony reached under the waistband of his pants and re-adjusted the long and bursting shaft of his cock.

'Aren't I worth the wait?'

'Tell me again – remind me what I'm missing.'

'Oyster silk French knickers, stockings and suspenders, the cutest little satin bra with peepholes for the nipples. The one I bought on that trip to Paris . . .'

'And what will you give me later, if I'm a good boy?'

'Ah, that would be telling.'

'Will you suck me off?'

'Maybe. Maybe not.'

'Will you let me soap your breasts and then come all over them?'

Anthea made a low, sexy growling sound in her throat. The prospect was tempting.

'Wait and see.'

She ran her finger lightly down the front of his pale grey trousers, and he shuddered, his prick painfully distended with longing.

'I thought we said no touching.'

Anthea shook her head.

'No, we said you couldn't touch me. I can do anything I like. Anything at all. I'm the mistress and you're the slave tonight. Rules of the game, remember?'

His eyes closed in mute agony.

'What's up now?'

'I need a pee.'

'So what's the problem? You're not shy, are you?'

'How the hell am I supposed to pee with a hard-on like this?' He unzipped himself and his dick sprang out, swollen with need. 'You're just going to have to let me fuck you. Call it an act of mercy, if you like.'

Anthea laughed, and popped her lipstick back into her bag.

'I've heard some chat-up lines in my time . . .'

'Anthea!' Tony tried to force her hand onto his dick but she pulled it gently away.

'Sorry, darling. You're flying solo on this one. See you downstairs when you've finished.'

Leaving him speechless, she unlocked the bathroom door and abandoned him to his tormenting fantasies.

Downstairs, she mingled again with the teeming throng of dedicated partygoers. Don Doonan, the record producer, certainly knew how to throw a party at his palatial riverside home.

Just as she was getting herself another drink from the kitchen, Anthea caught sight of someone she knew. Someone she knew, but habitually avoided like the plague. It was Terry Kestelman, and wasn't that a new escort he had with him tonight? She was certainly a looker: a tall, blonde woman with ice-blue eyes and thin, rather expressionless lips. Anthea vaguely recognised her as a new lecturer from St Alcuin's, and wondered how much Terry had had to pay her to accompany him to the party.

Anthea slipped away, but Terry had seen her and made a beeline for her, leaving the girl chatting to a group of his loud friends.

'Hello, Anthea. Fancy meeting you here.'

'I didn't know you were a friend of Don's,' observed Anthea. Evidently Don's taste had taken a nosedive.

'Oh you know, friend of a friend.'

'So you gatecrashed, then?'

'Now, Anthea, would I do a thing like that?' Terry's fat red face loomed too close in her field of vision, and she took a step back. 'Met Kirin, have you?'

'Yes, I've seen her around St Alcuin's. New, isn't she?'

'New, yes, but friendly too, if you know what I mean.' Undaunted by Anthea's frosty reception, Terry took a step nearer. She could smell his breath, and wondered how – and why – Kirin put up with it. 'Perhaps you ought to think about being a bit friendlier to me too, Anthea?'

She stared at him blankly, hoping she had misconstrued his clumsy advance.

'Friendly? Meaning what?'

'Meaning you could give me what your friend Maria wouldn't give me. Snooty cow. But you're not like that, are you, Anthea? You understand the benefits of being . . . cooperative towards me, don't you? Now I'm on the

85

Appointments Board, I have a lot of influence. There are some people it's better to have as friends than enemies, if you know what I mean.'

At that moment, Tony returned, and Anthea greeted him with a warm smile, grateful to be rescued from Terry Kestelman's lizard charm.

'I have to go now, Mr Kestelman.'

'Ah, right, yes.' Kestelman's face cracked into a filthy grin. 'I can see you two have got things you want to get on with. But think about what I said.'

'What did that creep want?' demanded Tony when Kestelman had gone.

'Oh it was nothing. Nothing to worry about,' replied Anthea. And in all honesty she wasn't really worrying about herself. There wasn't much that Kestelman could do to her. No, it was Maria she was really worried about. And Maria wasn't here to stand up for herself.

The morning was already golden and warm as Maria left the Duke of Gloucester and struck out alone for Brackwater Tor. Later that day, she would return to the village to see Theodore Myint; but first, she wanted to find out exactly what it was that she was supposed to have inherited.

A slight breeze ruffled her long red hair as she climbed the winding path from the valley floor, and she savoured the feel of the cool air on the bare skin of her arms. It felt good to be here, in this wild place where the ancient spirits felt strong and very real.

She did not see the tall, dark figure standing amongst the trees on the valley side, nor the brief flash as sunlight caught the silver rings on his right hand.

Pendorran's eyes narrowed with pleasure as he watched Maria Treharne walk up onto the moors, towards the tumbledown silhouette of Brackwater Hall. A quiet, ecstatic whisper escaped from his lips.

'Mistress . . .'

# Chapter Five

Maria pushed open the little wicket gate with a slight feeling of apprehension. The old wood yielded to a slightly harder shove, and she succeeded in opening it far enough to squeeze through into the front garden of Brackwater Hall.

The gardens were in a dreadful state. They obviously hadn't been tended for a long time – probably years. Ivy and ground elder had run riot, choking some of the more delicate plants and winding round the trunks and branches of trees like bizarre paperchains. But among the chaos and neglect were sprinklings of late spring flowers, splashes of vivid colour that caught the eye and drew it away from everything that was wrong with this poor, neglected place. There was even an orchard and a herb-garden – admittedly in complete disarray, but even from just inside the front gate Maria could smell the reassuring fragrance of sun-warmed chamomile, sweet basil and thyme.

The really strange thing about Brackwater Hall was the house itself. Despite the overgrown state of the garden, the façade of the house seemed completely unmarred by neglect. There were no cracked or broken panes of glass in the leaded windows, the white paint looked dusty but smooth, and the only external sign that the house was empty was the need for a good clean. Even the ornamental weatherboards beneath the eaves looked as if they had been freshly painted. Someone must have been making regular visits to the Hall to keep the building in good condition – so why hadn't they bothered to attend to the garden as well?

Puzzled, she walked slowly through the grounds, following a cracked flagstone path which took a vaguely circular route around the house. It meandered through straggling clumps of herbs and unpruned apple trees, and through an archway into a walled garden where the once elegant sunken pond reeked of stagnant decay. Maria made a mental note to find a gardener or handyman in the village – someone who would be able to knock the garden into shape quickly and efficiently. It looked so sad this way – like a pretty child in shabby, tattered clothes.

With a start, she realised that she was already making plans for the Hall, as though the formalities had been settled and the place was definitely hers. She reminded herself that she did not even know yet whether a mistake had been made over her 'inheritance'. Maybe it was some other Maria Treharne who had been the beneficiary of Clara Megawne's will, and next day she would find herself on the bus back to Truro.

And yet she felt at home here. It was quite odd really. She had been so apprehensive about coming anywhere near Lynmoor, let alone Brackwater Hall; and now here she was, happily strolling through the gardens as though she were already mistress of all she surveyed.

Mistress? She laughed, thinking of Jonathan and what he would make of it all. He had been so angry when she'd told him she was coming to Cornwall, his lower lip jutting out like a sulky little boy's. Even when she'd kissed away his anger, she'd sensed a tension still within him, a resentment that this mere woman should think she had found something more important than him.

She sighed. Although she was having a good time here, it would be better still if Jonathan were here too.

Even after knowing him for such a short time, she felt the lack of him keenly, like a sharp pang of loss.

It wasn't his affection she missed, of course. Jonathan Gresham wasn't a man you could love. It was the addictive pleasure of his company that she yearned for, the compulsive joy of his every subtle caress, his every perfect kiss – for Jonathan was knowing yet genuine in his lust, and Maria was flattered that his need for her seemed to match hers for him.

She thought of his body: young, tanned, golden and irresistible as some delicacy that she might treat herself to when she was feeling decadent. Yes, that was it – there was a real feeling of sensual decadence in her relationship with Jonathan. And as far as Maria was concerned, that was no bad thing.

Here, behind the think stone wall and overgrown hedges of Brackwater Hall, the cool breeze could not penetrate, and Maria felt the full force of the sun warming her back and shoulders, lending a fierce, flame-red lustre to her burnished copper hair. She walked on dreamily along the path, feeling the warmth soaking into her bones, making her lazy and sensual as a she-cat drowsing on sun-baked stones.

At each turn, Maria found something new in the house to marvel at, some new surprise. There was certainly no homogeneity about Brackwater Hall. It seemed to be an ad-hoc collage of styles stretching from mid-Victorian Neo-Gothic back to medieval and perhaps even beyond that. Some might call it a mess; Maria thought it beautiful – wild and mysterious and untamed as the north Cornish countryside over which it towered, and almost as ancient as the hills themselves.

She stroked the rounded stones of what might have once been a turret, back in the days of fortified manor houses, and the thrill of discovery raised gooseflesh on her bare arms. Although a follower of the Wicca religion and practitioner of white magic, she did not consider herself a particularly gifted sensitive. But this touch of bare flesh on ancient stone sent ripples of excitement through her. It was as though she could feel the whole of history in that stone; a history in which her own family had shared. Perhaps there was something for her here in Lynmoor, after all.

Turning away, she strolled across the remains of the vegetable garden and past the conservatory – a Victorian addition, but handsome in white-painted iron and local stone. More than one generation of gardeners must have blessed its south-facing aspect. On a whim, she tried the door – but of course it was locked, like all the other doors she had tried. It seemed her curiosity would have to wait until Mr Myint provided her with the keys to the Hall.

She walked on. Although the building itself seemed to be in good condition, a wild mat of creeper tangled over much of the eastern side of the house. Its growth had evidently not been checked for a long time, for its spidery fingers had crept across some of the stone-mullioned windows, almost obscuring them from view. Gently, Maria prised away some of the rampant greenery and found that the tiny leaded panes beneath were of pretty, painted glass, the colours still vibrant even though the glass must be centuries old.

She meant to turn and leave, but something in the centre of the wall caught her eye – something almost entirely hidden by the tight mesh of creeper. A splash of red glinted through the fresh green leaves, almost daring her to turn away and ignore it.

Fascinated, Maria pulled at the tenacious growth, tugging it away with difficulty from the wall where it had securely anchored itself. As it yielded, she realised what she had found. Hidden underneath the creeper, deeply set into the stone, was a small, red door.

Although the tangled creeper must have taken a long time to cover it up, the paint underneath the foliage curiously seemed as fresh and smooth as if it had only just been applied. It also struck Maria as faintly odd that this particular door should be painted red, when the rest of the paintwork on the house was a uniform white.

The handle was of bronze, and interestingly shaped like a serpent biting its own tail. Maria reached out to touch it, and to her immense surprise, she felt the door move slightly. Thinking she had imagined it, she turned the handle a little further to the right, and the door swung inwards on silent hinges. Beyond lay a twilit world, the darkness relieved by the small amount of coloured light that managed to filter into the house through the obscured windows.

Maria hesitated for a moment. Ought she to go in? It wasn't her house, at least not yet. Would she be trespassing?

But curiosity got the better of her, as she knew that it would. As excited as a child on a quest for buried treasure, she stepped inside.

Anthea put down her pen and stretched wearily. She'd spent all morning working, and her neck muscles were tight with fatigue; the last thing she ever wanted to do was mark another examination script. She cursed this time of year, when students were out celebrating the end of exams whilst their lecturers stayed up all hours of the day and night marking the damn things.

She glanced across at Tony, sprawled across her bed with a motorcycling magazine, and couldn't quite bring herself to curse him too. He had it made: young, rich, good-looking and clever. Everyone knew he had managed to get a First in History without really trying, and in all probability he had the ability to get a brilliant PhD too – but he was lazy. Up till now he'd been wily enough to get by on his wits, but sooner or later he was going to have to do some serious research, or the golden boy might find his arse kicked all the way back to Daddy's country estate.

Still, with Maria out of the way for a week or two, at least Tony had gained some extra time on that next chapter of his thesis. She looked at him with a gnawing ache of hunger she could not quite still. His face was turned away from her, but the yellow Chinese silk robe he was wearing was unbelted and open at the front, revealing the most tantalising glimpse of his penis.

It was large and thick even in repose, a slumbering python lying across his thigh, its head snaking under the richly-embroidered border of the robe. His pubic hair began at his navel as a thin line of golden-brown hairs, leading down to the fullness of his testicles and an abundant tangle of darker brown curls, soft and fragrant after his shower. Yes, Tony had it made. She ought to hate him, but she didn't of course. She looked at him and felt only hunger.

He glanced up from his reading and caught her watching him. Instantly he tossed aside his magazine.

'Is it time for lunch, then?'

Anthea allowed herself a lascivious smile.

'Could be.'

'You look like the cat who's got the cream.'

'And maybe I have,' replied Anthea playfully. It was no good, she couldn't do any more marking this afternoon – especially not with the delectable Tony so near at hand. It wouldn't do for him to feel neglected. She ran her fingers through her bobbed, dark-burgundy hair. 'I'm bushed. Never has so much crap been written by so many.'

Tony slid off the bed and came over to the desk. His hands felt cool and soothing on her sore, tired neck.

'Headache?'

'Mmm.'

'I'm not surprised. You've been marking those papers since after breakfast, and all you had then was a cup of black coffee.' His strong fingers started kneading her shoulders, and she winced. 'Your shoulders are all knotted up – the muscles are like iron. What you need is something to relax you, make you feel less uptight.'

Unseen by Tony, Anthea's lips curled into a sly smile. Her mind was racing ahead, imagining what might happen next. She hoped she wasn't mistaken . . .

'Oh yes? I don't suppose you'd have any suggestions to help me unwind, would you?'

'Take your shirt off, sweetheart. I'm going to give you a massage. You'd like that, wouldn't you?'

Arrogant little sod, thought Anthea, still concealing her smiling face from her young lover. He's so full of himself, he just *knows* I'm going to love everything he does to me. Trouble is, he's right.

She murmured her pleasure as Tony bent over her and nibbled her neck as his impatient young fingers fumbled with the buttons on the front of her blouse.

'How many dozen buttons are there on this thing?' he exclaimed in exasperation, the tiny mother-of-pearl discs defying even his skill and experience.

Anthea giggled.

'Don't be so impatient. Here, let me.' She prised his fingers from the buttons and unfastened them, quickly and easily, revealing the black half-cup bra she'd bought specially for Tony's benefit, from a sex-wear catalogue. It was a completely new adventure for her, but she was delighted with it.

As soon as she'd tried the bra on after her shower and seen herself in the mirror, she'd loved the way it looked. Her breasts might be only average in size, but in this underwired creation of black lace with red satin edging, they looked large and plump, round as juicy apples on a platter. The long, pink muzzles of her nipples peeped wickedly over the top of their lacy basket, the flesh puckered and hard in spite of her tiredness. She knew exactly what she looked like: she looked like a tart. And she revelled in it.

Tony drew in breath sharply.

'Well! You never said you'd been shopping . . .'

'I didn't want to spoil the surprise, did I?'

Still standing behind her, Tony let his hands slip round underneath Anthea's breasts, forming twin cups of flesh beneath the underwired shell of satin and lace. His thumbs flicked upwards, moving quickly back and forth across the very tips of Anthea's exposed nipples, and she could not suppress a little gasp of delight.

The feeling was an exquisite torment, reducing Anthea instantly to Tony's willing victim. It seemed a fitting revenge for the torments she had inflicted on him at Des Doonan's party. Within seconds she was half-laughing, half-sobbing with frustration.

'Stop, Tony, please! I thought you wanted to make me *less* tense!' she pleaded. 'I can't bear it, really I can't!'

His only response was to resume his kissing and biting, moving his lips and tongue round from the back of her neck to the side, then up to the soft, tender flesh of her right earlobe. His mouth felt wonderfully warm and wet, and his teeth teased and tormented her, his tongue working around the little diamond stud earring with a relentless devotion.

She writhed and murmured under the torture of his caresses, her backside sliding slowly backwards and forwards on the seat of her chair as her pelvis began to thrust instinctively under the force of her desire. Her legs were parted, and the shiny nylon of her black G-string stretched so tight across her pubis that the narrow gusset cut like a knife into her flesh, ruthlessly parting her love-lips and chafing her clitoris as she slid back and forth.

A warm ooze emerged from between her outspread thighs, moistening the G-string and escaping round the edges of the sodden fabric, to form a wet slick on the age-smoothened seat of the wooden chair.

'You're turned on,' remarked Tony, his voice triumphant with satisfaction. 'You've got the hots for me. I can smell you, you shameless hussy.'

Anthea squealed with astonishment as he pinched her nipples with a sudden violence that sent shivers of excitement through her, and a flood of sex-juice gushing out of her quim.

'Tony!'

'It's no good pretending to be little miss prim. I can smell your juice, Anthea. It *is* just your juice, isn't it?'

'What do you mean?'

'You haven't been screwing some other man, have you?'

There was a sly excitement in his voice. With a shiver of pleasure, Anthea realised that Tony, too, was incredibly turned on. Talking like this was one of the ways he liked to get off – imagining her with some other man, taking that man's dick into the sweet, wet haven of her yearning pussy. She wasn't surprised that it turned him on. It excited her, too.

Tony took his hands from her breasts, and she felt suddenly bereft. But a moment later he was pushing her chair away from the desk, and getting down on his knees between her parted thighs. She looked down. Tony's cock was as hard as an iron spike, and her skirt – already short – was practically up round her backside now, revealing the lacy tops of her seamed stockings. Suddenly she felt every inch the slut that Tony was making her out to be.

His fingers were on her thighs, pulling them further apart, making her reveal herself to him.

'No secrets, Anthea. I want to see everything. You can't hide your wickedness from me.'

'No.' Anthea was warming to this new game. 'I can't hide anything from you, can I?'

He pulled her thighs harder, but they could not open any further – the light fabric of her skirt was stretched as far as it would go.

'You'll tear it!' exclaimed Anthea, as he tried to force the way.

'No, I shan't,' he reassured her. 'I don't need to tear it.'

He reached behind him and found a pair of sharp scissors on Anthea's desk. Her eyes widened as he picked them up and ran the long, cold blades over her sheer black stockings and the inch or two of bare thigh that showed above them. The cold seemed to concentrate her attention, focusing her pleasure on the touch of the scissor-blade as it slid ever upward.

Tony was in an impatient mood today. A second later, and he had scissored open the fabric of her skirt from hem to waist. Her belly was bared, and the shameless mound of her sex was now divided into two fat lobes by the taut black G-string.

Tony ran his finger over the wet seat of the chair, then

along the narrow seam formed by the G-string. He put his finger to his lips and sampled the taste of her juice.

'You're very wet down there, Anthea. Wetter than you usually get for me.'

'I'm very excited.'

'Ah, but why are you excited? Is it because you've been thinking about fucking other men?' His eyes were sparkling. Anthea knew what he wanted her to do, the part he wanted her to play in this mischievous little playlet.

'What's it to you?' she said coolly.

'Or is it because you've already been fucking them? That's it, isn't it?' Tony breathed in the fragrance from his finger, the fragrance of his lover's sex. 'Yes, that's the shameful truth. I'm sure I can smell other men on you.'

'Perhaps you can,' replied Anthea. She was enjoying this, even if she had had to sacrifice one of her better skirts. 'Perhaps not.'

Tony picked up the scissors again, and ran the tip of the closed blades over the sensitive flesh of her inner thighs. She tried not to wriggle, slightly afraid of the blades, although they were not really very sharp. Playfully, Tony opened the jaws of the scissors and placed the blade under the gusset of the G-string. She trembled as the cold stainless steel touched the outer margin of her sex.

'It's no good trying to deceive me,' he continued. 'I know exactly what you've been doing. You've been opening your legs for these other men. Now I want you to tell me about them.'

So that's how you want to play it, thought Anthea. Another trickle of sex-juice oozed from her swollen pussy-lips, anointing the scissor-blades as she lay back in the chair and gave her imagination free rein.

'They were good, weren't they?' murmured Tony, slitting the sides of the G-string so that the insubstantial scrap of fabric fell away. He pulled the tattered remnant towards him, between her sex-lips, causing her the most agonising pleasure.

'Good. Oh yes . . .' Anthea savoured the feeling of the black nylon sliding between her pussy-lips, and across the head of her clitoris. 'They were so very good.'

'You're a little slut, Anthea,' growled Tony, his voice husky with excitement. 'A filthy-minded little slut who likes to have a cock in her crack.'

A groan of pleasure was the only response that Anthea could make as his muscular, ringed finger dived suddenly into the depths of her sex, almost shocking her into an instantaneous climax.

'How many cocks, Anthea? How many cocks do you like to take at once? Two, three, more?' He wanked her with his finger whilst the ball of his thumb brushed softly and tantalisingly over her hard love-button.

'Yes, yes!' screamed Anthea, caring nothing for the elderly couple in the next flat. All she cared about was the pleasure, the amazing pleasure of the fantasy in her head.

'One in your crack, and one in your mouth, and one in your hand, and one . . . one somewhere else.' A hand slid under her buttocks and searched out the tight moue of her anus with laser-beam precision. 'And one here, Anthea?'

Blushing scarlet with shameful pleasure – for it was a long time since she had let any lover touch her *there* – Anthea sobbed out her imagined penitence, dreaming up a lascivious fantasy-world that would drive both her and Tony to a frenzy of excitement.

'Yes, yes, yes! The first man's fucking me in my pussy, and I'm sucking the second one off – he's tall and dark-skinned, I think he must be an Arab. There's another cock in each of my hands. They're so big, so hard, I want them all inside me, now. These men have taken me as their slave, but I don't want to turn to run away from them, not any more. They've made me want it, you see. You do see, don't you? They've made me love all this wickedness. I couldn't help it. They used my body again and again, and now I want their cocks inside me, all the time.'

'More. Tell me more. If you want me to forgive you, I have to know it all. Every last sordid detail.'

Tony's voice was almost a whisper, the quiet whisper she recognised as the betrayal of his extreme excitement. She didn't know which was more stimulating – his finger sliding in and out of her quim, or the knowledge that she was bringing him to the point of climax with nothing more tangible than her voice.

She continued, describing the scene exactly as she pictured it in her mind. She had seldom fantasised like this in the past, and the power of her imagination astonished her. With Tony, she was learning not just how to screw well, but how to turn it into a wonderfully wicked game. Now that the fantasy was in her head, hot and so, so strong, she ached for it to come true. All of it . . .

'Now they're flipping me over onto my belly and there's a man fucking me in the arse. Oh! He's so big, so big, it hurts me . . . but it feels so good too. And the other men are wanking over me, I can feel the drops of semen falling on my back and my bum-cheeks as they climax . . .'

Suddenly she felt Tony's finger slide out of her, and when she opened her eyes he was standing over her, slipping off the yellow silk robe. She had seen him naked so many times before, but each time he surprised her with his arrogant young beauty; the self-assurance of those well-toned muscles and the set of that fine-featured, aristocratic head.

Her eyes moved from the unsmiling intensity of his face, down over the smoothness of torso and belly. She was magnetically drawn to the straining curve of his granite-hard penis, slick with moisture that made the head glisten like wet glass.

Silently he took her head and pulled it down towards his prick. She made no attempt to resist his desires; for they were hers too. Even before the fat cock-tip had slipped between her parted lips she could taste and smell him, and knew that she would need nothing more than the feel of him to push her to a climax.

98

She sucked him with genuine pleasure, her mouth and throat anointing him with saliva as her tongue worked him closer and closer to orgasm. Later, when the first urgency of his need was gone, he would carry her over to the bed and fill the emptiness of her sex with his own, ever-eager appetite. They would make love all afternoon to the lazy swish and drone of the passing traffic on the road outside, until at last they fell asleep in each other's arms, the game done.

As she sucked at Tony's prick and felt the final, wondrous hardening before he spurted into her throat, Anthea wondered vaguely if Maria was having this much fun. She hoped so. If there was one thing in the world that Maria Treharne craved more than anything else, it was pleasure.

Maria sat in the waiting-room, flicking through back-issues of *Country Life* and glancing from time to time at the ugly wooden clock on the mantelpiece.

'I'm sure he won't be long, Miss Treharne,' the receptionist reassured her with an uneasy smile. 'Mr Myint isn't normally running this late. Would you like another coffee?'

'No thanks, I'll just wait.' Maria tried to concentrate on the print but the words just swam in front of her eyes. It was silly. Dry-mouthed and twitchy, she felt as excited as a child on Christmas Eve. Now that she had seen the inside of Brackwater Hall for herself, she realised for the first time just how much she hoped there *hadn't* been a mistake over Clara Megawne's will.

It was the strangest place; but magnificent – magnificent in a way she would have found impossible to describe. Vast, silent rooms crowded with the heavy furniture and ornate *objets d'art* of an earlier age; simple rooms with whitewashed walls and plain stone floors; that huge, sweeping staircase; and stone-framed casement windows that opened out onto the wildest, most beautiful views that Maria had ever seen – these were mere snapshots in her mind, as she recalled single moments in the hour that she had spent at the Hall, exploring and at every instant discovering something new to astonish or delight.

And now, when the sharpness of memory had dulled to a confused jumble of images that ran into each other, the strongest impressions that remained with her were the impressions made by other senses – smell, and touch, and taste, and hearing. The smell of beeswax polish on polished mahogany; the touch of smooth stone and carved wood; the faint taste of salt and wild thyme on the air that blew in from the distant sea; and the gentle swishing sound of a warm wind in the apple trees.

She was far away in her thoughts when the door to Myint's office opened and a head peered out.

'Sorry to keep you waiting, Miss Tregawne. If you'd just like to come in . . .'

Maria looked up to see the thin, dried-up face of a middle-aged man with prematurely greying hair. He had thin, humourless lips and the smile on them seemed alien.

She got up, placed the magazine on a low coffee-table, and followed him into his office.

'Mr Myint?'

'Yes, indeed – but please call me Theodore. Everyone in Lynmoor does, and I'm sure I speak for all of us in saying that we hope you come to see this place as your home.'

Maria sat down, smoothing out the creases in her skirt.

'Well, I'm not sure about that, Mr Myint – Theodore. As you know, I'm a lecturer at Cambridge University, and when my Fellowship is confirmed I expect I shall have to spend a lot more time at my college.'

'St Alcuin's, is it? What a strange coincidence – my father read Law there. Beautiful old place. But I think you'll find Lynmoor has its charms, too. Few people who visit the village can resist coming back.'

'It's certainly a lovely part of the world. But I need to talk to you about my aunt's will . . .'

'Ah yes, the business in hand.'

Myint reached into his in-tray and took out a dusty folder tied with blue ribbon. He unfastened the knot with a meticulousness which Maria found rather irritating.

'Let me see, Miss Clara Megawne. She passed away almost two years ago to this very day, intestate I'm afraid – hence the difficulty I have had in tracking you down.'

'Indeed, Mr Myint – I'm rather concerned that I may not be the woman you're looking for. Frankly, I'm baffled. Megawne isn't a family name, and I'm quite certain I never had an Aunt Clara.'

Myint sat back in his chair, placed his fingertips lightly together, and surveyed her over the top of his half-moon glasses.

'I can assure you that the searches were carried out most meticulously.'

'Yes, I'm sure, but – who exactly was Clara Megawne?' insisted Maria.

'Of course, strictly speaking, Miss Megawne was not your aunt at all. It's a rather complicated relationship to describe, but as far as I can determine she was a remote cousin on your mother's side. That is surely all you need to know.'

'I suppose . . .' replied Maria weakly. 'But what sort of woman was she?'

Myint paused and gave a shrug, as though at a loss for the right words.

'She kept herself to herself.'

'What was she like, though? Can't you tell me anything about her?'

'You must understand that Miss Megawne was somewhat of a recluse, Miss Treharne. She did not mix easily with others. And so you see, I did not know her well. None of us did.'

With apparent relief, he made a deft and decisive change of subject.

'Now to the details of the will. The Hall and its

101

grounds are to pass to you in their entirety, and there is also a cash legacy which should provide you with quite a useful private income.'

Maria's jaw dropped.

'A private income? Just how much are we talking about?'

'The exact figures have yet to come to me. But the money is held in a trust fund, and each year the interest will accrue to you. Let us just say that it should prove sufficient to live modestly, but entirely comfortably.'

'I see.' Maria's head was reeling. 'I'd just been expecting the Hall, and nothing else.'

'I can see this has come as quite a shock to you,' remarked Myint. 'Perhaps you would like to clear your head with a walk in the fresh air? It's a beautiful afternoon, and I have the keys to the Hall here. You must be most eager to view your new possession.'

'Actually, er ... actually, I already have,' replied Maria sheepishly. 'I went up there this morning and had a nose around. Oddly enough, I found that one of the doors was unlocked, so I was able to have a look round the interior.'

'Indeed?' Myint's eyes gleamed with interest. 'And what was your opinion of the place?'

'Magnificent. Strange, but very beautiful. There are a few things I'd like to change, but hardly anything, really.'

'Good, good. Then perhaps if you'd just like to sign here for the keys ...'

Maria accepted the proffered fountain pen.

'There is just one other thing that puzzles me.'

'Of course.'

'I take it the house has been empty since Miss Megawne's death?'

'Certainly it has.'

'The thing is, the gardens are completely overgrown, but the house seems in an excellent condition. I take it the estate has been employing a handyman to make sure the Hall doesn't fall into disrepair?'

102

Myint's expression seemed to freeze momentarily; then he smiled.

'I'm afraid you're quite mistaken, Miss Treharne. Nobody has been near Brackwater Hall for at least two years. Not since the day Miss Megawne passed away.'

A few moments after Maria had gone back through into the reception area, a side door opened and a tall, dark figure entered Myint's office from the adjoining room.

Myint looked up questioningly, and Pendorran nodded his satisfaction.

'You have done well, Theodore,' he said. 'Now, at long last, the game may begin.'

Charles Allardyce brought the meeting to order with a look that could vaporise granite.

'Ladies and gentlemen, may I draw your attention to the rather fine scale model in the adjoining room. My colleague Mr Duvitski and I will of course be happy to answer any questions you may have about the Lynmoor Development.'

He shepherded the gaggle of City bankers and fat-cat industrialists into the ante-room, confident of his ability to persuade them to part with yet more of their capital, once they saw the ambitious plans for Phase Two and Phase Three. Of course, this was just the first stage in getting them really hooked. Once they'd expressed interest in the initial investment package he'd get them down to the Marketing Suite in Lynmoor, where Duvitski would use all his wiles to charm the money out of their wallets.

Not that this was in any way a con. Unlike some of the projects Allardyce had been involved in, the Lynmoor Development was not in the least bit dodgy. Once they'd ironed out the minor problems with local opposition – and iron them out they would – the investors would be putting their money on a cast-iron certainty.

'What is this, please, Mr Allardyce?'

Allardyce turned to answer the Japanese businessman's

103

question, following his jabbing finger to the centre of the scale model.

'That, Mr Takimoto, is our planned luxury hotel complex.'

'And why is it coloured blue? All the other buildings seem to be coloured white.'

'That is because we have not yet acquired the necessary land and buildings.'

'I see.' Allardyce could see Igushi Takimoto's mind turning over, examining the possibilities for his potential investment should CA Developments fail to obtain the necessary land and buildings. 'This is a problem, yes?'

'No,' replied Allardyce, firmly. 'It is not a problem at all.'

He wished Duvitski had something concrete from Grace Hawley and her sidekick – they hadn't heard from them in days.

'No, we don't anticipate any difficulties in carrying out our plans. The acquisition is a mere formality. In fact, Mr Takimoto, I can assure you that our purchase of Brackwater Hall and its surrounding land is certain to take place within the next few weeks.'

Maria sat in a deep, soft armchair and gazed out over the moors towards the thin blue smudge of the sea. The huge first-floor drawing room had already enchanted her, with its Victorian clutter of ornaments and the heavy, polished furniture of a byegone and more stately age.

The room was bigger than her entire set of rooms at Cambridge, and infinitely more gracious, mused Maria as she relaxed into the soft plush of the cushions. The centrepiece was an amazing fireplace in fine Italian marble, carved into an intricate tracery of leaves and flowers, and supported by two beautiful statues of naked men.

Above it was a heavy mirrored overmantel – perhaps not quite in keeping with the general tone of the room, but then that was the beauty of Brackwater Hall. It was quirky, unconventional, totally individual. Viewed with a critical eye, nothing seemed to quite go with anything else. The moth-eaten tigerskin rug clashed with the Egyptian Ushabti figurine; the massive grandfather clock seemed to be doing its best to ignore the tiny Goss Ware jug whose legend read 'Llandudno, 1906'. Each room was different in tone and colour and decor from the rest, and yet everything blended in together wonderfully well, into an harmonious whole.

Perhaps the oddest thing about this house was that it didn't seem to be quite the same as she'd remembered it from her first visit. She could have sworn the wallpaper had been a pale and rather insipid pink, not this bold Regency stripe – which she much preferred. Then there was the crack in the lintel above the kitchen door – had it really disappeared, or had it never been there in the first place? She put it down to tiredness; after all, this was an enormous house – how many bedrooms had she counted, seven, nine? The memory could easily play tricks in a place this size.

Heck, it was weird, it was insane; but already Maria was falling in love with Brackwater Hall. It was a place she could respond to – mind, body and soul. Never had she felt such sensuality in a place; a sensuality that had seemed to soak into her from the moment she set foot in the blissful tangle of the overgrown garden.

Her body ached for sexual release. It had been so long – too long. She thought of Jonathan and wondered if . . . But no, he was busy – he'd told her so. He had research to do. He couldn't afford the time to go on wild goose-chases to the wilds of north Cornwall. Tonight, she would have to rely on the sensual touch of her own skilful fingers.

She turned back to look out of the windows, which offered an unrivalled view of the surrounding countryside. A few fluffy grey clouds were gathering over the hills, and she had learned already that the climate around Lynmoor was fickle enough to change at a moment's notice. However, grey clouds and a few drops of rain were hardly sufficient to dampen her mood today.

This was going to be her first night at Brackwater Hall.

As she relaxed in the armchair, her fingertips stroking her breasts, two nagging thoughts insinuated themselves into the corners of her mind. First, why was there an abandoned car hidden in the scrubby trees near the back of the Hall? And second, why did she feel, even in her most intimate moments, that someone, somewhere, was watching her?

# Chapter Six

*T*he dream was so real, so seductive that Maria did not want to wake up. She was walking through velvety black darkness towards the warm, reddish glow of a distant light. Beneath her bare feet she felt the cool dampness of dewy grass, and the scent of crushed flowers rise all around her. Whispering voices soothed her fears, soft hands plucked at her clothing until at last she was naked. Naked and at the mercy of their touch.

She walked on slowly, the hands taking their pleasure of her body as she passed. No faces were visible in the darkness, not even the faintest shadow or the gleam of an eye. A moist tongue pressed itself against the bare flesh of her thigh, and she paused, wanting to give herself up to the wanton pleasure of the moment. The tongue wound a cool trail of saliva over her hip and lower belly, then dived into the moist warmth between her thighs. Hands stroked her back and belly, her neck and breasts. Fingers twisted long strands of her hair into snake-like coils, and still the tongue darted and probed the secret triangle of her sex.

Too excited to speak, she found herself moving on; different hands and different mouths speaking to her body with touch and taste. No one spoke; no sound was uttered save the low ebb and flow of Maria's own breathing. Her feet moved silently over the moist grass and slowly, very slowly, she moved towards the light.

Filmy tendrils of long grass brushed against her legs, catching at her as though unwilling to let her go. And then she was walking, not on grass, but on the mirror-smoothness of polished stone. It felt curiously warm beneath her feet, as though somewhere beneath it beat a heart of living flesh. In the red glow that brightened and enveloped her, Maria glimpsed the faint shapes of familiar objects: a heavy mahogany table, pictures and mirrors, and a carved banister rail winding upwards.

The door stood half-open, a red mist of light drifting through, making her skin shimmer with faint luminescence as she reached out to touch the handle. She had only to push it lightly, and the door would swing open. The air was so warm, as warm as a lover's embrace. And the points of her nipples stiffened as a soft breeze blew over them, teasing them like a lover's kisses.

She pushed the door open and stepped inside.

Rays of morning sunlight filtered in through the patterned fabric of the bedroom curtains, the red roses glowing as big as dinner-plates as the sun caught them.

Maria turned over in bed and the sheet slid away from her, exposing the swell of her right breast to the cool air from the half-open window. Patterns of red and white light danced across her closed eyelids, daring her to stay in the world of dreams. Seconds later, her eyes fluttered open, and she remembered where she was.

Brackwater Hall. Was she really the owner of Brackwater Hall? It had been a whole week since she'd arrived in Lynmoor, and still she awoke each morning with a sense of childlike wonderment. Maria felt almost like giggling. None of this made sense – the dream had felt far more real than this – but did that matter? She was here, and *that* was real.

Nine o'clock already. She had slept more soundly than she'd expected – and she had so many things planned for today. Still slightly dizzy with sleep, she pulled herself up into a sitting position and swung her legs out of bed. The carpet felt soft and springy underfoot, though to judge from the exquisitely-woven pattern it must surely be very old.

Reaching out to steady herself as she slid her feet into her slippers, she noticed that the bedside cabinet she had so disliked when she first arrived looked much better in the warm glow of daylight. Had she really never noticed the pretty marquetry and the delicate pink-white of the marble top? It was altogether strange how much she preferred this bedroom now that she was taking the time to look at it more closely.

How could she ever have imagined that the door to the little adjoining bathroom was stiff with rust? She turned the handle and it opened with silent ease. How could she have thought that the little sink was positioned too low on the wall? This morning, as she splashed her face with cold water, she found that it was exactly the right height. Perhaps she just wasn't very observant; or perhaps she was gradually getting used to this unusual place.

Crossing to the window, she drew back the curtain and gazed out over Lynmoor. Yesterday's grey clouds had vanished, though it had obviously rained in the night; a few fat drops still remained on the windowpanes, and there was a steady drip, drip from the tangle of vegetation in the gardens below.

She pushed the window open a little further and leaned out, breathing in the freshness of the morning. Like the Hall, the moors seemed different every time she looked at them. White clouds scudded over the high moorland, creating ever-changing patterns of light and shade on the many-coloured land. The yellow of gorse; the fresh green of grass cropped short by slow-moving flocks of sheep; the orange-brown of bracken and moist earth, interspersed with purplish heather; and the ashen grey of stones laid bare by millenia of wind and rain and relentless sun. Lynmoor was an ancient tapestry, its colours still vibrant, its every thread redolent with meaning.

Dressing quickly in a t-shirt and long velvet skirt, she sat down at the Victorian dressing table, and picked up a hairbrush which lay beside a matching comb and mirror. Curiously, despite two years of neglect, the polished silver backs showed no signs of tarnishing, and the bristles of the brush were as fine and soft as the day it had been made. Maria drew it through the thick mane of her hair and it slid through silkily, easing away the tangles effortlessly. She wondered if this had been her Aunt Clara's hairbrush, and how many other red-haired women like Maria Treharne had sat at this dressing table, brushing and combing the soft curtain of their hair as their heads filled with dreams and desires.

Filled with the spirit of adventure, she slid open a drawer and let out a little sigh of delight. Inside lay a jumble of antique costume jewellery – nothing especially valuable, but a real treasure-trove of Celtic brooches, pewter rings, necklaces of semi-precious stones, steel hat-pins decorated with marcasite and jewel-bright glass and ruby-red garnets. Lovely things – beautiful treasures that mirrored Maria's own tastes with uncanny accuracy. Evidently she and Clara Megawne had shared more than a tenuous ancestral link.

Selecting a jet hair-slide carved in the shape of a Celtic shield, she wound her hair up into a heavy knot, which she secured with the shield and a tiny silver spear. Wisps of unruly hair escaped and fell over her forehead, cheek and neck, but the look was rather fetching, showing off the elegance of her long, slender neck.

Maria hummed to herself as she walked out onto the landing and paused for a moment at the top of the huge sweeping staircase. She felt like Scarlett O'Hara. All she needed now was Rhett Butler to come striding up those stairs, take her struggling into his arms, and carry her off to bed.

The thought of bed brought wistful memories of Jonathan, and the days and nights of intense physical passion they had shared together. She wondered what they would be doing now if she was back in Cambridge with him. Would they be together? Perhaps they would be drifting down the Cam towards Grantchester, laughing under clear blue skies as they drank Pimms and shared the unspoken anticipation of the pleasure they would share. Or maybe they would already be making love beneath the sighing willows, their bodies moving together as they listened to the skylark singing above the softly-splashing waters.

Her body responded to the delicious daydream, a tingle of recognition budding in the secret garden between her thighs, then spreading out like spidery fingers of desire, touching thighs and belly and breasts, until her whole body vibrated to the rhythm of her need.

It had been too long. It wasn't natural. A woman like Maria Treharne had too, too much sensuality for it to be bottled up like this, and paganism had brought that sensuality to the surface. Sooner or later, she must have pleasure. She must have sex.

The doorbell rang with a suddenness that made her jump. She walked quickly to the top of the stairs and, peering over the banisters, saw a bulky shape silhouetted behind the thin curtain that covered the glass pane in the front door. Perhaps it was a neighbour, come to welcome her to Lynmoor – though it seemed pretty unlikely that she *had* any neighbours up here on Brackwater Tor. Or maybe it was Myint, wanting her to sign another of his endless bits of paper. Yes, that was probably it.

Quickly she ran down the stairs and opened the front door with a flourish.

'Hello – oh! I . . .'

'Morning, Miss. Nice one, ain't it?'

The grin was as wide as a Cheshire cat's, the blue eyes twinkling with an ingenuous delight. The look was boyish, mischievous, and disarming. Maria recognised him instantly. How could she fail to? He was a striking young man: blond hair as white as flax in the fierce light, skin deeply bronzed by sun and wind, and eyes as blue as the morning sky.

111

In some superficial way, he reminded Maria of Jonathan. But this was a very different kind of young man altogether. His clothes were not the well-cut flannels and hand-sewn shirts that Jonathan liked to wear with such studied casualness. His work-hardened, well-muscled body seemed to disdain his clothes – the torn check shirt, the faded, mud-stained jeans that hugged him so closely that the plump line of his cock was clearly visible beneath the tight blue denim.

His hand, nonchalantly resting on a stone ledge beside the door, was work-roughened, the fingers short and thick with muscle. Maria wondered fleetingly what it would be like to be touched by those fingers. Would their caresses be rough and urgent, or would they contain within them some unimagined gentleness? Would it feel good to be taken into those strong arms and crushed in a bear's-hug of an embrace?

The thought was a diverting one, and she did not reply for some seconds, mesmerised by the twinkling blue eyes and the slim pelvis, which seemed to throw into relief the pointing finger of cock-flesh beneath. But her silence did not seem to bother her visitor.

'Geraint Morgan – you remember me don't you, miss? We met last week, at the Duke of Gloucester. You was in a mortal hurry then, but I thought as how you might 'ave a bit more time for me today, now you've settled in. Wondered if we could maybe 'ave a chat about a bit of business, see.'

'Mr Morgan. Yes, of course . . . You'd better come in.'

She stood back to let him into the house and felt him brush against her as he walked past. Perhaps the touch was deliberate, perhaps not. Was Geraint Morgan really as rough and ready and innocent as he appeared, or did a keen and devious intelligence lurk within that undeniably attractive frame?

He turned, flashing her a smile that made her go weak at the knees.

'Geraint, miss. Call me Geraint – folks does, round 'ere. And seein' as we're friends already, perhaps I could call you Maria. Pretty name, Maria . . .'

She listened to him in silence as they walked together through the Hall towards the kitchen. His voice was melodious, his accent soft and quietly seductive.

'Amazin' place this, ain't it? Real nice, don't get me wrong, but sort of creepy.' He looked around at the dark furniture, and at the huge tapestry of a medieval hunting scene lining the main corridor which led from the front of the house to the kitchens and washrooms at the back. ' 'Spect you can't wait to sell up an' get back to your fancy college.'

'Well . . .' Maria's doubts surprised even her. But Geraint didn't seem to have noticed. He was in full flow now.

'You know, I ain't been in 'ere since . . . oh, years it is. Not since the year after I quit school. Fifteen, I'd be. The old woman lived 'ere then. Me and the boys from the village, we used to come up 'ere an' deliver her groceries once in a while. Good tips we 'ad off her, too.'

'You knew my aunt? Clara Megawne? What was she like?'

Geraint shrugged.

'Long as a piece o' string, and twice as skinny. Funny old stick, she were. Kept herself to herself, too. Didn't care for strangers, didn't Miss Clara.'

Maria felt frustrated and exasperated.

'Didn't anyone know her?'

He shook his head.

'Like I said, she kept herself to herself. Reckon you won't find no one in Lynmoor what knew 'er well.'

In the kitchen, Maria sat down at the old scrubbed-pine table with Geraint, and poured him a glass of orange juice. As he raised it to his lips a gleam of golden light haloed his blond head, making him look like a grubby archangel.

'So, what did you want to see me about?' enquired Maria as casually as she could manage. It wasn't easy, because Geraint was looking at her across the table, fixing her with those steady blue eyes that sent shivers running right through her. His tongue flicked the last drops of juice from his lips, and she found herself fantasising about doing the same thing herself; or maybe even savouring droplets of his semen on her tongue. What on earth was this place doing to her? All she could think about these days was sex.

'Bit of business, like I said.'

Geraint refilled his glass from the jug, and took a second drink. She could see a mist of fine golden curls peeping through the open neck of his shirt, and had an almost irresistible desire to kiss them. She looked down, making little patterns with her finger on the table-top.

'Such as?'

'Such as doin' your garden. Proper mess it's in, after all that time with no one givin' a damn for it. You'll be needin' someone to take care of things, now as you're livin' here. Ain't that so? Even if you want to sell it, you'll want it lookin' nice.'

His eyes challenged her to disagree with him, but of course she could not. She returned his gaze.

'I suppose you could be right. But why should I employ you?'

The corner of his mouth twitched, as though he were trying to suppress a smile.

'I'm very experienced. Ask anyone in the village.'

She felt something touch her ankle, and realised with a start that it was Geraint's foot. He was playing footsie with her, his prospective employer! His behaviour was completely outrageous, that went without saying; but what those mischievous blue eyes were proposing might just be fun. Might just fulfil the burning need within her . . .

She kept him waiting while she drank down her glass of orange juice, then set the glass down on the table-top, next to his. It was her turn to tantalise him. When she spoke again, her voice was heavy with irony, and she could hardly keep from laughing, though her heart was fluttering with excitement.

'So – if I take you on, do you think you could give *complete* satisfaction?'

114

He reached over the table and pushed a lock of hair back from Maria's face.

'Let's just say I've never had any complaints,' he replied. And his fingers moved slowly down from her cheek towards the hard-crested swell of her breasts.

It was after noon when Maria finally made it down to Lynmoor, sharing Geraint's battered old van for the bumpy drive down into the village.

Was it really only a week since she'd arrived in Lynmoor? It already felt like months since she'd left Cambridge, now little more than a blur at the back of her mind. Even her wistful longings for Jonathan had dimmed in the unexpected light of Geraint Morgan. Geraint was no sophisticate, it was true; and in the normal run of things perhaps she wouldn't even have given him a second look. But he had certain talents that could drive a woman crazy – particularly a highly-sensual woman whose appetites had been sharpened by long days of abstinence. And in this wild and beautiful place, her appetites seemed keener than ever.

Alone now, she strolled along the main street taking in all the details she had been too tired or too excited to notice on her arrival. Lynmoor had a weatherbeaten prettiness about it; almost chocolate-box pretty, but with the hard edge of a place that has withstood the elements for centuries. A working village; a place with attitude and edge. The village was busy today, bustling with activity, and she felt curious eyes looking her up and down; but whenever she turned round to make conversation, she found herself studiously ignored.

'Good afternoon.'

'Oh. Er . . . hello.'

Making contact with Geraint had been easy. Making contact with Lynmoor's other residents was proving more problematic. Outside the greengrocer's, Maria attempted to strike up a conversation with a gawky middle-aged woman laden with shopping; but the woman gave her a nervous smile and went on sorting

115

through a pile of cabbages, evidently not well-disposed towards 'foreigners'.

'My name's Maria Treharne. I've just come to live at Brackwater Hall.'

'So I believe.' The woman didn't even look up.

'Perhaps I shall see you up there sometime?'

'I doubt it.'

In exasperation, Maria gave up and moved on. Most of the population of Lynmoor seemed to have a similar attitude towards newcomers. Their idiotic suspicions irked Maria, reminding her of the way the male establishment had treated her when she first arrived at St Alcuin's. That had been a hard habit to break, and no doubt this would be, too. But she was determined to find a way of fitting in.

At the end of the high street – which was really little more than a narrow lane lined with lopsided shops evolved from lumps of stone and wood, rather than the subject of any deliberate planning attempt – she spotted a small wholefood shop: 'Greenways of Lynmoor', the sign read. Perhaps here, she would receive a warmer welcome. Intrigued, she went in.

Behind the counter a young woman of perhaps twenty-nine or thirty was chatting with an elderly man, and putting dark brown eggs into a box. The shop was filled with an agreeable aroma of citrus fruit, mixed with a faint, sweet, musky smell. Maria recognised it instantly. It was the same incense burned at gatherings of her coven. The corn-dolly hanging above the front door, and the row of painted candles on the window sill, were further clues that here, at least, her paganism might not meet with an entirely hostile response.

'There you are, Mr Driver. One dozen free range eggs, nice and brown, just how you like them.'

'I shall be glad when that new supermarket opens,' grunted the old man, putting the egg box into his bag. 'At least I shan't have to trudge halfway to Barncastle for my shopping.'

As Maria stood waiting, a man in his thirties – evidently the young woman's husband – came through from a back room in answer to the jangle of the doorbell. He, at least, seemed friendly enough.

'Good afternoon, miss – and what can we do for you?'

Maria set her basket down on the counter.

'I'll take some organic oranges please – two pounds should do. And a jar of honey. And, oh – that wholemeal bread looks nice.'

The young man wrapped the loaf carefully in tissue paper.

'Haven't I seen you up at the Duke of Gloucester? On holiday, are you?'

'Sort of. I've just come to live at Brackwater Hall. It belonged to my aunt Clara, but she died a couple of years ago. My name's Maria Treharne.'

'Really!' The young woman wiped a floury hand on her apron and extended it in greeting. 'Well I'm Emily Glover, and this is my husband, Ben.'

The shop-bell jangled as Mr Driver slammed the door behind him, trudging away down the street with considerable bad grace. Emily saw Maria's eyes following the bent figure and she laughed.

'Don't go taking any notice of him. He's just bad-tempered, like most of the people round here. We've been here five years, and they still see us as outsiders.'

'Doesn't stop 'em welcoming the developers though, does it?' grunted Ben, heaving a box of oranges onto the counter.

'Developers?'

Emily sighed.

'Some big London firm. They want to build a huge new development here – shops, offices, conference centre, leisure centre, you know the sort of thing. Of course, it would completely ruin Lynmoor but there's no talking sense into these people. All they can think about is not having to drive fifty miles to the nearest Marks & Spencer.'

'And now they've built the marketing suite . . .' added Ben. 'Well, a few free drinks and a fancy scale model,

117

and already they've got the local council eating out of their hands. It's only the New Age Travellers who seem to be putting up any show of opposition.'

'But what about building regulations?' protested Maria. 'And surely, there must be ancient monuments and sacred sites all over the place.'

Emily finished packing the food into Maria's basket.

'That'll be five pound forty please.' She took the money and rang it up on the ancient till. 'A few burial mounds won't stop them, you mark my words. In fact, I've heard a rumour they're going to move the old stone circle from Hilltop Tor fifteen miles to the other side of Lynmoor! Of course, if you want to know more you ought to go along and have a look at the plans yourself.'

'Maybe I will,' hazarded Maria. She didn't like the sound of this at all – major-league construction developments on Lynmoor? Moving ancient stone circles? It was a scandal!

Emily continued.

'The Marketing Suite's open today, isn't it, love?'

Ben nodded.

'Which is more than this place will be if CA Developments get their own way,' he commented gloomily.

Following Ben's directions, Maria walked on down to the end of the high street and turned left, in the direction of the old Corn Exchange, now the village museum. Since the War, tourism had declined markedly in Lynmoor, with the result that the museum was practically the village's only surviving amenity – and even that was only open from July to September.

Next door to the museum stood a brand-new, prefabricated building. Its lurid paintwork and angular construction were screamingly out of place in this ancient village, but the locals evidently didn't care. Several were standing outside, by the sign which read 'Marketing Suite', and peering into the interior through a vast plate-glass window. They were smiling.

Maria joined them, at first apprehensive and then downright curious. Maybe Emily had exaggerated, and the development wouldn't be half as bad as she had suggested.

At first glance, Maria realised that it was, in fact, much worse. The table-top scale model, gleaming-new in its square glass case, presented a landscape that looked more like Llandudno than Lynmoor. Blue and white boxes representing buildings straddled the moors, replacing the open moorland and ancient woodland with supermarkets, multiplex cinemas, giant swimming-pools and all-weather sports facilities. It was all utterly tasteless; and suddenly it was all very real.

But it wasn't until she looked at the model a second time that Maria noticed something rather peculiar.

Unless she was very much mistaken, the whole of the projected Lynmoor Development seemed to be centred on Brackwater Hall.

'What's the matter, Patsy love? Don't you like 'em?'

Patsy Polgarrow blinked in disbelief at the huge bunch of flowers in Geraint's arms.

'What you done now, Geraint?'

'I don't understand.'

'Well, you must 'ave done somethin' pretty bad, or you wouldn't be tryin' to buy me off with flowers, now would you?'

Geraint threw back his head and roared with laughter, dropping the bunch of flowers onto the table.

'You can take it from me, Patsy love; it ain't nothin' bad. It ain't nothin' bad at all.' He sat down on the old sofa – the one he'd courted Patsy on when she was just out of school and he was a knowing eighteen-year-old farm labourer with money in his pocket. 'Come an' sit 'ere. I got somethin' to tell you.'

Reluctantly she perched on the settee beside Geraint, her slight figure dominated by the soft vastness of her breasts.

'Not there. Here – on my knee.'

He put his arms around Patsy's waist but felt her stiffen at his touch.

'Not till you tell me what it is. You ain't gettin' round me that easily, Geraint Morgan.'

This was a game they played regularly as clockwork – so regularly that by now, Patsy knew the rules by heart. Geraint would do something he shouldn't have – like drink away all his wages at the Duke of Gloucester, or get some village girl in the family way – and then he'd come crawling back to her with some sob story and expect her to take him back, no questions asked. Well she wasn't having any of it, not this time.

'All right, all right.' His bright mood seemed undimmed, his temper not in the least frayed by Patsy's resistance. Undaunted, he slid his hand from Patsy's waist to her knee, ruching up the thin cotton of her dress with slow deliberateness until his fingers met bare, brown flesh. Patsy responded by placing her own small hand on top of his, curtailing further liberties.

'I said, tell me.'

Geraint beamed.

'I got a job.'

Patsy's eyes widened in astonishment.

'What – you mean your Dad's took you back? But I thought you said . . .'

'No, no, not my Dad – it's the big house. I got a job up at the Hall, diggin' the gardens, handyman and that.'

Patsy's fingers tightened round Geraint's hand and prised it from her knee. Her face darkened into the thunderous sulkiness that Geraint found so inexplicable – and so sexy. She snapped into his face:

'It's that woman, ain't it? That woman come down from some fancy Cambridge college? I seen her in the village, all long legs an' red 'air. I might have known you'd soon be sniffin' round her. Just can't keep it in your pants, can you?'

'It's not like that, Patsy,' protested Geraint, his face a picture of studied honesty. 'It's just a job, honest, working for Miss Treharne. You've seen what a state them gardens is in. They needs a proper seein' to.'

Patsy laughed humourlessly, trying to ignore the insistent way in which Geraint's fingers were climbing up her thigh.

'Oh yeah? An' what about Lady Muck? Does she need a proper seein' to, an' all?'

The venom in her words masked the trembling excitement Patsy felt vibrating through her, making her voice quaver and her mouth dry. Her own anger seemed to turn her on, and she could feel Geraint's excitement pulsing from his hot hand into the cool flesh of her thigh. The air seemed to crackle with erotic tension.

'I dunno, Patsy,' replied Geraint, his voice suddenly quiet and soft. 'You see, I don't give a damn about her. But what I do know is that it's been too long since I gave you what you need.'

'An' what might that be?'

'Give me a chance, an' I'll show you.' His fingers squeezed tight on the flesh of her inner thigh.

'Do you really think I'm going to let you do *that*? After what you've been doing to *her*?'

'I told you, I ain't bin doin' nothin' with her. All I want is to give you a darn good fuckin'.'

'Get your hands off me, Geraint Morgan!'

His arms encircled her, pulling her to him as he crushed his lips against hers, forcing her pride to submit to his hunger. Patsy fought him like a little hell-cat, her nails scratching his face and her teeth biting the hand that tried to unfasten the buttons down the front of her dress. But she was wet between her thighs, just like she always was when her errant lover touched her and kissed her. In a perverse way, even her own jealousy turned her on. Just thinking about Geraint with other women made her clitoris throb with an angry, shameful need. They both knew this was what she wanted.

She sank back onto the softness of the old settee, his body heavy and insistent upon hers. His hands pinned her arms down so that she could do nothing but wriggle and glare up at him, her dark eyes flashing with resentment. He smiled down at her as his denim-clad thigh insinuated itself between her legs until the hardness

121

made contact with the damp cotton stretched over her aching pubis.

'It's you I want all right,' he breathed, rubbing his thigh gently backwards and forwards across the wet gusset of Patsy's panties. She thought she might die of need, but she wasn't giving in that easily. 'You know it's true.'

'Why should I believe a word you say, Geraint Morgan?' she spat, but her voice was hardly more than a breathless gasp. 'You're a two-timing bastard, and you always will be.'

'But you want me, don't you, Patsy?' His thigh moved back and forth, her answering wetness emphasising the truth of his words.

'Get off me and go back to your fancy piece.'

Geraint ignored her protests. He just kept on rubbing his thigh between her legs, making her understand that what she really wanted was what he wanted too.

'C'mon Patsy. You want my cock in that greedy little pussy of yours.'

She writhed beneath him, but she was no longer really fighting him; the struggling was all for show, the slow bucking movements of her pelvis more in harmony with her desire than with her anger. Her breath was coming in short, thick gasps now, and her nipples were tingling with the need to be touched, licked, sucked, bitten.

Still Geraint's hard, muscular thigh moved up and down between her legs, pressing against the hard apex of her pubis, forcing apart the love-lips so imperfectly veiled by her thin cotton panties. The scent they released was powerful – so powerful that it seemed to fill the room like a warm, moist cloud of musky fragrance; a sex elixir that both soothed and aroused as it was breathed in.

Patsy made only the feeblest attempt to struggle free as Geraint released her left arm and used his right hand to undo the buttons that ran from the scooped neckline of her summer dress right down to the hem of the wide skirt. The taut fabric yielded gratefully, springing apart to reveal the creamy expanse of her breasts; large and soft under the simple white cotton bra.

Geraint tried to cup the twin globes but their bounty overflowed his greedy hands. His caresses were clumsy, almost rough, but Patsy shivered with reluctant need, her nipples huge and hard as brazil nuts under the stretchy cotton. Geraint might be a rogue, but he certainly knew how to turn her from spitting fury into soft, lascivious pleasure.

But Patsy knew a few things about pleasure, too. She was justly proud of her breasts – firm yet soft, they seemed huge in comparison with her tiny waist and modestly-rounded hips. Geraint was always telling her they were beautiful – and he wasn't the first man to have appreciated Patsy's very definite charms. She was only too aware of her lover's fascination, and often wore dresses that were tightly fitted in the bodice, expressly to drive him wild; to show him that his girl had something none of his other women had got.

Sometimes Geraint liked her to play with her breasts while he watched; taking out his dick and stroking it while Patsy rubbed baby oil or lather over the firm yet mobile flesh. At first she hadn't wanted to do it – it had felt dirty somehow, not quite decent. But later she'd grown to enjoy the feeling of control she always got, knowing that Geraint's entire sexual satisfaction depended on her beauty, her skill. And knowing that always made her feel hornier than ever ...

She moaned as Geraint's fingers slid under the bottom edge of her bra-cups and pulled them up over her breasts so that the fleshy globes lay bare and vulnerable, the stiffened nipples inviting kisses. His lips closed over the engorged flesh, his tongue winding round the puckered areola with an eager insistence which left Patsy almost helpless with delight. Surreptitiously, she slid her legs a little further apart, so that her right foot was on the carpet and her pubis was thrust slightly upwards, meeting the answering movements of Geraint's thigh.

She whimpered with need as he pinched her right nipple between finger and thumb, releasing the other nipple from his mouth. His lips were slick with wetness, like some ever-hungry child who has not yet drunk his fill of mother's milk. He smiled.

'Told you I knew what you wanted,' he whispered, his voice hoarse with excitement.

'Maybe,' retorted Patsy, still playing his game even though her thighs were running with the wetness from her sex.

His thigh pressed harder on her clitoris, and she gave a little squeal, half of surprise and half of mingled pain and pleasure.

'It ain't no good pretendin', Patsy love,' he panted, pulling himself up on his elbow and fumbling with the belt on his jeans. 'It's only natural. You love every minute of it.'

Lazy with desire, Patsy lay back and watched Geraint unfasten first his belt, then the top button of his old jeans. Torn and shabby they might be, but the skin-tight faded denim showed off his body to perfection, and little rips in the legs gave tantalising glimpses of the golden flesh beneath. Long before he had reached a hand into his pants, she had visualised and anticipated the sight of his wonderfully hard phallus.

A good seven inches long when erect, Geraint's manhood was a beautiful, smooth-skinned tyrant which ruled Patsy's life: lord of her pleasure, king of her desire, it had long since robbed her of the ability to resist Geraint's outrageous demands. She fought, she threatened, she parried, but she could not deny the need within her. Patsy Polgarrow was an addict: hopelessly hooked on the dazzling explosions of arousal that only Geraint could coax from her body. The taste, the smell, the thrust of his cock had made her a slave of her own lust.

'You ain't stickin' that thing in me,' she said defiantly, gazing straight up into Geraint's clear blue eyes. His cock was in his hand, its smooth, wet purple head peeping out from between his fingers as cradled the shaft, masturbating it gently. 'You bin stickin' it in *her*.'

'I told you, Patsy – you're the only woman for me.'
Geraint's voice was so smooth, so convincing that Patsy
almost began to believe his deceiving words. 'You know
that, don't you? You know you're the only woman who
really turns me on.'

He slid his thigh out from between her legs, and she
almost wept for the loss, for the yearning ache that he
had coaxed from the hot, wet heart of her sex. And then
his finger slid aside the gusset of her panties and she felt
it brush her sex with the lightness of a breeze, making
the hood of her clitoris slide backwards and forwards
with an agonising slowness.

'Tell me you want it, Patsy.'

'I . . . no!'

He pressed harder, and the need grew still more intolerable. She squirmed, longing for the void within her
to be filled.

'Tell me, Patsy. Tell me you want this nice fat dick in
you. I know you do . . .'

He lowered himself between her thighs, his stiffened
penis dancing over her pubic bone, a hair's-breadth
from the entrance to her quim. Patsy's head was swimming, her clitoris throbbing, her sex flooding with need.

'Geraint, I . . .'

His fingertips on her nipple, pressing, pinching, tormenting, brought a swift and brutal end to her show of
defiance; and eyes closed, lips moistened by the constant
flick of her hungry tongue-tip, she whispered her need.

'I . . . want it. I want it now.'

'Come on then. Come and get it.'

Playful in the assurance of his triumph, Geraint rolled
off Patsy's belly and onto his back on the carpeted floor.
Seizing her arm he dragged her off the sofa, and they fell
together in a tangled, disordered heap of limbs.

'Go on Patsy – you want it, take it.'

He looked up at his lover, half-kneeling, half-sitting
astride him, propping herself up on her strong, suntan-
ned arms. Her blonde hair was hanging in a cascade of
ringlets about her face, but it was not her face that he

was looking at. Patsy's dress was gaping at the front, the twisted string of her cotton bra pushed up high like a necklace, exposing the heavy globes of her breasts. And they were bulging through the gap in her bodice, hanging tantalisingly near; no longer plump spheres but pendulous and tempting as ripe fruit, just inches from his mouth. All he had to do was reach out and taste . . .

'What are you waitin' for?'

Patsy answered Geraint's question with a knowing smile. Slowly she sat up and stripped down the top of her short-sleeved dress, letting it fall so that the bodice hung from her waist, forming a loose peplum over the wide skirt. She savoured the look of wide-eyed covetousness on Geraint's face as she released the hooks on her bra and eased it off, dropping it on the floor.

'I'm waiting' for you to kiss me. Don't you know *where* I want you to kiss me? Look – my nipples are all hard.'

She lowered herself over his face, letting the pear-shaped, fleshy sacs of her breasts dangle teasingly close, swinging them gently so that the very tips of the nipples grazed his lips.

He reached up and took her right breast between his two hands, more lovingly than she remembered him ever doing so before. There was reverence in his touch as he weighed and stroked the heavy mass, caressing its coolness with calloused hands that radiated the furnace-heat of his desire.

'Go on Geraint – I'm waiting.'

She felt him trembling with excitement as his lips parted and took in the long, pink stalk of her nipple. The electricity of that first touch seemed to arc right through to Patsy's clitoris, and she squatted lower over her lover's body, rubbing her pubis up and down as he suckled her. A hot, sweet syrup emerged from her love-lips, smearing a wet trail over his belly from sternum to pubis, and she heard him moaning softly as his lips closed more tightly around her teat.

He teased her nipple with his tongue and teeth, his

cheeks hollowing as he sucked hard on the rubbery pink flesh. The fingers of his right hand moved to stroke and weigh the great hanging udder of her left breast; the blue veins standing out on the nacreous flesh as the comforting warmth of her desire began to kindle to a furious, white-hot need.

'Yes, yes, yes.' The rhythm of her whispered words was in step with the rhythm of Geraint's kisses on her breast; a lullaby of longing. She could almost imagine that he was no longer her lover but her greedy child, sucking the sweet white milk from her. But it was Geraint that she wanted to milk ...

Reaching behind her, she took hold of the curving sword of his dick. At the touch of her hand he gasped, and released her nipple for a few brief seconds, before raising his head and beginning to suck at her again, harder and more urgently than before. His eyes were closed, his breathing irregular and rasping.

Patsy looked down at her lover with a smile of perfect contentment. This was how she wanted to keep him for ever: docile and dependent, a happy captive between the soft prison-bars of her thighs. Lost in desire, so that he would never want to stray again, never want to do anything but give his lover the perfect pleasure she craved. That might never come true, but for a few moments, even a few hours, she could keep him under her soft spell, weaving a net of simple enchantment around him.

A single backward thrust of her hips took his cock-tip through the soft-fringed margin of her love-lips and into the deep red heart of her sex. And hip to hip, cock to quim, they began moving together in a glorious unison of desire.

Maria took her drink out into the front garden and surveyed the scene. Geraint was right: she did need a gardener, and pretty soon she was going to have to make sure he got down to work. She suppressed a giggle as she recollected that Geraint was right about one or two other things too. Doubtless she ought to feel guilty about what they'd been doing together for the last four days, but feeling any sort of guilt was so difficult. Here, in this place where nature's law was supreme, it seemed only natural to follow her deepest, most sensual instincts.

Savouring the warmth of the early evening sunlight on her back, she strolled through the remains of the old knot-garden, trying to visualise how it would all look when it was tidied up. Whether or not she eventually sold the Hall, she wanted the gardens to be restored to their former finery, and with the independent income promised to her from Aunt Clara's will, she could easily afford to pay Geraint to do all the heavy work. It just didn't feel right that a place as beautiful as this should be neglected.

She was so engrossed in her own thoughts that she did not hear the sound of soft footsteps on the overgrown path until a voice sounded behind her.

'Maria? Miss Treharne?'

She wheeled round, astonished and a little disconcerted to find that she was not alone.

'I'm sorry, did I startle you?'

The stranger's eyes met hers, and for a fleeting instant Maria felt an electricity pass between them, almost a sense of déjà-vu; yet she was certain she had never seen this man before. Over six feet tall and slender, but with broad shoulders and strong hands, he cut a striking figure, towering over Maria's average frame. The black leather jacket and trousers he wore accentuated his height and echoed the glossy black of his shoulder-length hair. Sea-grey eyes glittered in a handsome face, the features sharp as an eagle's, the skin smooth but deeply tanned.

'Forgive me,' he repeated, and he reached out his right hand, on which glittered a series of heavy silver rings. 'My name is Anthony Pendorran. I heard that you had moved into the old Hall, and thought I would come and introduce myself.'

She took his hand and the clasp was strong, almost painful.

'I didn't hear you come into the garden,' said Maria. She felt awkward and stupid beside this beautiful and infinitely desirable stranger, whose grey eyes seemed to see into the very depths of her soul.

Pendorran smiled, and Maria found herself thinking that she could lose herself in that smile, in those eyes. From a man like Pendorran, a smile could be a kiss, the lightest touch as blissful as a passionate caress. Not for the first time that day, she felt herself carried away on a tide of aching desire.

'You seemed far away – lost in your thoughts,' observed Pendorran.

'Oh, I was just daydreaming about what to do with this garden. It's such a mess.'

His hands in his pockets, Pendorran surveyed the tangle of leaves and branches, the anarchic sprawl of weeds and flowers.

'The power of the Goddess is not to be scorned,' he remarked. 'In two short years she has well-nigh reclaimed this place.'

Maria looked up at him sharply.

'The Goddess?' Of course, she should have understood with that first flash of recognition. Pendorran, too, must be of the old faith.

'She who is the soul of earth and the mother of all.'

'You are a pagan?'

Pendorran shrugged.

'I do not care for names. But yes, I am a follower of the Goddess. As you are yourself, is that not so?'

Maria looked up at him sharply. He seemed to be watching, waiting for her response so that he could judge her by it. That made her feel faintly uneasy.

'How did you . . ?'

'How is not important. Let us just say that I know many things.' He took her hand and pressed it to his lips, the touch lingering long beyond a simple greeting. 'I have come here today to welcome you, Maria, and to tell you that you are all that I had imagined you would be. Perhaps you may yet be more.'

Maria understood nothing of what Pendorran was saying. His words were a crazy jumble in her head, as meaningless as the slow drone of the bees moving like fat aeroplanes from flower to flower. But his touch spoke to her of many things; of exotic lands and silken nights, of kisses hot with passion and caresses far more eloquent than words. Her mind was a whirl of colours and desires, the touch of his kiss still warm on her hand.

'I live about ten miles from here,' continued Pendorran, apparently oblivious to Maria's confusion. 'My house stands on the cliffs above Polmadoc Point. Perhaps you would care to dine there with me tomorrow evening?'

He let her hand fall, and she felt bereft. There could be no doubt of her response.

'I'd love to,' she replied.

Anthea left Tony's bed early on Saturday morning, leaving him still slumbering peacefully, his golden body sprawled across the sheets they had so effectively dampened with their passion, throughout the long, warm night.

All in all, things were progressing much more satisfactorily with Tony than she'd expected. Oh, he was a bastard – she'd known that from the start; given half a chance, he'd take what he wanted and discard her, like all the others. But what if she kept on giving him more and more of what he wanted? At any rate, it would be fun to try keeping the luscious Tony Fitzhardinge dangling on a string, panting for the little sex-games she played so well.

As she wheeled her bike out through the porter's lodge into Trumpington Street, Anthea glanced across the road and caught sight of a striking blond figure. She might not have given him a second glance if he hadn't been standing on the steps of a discreet private hotel she'd once used when going out with a deacon from the theological college. Wasn't that ..? Yes, she was sure it was Jonathan Gresham. She'd recognise that golden hair and sardonic smile anywhere.

As she stood and watched, the front door of the hotel opened and a second figure slipped out. Anthea's curiosity turned to horror and then mute fury as she saw Jonathan put his arms round the Japanese girl's waist and plant a passionate kiss on her upraised lips.

So that was Jonathan's little game, was it? Anthea pushed the bike into the roadway and stepped furiously on the pedals, silently cursing as her bike slid into the middle of the early-morning traffic, narrowly missing an oncoming taxi. First Terry Kestelman and his clumsy threats; and now that slime Jonathan was showing his true colours. It was about time someone told poor Maria what the bastards were getting up to behind her back.

# Chapter Seven

*A* watery sun was shining down from a pale greyish sky as Patsy closed the door of Hawthorn Cottage behind her. She glanced up and felt a wave of depression wash over her. Grey, everything grey and unremarkable, and dull, dull, dull – that was how she saw Lynmoor.

It was all right for the tourists of course – they only saw the place for two weeks a year; and the few weekenders never stepped outside their centrally-heated bijou cottages. But Patsy had lived in Lynmoor for the whole of her twenty-three years, and frankly it had long since ceased to exert any fascination for her. She was young, she was pretty, she wanted to get out and enjoy herself; something it was virtually impossible to do in deader-than-dead Lynmoor.

Her feet slid on the wet cobblestones as she descended the hill, walking past shuttered cottages where nobody lived any more because there was no work in Lynmoor, not since they closed the old Wheal Garew over by Polmadoc. What this place really needed, mused Patsy, was dragging into the twentieth century – and the new development promised to do precisely that.

The narrow street twisted sharply to the left and Patsy had to step aside suddenly to avoid a boy on a rusty bicycle, freewheeling recklessly down the hill. Cursing him under her breath, she recognised him instantly as one of the grubby little urchins who lived on the moor above the village, in that weird hippie camp. 'Travellers' they called themselves; layabouts was what Geraint was apt to call them when he was drinking with his mates, in the Duke of Goucester.

Patsy reached the bottom of the hill and turned into the main street. She hadn't intended going to the Glovers' health food store (the prices were enough to put anyone off), but, now they'd closed down the sub post office, it was the only place you could buy stamps. As she got nearer, Patsy made out a gaggle of perhaps three or four scruffily-dressed figures, and spotted the urchin-boy's bike, leaning up against the front of the shop. A home-made banner made from a torn sheet and two fence-posts completed the scene. In crudely-painted black letters, it proclaimed:

HANDS OFF OUR HISTORY. PLANNERS GO HOME.

Patsy felt a rush of indignation. *Their* history? These New Age hippies hadn't been here five minutes, and already they were telling honest Lynmoor folk what they ought to think.

'Keep Lynmoor free from the fascist developers.'

A hand gripped her arm and she leapt away as though burnt. She turned to glare at the speaker; a thin young man with a shaven head and a spider tattoo on the side of his neck.

'Get off me! Who d'you think you are, anyway? Bloody cheek.'

'Leave her alone, Jak. If she don't want to, she don't want to.'

The second man defused her anger with a grin that reminded her of Geraint in one of his rare good moods. On the surface of it, this was an unremarkable man; average height and build, tattily-dressed, with straggling mud-coloured hair and an unkempt beard. But there

133

was something about him that drew the gaze. Was it those deep-set dark brown eyes, twinkling with a hint of roguish charm? Was it his voice, soft and musical; or the way his mouth curled at the corners when he smiled?

Whatever it was, Patsy found herself lost for words, listening in silence to his apology.

'He's a bit rough and ready, is our Jak, but he don't mean no harm. Do you, Jak?'

He flashed a meaningful stare at his companion, who shuffled his feet awkwardly on the cobbles, hands thrust in pockets, eyes downcast.

'Reckon not.'

'Why not sign our petition?' He indicated a crumpled sheet of paper adorned with five or six scrawled names, and a ballpoint pen secured to the clipboard with a length of hairy string. 'After all, it's our heritage they're trying to destroy. Isn't that right?'

The brown eyes argued the case so prettily that for a split second Patsy almost wondered if he was right. That gaze was like a warm caress, an hypnotic lure that would promise all the lies in the world to get what it wanted. But Patsy was used to the technique; she'd been with Geraint long enough to recognise bullshit when she saw it, no matter how seductively gift-wrapped that bullshit might be.

'It ain't your heritage,' snapped Patsy. 'It's mine – and it ain't got nothin' to do with you an' your sort. Why don't you just go away and leave us all in peace?'

When she came out of the shop, five minutes later, the travellers had moved on to the far end of the street. Oddly enough, Patsy almost admitted to a twinge of regret. There'd been something about that guy, something that turned her on in spite of herself. Had he been turned on by her, too? Had she caught the faintest glimmer of lust in his eyes?

Maybe it was just too long since she'd had a man – except Geraint, of course, but he never really appreciated her for the sensual woman she was. Lost in thought, she turned back towards the baker's shop, only to feel a tap on her shoulder. She wheeled round.

'Morning, Patsy. You're looking well.'

'Clive!'

It was several weeks since Patsy had seen Clive Fallowfield, the village constable. Geraint didn't like to see her talking to other men, particularly not Fallowfield, as he was painfully aware that Patsy had had a fling with him during one of her periodic bust-ups with him. She greeted Clive with an enthusiasm which surprised them both, and he beamed with pleasure at her kiss on his cheek. He nodded in the direction of the retreating demonstrators.

'Hope that shower didn't cause you any problems.'

'Not really.' Patsy reflected on the man with the brown eyes. Perhaps he had not really been quite as interesting as she'd imagined at the time. 'That lot are just a waste of space.'

'If you ask me,' remarked Clive, bending closer to Patsy's face as his voice became conspiratorial, 'we should bundle the whole bloody lot of 'em into the back of a van and drop them off the cliffs at Polmadoc. Nobody'd miss them.'

Patsy giggled; she liked Clive's outrageous solutions. At least he believed in getting things done. She still quite fancied him, too. He didn't have Geraint's raw, rough energy of course, but he knew how to treat a woman and besides, uniforms had always turned her on.

'Never mind,' she soothed. 'They'll be gone soon. Once the plans go through they'll be evicted, won't they?'

'*If* the plans go through,' Clive reminded her. 'It's scum like them that drive away people who want to invest their money in Lynmoor. That Carolan or whatever he calls himself may want to live like a pig and scrounge off the state, but there's honest, hard-working people in Lynmoor who want jobs. This village and that riff-raff could do with a damn good kick up the arse.'

As she stood looking in the baker's shop window, Patsy felt Clive's arm sneak round her waist, his leathergloved hand slipping down to cup the fullness of her backside. She made no attempt to pull away.

'I'm off at two,' murmured Clive. 'I wondered if maybe we could get together . . .'

Patsy did not look across at Clive; she smiled back at her own reflection in the window-pane, sly and triumphant. If Geraint insisted on screwing that woman up at the big house, well, she'd show him that she could play that game too. Best of all, Geraint was out this afternoon, up at the Hall doing some job or other for that precious Miss Treharne of his. There was no reason why he should ever find out who Patsy had been entertaining in his absence.

Unless, of course, she told him.

Maria glanced at the clock on the marble mantelpiece in her bedroom. Its heavy brass hands clicked on inexorably towards seven o'clock, when Anthony had said he would send someone for her. It was a bind not having a car; she'd have to see about that, find out if Geraint knew anyone who had an old banger going cheap. If there was one thing Maria really disliked, it was being robbed of her independence – even by a man as desirable as Anthony Pendorran.

After their brief acquaintance yesterday, Pendorran remained a complete enigma to Maria. As she undressed, she reviewed what she knew about him – that he was a pagan, and that he lived in a house overlooking the sea at Polmadoc. Add to this that he was certainly an individualist, and more than a little arrogant too, and you had the sum total of her knowledge. When she tried to think about him, she even found it difficult to picture his face in any detail. All she could remember were those compelling, sea-grey eyes, and the feeling of frantic excitement that had overwhelmed her at the first touch of their fingers.

She went through into the adjoining bathroom and turned on the shower. When she'd first moved in, the plumbing had seemed dodgy to say the least – you never knew whether the water would come out ice-cold or raging hot, and sometimes it didn't come out at all.

She'd been on the point of calling in a plumber when, as if by some miracle, the problem had righted itself. She sincerely hoped it would stay righted – until Myint came up with the precise details of this alleged private income, she was forced to live on her own resources; and St Alcuin's did not believe in paying its assistant lecturers any more than it absolutely had to. The sooner that Fellowship came through, the better.

Already she had become inordinately fond of this cosy little private bathroom. The Hall boasted three other bathrooms – or was it four? – but of all of them, this was Maria's favourite. She loved the antique feel of the room: the thick, syrupy glaze on the Victorian tiles that surrounded an old cast-iron bath with elegant lion's-paw feet and gleaming brass fittings; the pretty mosaic floor; and the roomy shower-cabinet with doors of antique etched glass.

She stepped inside. Today, the water was just right: an even warmth that spread over her bare skin in high-pressure jets that tingled where they touched. Maria moved slowly round, allowing the water to caress her in new and secret places; offering herself up to the inquisitive jets that expored her every fold and swell. She reached up to push the wet hair back from her forehead, and the warm water fell like tropical rain on her up-turned face, cascading down her cheeks and neck, running down into the deep valley between her breasts, and falling in huge, slow drops from the swelling crests of her nipples.

She reached out for the shower-gel and squeezed a little into the palm of her hand. The sharp, piney fragrance of horse chestnut wafted around her as she smoothed the cool gel over her shoulders, back and breasts, which had grown pink with the warm, tingling massage.

With slow, luxurious, circular movements she worked the gel into a foamy lather which mingled with the trickles of steaming water coursing down over her belly and flanks. The touch awakened new reserves of desire

137

that even Geraint's enthusiastic love-making had neither reached nor satisfied, and her fingers slid inexorably downwards, towards the plump swell of her pubis.

Maria could not recall a time when she had felt so sexually aroused over such a long period. She had always enjoyed an active sex-life of course, but since she had arrived in Lynmoor, it was as though a dam had burst, releasing great floods of sexual desire that had been pent up inside her since ... for ever. Her whole body had become hypersensitive, each nerve-ending crying out for a touch, a kiss, a caress.

The reason was probably nothing more unusual than a release of tension, after a long and tense academic year that had left her strung up tighter than a steel wire. But all the same, there was definitely something about this place, this house in particular, that was uniquely conducive to the sweet, seductive warmth of lust, and the pleasures of the flesh.

Take this afternoon, for example. She had been talking to Geraint whilst he swung a scythe over the chaotic tangle of brambles and woodbine just outside the back wall of the Hall gardens. She'd initially intended leaving this part of the land until the formal gardens were properly cleared, but out walking yesterday evening she'd discovered a couple of small apparently carved stones, peeping through the tight-knit vegetation.

On closer investigation, when they'd scythed away the long grass and brambles around them, Geraint and Maria had gradually uncovered not two, but seven small stones, some broken, and all cracked and worn, but arranged in a perfect circle, about six feet across.

She'd known instantly that this was something very special; but it wasn't until she'd stepped into the circle that Maria had felt the power – like a hot wind blowing over her skin, dragging at her clothes and hair, caressing her like lewd fingers intent on exploring every nook and cranny of her body.

Could she possibly have imagined it, or had she really got in touch with some immense spiritual truth, hidden for years beneath an impenetrable carpet of bramble and woodbine? The initial exhilaration had lasted only a few seconds at most, and then it was gone from her, leaving a hot, sensual glow. Gone, leaving her standing alone in the circle, whilst Geraint watched her with a curious look in his eyes, not understanding, yet wanting – wanting so badly to share what Maria was experiencing.

'You all right, Maria? Thought you was goin' to faint just then.'

'I . . . I'm fine, Geraint. Why don't you come and join me? Come on, come and stand here next to me.'

'Whatever you say.'

With a shrug of his broad shoulders, he took two long strides which brought him into the centre of the circle.

'What happens now, then?'

Could he not feel it? Could he not feel the hot, trembling lust running through her body to her very fingertips as she reached out and touched his cheek? As if reading her thoughts he caught her hand and kissed it, and she felt a new electricity tingle through her, raising goose-flesh on her bare arms.

'This. This is what happens, Geraint. If you want it to happen.'

She sank to her knees on the rough-cut grass, paying no heed to the sharp bramble twigs which stuck up out of the ground and dug into her bare flesh. Pressing her face against the crotch of Geraint's jeans, she breathed in the bitter tang of his sweat, and let her teeth bite gently along the hard, smooth outline of his cock; a swollen, slanting baton beneath the tight fabric. Geraint shuddered with excitement, his fingers gripping her shoulders and winding her hair into corkscrew tendrils as her hot, moist breath soaked through the skin-tight denim, exciting the flesh beneath.

Geraint's cock was so swollen that the flies of his 501s bulged, pushing out the material so that the buttons were clearly visible, and straining fit to burst. Maria tasted them with the tip of her tongue; the metal was cold and slightly rough to the touch, but it excited her.

She wished she had the teeth of a wild she-cat, sharp enough and strong enough to slice through thick fabric, bite away the buttons and free her lover's cock from the prison of its covering.

She looked up at Geraint. His eyes were fixed on her, watchful and excited. She could sense how it was turning him on, just watching her playing the harlot with his arrogant young body. And she was incredibly turned on, too. She smiled, and she saw Geraint's eyes glitter with mischievous complicity.

'Unbutton yourself,' she whispered. 'Please. For me.'

She took his hand and placed it on his flies, kissing his fingers one by one as they unfastened the fly-buttons, baring the tight white cotton briefs underneath.

'Now take out your beautiful cock for me,' she urged him, her eyes following every movement as he slid his fingers under the waistband of his briefs. 'I want to taste you.'

His fingers lingered for a little while, teasing her as they curled about the turgid flesh. Perhaps he was showing her that he did not need her to give him pleasure. Then, in a single rapid movement, he pulled on his cock and it sprang out like a flick-knife, wickedly hard and so tempting that she could not resist opening her lips and taking it into her throat in a single greedy thrust of her head.

Standing under the shower, massaging the creamy lather over her belly, Maria recalled the salty taste of Geraint's cock. She remembered the divine slipperiness of the sex-fluid that oozed from the tip as she ran her tongue over it again and again, closing her lips very tight about the shaft so that each movement of her mouth became an unforgiving caress.

The remembered taste of Geraint's hot, white sperm on her tongue made Maria shudder with delicious excitement. There had been floods of it – great, creamy jets with a bitter aftertaste that only served to renew her thirst for more and yet more. And when she had swallowed down every last drop, she had forced her lips

140

against Geraint's, so that he too could enjoy the taste of their shared lust.

Smiling at the recollection of their joining, there in the sunshine amid the broken stones, Maria let her fingers wander slowly down over the soapy-smooth skin to the dripping-wet curls that adorned her pubis, their auburn glow now darkened by the water. She shifted her position slightly so that her feet moved further apart, and her love-lips parted gently, revealing the path to the hidden heart of her sex. As they opened, a trickle of warm, soapy water coursed down her belly and found its way into the interior, teasing and tickling as it ran, like an infinitely long, infinitely playful tongue.

Why hold out any longer against the sensual hunger that was gnawing away at her? Maria unhooked the shower-head and directed it between her sex-lips, shuddering with the explosion of sudden, brutal pleasure as the hot water-jets made contact with the hard rosebud of her desire.

She knew it would not last long; the need was too urgent, the hunger too immediate, the touch too brutal. But the pleasure was immense and all-consuming. Leaning back against the tiled wall, trickles of water from her wet hair still running over her neck and breasts, she began moving the shower-head over the inner lips of her sex, at first quite slowly and languidly, then with increasing rapidity, so that the water-jets flicked over her clitoris like a hundred needle-sharp tongues.

Images of her most skilful lovers flickered on the dark screen of her mind: Jonathan and Geraint – and another man: the dark and enigmatic figure of Anthony Pendorran. Which of them was running his tongue-tip over her pussy? Which of these imagined lovers was here with her now, manipulating her desire, summoning her to the heights of orgasm? All of their faces were blurring into one . . .

Jerking and moaning with pleasure, she abandoned herself to a climax that left her gasping. Her head reeled as she put a hand out to steady herself and as the last delicious spasms died away, the honeydew of her sex mingled with the hot, soapy water spiralling around her feet.

Drying herself with a fluffy pink towel, Maria padded across the tiled floor towards the bedroom. She glanced at the clock as she put on her stockings and suspenders: half-past six, and she'd only just showered. Only half an hour to get herself ready – for what? For a big dinner-date; or just a neighbourly get-together? Even on their short acquaintance, Maria had the feeling that there would be more to it than that.

Opening the door of the massive wardrobe, Maria scanned the row of clothes with growing dismay. The red dress with the embroidered yoke? No, no, far too gauche and unsophisticated. The dark green, then? The one that everyone said brought out the green in her hazel eyes? She ran the fabric between her fingers, but it felt coarse and alien. Nothing pleased her, not one of the dresses and blouses and skirts she had always felt happy in before. It was as though a change had come over her, as though this place belonged to a different Maria Treharne, with different tastes and different needs.

Well, she would have to choose something – she could hardly go out to dinner stark naked, though the idea was a diverting one. On a whim, she pulled open one of the drawers inside the wardrobe. Empty of course, except . . .

Except for a dress in an opulent purple silk; a dress which, frankly, Maria had never seen before in her life. She unfolded it carefully from its layers of tissue-paper and a few dried rose-petals fluttered out, still full of their rich, musky perfume.

She held the dress up against herself and admired the effect in the mirror. It must be very old – the quality of the workmanship and styling placed it way back some time in the thirties or forties – yet it was in near-perfect condition, as though it had been worn no more than once or twice, then put away in the drawer and forgotten. Which was probably exactly what had happened, reflected Maria, turning sideways to get a different perspective. Had this once been one of the mysterious Clara Megawne's favourite evening gowns? It was lovely, but no, she couldn't. It wasn't a colour she could wear, not ever. Surely not.

It seemed impossibly small, impossibly fragile, but curiosity got the better of her and she slipped the dress over her head, astonished to feel her body slide easily into the narrow shape, her breasts swelling the tight bodice so that a deep cleavage showed above the sweet-heart neckline. She tugged the heavy, old-fashioned zipper up and turned slowly round, so that the full, calf-length skirt swirled round her legs.

She felt good in the dress; surprisingly good. The fit wasn't quite perfect, but it was better than she could possibly have imagined, and the colour seemed to complement rather than clash with her tumbling red hair. The sleeves, full at the shoulders but tapering to three neat buttons at a tight wrist, flattered her hands, making the fingers look longer and more slender. Her breasts, which she had always thought a little too heavy for her tall, spare frame, seemed perfectly balanced by the full skirt, flaring out from a yoke which moulded tightly to her rounded hips and flat belly.

It might do. It might just do, at that. She rummaged in the bottom of the wardrobe for a pair of shoes and took out her favourites – a pair of thirties-style bar shoes with a Louis heel. Why not? And there was that dragon brooch she'd found the other day . . .

By the time the doorbell rang, she was downstairs in the hallway, gazing into the mirror at a red-haired woman in a violet dress, her eyes sparkling with anticipation. She was ready now; ready for anything – even the enigmatic Mr Pendorran.

Jonathan Gresham had been wrong; he knew that now. He had been quite wrong to assume that just because the delicious Lim Pei was Japanese, she would be submissive and infinitely suggestible.

Lim Pei was open to suggestions, certainly – but most of them were her own. As Jonathan was fast discovering, his new protégée had just as much to show him as he had to teach her. He had chosen even better than he had thought.

'You have tea now, yes?'

He rolled over in bed and observed the girl's entirely delectable nakedness, framed in the doorway to the poky little kitchenette. He wished he had a better flat to entertain her in; bringing her here was like putting a work of art in a Woolworth's frame.

'Not tea, not now.' He grinned. 'You.'

She put the kettle back down on the draining board and glided towards him, her face a mask of smiling mystery, her body a sinuous serpent of graceful lechery, taut and smooth and beautiful. And all he had to do . . . all he had to do was just lie back and enjoy it. She was crazy about him and the whole thing was indecently easy.

As Lim Pei sank down onto his upraised prick, taking him into her with a sudden smoothness that drove him to the point of madness, she turned her head away, hiding from him the laughter in her eyes, and the stifled yawn that made a mockery of his arrogant self-assurance. If anyone here is a fool, she told herself silently, it is not Lim Pei. And she thought of the money her new lover would lavish on her, the clothes he would buy her, and the other, richer men to whom he would introduce her.

As for Jonathan, he was in seventh heaven. His prick felt like it was on fire, and as Lim Pei's tight, wet pussy took him to the brink of climaxing, he realised that he had almost completely forgotten about Maria. But what did he care? Lim Pei was here and now, and Maria Treharne was relegated to a fast-fading memory.

'But Anthony . . . a horse and carriage!'

Maria allowed Joseph, Pendorran's manservant, to take her coat, then followed Pendorran along a rather dark corridor into a spacious but sparsely-furnished dining hall. He walked very close to her but without touching, without even looking at her so that in the end she almost willed him to turn his head so that she could gaze once more into those wild grey eyes.

At last he turned, his lips twisted by that curious half-smile that made him look just a little demonic in the dancing light cast by the candles arranged along the length of the heavy oak dining table.

'You must think me very old-fashioned,' he observed, ushering Maria to her seat at one end of the long table. 'But you see, I have always infinitely preferred horses to cars. And of course, I make a great deal of my income from breeding thoroughbreds, so horses are my livelihood as well as my transport.'

He sat himself down at the other end of the table, a good ten feet away, and nodded to his manservant to pour the wine. When he spoke again, there was a slight quavering in his sonorous voice, as though he were trying not to laugh.

'However, I do also own a 1200cc Harley-Davidson and a 1932 Velocette. Perhaps they would be more to your taste?'

Maria wasn't sure whether to laugh or squirm. This guy was like no one she'd ever met in her life before. He seemed to have the power to make her feel at once insignificant and important, beautiful and impossibly gauche.

She blushed.

'I'm sorry. I didn't mean to be rude. It was just rather a surprise, that's all.'

Pendorran raised his hand to silence her.

'Please, I understand. No offence was intended and none is taken. I realise that I am a somewhat ... unusual man; but then you are an unusual woman, Maria Treharne.' He raised his glass in a toast and the red wine glittered like rubies in the candlelight. 'Welcome to Polmadoc, Maria. I trust we shall none of us disappoint you.'

145

The first course arrived – a cold watercress soup elegantly swirled with cream. It was delicious, but seemed slightly out of place in the vastness of this essentially primitive building. The roughness of the stone walls were barely softened by a coat of whitewash, and the ceiling of the hall rose a good thirty feet to a vault of ancient timbers, blackened and bowed like the ribs of some ancient ship.

'You have a very interesting house,' observed Maria.

Even as she spoke the words sounded idiotic, embarrassingly meaningless, but this man had the ability to regress her to the quivering sixteen-year-old she had been twelve years ago; tongue-tied and dry-mouthed in the presence of her oh-so-cool, oh-so-sarcastic music master. She had those same feelings now – the head-spinning intoxication, the inability to string two words together sensibly, the throbbing ache between her thighs that made her want to writhe on her seat, hotter than a bitch in season.

But Pendorran seemed not to have noticed her confusion; or if he had, he chose to ignore it. Instead, he followed her eyes up to the ceiling.

'This used to be a Celtic longhouse,' he explained. 'No one is quite sure of its precise history before then, but its origins certainly lie far back in antiquity. The rest of the house was added on later, mostly in the sixteenth century, when my family was favoured with money by the Crown.'

Maria glanced up at him in surprise.

'Your family has been here all that time?'

Pendorran raised his glass and gazed into the ruby depths, as though he could perceive something fascinating within the clear, blood-red liquid.

'There has always been a Pendorran at Polmadoc,' he replied simply. 'And if the Goddess wills it, there always will be.'

A breeze rolled in from the sea and ruffled the curtains, making the candles flicker and striking a shower of sparkling lights from the cut facets of the glass he was rolling slowly between finger and thumb. Half-mesmerised, Maria lifted her own glass to her lips and drank deeply, savouring the sharp aftertaste of the full-bodied, velvety wine as it slipped down her throat. And all the time her eyes were locked to Pendorran's gaze, his grey eyes steady and compelling in the ebb and flow of the orange-yellow light.

Out of the silence he spoke again, his words unexpected and, for a few seconds, inexplicable.

'They will destroy Lynmoor.'

Maria paused, a forkful of food halfway between her plate and her lips.

'I'm sorry?'

'The developers, Maria.' Pendorran's voice was quiet but very distinct, a note of urgency hardening the soft tones into an insistent hiss. 'You must understand. They will destroy all that is ancient and good in this place. Will you stand by and see it happen?'

Maria laid down her fork on the plate. Pendorran's almost aggressive insistence disturbed her, but not as much as the steady gaze of those eyes, deep and grey and wild as the ocean breakers that crashed on the rocky coastline, two hundred feet below in Polmadoc Cove.

'I don't see what I can do. It disturbs me, of course it does, but what can I do to stop it happening? I've hardly been in Lynmoor five minutes.'

Pendorran got to his feet, pushing back his carved wooden chair with a sudden grating noise that filled the vast dining hall with a cacophony of echoes.

'What can you do? By all that is sacred, Maria, use what is within you! Stop fighting it, accept the Goddess's command.'

She stared at him in astonishment as he walked towards her, the steel-tipped heels of his heavy riding-boots striking out a staccato rhythm on the polished wooden floor. He was beautiful in the half-light, but his beauty frightened her. He seemed to threaten her with some secret knowledge he demanded she must share.

He towered over her, his face pale and his eyes grey shadows against the soft blackness of his glossy, swept-

147

back hair, and the midnight darkness of his clothes. Only his silver belt buckle gleamed amid the black linen and leather, the raven's one crystal eye flashing fire as it caught the light from the seven-branched candelabrum, its bronze frame curiously gnarled and twisted like the trunk and branches of some ancient forest giant.

Maria's whole body trembled as Pendorran's fingers skimmed her cheek, tracing the soft white curves of her face, and the slight pout of her full, red lips.

'Accept the Goddess,' he whispered. 'Accept me.'

In spite of her apprehension she found herself responding to his touch, her body calling out to his; but her response was instinctive, totally independent of her will, and its intensity stunned and alarmed her.

'What is it that you're asking of me?' she murmured. 'I don't understand, I really don't think I *want* to understand any of this.'

But Anthony's hands were on her shoulders now, coaxing her, drawing her to her feet; and suddenly she was obeying the call of his need, the need that was also hers, and was flooding through her like a fast-moving stream. Outside the thick stone walls, the Atlantic breakers were crashing against the rocky shoreline, the sound no less elemental than the thundering of Maria's heart; the pounding, surging pulse of the blood rushing through her head, making her dizzy and disorientated.

They stood together, Pendorran's hand still on her shoulders, holding her close, whilst the other slid the silver pin from her hair, so that it came tumbling down about her shoulders in a mad disarray of russet waves.

'This is how I want you to come to me, Maria. Wild and untamed as your own heart.'

He let his hand fall from her hair and slide smoothly down her back to the firm roundness of her buttock, pressing her even more closely to him, so that she could not fail to be aware of his erection; a bold, pointing finger of swollen flesh beneath his leather trousers. It seemed huge, self-confident, insolent even – infinitely desirable yet flawed by its own arrogance, just like its master.

She tilted her head slightly back, so that she was looking up into Pendorran's wild grey eyes. They seemed filled with a yearning intensity, and the depth of his need was intoxicating. His kiss on her throat burned with a flame of passion so strong it seemed to sear her flesh with an exquisite pain. Could a man really want her this much; so much that his desire maddened him, turning gentle lust into a savage, unstoppable hunger? And was this what she wanted . . ?

He massaged her backside gently but firmly, with broad circular movements that forced her whole body to move, sliding her belly up and down the front of his trousers. Part of her wanted to resist him, but she could not. Her pubis, perfectly bare beneath the purple silk dress save for the tangled thicket of her maiden curls, responded eagerly to the rough caress; and it seemed to Maria that she was thrusting herself against him instinctively, her body making the decision that her mind was much too afraid to make.

Afraid? But why on earth should anyone be afraid of Anthony Pendorran? He was just a man; a handsome, desirable, self-possessed man who was accustomed to getting exactly what he wanted. And her body was telling her, more strongly than she could have believed possible, that this was what she wanted, too . . .

The sounds of wind-blown ocean spray, driving against the windows of the house, filled Maria's mind with images of foam-white semen, bubbling and seething and spitting like magma in the belly of some great volcano, waiting only for the moment when it would boil and overflow, engulfing all in its path.

She felt a deep, burning warmth spreading through her belly, making her prickle with need. Pendorran's arms slid round her and he lowered his face to hers, planting kisses on her upturned lips, her brow, her cheeks.

'Give yourself to me, Maria. Here and now. The need is so, so strong.'

'But Anthony . . .'

He pushed her gently backwards, and she felt the hard edge of the table against her backside. She put out a hand to steady herself as he lowered her towards the smooth, polished surface, and a silver salt-cellar over-turned, rolling slowly away from her towards the far end of the table. She turned her head and watched it go, mesmerised for a moment by the way the light caught the silver cylinder as it rolled over and over and then was lost in the shadows. It was like watching her own free will disappearing before her eyes, escaping from her grasp and rolling away, to be lost in the darkness of Pendorran's uncompromising desire.

In a daze of need, she heard Pendorran's low whisper: 'Maria, the power. Reach out for the power . . .'

His hand ruched up the skirt of the purple silk gown, exposing the lacy top of her black-stockinged thigh, and the margin of milk-white flesh beyond it. A cool draught of air swirled around Maria's bare skin, caressing her responsive flesh as though it were the strings of an Aeolian harp, playing the music of her desire. Smooth and slow, Pendorran's fingers slid up towards the naked secret of her sex, and she writhed at his touch, her body at once hiding from him and offering itself to his need.

'Anthony, please, I'm not ready . . .'

'Do not be afraid, Maria. All is as it must be.'

'No. Please . . .'

'Maria. What the Goddess wills, no one must deny.'

His voice was hoarse and heavy with sex, and suddenly Anthony Pendorran was no longer the magical seducer, the master of her sexual enchantment. He was breathing heavily as he lay across her, and Maria smelt the spicy tang of wine on his breath. This was a man – an ordinary man with ordinary desires – and she was a fool. All this talk of obeying the Goddess's will was just insincere rubbish, designed to make her fall obligingly into his arms. Well, if Anthony Pendorran thought she was so easily deceived, he had another think coming.

With a suddenness that caught Pendorran unawares, she pushed him hard and he staggered backwards, leaving her sprawled over the table-top with her dress-skirt pushed high up her thigh. His eyes widened in astonishment, and then clouded a moment later with the unmistakable thunder of annoyance.

'What the hell was that for?'

Maria rolled sideways and got up, tugging down her skirt with little irritated movements of her fingers.

'For pity's sake, Anthony – did you really think I was so naïve?'

'Stubborn certainly; naïve, no.'

Anthony leaned back against the whitewashed wall, the heavy curtain over the window billowing round him like a cape as the wind rolled in off the ocean. He looked more demonic than ever, thought Maria as she smoothed the creases out of her dress. More demonic, yet more potently attractive than ever. She forced herself to be angry with him, but in all honesty she was angry with herself. Angry for the weakness that made her desire this beautiful but insensitive man.

'Oh come on, Anthony. You didn't bring me here to talk about the Goddess, did you? You brought me here because you fancied your chances of getting me into bed.'

Maria paused, waiting for Pendorran to retaliate or defend himself; but to her annoyance he said nothing at all. His own initial anger seemed completely under control now, his hawk's face settling into its habitual expression of faintly cynical composure. She looked at him and hated him for being so impossibly cool, so nearly the master of her desire. Hated herself, too, for the lust that still pulsed through her, demanding to be satisfied.

Maria picked up the silver pin that Pendorran had pulled from her hair, and slipped it into the pocket of her evening jacket, which she slung round her shoulders.

'Take me home. Now, this minute.'

When Pendorran finally spoke, she wondered if he had even heard her demand.

'What I have told you is no lie, Maria. Without you,

Lynmoor will die – and with it, Brackwater Hall.' Pendorran shifted his position slightly, and Maria could not help noticing the fat, swollen line of his cock, and the kiss of his glossy black hair on his tanned throat. His beauty made her half-mad with desire for him, but she defied him with a scornful sneer.

'Do you honestly expect me to believe that?'

Pendorran's grey eyes gazed unblinkingly into hers as he walked slowly back towards her.

'You are a seer of spirits, Maria, an unlocker of souls. I understood that the first moment I saw you. Belief is natural to you, though the truth may be stranger and more frightening than the lie.'

Maria hesitated, disconcerted by the excitement that refused to die down inside her.

'Just who do you think you are?'

'I know who I am, Maria. Can you say that much about yourself?'

'I don't believe it, really I don't.'

Leon Duvitski looked up to see Janis peering out of the front window of Lynmoor's marketing suite, the morning sunlight half blocked-out by the grubby backs of six or seven of the great unwashed.

'Something the matter, Janis?' enquired Duvitski casually as she turned away from the window and set down a cup of espresso on his desk.

'It's those New Age hippies, or whatever they call themselves. They're back again, staging another of their so-called demonstrations. It's not doing our reputation any good, you know, having them outside the marketing suite with their banners and their flea-bitten mongrels.'

'I shouldn't worry, Janis,' replied Duvitski smoothly. 'It's all under control.' He recalled the brief conversation he had had with Carolan the previous day, and how much more co-operative he had become about the proposition when he heard about Allardyce's promises of money.

'But don't you think you should *do* something?' demanded Janis, taking a further peek at the demonstrators and wrinkling her nose in disgust.

'Yes, Janis, as a matter of fact I do,' replied Duvitski rather distractedly as he got to his feet and wandered over to the window. Something – or rather someone – had caught his eye. She was worth stopping to look at, too: a tall, leggy redhead with hair that reached almost to her waist and flowed in rippling waves over the soft swell of her breasts.

Despite Grace and Benedict's inexplicable disappearance, Duvitski had learned with interest of Maria Treharne's arrival at Brackwater Hall. Although their paths hadn't yet crossed, he had no doubt that this was she. There couldn't be two women like that in a place like Lynmoor.

'Yes, Janis, you're right,' he murmured to himself.

'What's that?'

He turned round and smiled at his immaculately-groomed PA. So what if she was screwing Charles Allardyce? Janis Faversham wasn't the only woman in the world. He scratched his chin reflectively as he watched the young woman pause and talk to the group of demonstrators.

'Nothing, Janis. I was just reminding myself that there's something else I need to attend to.'

Maria walked down the village high-street in a dream. She was still trying to figure out the previous night, trying to get to the heart of what had happened and work out exactly what game Pendorran was playing.

It was all very odd. One moment she had been on the point of giving herself to him, the next she was pushing him away, spitting venom at him as she ordered him to take her home. She still didn't quite understand why she'd reacted so violently to his advances, or refused quite so resolutely to listen to any of his explanations.

Not that they had made any sense. Nothing Anthony Pendorran said made sense. He spoke in hints and riddles, like a man at the far edge of a dream. Perhaps that was what both attracted and frightened her about him – he seemed to have only the most tenuous of links with reality.

Reality hit her full in the face as she approached the CA Developments marketing suite, where a group of dishevelled young men and women were chanting protests under the watchful eye of the village constable and a one-eyed mongrel dog.

'HANDS OFF OUR HISTORY. PLANNERS GO HOME.' The words bounced into her brain with an insolent energy, refusing to be ignored. She stopped and turned back.

'Sign our petition, lady?' A shaven-headed young man with a spider tattoo indicated a much-fingered sheet of paper, attached to a piece of board with a bulldog clip. 'Keep the fascist developers out of Lynmoor.'

She hesitated, then picked up the pen and scrawled her name across the sheet. Anthony Pendorran might be faintly unhinged, but he was right about one thing, at least: Lynmoor must not be abandoned to men who wanted to tear the very guts out of the place.

'You're from the travellers' camp? she enquired.

'That's right.' She turned to face the new arrival; a bearded man with dull brown hair and eyes that twinkled like two brown diamonds. 'And you're the young lady from the Hall, am I right?'

'Yes, you are – how did you know?'

He chuckled.

'Folk round here may not like passing the time of day with us, but we get to hear a lot of things. We keep our eyes and ears open, see. It pays when you're dealing with scum like Charles Allardyce.' He turned and spat in the direction of Duvitski's office, the spittle landing on the glass in a single gobbet and trickling slowly down the pane.

His accent held residual hints of a faint brogue – Scottish perhaps, or southern Irish. Maria found it quite pleasantly lyrical, though its owner looked more like a down-at-heel young tinker than a Celtic bard. She guessed that the amiable smile might conceal a wealth of secrets, by no means all respectable or pleasant. Nevertheless, there was something fascinating about the man – an intangible, dynamic quality that marked him out as a leader.

'Let me see – your name's Maria, and you're from Cambridge, though that's a Liverpool accent if I'm not much mistaken. Your auntie left you that great big house, and now you're wondering what to do with it. I'm right, aren't I?'

Maria laughed.

'In every last detail. But how ..?'

The traveller silenced her with a shake of the head, wiped his right hand on his waistcoat and extended it in greeting.

'Let's just say we have our ways. Carolan's the name.' He carefully omitted to mention that, as far as the East Midlands Constabulary were concerned, he was still plain old Benjamin Tarrant. Maria slid her hand into his; its grip was vice-like. So this was the legendary New Age hellraiser she'd heard about from Geraint. At last he released her fingers. 'I've been waiting for a chance to get to talk to you.'

'Really?'

'Just come over here a little way, where we can talk without the whole world listening.' Carolan led her a few yards down the street, and sat down on the steps of the old museum. He lowered his voice to a conspiratorial whisper. 'I hear you are ... of the ancient faith.'

Maria nodded.

'I worship the Goddess.' A faint irritation mingled with her surprise. Were there no secrets at all in this place? Did the whole of Lynmoor know who and what she was?

'We too try to live our lives in harmony with nature,' continued Carolan, an edge of bitterness entering his voice. 'But the Establishment's only too happy to let men like Allardyce ruin it for us – and our kids.

155

'The thing is, we're doing our damnedest to get this Lynmoor Development scrapped, but alone, we're not strong enough. We need help.'

'I don't see what I can do,' chipped in Maria quickly, her mind suddenly filled with uncomfortable recollections of the previous night. 'I've no more power than you, and I've only just come to stay here. I don't even belong to Lynmoor.'

Carolan seized hold of her wrist with an unexpected energy that demanded her undivided attention.

'We must get in touch with the power,' he hissed. 'The ancient spirit. You can help us, you have the knowledge and the skill.'

'I think you're over-estimating my abilities,' protested Maria. But Carolan was not easily put off.

'A ritual, that's what we're planning,' he continued. 'Up among the old standing stones on Hilltop Tor – the ones Allardyce wants to move halfway to bloody Barncastle. A rite of conjuration, using sensual and sexual power; but we need your help.'

Maria released her wrist from Carolan's grip.

'Let me get this straight. You're asking me to take part in this . . . sexual rite?'

She saw Carolan's eyes gleam – with triumph? – and wondered just how far she could trust him. Was he really the Robin Hood of Lynmoor, or just a tatty little man with an eye for the main chance? As though in a sudden gesture of supplication, he took hold of her hand and pressed his lips against it.

'Think of the power you would bring to the ritual,' he urged. 'Join with us. In two weeks from now, on the night of the new moon.'

She gave no promise, but walked slowly away, painfully aware of Carolan's bright, bird-like eyes boring holes in the back of her thin cotton dress. First Pendorran, and now Carolan. Why did she have the uneasy feeling that – given half a chance – both of them would lead her into disaster?

* * *

Amid the rich furnishings of the attic chamber, the lovers who had once been Grace Hawley and Benedict Green entwined in a new frenzy of unquenchable passion.

Time had passed. Long, luxurious days that stretched into weeks as, in the valley below Brackwater Hall, spring melted into high summer. But in this world there was no time, no space. Even the lovers' identities had been long forgotten in this never-ending festival of lust. They were oblivious to the colours and the textures of the silks and velvets strewn on the floor about them; the myriad coloured lights cast through painted glass onto their naked, famished flesh.

As their bodies moved together in silent, savage hunger, their fingers clawing, their teeth biting, the spider's-web crack in the painted windowpane began to recede and mend, the yellowing paintwork on the attic door gradually brightening to a smooth and dazzling white.

Slowly, almost imperceptibly, the lovers' bodies were growing less and less substantial, their united flesh becoming as transparent as a projected image, until at last the force of ecstasy melted their very souls into the ancient fabric of Brackwater Hall.

And even their memory had disappeared.

# Chapter Eight

July heat shimmered over the high moorland, a bluish haze blurring the distant horizon. Anthony Pendorran looked up at the sun through narrowed eyes. It was almost noon; almost time.

Seconds ticked away in the silence of his brain as he sat there, cross-legged on the stony ground, watching for a sign. Nothing moved in the still, scorching air: no blade of grass, not a bird in the sky. Nothing.

Slowly he got to his feet, untied the pouch from his belt and loosened the drawstring which held it closed. The whitish powder inside was coarse and crystalline. He tipped a handful into his gloved palm, then closed his fingers over it, feeling its grittiness as the grains slid over the smooth black leather.

A black shape darted across the white-gold disc of the sun; a raven with outspread wings, its beak open in a raucous greeting as it cut through the steel-blue sky.

Time.

Raising his clenched fist to the sky, Pendorran hurled the handful of white dust into the stagnant air; and the white grains glittered like a shower of sparks in the fierce sunlight.

Almost immediately, he felt it. The first stirrings of the breeze, cold as ice on his sun-warmed cheek. A breeze that was but the herald of a wild wind bearing mischief in its sharpened claws.

Warm cascades of afternoon sunlight flooded through the casement window, casting a golden sheen on smooth, tanned flesh.

Maria stretched out luxuriously, then wriggled across the bed to where her lover was sleeping, moulding herself to him so that the hollow of her belly cradled the hard smooth curve of his backside. Her playful fingers walked teasingly over the bronzed flesh, stroking Geraint's muscular young body. His irresistible warmth flooded into her on a spring tide of desire. But still he lay with his back towards her, his breathing regular and deep.

She snuggled close, pressing her chin into the crook of his neck and whispering endearments into the soft mat of his golden hair.

'Geraint – please wake up. I'm lonely . . .'

No response came, but Maria had no intention of giving up so easily. She slid the flat of her hand down the amber curve of his shoulder and back, then slipped teasing fingers over the taut flesh of his belly, toned iron-hard from long days spent working in his father's fields. Surfacing towards wakefulness, he murmured his sleepy pleasure, and she nuzzled the back of his neck, moist now with the sweat of their lovemaking, and fragrant with the sweetness of new-mown hay.

'Don't you want to play?' Hunger kindling inside her by the moment, Maria hardly recognised her own words. Her whisper was smooth as silk, her voice caressing and cajoling him to come back to her and answer her need. She tried a different tack. 'Don't you want me to give you pleasure?'

Geraint gave a shuddering sigh and rolled onto his back, his eyes flickering open to gaze at her. They were a clear amethyst blue. Maria returned his smile, bending over to kiss him, the tips of her breasts brushing across the little blond hairs on his well-muscled chest as she

159

did so. They'd already made love twice this afternoon, but she wasn't tired; and she could see from the sap-filled bough of Geraint's prick that he wasn't either. She ran the tip of her tongue over her parched lips, her belly famished and aching for love.

'At last! I thought you were going to sleep all after-noon.'

The young farmworker grinned and pulled Maria's face down to his, almost crushing her with his kiss. The tip of his tongue parted her lips, filling her mouth with the unashamedly spicy taste of her own juices. Geraint might be unsophisticated compared to Jonathan Gresham or Tony Fitzhardinge, but you couldn't say he wasn't an energetic and willing lover. At last he pulled away, leaving Maria breathless for more. The rawness of this young buck of a lover served only to whet her appetite for him.

There was a mischievous glint in Geraint's eyes as he stretched and yawned, the inside of his mouth pink as a cat's as it lazes in the sun.

'S'pose you'll want me to get up an' do your garden,' he observed, sprawling back on the pillows, his blond curls forming a golden halo around his wind-tanned face.

'Is *that* what you think?'

'Can't go shirkin' my duties now, can I?'

Maria's lips curled a wicked smile as she bent over her lover, her voice a seductive whisper:

'You know damn well that wasn't what I had in mind.'

Her head was full of possibilities, all of them far more interesting than digging the garden. More enjoyable, too. She didn't need reminding that you could have a lot of fun with a cocksure young buck like Geraint Morgan; the sort of carefree, roistering fun that made Anthony Pendorran seem cranky and weird, and not worth the bother of worrying about. Anthony Pendorran – damn him. That man kept sneaking into her thoughts even here, as Geraint's impertinent fingers worked away at the malleable flesh of her backside.

She dismissed Pendorran from her thoughts with a rush of angry stubbornness that evaporated as soon as she glanced back into Geraint's twinkling blue eyes. They seemed to be daring her, inviting her to new and delicious liberties.

Playful as a kitten, she slid down Geraint's body and planted a trail of little kisses leading up his thighs to the golden tangle of his pubic curls. Then she looked at him and smiled. Her red lips pouted seductively as they framed the words that made Geraint's cock twitch with a secret inner life of its own:

'Want to fuck?'

Geraint did not reply – his skill lay in actions rather than words. Rolling suddenly sideways, he flipped Maria onto her back and knelt over her, straddling her with his strong thighs, tanned columns of flesh that seemed firm as marble. Giggling, she reached out and ran a questing finger over the bronzed flesh, which rippled as he moved with an alluring hint of work-hardened muscle.

Sex-hardened, too: Maria was under no illusions about her new lover. In any case, it was an open secret that Geraint Morgan had lovers in just about every house in and around Lynmoor. Mind you, his girlfriend Patsy seemed to be remarkably accommodating about it all, letting him return to her bed time after time. What was it about Geraint? He was good-looking but not exceptionally so; an instinctive rather than a skilled or sophisticated lover. Viewed objectively, he wasn't a patch on Jonathan. And yet . . .

And yet Geraint Morgan had only to strip off his shirt and Maria wanted to run her tongue all over his shoulders and chest, licking the salty sweat from the skin, feeling the firmness of muscle and flesh beneath the eager probe of her tongue. This attraction made no better sense than any other addiction, but Maria Treharne was developing a definite appetite for Geraint Morgan's lusty lovemaking.

So now, without even putting up the semblance of a

fight, Maria had joined the long list of Geraint's conquests. Or was Geraint one of hers? She preferred to think he was. She emphatically wasn't the sort of woman who enjoyed being anybody's victim. No, Maria liked to feel she was in control at every moment, savouring the agreeable sensation of having a man's pleasure in her hands or on her tongue.

Hungry for Geraint's sex, she caressed him; and he shuddered with anticipation as her scarlet fingernail travelled lightly up his inner thigh towards the velvety pouch of his balls. Pendulous and heavy, they hung over her belly like ripe fruit, tempting and full of delicious juice. Maria cradled them gently in her hand and smiled up into Geraint's amethyst-blue eyes.

'Why don't we have some more fun?'

She smoothed her fingers over his balls, squeezing and kneading them with the utmost gentleness until they ached with need: the need to shoot their creamy-white tribute all over Maria's full, firm breasts. When her fingers left his balls and climbed steadily up his shaft, he thought he might die of pleasure.

He laid his hand on Maria's with a sudden urgency.

'You'd better stop right there, or I'll come all over you, I swear I will . . .'

Maria shook her head.

'Oh no. Not before I'm ready for you,' she promised. And she began gently wanking Geraint's stiffened shaft, using the flat of her thumb to smooth droplets of clear pre-come across the head of his swollen glans. 'I just want to make you *really* ready for me.' The long, slow strokes were luxuriously, perfectly judged to impart the maximum sensation but leave her lover gasping for more.

She loved the feel of a stiff, thick shaft between her fingers, and the knowledge that her lover was hard for her and her alone. She loved the ripples of excitement that ran through her as she watched the little eye at the cock-tip dilate and weep clear, salty tears of longing.

Just when Geraint thought he could hold back no lon-

162

ger, Maria stopped stroking his shaft, and slid her hand down to his balls, gently squeezing their ripeness in her covetous fingers. There was a madness in her eyes, a wild desire that could only be sated by the delicious friction of sex. Her clitoris was throbbing, hungry for the grind of flesh on flesh. She had to have him.

'I want it,' she breathed. 'I want it now.'

Even in the haze of his desire, Geraint managed to play the tease. He gave her a malicious smile.

'What is it you want? Go on then, I want to 'ear you tell me.' Reaching down, he seized her nipple between finger and thumb and pinched it; hard, so that a tiny sob escaped from her lips.

Maria's body rippled with excitement, responding instinctively to Geraint's game.

'Give it to me,' she pleaded, her hips writhing sinuously as Geraint rolled her nipple backwards and forwards, making it tingle and ache with frustrated need.

'Tell me then, little miss prim,' taunted Geraint. 'I want to 'ear you talk dirty.'

Maria's thighs were jerking apart, but her lips formed a perfect moue of pretended disdain.

'You're an animal!' she retorted joyfully, sensing the laughter that was bubbling up within the flood-tide of desire. She wriggled, but Geraint had no intention of letting her go. He knew that was not what she wanted from him at all.

He crushed her lips with his, and left her gasping.

'Maybe I am,' he replied triumphantly. 'But I've got what you want, ain't I?' He forced her hand back onto his cock, and an immense shudder of desire shook her entire body. 'You city girls can't get enough of it, can you? But if you want it, you'd better tell me – else I shan't know what you want, shall I? Stands to reason ...'

Maria squeezed Geraint's shaft hard, trying desperately to pull him into her.

'Tell me,' he insisted, smiling all over his wind-bronzed face.

'All right then,' replied Maria sweetly, her feigned modesty evaporating as the urgency of need superseded the desire to tease. 'I want to be fucked, Geraint. Do you hear? I want you to screw the arse off me. I want you to spear me with that big fat cock of yours . . .'

The time for talking was long gone. Before Maria had finished speaking he was inside her, his breathing hoarse with need as he slid between her fringed love-lips and far into the silken depths of her haven. He was so beautifully big that she could feel his cock-tip nudging against the neck of her womb, her well-lubricated flesh distending to accommodate its oh-so-welcome guest. And her hips rose to meet him, eager and insistent in their hunger.

The summer sunshine lay like a golden pool across the bed as they coupled, picking out the dewdrops of sweat like tiny diamonds on their skin. They moved well together, their bodies synchronising in an instinctive harmony of mutual desire. The sunlight seemed warm, friendly, welcoming.

Answering Geraint's thrusts with a rhythmic tilting of her hips, Maria luxuriated in the pure, uncomplicated delight of their coupling. She felt so good in this place; so sexually complete. Despite her worries about the threat to Lynmoor from the developers, it was curious how many aspects of her life seemed to be coming into focus since she had arrived at Brackwater Hall: her work, her happiness, even aspects of her ritual magic. There seemed to be something about this ancient place that made all things sacred and special.

Sex, especially, had never been so good. She asked herself, as a familiar tingle began to spread through her belly, why she had even bothered to accept Anthony Pendorran's dinner invitation, let alone almost let him make love to her. What brainstorm had taken her so close to losing her senses? Darkly attractive he might be, but she didn't need some screwed-up egomaniac to make her feel good. And what could make her feel better than this . . ?

Warm, sweet languor washed over her, making her relaxed and excited and dizzy, all at the same time. On a day like this, Anthony Pendorran, Alcuin College and CA Developments all seemed light years away. All Maria needed or wanted right now was the Cornish sun on her back, and the sublime hardness of a prick, deep within her belly.

Now. Now. Now. Pleasure was a sunlit ocean, ecstasy crashing down upon her in wave upon wild wave.

'I'm coming, coming, hold me . . .'

As her womanhood tensed in the powerful spasms of orgasm, Geraint answered with a final thrust, and she felt the twitch of his cock as he came, clasping her tightly to him.

It had been good. So very good. But today, passion's hunger was not quite so easily satisfied. Minutes later, as lengthening shadows ran curious fingers over the lovers' bodies, their pleasure began all over again.

Maria dried her hair, slipped on a bathrobe and went down the back stairs to the kitchen for a cool, decadent glass of wine. Geraint's enthusiastic lovemaking had left her feeling languid and lazy, and it was more difficult than ever to contemplate work. Once again it struck her how completely her life had changed in a matter of a few short weeks: St Alcuin's seemed a whole world away. Thoughts of dour Cambridge dons and dreary formal dinners had no place in this land of wild, unforgiving beauty.

As she brought the opened bottle from the fridge to the old scrubbed-oak table, she paused by the kitchen window and saw that the sky was beginning to darken; graduating from deep azure to a threatening purple over the hills towards the sea, where storm-clouds were already gathering. But she gave it little thought, for she had already grown accustomed to Lynmoor's capricious changes of weather.

Other, less welcome thoughts were crowding in on her, refusing to go away. Those lecture notes, for example – the ones she had absolutely promised to have ready for the late summer school she was supposed to be returning to Cambridge to teach in August. Like it or not, they weren't going to wait for ever. With a sigh of resignation, she reached into one of the kitchen cupboards and, selecting the biggest wine-glass she could find, filled it to the brim, grateful for the iciness of the chilled white wine in the sweltering August heat. Perhaps a storm would help clear the air – clear her thoughts too, maybe. Pendorran had been right about one thing, that was for sure: with or without his questionable assistance, there was the Lynmoor protest campaign to think about; and of course there were those bloody lecture notes to get started on, too.

Maria grinned to herself. Well, it was no good staying here in the kitchen – she'd only drink her way through every bottle in the wine-rack, and then start on the contents of the fridge. Time to put pen to paper. She'd found she worked best in the huge first-floor drawing-room, with its panoramic views of the moors and its assortment of Victorian clutter: dark beeswax-scented furniture, Indian carpets and chenilles. She liked to sit there, at the big carved dining-table, gazing out towards the far-distant sea and imagining how her mysterious Aunt Clara and her ancestors must once have sat there, entertaining their elegant friends to afternoon tea. Why, the way it was furnished and decorated, this house could hardly have changed in a hundred years.

Still thinking of Aunt Clara, she drained her glass and walked out into the hallway. Immediately she noticed the wire basket on the back of the front door, a few brown envelopes jumbled at the bottom in an untidy heap. These little sexual interludes were making her lazy. All day the post must have been sitting there, but of course she'd been much too busy to think about what the postman had delivered. The question was, did she really want to know? Knowing her luck, Myint would finally have got his act together, and it would be that solicitor's bill she'd been dreading ever since she arrived.

At first sight there was nothing but junk: an invitation to a vegetarian barbeque with Emily and Ben, an Ars Magica catalogue from Kai ... but wait a minute; right at the bottom of the pile there was an official-looking letter postmarked 'Cambridge'. She brightened. At last! The confirmation of her long-awaited appointment as a Fellow of St Alcuin's – and about time too. The Appointments Board had been dragging their feet all year. Perhaps the publication of her acclaimed book, *Goddess Worship and the Celts*, had finally prompted them into action. Eagerly she tore open the envelope and unfolded the crisp white sheet of paper.

What? No. It couldn't be ...

The letter was from the Master of St Alcuin's all right, but it wasn't the coveted rubber-stamp on her Fellowship – in fact, it was the complete opposite.

Words swam before her eyes, refusing to resolve themselves into any familiar pattern. None of this made sense. How could it? She must have got it wrong. Surely ... Dazed, she sat down and read the letter again, more slowly this time, convinced that she had missed something vital that would make everything clear. But no matter how many times she read it, the message kept adding up to the same thing.

The sack.

"Dear Dr Treharne," she read for the umpteenth time, "it is with regret that I have to inform you that, owing to the current retrenchment in Government funding for university posts ..."

'Government retrenchment'? 'Financial constraints'? Did Armstrong-Baker really expect her to believe that crap? 'Regret'? At this very moment he was probably rubbing his sweaty little hands with glee. He and his chauvinistic friends on the College Appointments Board had been doing their damnedest to make life difficult for her these last eighteen months – and now they'd found a way of getting exactly what they wanted. Frankly, she didn't know whether to laugh or cry.

Mad as hell, she ripped the letter up, and threw it in

the wastepaper bin; then thought better of it, and rummaged for the crumpled pieces. Maybe there was a more constructive outlet for her anger. Let's calm down and think clearly, she told herself. Right. If they wanted to get rid of her, they were going to have a fight on their hands. Her mind worked fast, thought succeeding thought with an icy clarity. She'd sue for unfair dismissal, that's what she'd do. It was only fair. The bastards needn't think they were going to get away with it this easily.

She glanced at the grandfather clock in the hallway, the heavy pendulum marking out the passing seconds. Ten to five. There should just be time to catch Armstrong-Baker at his College rooms before he left for another dirty weekend with the Assistant Bursar. Huh! She bet he wouldn't be dispensing with *her* services in a hurry.

Still trembling with fury, she dialled the College number on the antiquated hall phone – a Bakelite monstrosity so out of date that it would probably represent the height of retro chic in a Mayfair penthouse suite. Her fingers drumming impatiently on the hall table, she waited for Armstrong-Baker to pick up the receiver.

Come on. Come on. I know you're there.

'Yes?'

The woman's voice was unfamiliar, peculiarly crackly and distant. It didn't sound like Armstrong-Baker's secretary, but maybe it was just a bad line.

'Hello – is that St Alcuin's College?'

'I'm sorry, who is that? I can hardly hear you.'

'It's Maria Treharne. Dr Treharne. I need to speak to Dr Armstrong-Baker right away.'

'I beg your pardon? This is Rokeby 5465.'

'Oh. Sorry, wrong number.'

In exasperation, Maria slammed down the receiver. Just her luck. This damned weather must be affecting the telephone lines. She checked the time with mounting irritation. Nearly five to. Still, he shouldn't have left yet. With a deep breath, she tried again. After four rings, an answering machine whirred into action. Damn.

'This is Dr Armstrong-Baker's office. I am sorry, but there is no one here to answer your call at the moment. Please leave your name, number and message after the tone, and we will return your call at our earliest opportunity.'

'This is Maria Treharne,' began Maria, her words icily precise. Armstrong-Baker might not be there, but he was sure as hell going to get the full force of her venom. 'I just wanted you to know what I think of your bloody . . .'

Click.

Maria stared at the receiver, shook it and listened again. The line had gone completely dead. Maybe it was the weather. It *did* seem to be working its way up to a massive electrical storm out there – the sky was turning all colours of the rainbow. Puzzled, she dialled again, but it was pointless – there was no dialling tone. No sound at all. Nothing.

She could smell something, too – like . . . burning? Glancing down, she saw why the telephone wasn't working. It was no longer plugged in at all. The end of the flex was hanging limp and useless, neatly amputated just short of the wall socket, a little molten plastic dripping slowly onto the carpet beneath.

Maria picked up the end of the flex and stared at it for a few seconds, dumbfounded. The flex seemed to have burned right through.


Angry sunlight glinted through the plate-glass windows of Charles Allardyce's tenth-floor London office. But Allardyce had no time to notice the weather. His thoughts were fully occupied with his latest – and most impressive – development.

'So you see, Mr Carolan, it is in all our interests for the Lynmoor project to go ahead exactly as planned. As you have seen from the prospectus, this innovative development will bring employment and prosperity to a remote and economically-depressed area of the country.'

'Yeah. Right.'

'And you understand, of course, that this extensive development will in no way damage Lynmoor – simply maximise the accessibility of all its ... how shall we say ... natural amenities.'

Charles Allardyce smiled behind the massive mahogany desk, smug and patronising in his Savile Row suit and gold designer cufflinks. The travellers' leader irritated him; but he was willing to do whatever was necessary to ensure the success of his plans. Like his father before him, he'd happily have made a pact with the Devil if it looked cost-effective. Besides, Lynmoor was the big one: the project that would transform him from merely filthy rich into the sort of mega-tycoon who could buy up the whole of Luxembourg ... if the fancy took him.

Carolan snorted with ill-concealed mirth, drained the glass and wiped his mouth on the back of his hand. Allardyce might be a prize prick, but he knew his brandy – it was bloody good. A whole lot better than the piss-poor elderberry wine the women made back at the camp. And talking of women ...

The immaculately-coiffured secretary with the long, long legs refilled his glass, and he amused himself by giving her arse a good grope as she bent over. Her sleeveless silk blouse was cut low at the neck, providing a tantalising glimpse of generous breasts. Obviously Allardyce shared his taste in women as well as brandy.

'You can cut the PR,' he observed. 'I'm not interested in that shit. Just tell me what's in it for me.'

Allardyce raised an eyebrow and beckoned a male PA with a snap of his fingers.

'The Brackwater file. Now.'

'At once, sir.'

He resumed his contemplation of Carolan.

'I thought you ... travellers ... were supposed to be back-to-nature types, in harmony with the suffering earth.' His voice was heavy with irony. 'Aren't you interested in the future of the natural landscape where your people live? What do they think about all this?'

Carolan grunted.

'They'll think whatever I tell them to think. Besides – if you'd thought I was some sort of New Age do-gooder, you wouldn't have asked me here. You and I both know where we stand.'

It was true. Allardyce needed Carolan as an informant and as a fifth columnist – undermining effective opposition to CA Developments from within. For his part, Carolan coveted what Allardyce could offer ... including his discretion. No, it really wouldn't do for the rest of the camp to hear about their leader's string of convictions for petty theft and deception.

A slim manila file arrived on Allardyce's desk.

'I can be a generous man, Carolan. If that generosity is deserved.'

'Talk's cheap, Mr Allardyce.'

Allardyce opened the folder and took out a cheque for a four-figure sum. He pushed it across the desk towards Carolan.

'Call this the first instalment. There will be plenty more if you can prove to me that it's money well spent.'

'I prefer cash.'

Allardyce shrugged dismissively.

'That can be arranged. Anything can be arranged – if you're prepared to cooperate.' He sat back in his chair and pressed the tips of his fingers together. 'Now, tell me about the Treharne woman. How is she likely to re-act when we apply for a compulsory purchase order on Brackwater Hall? Is she the sort of woman who likes to cause trouble?'

'Maria Treharne? Daft tart's hardly been in that house five minutes. You make her a good offer, and she'll be quick enough to take it. And in any case I've got plans to fix her, don't you worry.' He chuckled maliciously. 'She's not as clever as she thinks, that girl. Soon have her running back to her fancy college with her tail between her legs. Besides,' he grinned. 'I've never met a woman yet who could resist me.'

'I sincerely hope you're right,' replied Allardyce.

'Obtaining possession of Brackwater Hall is central to our plans. It may yet be necessary for myself and Mr Duvitski to pay Ms Treharne a little personal visit.'

He glanced at his Rolex and got up from his chair, smoothing imaginary creases out of his immaculate grey suit. His handshake was bone-crushingly firm.

'If I don't leave now I shall be late. I have an important meeting at County Hall. Don't forget – I want the rest of that information by the middle of next week at the latest.'

'No problem.'

Allardyce and his acolytes were leaving, but Carolan couldn't help noticing that the immaculate secretary was making no attempt to follow her boss out of the office. In fact, she was still perched rather prettily on the chair beside him, her short skirt hitched high on her slender thighs. Carolan gave Allardyce a quizzical look.

'Miss Grayston will attend to you now,' remarked Allardyce casually, as he opened the door to leave. 'I trust you will enjoy her hospitality – it is just a small taste of what you can expect if you show complete loyalty to the organisation.'

As the door swung shut, Carolan felt Deborah Grayston's well-manicured hand sliding its way up his thigh. If he wasn't very much mistaken, he was going to enjoy working for Charles Allardyce.

'Come away with me, Anthea. My father has this amazing villa in Tuscany. If we left tomorrow morning, we could drive down in a couple of days. It would be heaven on earth.'

Anthea Redwood responded enthusiastically to her lover's kiss as he pulled her towards the shower cubicle. It was completely against her landlord's rules and regulations, of course, but Tony Fitzhardinge had been sharing her flat for several weeks now. Luckily, no one had yet noticed. If they were luckier still, they might make it to the end of the long vacation without anyone ever being the wiser. And once Michaelmas Term began, Tony would be able to move back into his student room at St Bride's – if, that is, Anthea hadn't decided to move out of her flat altogether and set up house with Tony in bold, glorious sin. If Tony didn't get himself sent down for not getting on with his thesis . . .

She couldn't quite make up her mind. If Maria was here, she'd be able to help her decide if young Tony was worth the hassle. Maria was such a connoisseur of sexy young PhD students. Mind you, Anthea had a pretty fair idea of what Maria would think of any woman daft enough to get mixed up with Tony Fitzhardinge. In any case, Maria was off in some godforsaken corner of north Cornwall where the phone lines were always down. Now the latest vicious rumour doing the rounds in Cambridge was that that creep Armstrong-Baker was planning to get her kicked out of her lectureship.

There was worse to come, too. Anthea had been putting it off for too long, and she was beginning to feel guilty. But it wasn't an easy thing to contemplate. How was Maria going to take it when Anthea told her her precious Jonathan had been seen leaving a cheap hotel with some high-class tart from Kyoto? Yes, there were one or two things Maria ought to know, before it was too late.

She stepped under the warm shower-jet and pressed her nakedness up against Tony's hunky young body. OK, so he had a reputation as a bit of a bastard, but let's face it, he was a good-looking bastard. In fact, he was just about everything a girl could ever want: young, with a body to die for, clever but not too clever . . . and very, very over-sexed. On the other hand, Cambridge was full of personable young hunks with wealthy fathers, and not *all* of them were bastards you couldn't trust any further than you could throw them. Maybe Tuscany was that way, too. Decisions, decisions . . .

'No, I can't come to Tuscany, sweetheart,' she sighed, smoothing shower-gel over Tony's back and belly.

'Of course you can.' His kisses were moving down from her throat to her breasts, tormenting the stiff buds of her nipples. 'The long vacation's hardly started, and you don't have to be back here until . . . oh, late September at a push. We could have weeks and weeks out there. Just you and me in the sunshine . . .'

She gripped his manhood and slid her fingers lovingly up the smooth shaft. Tuscany would be great; but maybe it was better if she didn't give Tony everything he wanted – maybe she should try to keep him wanting more. If she was going to maintain Tony's interest, she was going to have to stay one step ahead of him in the game.

'No, no, you don't understand,' she protested, fighting to maintain control as Tony's fingers worked warm, soapy lather over her pubis and between her thighs. 'I've decided to go to Cornwall.'

He stopped kissing Anthea and looked at her in surprise.

'Cornwall? What the hell for?'

'To see Maria.' She held Tony close and kissed him passionately. 'I had a letter from her the other day. She's invited me to stay at Brackwater Hall.'

The first peal of thunder awoke Maria, jolting her from sleep into the turbulent world of the storm. The air was unbreathable, filled with a heavy, nerve-jangling electricity.

A hot, arid wind was blowing across the moors, and the bedroom curtains were billowing inwards, casting bizarre shadows on the walls as lightning flashed: orange, purple, crimson, cutting through the inky darkness.

Suddenly very awake, Maria slipped from between the crisp cotton sheets and hurried to the window to close it. Drawing open the curtains to lower the sash, she was in time to see the whole of Lynmoor suddenly illuminated by a garish zig-zag of multi-coloured lightning that seemed to cut the sky in two like a razor-gash in deep violet silk.

A moment later, thunder rolled a second time and the

rain began: huge, fat droplets at first, falling sluggishly out of the heavy sky, then quickening into a torrent that drove with increasing violence against the ancient stone walls of Brackwater Hall.

Fascinated by the passionate energy of the storm, Maria remained standing there for a few moments, enjoying the feel of cool raindrops on her hot, naked flesh. But lightning flashed again across the night sky, and this time a vicious gust of wind drove through the open window, knocking over a table lamp with the tinkling of shattered glass.

With a cry of annoyance, Maria turned from the window. But it was not the broken fragments of the lamp which drew Maria's gaze. It was the small bronze mirror hanging on the wall opposite the window, its ancient frame moulded into the shapes of many-headed dragons with ruby eyes. As the storm lit up the room momentarily, filling it with multicoloured light, Maria caught sight of something strange about the mirror. Something within its secret depths, that was and was not a true reflection. It was a fleeting glimpse, a pretty deception, a trick of this crazy storm-light which left her feeling dizzy and yet exhilarated.

As the storm raged on outside, Maria stepped forward to touch the ornate bronzework, smoothing her fingertips across the beautiful, snarling dragon-heads. Lightning flashed again, and she was startled by the flickering image which greeted her not from the surface of the mirror, but from somewhere, it seemed, deep within.

It was her own face which gazed back at her, her own flesh reflected within the bronze frame, and yet she did not recognise the woman in the mirror. In place of her own nakedness, she saw herself dressed in a rich, crimson gown cut low at the breast; her chestnut hair plaited into long braids, and crowned by a red-gold circlet studded with glittering rubies. Then darkness came once again, and the image was gone.

Spellbound, Maria reached out to touch the surface of the mirror, trying to understand what trick of the light could do this. But her fingers did not meet cold, inert glass and metal. The surface of the mirror was warm and yielding as flesh to the touch; it seemed to vibrate to some secret inner rhythm ... the pulse of an inner life?

Alarmed now, Maria drew back. If this was a dream, she wanted it to stop. If it was sorcery, it was not any magic that she could understand. She closed her eyes, but she could not banish the room, nor the storm-lit face of the woman who was and was not Maria Treharne, calling to her from beyond a living mirror.

And now there was a whispering in her head, a desperate pleading that refused to go away. She could not grasp what it might mean. A single word, over and over again; in time with her heart, synchronised to her fear:

'Deliverance.'

Thunder rolled from a lowering sky, orange and purple clouds hanging low over Brackwater Tor. It was a wild Cornish night, fit for neither man nor beast.

But a lone figure strode the heights of Lynmoor, his tall, powerful figure silhouetted against the angry sky-line.

Anthony Pendorran did not fear the storm. He welcomed it, revelling in the energy of the elements battling in the skies above him. Rain was lashing his face, wind tearing at his long black coat so that it flew out behind him like a raven's wings. But his eyes were shining with a fanatical joy.

The ancient promise had been fulfilled. The Mistress had come to Brackwater Tor.

# Chapter Nine

'*A*nd so, ladies and gentlemen, those are my detailed proposals for Phases Three and Four of the Lynmoor Development.'

Charles Allardyce addressed his assembled business partners with instinctive authority. One or two of them could buy him out several times over, but he wasn't the type to be cowed by another man's money. He knew he was the man of the moment: the only man who could bring the Lynmoor Development to fruition.

And let's face it, tonight's meeting was going rather well. After plying them with a first-rate dinner and plenty of wine, he could feel his audience warming to his point of view. Putty in his hands, that's what they were.

In the centre of the polished boardroom table at CA Developments' London headquarters stood a brand-new scale model. It was quite an advance on earlier versions, amended to make room for the much more prestigious third and fourth phases of the development. Now that he was a mere hairsbreadth from obtaining blanket planning permission, Allardyce felt he could afford to start planning ahead on a more grandiose scale.

True, Phase One was still causing a few minor teething problems, because of the need to relocate some rather insignificant Bronze Age burials and a stone circle that would look much more picturesque on the other side of the valley; but Allardyce saw no reason to suppose that they would pose any serious hindrance. For one thing, it was surprising how quickly the county planners had come round to his way of thinking, once he'd had a private chat with them. His money talked even more eloquently than he did.

Even now the construction teams were preparing to move on to the site of the new leisure and theatre complex, just above Lynmoor village – and Allardyce didn't anticipate any real problems from the villagers. Admittedly some of the locals had been opposed to the development at first, but then that was just their typical peasant suspicion of anything new. Duvitski had worked on them with his usual evangelical skill, and now most of them seemed to welcome the opportunities it would bring them.

When the time came and Allardyce wanted them out of Hilltop Tor, the hippy layabouts would be made to see reason, too. And of course, with Carolan to sabotage the protest movement from within ... No, there could be no question of failure.

'Are the works still on schedule?' demanded Lorinda Crawley, interrupting his self-congratulatory train of thought with a small note of discord. Allardyce had spent a few diverting nights with the icily-sensual Financial Director of Clone Investments, but an initially promising relationship had never quite got off the starting-blocks. Allardyce preferred his women less intelligent and a good deal more accommodating. 'I've heard some disturbing reports about a local protest campaign.'

Nods and murmurs of assent ran round the table as the decanter of vintage port was passed from hand to hand.

'That's right,' butted in Jeremy James, whose father owned most of Pembrokeshire. 'Hippy convoys and demonstrations – not very good for our image, is it?'

Allardyce smirked, his handsome face a picture of self-satisfied smugness.

'No problems, I can assure you. The bulldozers will shortly be moving in to prepare the area above the village, for the new theatre and leisure complex. Once that's under way, we'll turn our attentions to Hilltop Tor. Frankly I don't imagine for one moment that that flea-bitten rabble will be presenting us with any serious opposition.'

He leaned over the table, as though getting closer to his audience so that he could draw them into his secret. His smirk grew wider.

'For some unaccountable reason, it seems the New Age hippies and their friends are having trouble getting their act together.'

'*Très bien, mais* ... what of the next phase?' enquired Olivier Ducasse, a Breton hotelier who had made his money in the international vice industry, and now had legitimate business interests across three continents. He scanned the scale model, taking in the golf course, theatre, all-weather 'dome' leisure centre, cross-country horse riding trail – and dominating it all, the craggy prominence of Brackwater Tor. He jabbed his finger at it. 'How are negotiations proceeding on the purchase of Brackwater Hall?'

Allardyce's composure did not slip for a second.

'It is in hand, I can assure you. If by chance we should fail to reach agreement on a fair price – and I cannot imagine that the new owner would be foolish enough to turn down our offer – we shall doubtless be serving a compulsory purchase order on her in the very near future.'

'But what about this Treharne woman?' Lorinda Crawley interjected. 'I've heard she has strong links with the pagan movement, and with her academic background she might exert a certain ... influence. Couldn't she be a problem?'

Allardyce exchanged amused glances with Leon Duvitski, his deputy.

'Personally,' replied Duvitski with a grin, 'I have *never* found women a problem.'

'Be that as it may,' replied Ducasse, scarcely warming to Allardyce's breezy self-assurance or Duvitski's flippant sexism. 'My own company's investment is, as you know, directed specifically at the hotel complex. Were that not to proceed according to plan . . .'

'It will proceed *exactly* as we have planned it,' replied Allardyce, his look clearly stating that the matter was closed. 'Rest assured, Monsieur Ducasse; I shall see to it that nothing gets in the way of a successful outcome. You see, ladies and gentlemen, the Lynmoor Development is going to make everyone in this room very, very rich.'

Maria stood in the centre of the tiny stone circle that she and Geraint had uncovered behind Brackwater Hall. Her arms were raised above her shoulders, her hands outstretched to the rising sun of a matchless new dawn. In the right she held a spray of dog-rose, the pink-white petals translucent as an infant's flesh against the luminescent sky.

> 'Mother of all, hear my prayer.
> Mother of all, accept my worship.'

A cool breeze rolled across the open moorland, stirring the branches of the stunted trees and flicking Maria's long chestnut hair from her face. A cascade of rose-petals detached themselves from their stems, fluttering and dancing like snowflakes before settling on the ground about Maria's bare feet.

There was not a trace now of the storm which had raged across the moors, three nights ago. Lynmoor felt tranquil, at peace. It seemed impossible to believe that even now, bulldozers were moving in at the far end of the valley, and that the face of Lynmoor would soon be changed for ever. If Charles Allardyce had his way, it wouldn't just be a theatre and a new supermarket that Lynmoor would be getting – the jackbooted march of progress would ensure that the spirit of this place was well and truly suffocated and exterminated for ever. Pendorran's words echoed with an irritating regularity in her brain: 'Without you, Lynmoor will die.'

She didn't understand the role that Pendorran was ascribing to her, she didn't want to understand it, perhaps; yet there was an ache of truth in her heart, like a deep, gnawing hunger. She wouldn't, couldn't, ignore it. But how could one woman, alone, oppose the might of a multi-million City consortium?

> 'Mother of all, for all is thine,
> Make light the way which I must tread.'

It seemed right that she should come here, to the little stone circle that was her own, a gift – or so it seemed – from the Mother-spirit herself. This must surely be a fitting place to make supplication to the old spirits who had watched over these valleys and moors for so many centuries. Perhaps if she could gain their favour, they would watch over her too, granting her power and sight. Understanding, also: of the reflection that she had seen in the bronze mirror, three nights ago.

The sun rose a little higher in the lightening sky, casting a rosy blush across the valley to the distant swell of Hilltop Tor; and beside it, the jagged outline of the much bigger and more magnificent stone circle where Carolan and his Travellers were encamped.

Carolan. Should she go to the camp on the night of the new moon, as he had urged her to? Indecision crippled her will. This planned sexual rite of dedication to the earth-mother might seem like a good idea on the surface, but the doubts would not go away. She couldn't get rid of the feeling that there was something bogus about Carolan; instinct whispered to her that he was as much the charlatan as the shaman. Something else bothered her, too. Did Carolan and his self-styled New Age followers fully comprehend that pagan ritual was much more than just a pretty game with sex as the prize? Did he understand that in conjuring up the forces of nature, there might be danger involved as well as pleasure?

With an effort of will, Maria emptied her mind. To allow such discordant thoughts to impinge on her act of worship would be disrespectful to the Mother-goddess. Kneeling down on the dew-covered grass, Maria bowed low and planted a reverential kiss upon the earth. And, as her lips touched the exact centre of the circle, she thought of Hilltop Tor where, four thousand years ago, a Bronze Age priestess had buried an exquisite ceremonial jade axe.

An axe which was now in a glass case in Truro Museum, for a procession of tourists to gawp at. If Charles Allardyce got what he wanted, the entire stone circle at Hilltop Tor would soon be dug up and transported miles away, to the other side of Lynmoor. Anger flared inside Maria; anger and fear. How could people be so stupid, so greedy? Why must they risk all by desecrating what they did not understand?

Laying the stem of dog-rose on the trodden grass, Maria got to her feet. The sky was streaked with purple, pink and orange now. Soon it would be completely light, and the hour of mysteries would be gone.

Slowly she began to unbutton her light summer blouse. To achieve spiritual tranquillity and receive the full blessing of the spirits, she must go sky-clad.

It excited her to feel the cool breeze on each new inch of bare flesh as she peeled the blouse away, exposing naked shoulders, breasts, and belly. Her nipples were erect, but not with cold. They were responding to the caress of cool air on firm, young, hypersensitive flesh; stiffening as the breeze lapped at them like a slick, smooth tongue, flicking playfully across their tips.

Next came the skirt. It slid down over her hips with a faint whisper of silk and joined the blouse in a discarded heap outside the margin of the circle. As she stepped out of her panties, Maria felt excitement welling up inside her. The stones seemed to crowd about her more closely now, silent yet knowing; each one the host of a proud pagan spirit summoned to watch and covet her nakedness.

Her pleasure in this simple rite would be theirs also.

> 'Mother of all,
> Great spirits of earth, sea and sky,
> Accept this tribute of desire,
> This worship of sweet flesh.'

Maria raised her face to the sunlight that glowed red through her closed eyelids; and began to run her fingers with all the gentle eagerness of a lover over the tanned, taut flesh of belly and breasts. Already there was a warm ooze of moisture between her thighs, a fragrant nectar that dripped in clear, sweet droplets from the very heart of her womanhood.

She had deprived herself of pleasure for three full days in preparation for this rite, and her clitoris was throbbing to the quickening drumbeat of her desire. But she would not touch it. Not yet. The longer she kept her desire in check, the more powerful it would become; and the more delicious her pleasure, the better pleased the spirits would be, and the more potent the mark of their favour.

Gently she cupped her right breast in her hand and pinched the nipple between finger and thumb. A little gasp of delight escaped from her parted lips, and she began kneading and pinching her breasts with a joyful hunger, taking her pleasure to the delicious margin of pain and beyond; until nothing existed but the silent world of touch and caress. Little by little, she was transported far from Lynmoor onto an ethereal plane where the only reality was sensual enjoyment.

At first she did not even notice the light touch of a hand, skimming her shoulder with a teasing gentleness.

'And so I find you here.'

Startled out of her meditation, Maria wheeled round to confront a tall, black-clad figure, a pair of leather gauntlets tucked through the belt of his trousers.

'Anthony Pendorran! What the hell . . ?'

He was too close, invading her space; a dark shadow of self-assurance cutting out the warmth and light of dawn. Maria took a step backwards but he followed her, pursuing her with all the force of his will; and she trembled as he seized her by the shoulders, ran his hand over the ample swell of her breast, gathering her into the dark enfolding cloak of his embrace. His fingers were long and slim yet powerful, radiating an animal warmth that dared her body not to respond as it slid from shoulder to breast and then down the curve of her belly. He bent forward and placed a kiss on her throat. His voice was soft, seductive, almost a whisper.

'Don't lose the moment, Maria. Not this time.'

His steel-grey eyes glittered as he pushed a lock of unruly black hair off his forehead with a slender, ringed hand. Maria felt a shiver run through her. He was beautiful, more beautiful even than she remembered. So much so, that his touch awoke a thousand exotic desires. You could not look into those fathomless grey eyes and not feel hunger. Hunger and the cold frisson of fear.

For there was a darkness about the man, too – a darkness which went far deeper than his preference for dressing in black. She sensed that it was that spirit-deep darkness which had held her back before, and prevented her from sharing his bed that night when it would have been so easy to say yes; take me, enjoy me, give me pleasure. What other reason could there be? She mistrusted the hunger she felt for this man, this mysterious man; and yet, as she met his gaze, she could not remember ever desiring a man as powerfully as she desired Anthony Pendorran. She wanted to hate herself for this weakness; but all she felt was need, need, burning need.

His voice was a burning caress, making Maria writhe and twist in his embrace.

'The moment is now, Maria: why not seize it?'

His strong arms were about her waist, pulling her towards him so insistently that the iron-hard points of her nipples ground against the rough linen fabric of his shirt. The feel of the rough material on her sensitive skin only made the longing more intolerable. Pride urged her to push him away, but she wanted so much more to submit to the force of his desire; the hungry kisses he was planting on her face, neck and breasts.

'You're not afraid of me, are you, Maria? You who claim to fear nothing?'

'No. No of course I'm not afraid. Why should I fear you?' A surge of defiance broke through the successive waves of need.

He paused, fixing his gaze on hers so that she felt like some hapless butterfly, captured and pinned out under glass.

'You were afraid of me ... the last time.'

'No. Not afraid; I was angry, that's all. You behaved intolerably.'

He slid his hand down her naked belly and twisted a little knot of russet pubic curls about his fingers. It hurt deliciously.

'Are you angry with me now?'

'Yes, no ... I don't no. No, I suppose not.'

'Then what's holding you back?'

Maria was painfully aware of how pathetic her reply must sound, but there were no words adequate to describe the turmoil inside her.

'I ... really don't know. I don't even know what I want any more.'

'But I know. I know that you want me, Maria Treharne.'

He kissed her again, crushing his lips against hers; and with the force of that kiss all the last vestiges of her resistance evaporated. Her willing mouth opened like a flower, her tongue welcoming him in. His hand sought hers, and guided it to the front of his skin-tight black jeans. The cock beneath was hot, hard and throbbing, and her hand rested there willingly, her fingers tracing the telltale outline of his swollen flesh. He was more than ready for her, and she sensed that this time, his passion would not wait.

The kiss ended, leaving Maria gasping for breath and yearning for the feel of Anthony's hardness deep within her belly.

'It's no use pretending, Maria,' breathed Anthony, deftly unbuttoning his jeans and sliding down the zip. 'You wanted me the moment you set eyes on me, you know it's true. You wanted me that night at Polmadoc, when you let me caress you, but then you were too afraid. Banish the fear, Maria. Fear is negative, it blocks our spiritual energies. I understand you, I know what you crave.'

The yearning was almost unbearable now. His index finger was probing between Maria's thighs, pressing against the tender flesh that longed for release. His voice was smooth and bittersweet as dark chocolate. Like an exotic sweetmeat, she melted at his touch.

'You can't tell me you don't want me, Maria. You've been dreaming about this moment, ever since the night we met. The Goddess wishes it, Maria, and she will not be denied. Our joining is preordained. Don't fight it . . .'

'Yes . . .'

It was true, every word was true. Suddenly acceptance flooded into her. The fear did not matter, only the hunger and the worship of the flesh.

Maria's hand slipped through Anthony's open flies and discovered that he was naked under his jeans. He was big. Big enough to stretch her sex-lips almost to the limit, filling her up with the arrogant pleasure of his possession. Her fingers stroked his shaft and she discovered, also, that his big, swollen cock was not like others that had entered her. A smooth ring of polished black stone pierced the flesh, passing right through the glans. Her fingers explored it, delighting in their new toy.

'You want it inside you, don't you?'

'Oh yes,' sighed Maria. 'I want to be joined with you, I want to know how it feels deep inside me.'

She cupped Anthony's balls in her cool, gentle fingers. They were big and heavy with semen, and Pendorran groaned at her touch. So this man of stone had human feelings after all. A sudden delicious thought made her slide down Anthony's body until she was on her knees before him, pulling out his shaft from his jeans.

'But first, I want to know how it tastes.'

If Pendorran was surprised, he did not show it. But his eyes closed in mute pleasure as Maria's skilful mouth closed about the tip of his erect penis in a kiss of consummation.

Maria ran her tongue around Anthony's glans, delighting in the saltiness of his slippery sex-fluid. The haematite ring was smooth and cold on her tongue, and as she toyed with it she felt his shaft stiffen with pleasure. Pleased with her success, she eased down his pants, exposing the heavy globes of his balls, pendulous and juicy in their velvety pouch. As her scarlet fingernails gently raked the sensitive flesh of his scrotum, his breathing grew more rapid and shallow, testifying to his increasing excitement.

His hands were stroking Maria's long chestnut mane as he began to thrust in and out of her mouth. She was good; very good. His judgement rarely failed him, and he had correctly judged that Maria Treharne would be a creature of sensual excess.

Maria rejoiced in the taste of Pendorran's cock, and the novelty of toying with the stone ring that passed through its very tip. By now, the identity of her lover was no longer of any consequence. All that mattered now was the taste of salty cock-juice on her tongue, and the hardness of cold stone and warm, warm flesh.

With a sudden spurt, he came into her mouth, jerking his massive hardness so far down her throat that she almost choked in her eagerness to swallow down the creamy-white tribute. He tasted so good that she wanted more, more, more; and the intimate heart of her ached for the comfort of his cock.

Pendorran pulled Maria to her feet and kissed the droplets of semen from her lips. He could hardly fail to notice the mist of regret in her eyes.

'The power is all around us, Maria. Here, within the Circle, the Goddess has provided for our pleasure – pleasure that ends only when our passion is spent. I hunger still for you, Maria Treharne.'

Maria was already pulling at her lover's clothes, fumbling with the buttons on his shirt as he struggled out of his jeans.

'Now,' she pleaded. 'Join with me now.'

The revelation of his nakedness was a delight to her, and she ran her eager tongue over his tanned shoulders and torso, bending to skim the flesh of his belly and inner thighs. He tasted good, indecently good; and his strong hands on her breasts and buttocks felt like heaven.

'Then kneel for me. Kneel and let me enter you.'

This time she obeyed without question, getting down on her hands and knees at the centre of the stone circle, her nakedness caressed by the early-morning sunlight. In her mind it seemed that she was no longer Maria Treharne, but a nameless creature of purest passion. Instinct alone drove her now, and she arched her back to accept the tribute of his sex.

Pendorran knelt behind her on the grass, and began biting her flesh – at first gently, then with a greater passion. Maria began whimpering, not in distress but with the exquisite pleasure of the sweet pain. Seconds later, his cock-tip was thrusting eagerly between her thighs, seeking out the moist, hot heart of her womanhood; and all at once she was gasping with pleasure, thrusting out her buttocks to receive the gift of her lover's cock.

As soon as he entered her, Anthony knew that he had not been mistaken. She was indeed the one. Coupled together now, they were wild creatures in some primeval forest, their only imperative the rhythm of rutting beasts. The pleasure was primitive, exquisitely raw. But the excitement of Pendorran's physical pleasure was almost overtaken by the exhilaration of recognition: the pure joy of feeling the power within Maria as he toiled within her. Sexual and psychic forces were fizzing and bubbling inside her with an elemental energy; he had never before encountered anything remotely as powerful as this.

He thrust his cock deeper into her, and she shuddered with delight as his fingers slid over her belly and down towards her pubis, seeking out the hot, hard centre of her pleasure.

Sobbing with excitement, Maria thrust out her backside to take in Pendorran's iron-hard shaft a little deeper, as he smoothed and rubbed her clitoris. He slid its hood back and forth over the sex-swollen head until at last she knew there could be no escape from the shuddering, ecstatic climax. A moment later, his cock jerked within her, and thrusting deep into her womanhood, their pleasure met and mingled.

Time had moved on. Now, the sun was riding high in the cloudless vault of a perfect summer sky; all mystery and all shadows were banished. They lay together for no more than a few moments at the centre of the circle. Such savage, spontaneous passion scorned tenderness, and if there had been any between them, it was now gone.

'I must go,' announced Anthony, getting to his feet. All the mystery seemed to have gone from his voice. He sounded casual, almost cold. 'I have things to do.'

Maria remained lying on the grass, regret mingling with faint resentment as she watched her transient lover get dressed. The same question kept coming back into her head, demanding an answer. Finally she gave it voice.

'How did you know I would be here?'

Pendorran brushed aside the question as though it were a child's foolishness.

'Did I? It seemed a reasonable enough assumption. And surely a man may take an early morning walk on the moors if he has a mind to.'

Maria's eyebrows rose in a cynical arc.

'It's a good ten miles from here to Polmadoc,' she

pointed out. 'Quite some way to come for a walk on the moors.'

Pendorran zipped up his tight black jeans and fastened the belt. For the first time, Maria noticed the exquisitely-worked detail on the ornate buckle: a silver raven with a sliver of mistletoe in its beak. He shrugged.

'I like long walks.'

'In the dark?'

He didn't reply, silently and methodically buttoning his shirt as though Maria simply wasn't there.

Maria felt annoyance subdue any lingering pangs of regret. The situation was ridiculous, the conversation even more so. Pendorran seemed so irritatingly cool and collected now, that it was difficult to believe they had even touched, let alone enjoyed the rawest, most passionate joining she'd ever shared. Maybe he was like this with all the women who took his fancy. Had he used her and made a fool of her, or had there really been more to it . . . something genuinely magical?

Well, it was about time Pendorran realised that Maria Treharne wasn't just any woman. A fleeting encounter was one thing, but she certainly wasn't going to let herself become the occasional plaything of some over-sexed egotist. She looked up at him, taking in the smooth lines of his body, and the fulness where his cock pushed against the black denim of his jeans. If only she didn't want him quite so much.

She searched around for words to break the awkward silence.

'The pagans,' she began, 'over at the ancient circle on Hilltop Tor.'

Anthony raised an eyebrow.

'Carolan and his band of merry men? What about them?'

'I was talking to Carolan in the village the other day, outside the marketing suite. His people are planning some sort of sexual rite of dedication to the Goddess. In the stone circle, on the night of the new moon. I'm not sure about it, but Carolan thinks it might help empower the protest campaign.'

Pendorran laughed drily as he bent to pick up his leather jacket and slung it over his shoulder, the silver rings on his right hand glinting in the clear morning sunlight.

'I'm sure he does. Carolan never misses an opportunity to screw a few pretty girls.'

'So you think he's just a charlatan, then? You think the whole thing's a waste of time?'

'I didn't say that.'

'But ...' Maria felt more than irritated now; she felt angry and foolish. Why did Anthony Pendorran have to play these silly power-games with her? Her annoyance spilled out. 'Look, Anthony, it's about time you told me what you're playing at.'

'I'm not playing, Maria. Are you?'

'Why do you have to be so bloody enigmatic all the time? You keep telling me you want me to do something to help Lynmoor – but will you help me? Will you hell! Are you in with the developers on this or something – is that it?'

Pendorran looked genuinely surprised.

'You know that's not true.'

'Then *help* me. You know these people better than anybody around here. You're the one who keeps going on about how much Lynmoor needs me. So tell me: should I go to Carolan's camp, or not?'

'You could do,' replied Pendorran. 'Or then again, you might tell him to go to hell.'

'For God's sake!' snapped Maria. 'Just what exactly are you saying?'

Pendorran smiled, his strong features softening as he took her face between his hands and kissed her lightly on the forehead.

'I'm saying this,' he replied. 'You don't need Carolan and his travelling circus. You don't need anyone. Look within yourself. The answer lies there – and all around you.'

'I still don't understand,' protested Maria as he turned to leave her.

191

'You will, soon. Have patience. The Goddess makes all things clear.'

'You've been with her, haven't you? I just know you have!'

Geraint groaned inwardly as he locked the van and pushed open the front gate of Hawthorn Cottage. That was the trouble with Patsy, she had such a suspicious mind. And it didn't make life any easier for him that her suspicions were usually well-founded. Now she was playing that well-worn record again, making out he'd been getting it from the Treharne woman. And what if he had?

He switched on a beaming smile and followed Patsy into the living room.

'Been with who?'

'With that slut at the Hall, who do you think?'

' 'Course I've been with her – I do 'er garden, don't I?'

'Gardening! You really expect me to believe that, do you?'

'Oh, come on, Patsy. It ain't her fault if the village don't like her. But you know you're the only woman for me.' He pulled her towards him and attempted to kiss her, but she wriggled free.

'It's no good sweet-talking me, Geraint Thomas. I can smell 'er perfume on you. You've been screwing her, ain't you?'

'No, of course I haven't. I . . .'

'Good, was she?' She spun round, eyes flashing. There was a heavy flower vase in her hand. Geraint dodged it and it smashed into the fireplace.

'Don't talk daft, Patsy. Come here and I'll show you how much I care about Maria Treharne.'

And it wasn't a lie either, well not really. He might screw around a bit, but he did have the hots for Patsy – and there was something irresistibly sexy about her when she was mad at him. Maybe it was the way she thrust out her breasts at him, or the way her red lips pouted defiance. At any rate, he didn't know what it

192

was, but it worked every time. He was hard for her already.

He ran his fingers playfully down the crotch of his trousers, pleased to see the way her eyes followed him as he traced the outline of his swelling hardness.

'See – I don't get stiff for no one like I do for you, Patsy Polgarrow.'

But Patsy was still indignant.

'Suck you off, did she?'

She had done, too. The memory of Maria's soft lips round his cock only served to make Geraint even harder. He reached out and put his arm round Patsy's waist. This time she flinched but did not pull away. Geraint breathed a sigh of relief, knowing he had won.

'Think you can sweet-talk me, I suppose,' she muttered bitterly.

Emboldened, he pulled her close to him and kissed her, running his hands over her backside. It was firm, juicy and tempting, and his cock was straining to get inside that tight, wet haven. Why couldn't Patsy understand that, no matter how many other women he screwed, there'd always be plenty left for her?

'Look, sweetheart,' he pleaded. 'I'm really sorry if I've upset you, but I ain't done nothin' wrong, honest I ain't.'

'Yeah, well . . . maybe.'

Patsy relented with a sigh. Maybe she'd forgive and forget – this time. She didn't know for sure that Geraint had been servicing the lady of the manor. For all she knew, Maria Treharne had better taste. At any rate, it stood to reason that the Treharne woman wouldn't be around for ever. Her sort always got tired of the country once the novelty value wore off – and once the locals made it plain that their meddling wasn't welcome.

What's more, however often he strayed, Geraint always came back to her – and when he did, he was always so full of remorse that he'd move heaven and earth to please his Patsy. Sex was never better than when Geraint was on a guilt trip. Smiling to herself, she took hold of his hand and slid it up underneath her skirt, placing it on the soft, throbbing mound of her sex.

'Now *show* me you're sorry,' she said.

Maria sat down at the kitchen table and eased off her shoes. After a five-mile round-trip to the nearest working phone box, she needed a rest and a drink. She must do something about getting the phone reconnected, and take up Geraint's offer to find her a cheap car to get about in. Still, she felt better after leaving that acrimonious telephone message with Armstrong-Baker's secretary. Tomorrow, she'd go into the village, visit the solicitor's and ask Theodore Myint about petitioning for unfair dismissal. Positive action, that's what was needed.

She was just about to undress and have a bath when the front doorbell rang. Funny. She wasn't expecting anyone – and she was a long way out of the village for casual house-calls.

As she walked towards the door, she saw two shapes silhouetted against the frosted glass: one man tall with mid-brown hair, the other shorter and darker.

She opened the door.

'Yes?'

The brown-haired man greeted her with an alligator smile.

'Good afternoon, Dr Treharne,' he said. 'My name's Charles Allardyce, and this is my associate, Leon Duvitski. We've been so looking forward to meeting you.'

# Chapter Ten

$M$ aria stared down at the business card in her hand. *'The* Charles Allardyce?'

'Of CA Developments, that's right. May we come in?'

Allardyce smiled – an upward curling of the lips which did not quite take in the smouldering coals of his eyes – and extended a hand. Without waiting for Maria to take it, he slid smoothly past her and into the interior of the house. His companion hung back; either he was more polite, or was just out to make a better impression on Maria.

'Leon Duvitski. I'm sorry about Charles, he's very impetuous when he's got a head full of plans.'

Maria did not accept Duvitski's handshake. Her immediate instinct was to tell him, and his friend Allardyce, to get the hell out of here. How dare they come here, and what did they think they would gain, anyway? They must have heard about her involvement with the protesters.

Irritated but curious, she followed Allardyce down the corridor. He was already looking round, scanning the entrance hall, taking it all in like an interior decorator working out the number of rolls of wallpaper he was going to need. What *was* he up to? She touched his arm, and he turned round to face her; that perfect plastic smile flashing on as soon as her eyes met his. As he turned towards her, the hall light suddenly flickered on; then off; and on again, the single dingy bulb gleaming a dull and dusty yellow in its Edwardian glass shade.

'Terrible wiring you get in these old places,' observed Allardyce, not allowing the smile to leave his face for a second. 'It can cost a fortune to put it right.'

'I suppose it can,' replied Maria. 'But I'm sure it's nothing – just an intermittent fault. I mean, it's never done that before.'

'Still, a thing like that can be dangerous,' continued Allardyce, running his finger thoughtfully along the top of the old dado rail. 'A woman on her own, like you, can't be too careful.'

Maria tried to ignore the bulb, which was now switching itself on and off in a constant blur of flickering yellow light. Damn it. She reached out for the antiquated Bakelite switch and clicked it firmly down, but to her surprise nothing happened. If anything, it made things worse. The light just kept flashing on and off, so quickly that it became an almost stroboscopic flicker. Allardyce watched her in a faintly amused silence that reminded her of the elegantly repellent Armstrong-Baker. Slightly flustered by her own ineptitude, she rounded on him.

'Have you quite finished casing the joint, or was there something else you wanted?'

'Actually there was.'

Duvitski stepped forward, his stocky frame almost filling the square of light that filtered in through the pane of glass in the front door. There was something faintly disreputable about him, but Maria had already decided that she preferred him to his companion. Despite his studiously groomed good looks, Allardyce had all the charm of a hungry rattlesnake. 'We wondered if we might sit down and have a little chat with you, Ms Treharne.'

'Did you, now? A chat about what?'

'About the future, Maria.' She noted with irritation that Allardyce was using her first name as casually as if she were some sort of junior servant, or a naïve little sister who could be patronised with impunity. But she couldn't be bothered to make an issue out of it. 'Yours, and the future of this house.'

Allardyce reached the end of the passageway and pushed through the door into the kitchen.

'Nice. Very nice. Quaint, you might call it.'

Maria followed him in, holding her annoyance firmly in check. It wasn't an easy task.

'I like it,' she replied coolly.

'Bit old fashioned though,' observed Allardyce, making himself at home in one of the kitchen chairs and surveying the room in a single critical sweep of his brown eyes. 'Can't have had any money spent on it for donkey's years.' He leaned back in his chair and folded his hands, obviously perfectly at ease. Maria half expected him to put his feet up on the table. 'For God's sake sit down, Leon, you look like a spare prick at a wedding. Miss Treharne hasn't got all day, have you, dear?'

Maria pulled up a chair opposite Allardyce and Duvitski sat down in silence beside her, setting down his briefcase on the table. The polished brass and shiny black leather looked curiously out of place against the scrubbed oak of the much-used table-top. He flashed Maria a smile, but she did not return it. Clearing his throat, he began:

'Perhaps we could get down to business?'

Maria tossed the long hair back from her face.

'Don't let me stop you.'

'What a charming old house this is,' purred Allardyce. He was watching her through half-closed eyelids, snake-like. 'One could do such a lot with it, don't you think?'

'I fully intend to,' replied Maria frostily.

'Ah, but the cost of full restoration and modernisation – it would surely be prohibitive for a private individual such as yourself,' chipped in Duvitski.

'It might,' conceded Maria. 'If I had any intention of modernising it. But you see, Mr Allardyce, I like

Brackwater Hall the way it is. Now, gentlemen, if you've finished giving me the benefit of your advice on interior decoration . . .'

Allardyce put up his hand to silence her objections.

'Forgive me, Maria. I am apt to digress when something catches my eye – something that I'm really excited about. And I'm really excited about this, Maria.' It wasn't difficult to work out that there was more than one layer of meaning to Allardyce's words. His eyes seemed to be boring right into her, daring her to look away. But she brazened out his challenge with a steady stare.

'As a matter of fact,' observed Duvitski, 'we've been trying to make contact with you for a while. A couple of my . . . associates . . . came up here recently to try and find you – a Ms Harmer and a Mr Green. I don't suppose you came across them . . ?'

Maria shook her head.

'As you can imagine, I don't get many visitors up here.' It crossed her mind fleetingly that these two people might just possibly have something to do with the abandoned car she'd found near the outer wall of the grounds; but then again there might be no connection at all, and in any case, what reason did she have to help Duvitski or his boss? She kept silent.

Duvitski clicked open the locks of his briefcase, lifting the lid to reveal a few sheets of closely-typed white paper.

'You have heard of the Lynmoor Development?' he enquired.

'I could hardly fail to miss it,' replied Maria acidly. 'If your people get their way, it looks like I shall be practically surrounded by it.'

'Quite so.' Allardyce leaned over the table towards her, his brown eyes opening wide in emphasis. 'Under the existing plans, the Hall and its grounds would be almost entirely surrounded – and indeed isolated – by the new complex. Wouldn't it be infinitely preferable, don't you think, for Brackwater Hall to become a functioning *part* of the Development? Not just to stand here as a crumbling relic of the past, but to be transformed into a dazzling symbol of Lynmoor's bright future?'

'What precisely are you suggesting?' Maria had already guessed that she wasn't going to like what she heard.

'We are willing to make you a very generous offer for Brackwater Hall and the surrounding land,' continued Duvitski, sliding a crisp sheet of paper towards her. 'Very generous indeed.'

What happened next, Maria could not satisfactorily explain, no matter how long and hard she thought about it afterwards. But she could feel anger rising inside her and suddenly it was as though that anger was spurting out of her like blood from a cut artery, flooding the room in a bright crimson tide. She wanted to speak, but she could not. All her energy was being channelled into the boiling cauldron of rage within her.

Reaching out a shaking hand to touch the paper, she felt the table move; at first just a tiny jerk, as though it had been pushed, but then a violent trembling that turned to a rattling cacophony as the table-legs began to dance on the stone-flagged floor. Looking across at Allardyce, she saw his expression change from patronising smugness to disbelief. As another jerk of the table threw her against Duvitski, she felt him tense, his whole body stiffening with alarm.

'What the hell . . .' Allardyce tried to stand up, but it felt as though an enormously heavy weight was pinning him to his chair, preventing him from moving. The pressure on his chest was so great that he could scarcely catch his breath. 'Is this some kind of sick joke?'

Maria could not explain what was happening, but she knew that it was anything but a joke. It was like a virulent infection, spreading first from the table to the sink, where a bowlful of unwashed cups and glasses clinked and shattered as they were jostled together; from there to the old pine dresser, sending a cascade of patterned dinner-plates crashing to the floor; and then to the hooks above the Aga, making the shiny copper pans swing and crash against each other again and again, like cymbals in some hellish orchestra.

Maria tried to pull herself to her feet, but now the whole room seemed to be shaking, shaking with the anger that she felt so keenly within herself. Above her head the lampshade was swinging wildly, casting the shadow of a huge black pendulum across the sunny table. Something very strange and quite uncontrollable was going on here. She knew that she ought to be afraid, but she was more intrigued than scared; she realised that she was not so much a victim, but a part of what was happening around her.

As she clutched at the table-edge and used all her strength to lever herself up, she quite clearly saw a glass jug rise several inches above the dresser, hang there for a moment and then hurl itself through the air, landing only inches from Duvitski's head in a shower of needle-sharp fragments. She turned to look at him, and it was like watching an old silent film; his mouth was opening in alarm, and his eyes were round as saucers, but no sound was coming out.

A high-pitched electrical whine mingled with the rhythmic clatter of the pans, filling the air, shrill and unpleasant as fingernails on a school blackboard. She covered her ears, but the sound was still there, filling her head, refusing to let go of her. And above it, in the deepest recesses of her mind, she could hear that one word repeated over and over again – not whispered now, but screamed; a voice filled with rage and madness.

Deliverance. Deliverance. Deliverance.

'Stop! For pity's sake . . .'

Her own voice screamed above the tumult in her head, cutting through the painful cacophony like a hot knife through butter; and suddenly everything stopped.

'Bloody hell.'

Duvitski's voice sounded inordinately loud in the sudden silence. Maria looked down at him and their eyes met. His seemed brighter and darker, the pupils contracted to tiny points by the adrenalin rush of fear. Maria opened her mouth to speak, but her throat was dry as parchment.

A quiet click made her wheel round.

'And now, on Radio 4 FM, it's time for our afternoon play, *Women of Power* . . .'

Three pairs of eyes stared at the small battery radio, still standing on the dresser amid the debris of what amounted to a minor earthquake. Had it really switched itself on? No, surely that wasn't possible. But then, none of this was possible, was it?

Allardyce was the first to recover. His smile was still there, but now it was glacial beneath eyes as expressionless as a doll's. He picked up the piece of paper, swept off the fragments of broken glass and placed it in front of Maria, as if nothing had happened.

'Our offer, Ms Treharne. You won't get a better one. And by the look of this place . . .' He glanced around the chaotic jumble of broken china and overturned chairs. 'You'll probably be glad to see the back of it.'

He got to his feet, dusting down his jacket with a studied nonchalance that Maria could not help admiring. Duvitski followed suit, but Maria could see that he was genuinely shaken. His normally olive complexion was ashen-pale, and his hands were trembling as he clicked shut the locks on his briefcase.

She was shaken too, but she was damned if she was going to show it. In any case, she felt curiously exhilarated by the power that had erupted around her, and Duvitski's confusion gave her a certain malicious satisfaction. How dare these people come here, trying to take away what was rightfully hers? How dare they try to bulldoze an ancient burial ground, and then tell the world it was all in the name of the great god of progress?

Perhaps what they had seen and felt here today had shown them that there were forces greater than the persuasive power of money. She could not begin to interpret what had happened, only understand that there was anger in her, and greater anger still in this place; something had to be done, and soon. In that instant, Maria made her decision. Pendorran or no Pendorran, she would go to the ritual at Carolan's camp.

'You will consider our offer, of course.' Allardyce's unshatterable self-confidence alone was enough to make Maria defy him; but that, in any case, was a foregone conclusion. Still, no sense in giving him the satisfaction of a quick reply. She would spin it out a little, make him sweat for her answer.

'Of course,' she replied. She saw how Allardyce's eyes travelled over her body, noting the fullness of breast and hip, his connoisseur's gaze appreciating the way her small waist nipped in beneath her tight t-shirt. So he wanted her; good. He could wait for that too – and he'd wait a long, long time. With deliberate and gleeful malevolence she leaned forward until her face was only inches from his, making sure that Allardyce got a really tantalising look down the front of her low-cut t-shirt. 'And now, if you don't mind, I've got things to do.'

His gaze lingered for a few seconds, then snapped away, wandering gradually upwards.

'Great ceiling you've got there, Maria. I could do a lot with that ceiling. Some of those injection-moulded plastic beams are practically indistinguishable from the real thing, you know. That's what this place could do with – a bit of technology.'

'Really.' Maria stalked towards the front door, wrenched it open and breathed in gratefully, filling her lungs with the warm, sunlit air of a summer's afternoon. Duvitski looked grateful, too. He practically leapt out through the front door. But Allardyce sauntered out, pausing to turn and take a final look at the interior of the Hall.

'When the deal is signed and sealed, Maria, perhaps we could have dinner together?'

Maria hardly knew whether to laugh or knee him in the balls.

'*When* it's signed and sealed,' she replied with a smile as phoney as Allardyce's 'generous' offer. Which means when Hell freezes over, she thought, slamming the door behind the two men and watching their dark shapes retreat into the distance as they disappeared down the drive towards their car.

She walked slowly back into the kitchen. It certainly was one hell of a mess in there. Broken bits of china and glass everywhere, the radio blaring out 'Women of Power', and Duvitski's clean white piece of paper lying on the table in the middle of it all. She picked it up and glanced at the figures – there were a lot of noughts in that offer, more than she'd imagined. Maybe . . ? But no. Of course not. It was unthinkable that she could even consider it.

Crumpling it up, she laughed humourlessly. Did Allardyce really imagine she would give in to him so easily? She dropped the scrap of paper into the kitchen bin and surveyed the mess. Later. She would sweep it up later. What she needed now was fresh, clean air and the freedom of the moors.

She placed her hand on the back door handle. It turned, but nothing happened. Puzzled, she gave the door a gentle shove, but still it refused to move, and she shouldered it with all her weight, to no avail. It seemed completely jammed.

And then, at long last, she began to understand. No matter what Allardyce might think, there was no question of her leaving Brackwater Hall. The Hall would never let her go.


Anthea had been driving round the one-way system in Reading for a full half-hour. It was almost tea-time, she hadn't eaten since breakfast, and her patience was wearing thin.

She hadn't even intended to come anywhere near Reading, until Tony had suggested she drop in on a friend of his and pick up a box of books he'd left with him for safe-keeping. She'd managed that easily enough, but on the way out of the city she'd got lost and ... was that the third or the fourth time she'd driven past the Hexagon?

In desperation, she took the first left turn she came across and found herself heading off across a flyover in a completely unknown and unexpected direction. Ah well, at least it was an adventure – and at least she was finally getting out of this concrete mess of a town.

Settling back in her seat, she thought of the torrid nights she'd spent with Tony over the past week; of how good it had been with him, and how hard he had pleaded with her to change her mind about going to Cornwall. He had almost convinced her, too, with his so-persuasive kisses and caresses, that it would be much more fun to go to Tuscany with him than to spend the time in Cornwall with Maria Treharne.

Last night, they'd dined at La Margherita in Magdalene Street, then walked along the banks of the Cam towards the boathouse. At that time of night there were few people around, and Tony and Anthea were just drunk enough to be foolhardy. So it was hardly surprising that their instincts had taken over, turning a pleasant evening walk into a night of lust.

Easing the car through a sharp right turn, Anthea smiled to herself as she recalled how they had kissed under a canopy of stars, their tongues winding into a knot of pleasure as their hands explored the shadowy world of each other's flesh.

They walked on, two dark silhouettes edged with silver; and beyond, the broad ribbon of the river, sliding smoothly on with the faintest plash of water against shored-up banks. A few yards further on, the dark shape of the University boathouse loomed up, blacker than the surrounding blackness.

She felt Tony's hand touch hers.

'I bet you love it, don't you?'

She turned to look at him; his eyes were the only visible feature of his face, two glittering stars against a dark shadow.

'Love what?'

His voice purred with lust.

'Doing it in the open air. What else?' He slid his arm round Anthea's waist. 'Go on, tell me about it. Tell me about all the times you've had a bloke in the great outdoors.'

Anthea responded to Tony's game more enthusiastically even than she had expected. He seemed to know exactly the right buttons to press to excite her, and set her imagination racing so that she turned herself on. She fantasised with consummate ease, mingling fact and fiction in a picture that mirrored her own lust.

'Well, there were these two blokes . . .'

'Go on,' Tony urged her, his hand sliding down from her waist to her backside, gently squeezing the flesh through the thin stretchy material of her skirt.

'I was just about to start at college, and I was amazingly innocent. I mean, I'd had one or two boyfriends and we'd got pretty intimate, but I was still a virgin – can you believe that? Seventeen years old, and I'd never had full-on sex. Mummy used to watch me like a hawk, in case I got myself pregnant before she'd married me off to some ghastly Guards officer. Honestly, she and Daddy seemed to see me as some sort of prize heifer.'

Anthea giggled. The memory of her teenage years seemed hilarious with hindsight.

'Anyhow, this particular summer I escaped from them both. I managed to persuade them to let me go on this working holiday to France, picking grapes, and well, I met these two French guys. To be honest I can't even remember their names, but I can remember what we did together.'

'Don't stop. I want to hear it all.' His fingers traced the deep groove between her buttocks, pressing lightly yet with sufficient firmness to make her want to thrust her bum against his hand, trying to make his fingertip caress the hidden rosebud of her arse. 'Don't hide anything from me.'

'Well, one night, the night after we'd finished the last

of the picking, we had a bit of a party. You know, it's sort of traditional, and there was loads and loads of this incredibly rough red wine, and it was all free, so we all got incredibly pissed. We must have been half out of our brains on the stuff, but it didn't matter. Nothing mattered except having fun. And I felt so, so randy.

'Anyhow, I wandered off a little way with a bottle of wine, up the hillside to where the vines were. It was a gorgeous night, warm and clear, and all the stars were out. I could see this guy standing in front of me, and he was pissing on the ground, in between the vines. I'd never seen a man piss before, do you know that? Not even my brother Giles. Anyhow, this guy was holding his cock and even in the moonlight I could see it was enormous.'

'Bigger than me?' Tony took hold of Anthea's hand and pressed it against the hard swelling beneath the fly of his trousers. She laughed, her head spinning from the drink and the desire.

'Yes, even bigger than you, Tony. A full nine inches of pleasure when he was stiff – bigger than any other man I've ever had. He must have seen me standing there, because he turned his head towards me and said: "Tu veux? Tu voudrais un peu?" I could hardly deny it, now, could I? I didn't know what to say or do. I just stood and stared at him and he kept walking towards me, with his dick still in his hand and it seemed to be getting bigger all the time, swelling up like a great big fat snake.'

'What about this other guy you told me about?' Tony rubbed Anthea's hand up and down the long, hard line of his cock. Hell, he didn't like to make a habit of getting too involved with his women, but he was certainly going to miss Anthea if she carried through this ridiculous decision not to come to Tuscany. 'I want to hear about the other guy.'

Anthea gave a long, luxurious sigh. She was remembering, savouring the memory, augmented now by the full force of her imagination. There never had been a second guy, but now, in the fantasy-land she had created for herself and Tony, he was even now looming out of the shadows, a tall dark shape imbued with gallons of Gallic charm.

'Oh, he was the other guy's friend. He'd been watching us all the time, I think. I was standing there like an idiot, just staring and not saying anything, and suddenly this second guy turns up, puts his arms round me, and forces me to kiss him. He's holding me very tightly and I'm wriggling and saying, "*Non, non, laisse-moi tranquille,*" but of course he's taking absolutely no notice and that's exactly what I want. I'm scared as hell, but he's rubbing himself against me and I can feel him through my dress, getting hard as an iron bar.

'So the first guy comes up to me and takes hold of my hand, and do you know what he does?'

'I can guess. But tell me.'

'He grabs it, and he makes me take hold of his cock! Wraps my fingers round it and holds them there, making me wank him up and down like I'm some kind of sex-machine. I could feel my cheeks burning, and my face must have been absolutely crimson, but at least it was too dark for him to see how amazingly embarrassed I was. Embarrassed and excited, because believe me, I was getting so, so wet between my legs. I'd never felt anything like it before. I didn't even know how to masturbate, I was so innocent!'

Tony laughed; a gentle, husky laugh thick with sex. She didn't resist as he led her across the grass to the boathouse and pressed her up against the wooden exterior. His fingers closed on Anthea's and guided them to the smooth, naked baton of his prick, in a wickedly delicious *aide-mémoire*.

'More, Anthea. I want to know it all.'

She smiled in the darkness, remembering how wonderful and how terrifying it had felt to be so naïve; so full of unknown sensations that came tumbling out as she held the Frenchman's cock with a fearful wonderment. Memories and fantasies were tumbling out of her now, the words forming a seamless embroidery of mingled fact and fiction.

'He's holding my hand on his cock, sliding it up and down, and there's all this slippery stuff coming out of him all over my hand, and I'm going crazy. I think I'm shouting out but it sounds like someone else's voice; I'm delirious, I don't know what I'm doing any more, but my nipples are hard like rubber teats, and each time I move I can feel them rubbing backwards and forwards over the inside of my shirt.

'Now the other guy's behind me again, and he's pulling down my jeans. I wonder if he knows I've never done this sort of thing before, but I don't really care. All I care about is the fact that he's pulling down my pants, and his hands are so rough and hot on the smooth skin of my bottom. He smells of wine and garlic and sweat, and it makes my head swim because I've had too much to drink and I'm half-crazy with lust. All I want is for him to keep on touching me.'

Tony slid up Anthea's skirt and ran his hand over her bare thigh.

'You like being touched, don't you?' His fingers moved upwards, getting tantalisingly close to the pouting swell of Anthea's fat, juicy love-lips. 'Tell me how he touched you, this French guy. Did you like that, too?'

'He pulls down my pants and I step out of them,' recited Anthea, with closed eyes, strangely detached from reality. She hardly cared about the hard wooden wall of the boathouse, its ridges pressing against her back. 'My jeans are lying on the ground and I'm naked from the waist down, with just a man's old shirt to cover my modesty. The second guy's hands slide up underneath the shirt, and cup my breasts. I hear him make this kind of grunt in his throat, a noise like an animal makes, and that makes me even more excited. He's kneading and squeezing my boobs and I can hear myself going 'yes, yes, yes', even though he's rough and it hurts just a little bit.

'And the first guy's cock is hot and slippery in my

hand. Everything feels smooth and rhythmic, and it's like I'm a cog in some huge well-oiled machine, and it's going to go on forever. Only it doesn't, because the next thing I know the first guy's taking my hand from his cock, and licking his own sex-juice from it. It feels so good, having his tongue lick my fingers. He leaves them all cold and slippery.

'And then his own fingers are moving down over my belly, brushing my little dark bush and suddenly diving between my thighs. His forefinger darts right up inside me, and I'm crying out "No, no, please!", but of course he's taking no notice, and I can hear him laughing: "*Ah, la petite vierge, la petite vierge anglaise, qu'elle sent bon!*" His fingertip is right up against my hymen, and he's twisting his finger round and round, making me wet all over him . . .'

'I make you wet, don't I, Anthea? You're all wet now, aren't you?' Tony's finger slid under the elasticated band of Anthea's tiny black panties and down into the deep, deep well of her sex. She writhed at the pleasure of his touch, and the musky odour of her sex wafted up into the warm night air. 'Tell me how the French guy made you wet.'

'He lifted me up,' gasped Anthea. 'He lifted me up and my thighs were wide apart and the breeze was so cold on my bare backside – I could feel it coming up in goose-bumps, but all I could think about was what he was going to do to me next. He lifted me up as if I was light as a feather, and all the time his friend was stroking and pinching and squeezing my tits. I could feel the tip of this huge, hard dick just tickling and nuzzling at the entrance to my pussy, and then suddenly he drove up hard into me.

'I don't know what's happening to me. I'm screaming, and shouting, and crying, but he's taking no notice and the next thing I know, he's thrusting into me again and this time he gets right inside. There's one endless second of pure agony, and then it's all gone, and the pleasure's just incredible.'

Tony pressed harder against her, his breath hot and alcoholic on her cheek.

'Poor little Anthea,' he chuckled. 'Sweet seventeen and never been fucked. And suddenly you had nine inches all at once.' His fingers probed more deeply, stretching and pressing the walls of her vagina in remembrance of that first night of pleasure. 'Was it good? Did he make you come, with his big fat cock?'

Anthea shivered, her mind filled with the images she would carry for ever. How could she ever forget how it had felt to be borne aloft on that great, curving spike of a penis, so thick that it felt as though he had thrust his whole arm inside her? How could she ever banish the memory of her second lover, cupping her breasts and kissing and biting her neck as she rode her bucking bronco towards the dazzling heights of ecstasy? Good? It had been pure heaven.

'You could say it was fun,' she replied, smiling at Tony in the darkness. 'Yes, you could say that.'

'Ah, but what can we possibly do to improve on a night like that?' Tony wriggled his finger a little deeper into Anthea's warm, welcoming hole. 'What indeed .. ?'

Anthea met his lips with her own, her heart thumping as they kissed and their saliva met and mingled. Tony's finger worked in and out of her, the side of his hand brushing backwards and forwards lightly over her clitoris. In her mind, she was back in that French vineyard, savouring all the fearful excitement of her first time. Tony had become that first lover, that benevolent tyrant whose egotistical desire would show her the glittering way to pleasure.

'I know,' whispered Tony, easing slightly away from Anthea. 'I know just what we can do.' His hands moved over her skilfully, cajoling and caressing as he persuaded her to turn round until she faced the side wall of the boathouse, her cheek pressed up against the dark, roughened wood. His fingers slid her skirt up, exposing the twin moons of her backside, neatly divided by the dark line of her panties.

It took only seconds to slide those panties down and discard them on the dew-damp grass. In no time at all he was cupping the soft flesh of Anthea's bum-cheeks and prising them firmly, unforgivingly apart. He pressed himself against her, and she shuddered with realisation.

'My little English virgin,' he murmured: and in Anthea's mind he truly was that first lover of her dreams. 'You wanted to give him your second virginity that night, isn't that so?' She felt the tip of his prick slip between her buttocks, blindly searching out the epicentre of her shameful desire. 'But you gave it to me, Anthea, didn't you? And you know you want to give it to me again . . .'

Driving along the bypass, Anthea laughed aloud at the recollection of the previous evening's little adventure. Yes, Tony had been persuasive and she'd damn near given in to his pleas for her to stay. But she'd made up her mind, and perhaps there would be adventure to be had in Cornwall, just as there had been in Cambridge. Tony was not the only guy in the world worth screwing.

Glancing at the fuel gauge, she pulled in to a petrol station and switched off the engine. Across the forecourt she saw him, the young mechanic, the top two buttons of his oil-stained shirt open to reveal golden flesh. His small, eminently kissable backside was encased in the tightest jeans imaginable, and as he turned and walked towards the car Anthea smiled to herself, sat back and waited for the next adventure to begin.

'So how old are you, then?'

Megan Rothermead replied without hesitation.

'Twenty.'

'Oh yeah?' Jak spat on the ground reflectively, unsure of whether he ought to throw the girl out or take advantage of her obvious willingness to please. Delma, the spike-haired punk with the ring through her nose, let out a high-pitched giggle. When she laughed like that, the Egyptian ankh between her small breasts jiggled alarmingly, and her lips drew back, revealing teeth as long and yellow as a horse's.

'Is that months or years, darlin'?'

Megan didn't care whether they believed her or not, only that they accepted her and let her join them. She had come a long way to the camp on Hilltop Tor, and she had no intention of going back to the prison camp her parents called a boarding school.

She was seventeen years old; she had a right to do whatever she damn well wanted, and fight the causes she believed in so passionately. As soon as she'd heard what was about to happen to the ancient stone circle above Lynmoor, she'd known what she must do. Hitching from Inverness had taken a few days, but at last she'd made it. It would take more than a little scepticism to get rid of her now.

'So exactly what is it you want?' demanded Jak. She felt his eyes travelling up and down her body, and hoped her blouse was sufficiently tight to awaken his interest. She could do with an ally.

'To join you,' she replied simply.

'And why would you want to do that?' Jak leaned back against the rusting van which might once have been an ambulance. When he threw his head back like that, thought Megan, the evening sunlight caught the side of his face and you could make out the spider's-web tattoo really clearly.

Jak's was a good question. Even idealistic Megan had to admit that the camp was not entirely what she'd expected. For one thing, it was a great deal less romantic; just a collection of old vans and tents pitched higgledy-piggledy in and around the ancient stones. And if this was their leader, well frankly she wasn't that impressed. None the less, she was determined; whatever it took to persuade him to let her stay, she'd do it. She tossed her long, loose plait of mid-brown hair over her shoulder, wishing she'd worn it loose so as to look less like a runaway sixth-former.

'I want to join the protest campaign and save Lynmoor. I think it's a crime, what they're going to do to this place.' She stood up a little straighter, cynically aware that this would thrust her breasts out to best advantage. She wasn't averse to using sex if it would get her what she wanted.

Jak felt a commotion in his pants as he took in the sinuous, willow-slim form of this half-budded flower of young womanhood. She was classy, and you didn't get many classy birds in a place like this. Nine times out of ten, Carolan got the girl and Jak was left playing the faithful bodyguard. It wasn't a role he relished. Sometimes he thought life had been better in the open prison where he and Carolan – plain old Ben Tarrant in those days – had shared a cell. Certainly he'd got to screw more girls when he was in jail, what with the warders being so accommodating.

Yes, Delma was all very well, but when it came down to it, she'd go with anyone, and that fact alone was bound to take the edge off his desire. This one though; well, this one was a bit different – a regular little convent girl. He knew he ought to send her off home to her mummy, but surely there'd be no harm in having a bit of fun with her first?

'Why don't you come inside the van? We could talk about it, if you like.' Jak threw Delma a glance that said piss off, I think I'm on to a good thing here.

'And if I do, will you let me stay?' Megan picked up her kitbag and slung it onto her shoulder. The weight of it pulled the strap down, stretching the fabric of her shirt even more tightly across her small, firm breasts.

'Well, we'll have to see, won't we?' Jak thrust his hand into his jeans pocket, hoping he looked cool. 'But if you're nice to me . . .'

A voice from behind made Jak's heart sink.

'Well, well, Jak – what have we here? Not trying to keep our guest from me, I hope?'

Megan followed the direction of Jak's gaze and saw a bearded man with straggling brown hair and the most remarkable eyes: dark brown but bright with the sharpness of cut diamonds. He was standing in the doorway to a large tepee in the centre of the stone circle. With his dishevelled hippy clothes and unkempt hair, he had a peculiarly messianic appearance, and Megan guessed who he was instantly. She turned to Jak with a glare of resentment, her bottom lip jutting out slightly like a sulky child's.

'You're *not* Carolan, are you? You told me . . .'

Jak shook his head, putting up his hands.

'Uh-huh, little lady. You assumed I was Carolan, I just didn't contradict you, remember? Didn't want to bother our leader, that's all. He's got more important things on his mind than runaway girls.'

'I'm not . . !' protested Megan.

Carolan took a step forward.

'Is that so, Jak? How very thoughtful of you to spare me all that worry.' His voice was thick with sarcasm. 'But it just so happens that I have nothing else on my mind just now, so perhaps you'd be good enough to introduce us?'

'My name's Megan,' she blurted out, pre-empting the extremely pissed-off Jak. 'Megan Rothermead. I've come here because I want to join with you. I believe in the cause.'

Carolan's face betrayed no trace of expression. Megan gazed deep into his eyes, a wave of utter devotion washing over her. For all his disreputable appearance, there was a charismatic quality about the man that compelled attention. She looked into his face and knew that he was all that she had heard, and more. Instantly all her cocky self-assurance evaporated, leaving her overawed and curiously excited.

'I only want to serve,' she whispered. 'Please don't send me away.'

He was standing over her now, and she looked up, hoping for a sign. Miraculously, he blessed her with a smile.

'You are sure that you wish to join us?'

'Absolutely.'

'Then there are things which you must know. In this community we share everything, and we believe that everything is sacred. *Everything*, including the worship and humble service of our bodies.'

'Yes, yes; I understand.'

'Sex is power, and power is sex. The two forces are interchangeable and complementary. It is our belief that in building up our sexual energies, we shall in turn empower this ancient place to resist the evil forces which threaten to destroy it. Each of us must show that he or she is equal to this sacred task.

'Consequently, there are certain rituals, certain ... proofs of obedience and devotion which the Mother-spirit requires of all her disciples before they are deemed fit to serve her.'

Megan's fingers tensed around his hand.

'Anything. I will do anything.'

Carolan's smile grew broader, and Megan's heart soared. She felt certain, now, that her journey here had not been in vain. It was going to be all right. Everything was going to be all right.


'I see Kestelman's over-reaching himself again.'

David Armstrong-Baker put down his fork and took a sip of wine. It was not a very good wine – St Alcuin's was not a wealthy college with a fine cellar like Trinity or John's – but it tasted all the better for being cheap. Armstrong-Baker abhorred wanton expenditure almost as much as he deplored interfering women like Maria Treharne, and ill-bred oafs like Terry Kestelman.

Sir Hilary Lloyd, Master of St Alcuin's, did not even raise his eyes from his plate.

'Kestelman's a prick.'

A man of few words – all of them pithy – Sir Hilary had worked his way up from lower middle-class obscurity to academic honours. His climb up the social ladder, although ruthless, had been admirably discreet, and there was nothing he despised more than a man who shot his big mouth off in public.

Terry Kestelman's indiscreet remarks about the extent of his influence, together with his rather vulgar sexual associations with a number of female staff and students, was the talk of St Alcuin's. Armstrong-Baker glanced around the great vaulted dining-hall where the great and the good had attended college formal dinners for nigh on seven centuries; and was forced to conclude that Kestelman was neither.

'Evidently; but what are we going to *do* about him?' he enquired.

Sir Hilary finished munching and glanced up.

'Do? Nothing.'

'But Sir . . .'

'I said nothing. We won't have to. Sooner or later, a man like Kestelman always ends up hanging himself – if you give him enough rope. Now, can we discuss something else? All this talk of Terry Kestelman is giving me indigestion.'

It was late, but Maria could not sleep. She sat cross-legged on the bed, trying to focus her mind on the rhythmic rise and fall of her breathing; meditating, trying to get in touch with the protecting spirits who had the power to guide and empower her. Something strange was happening to her, as though her meditation had taken on a life of its own, and she had stepped through a doorway into a world which obeyed no rule that she could understand.

'Hear me, guide me.' Her whispered words seemed to echo back to her on the ebb-tide of her own outward breath, mocking her foolishness in believing that she could control what she could not understand.

In the darkness, she felt a warmth surround her, and suddenly she realised that her breathing was no longer a single, rhythmic sound. Above it, she could hear a halting counterpoint; a discordance of breathing as though the entire room were filled with it.

Maria . . .

She started at the sound of her own name, whispered

so clearly that she almost believed it had been spoken by someone in the same room. She opened her eyes, but nothing surrounded her but the velvet blackness of night, and the grey rectangle of faint light beyond the bedroom curtains.

Maria. Maria . . .

This time she had not been mistaken. She had heard the whispering voice as clearly as if the speaker had been right next to her. Now it was joined by a second voice; slightly deeper, a man's perhaps, repeating her name over and over again, with an urgency that seemed like a desperate yearning.

Maria, Maria, Maria, Maria.

She put her hands over her ears, but the voices just carried on whispering, groaning, panting; the voices of lovers in the heat of passion, calling out not each other's names, but hers.

And as she closed her eyes, she saw them for the first time; writhing, twisting silhouettes of pale flesh against a deep crimson background. She could not see their faces, but she made out the figures of a man and a woman, their bodies slick with sweat and falling, falling endlessly through space as they coupled, th r hands clawing at each other in a frenzy of passion that could never, ever be sated.

As she watched, fearful but without understanding, the warmth in her own belly kindled to a furnace of need, and her fingers slipped down the gentle slope of her belly towards the pouting kiss of her sex-lips. Only her own touch could satisfy, and she yearned for the brutal pleasure her fingers would bring as they rubbed the hard pink pearl of her desire.

Her fingers slipped between her thighs and, mesmerised by the images before her eyes, she began stroking and rubbing at her clitoris, caring nothing for gentleness as she forced herself to orgasm. The urgency of her need was everything now, the touch of her fingertips an electric shock of pain-racked pleasure that brought her, sobbing with distress, to the sudden precipice of ecstasy.

217

And beyond.

Panting and disoriented she forced her eyes open, and the images were gone as quickly as they had come. When she closed her eyelids once more, they did not reappear. She was very alone, very confused; and just a little afraid.

Why did she have the feeling that something was playing a dangerous game with her body and soul? What unknown power had torn through the Hall that afternoon, when Allardyce and Duvitski had paid her their ill-fated visit? And had the house really wanted to prevent her from leaving? In daylight it had all seemed faintly ludicrous, but here, in the solitary blackness of her bedroom, where the dark shapes of the furniture seemed to crowd in on her like greedy ghosts, anything seemed possible.

Some vestige of the sight was in her – she knew that. She had known it since, as a child, she had predicted the accident that stole away her young sister's life. But since that one manifestation it had never been powerful within her; it had never given her reason to believe that she was anything other than a minor sensitive.

And now? What now? Was she supposed to believe that something was trying to channel itself through her? Or was the whole damn thing some sort of clever, hallucinogenic trick dreamed up by Allardyce or Carolan, or both?

She had to find out more; she had to arm herself with information that would help her to work out what was happening. Perhaps Pendorran . . ?

But no. She had her pride, and Pendorran had made it very clear where he stood. No, she would not ask Pendorran for his help, at least not yet. For now, she would face whatever was to come as she had always done: alone.

In the bar at the Duke of Gloucester, Leon Duvitski and Charles Allardyce were sharing a discreet after-hours bottle of vodka.

'I reckon she's crazy,' observed Duvitski, topping up his glass with the merest splash of orange juice. 'Mad as a hatter. Nice legs though,' he added as an afterthought.

Allardyce chuckled and tossed his drink back in a single gulp.

'You shouldn't be deceived, Leon,' he replied. 'Not by an elaborate charade staged entirely for our benefit.'

'But . . .'

'Oh come on, Leon – you don't seriously think what happened back there was *supernatural*, do you? I know you eastern Europeans are peasants, but I thought you'd dragged yourselves out of the dark ages.'

Duvitski threw him a black look, but it was completely lost on Allardyce.

'Like I said, Leon, it was a charade. Now, don't ask me how she did it – it was certainly clever, professional even, and I'm not disputing that – but she was setting us up, trying to frighten us off.'

'If you say so,' replied Duvitski, pouring himself another double vodka.

'Anyhow, it won't work and I reckon she knows it. First thing tomorrow, we'll get Janis to do a bit of research into the woman, find out what makes her tick, what her weak spots are.' He took a peanut and flicked it neatly into his open mouth. 'Don't you worry, Brackwater Hall is as good as ours. By the time I've finished with her, Miss Maria Treharne will be begging us to buy her damn house.'

'Yeah, yeah. Sure,' replied Duvitski dreamily. He was doing his best to share Allardyce's optimism, but a fatal uneasiness kept stealing over him, no matter how much vodka he put away. The thing was, Allardyce might say it was a charade and heck, it probably *was* a charade; but on the other hand, it had seemed pretty damn real to him.

# Chapter Eleven

*H*oofbeats thudded into the soft earth as the white stallion galloped over the high moors in a rhythmic jingle of harness. On his back sat Anthony Pendorran, a dark silhouette against a dimming sky, high and haughty in the saddle.

He seemed distracted, his gaze roaming aimlessly over the darkening horizon, but Pendorran missed nothing. The plover on the nest, crying softly to its chicks; the high, hovering shadow of a kestrel hungry for prey; the quiet rattle of dry grasses, shaken by the wind: all pleased him, symbols of the order that should be, the effortless supremacy of nature.

But all was not as it should be. Even as he rode towards Polmadoc, the bulldozers were moving on to the site of the new theatre complex, and thin-lipped men in grey suits were smiling as they signed away the sacred past and present and future of Lynmoor. The threat had not been dispelled; in fact, it had never been greater.

Dusk was moving in quickly, and soon Lynmoor would slumber beneath the conspiratorial blanket of night. But some would not sleep tonight. For some, there was work still to be done.

He reined in the stallion and it trotted to a reluctant halt on the brow of the hill, pawing the ground in its resentment. He was a magnificent beast; proud and impulsive as his master. Only Pendorran could control him.

'Later, Jupiter; later you shall have your way.' He patted the animal's neck thoughtfully, trying to make sense of his thoughts. 'And soon, perhaps, I shall have mine also.'

Though the Mother-goddess, in her wisdom, had sent him the instrument of Lynmoor's salvation, Maria Treharne was both less and infinitely more than he had bargained for. She puzzled and intrigued, angered and aroused him; all that raw, untutored energy spilling and crackling out of her like a sensual storm. He doubted that even she had yet experienced the full power of that energy, and he ached to release it from her, to bask in the violence of her unleashed passion.

That fleeting dawn encounter had been no more than a beginning, an opening up of the channel that might enable Maria to understand and learn to harness the potential that was within her. The memory of their coupling was strong in Pendorran's mind, and even now he was reliving it, feeling the silk-softness of her cool white skin against him; savouring the sweet spice of her anger as she fought him, resisting him for a brief moment before she sank into the harbour of his embrace, abandoning herself to him even though he knew she did not trust him.

Did she also fear him? That thought produced a sardonic smile. For what had Maria Treharne to fear from him that he had not also to fear from her? When dark power met light, the result might ultimately be destruction for both.

But Pendorran felt no fear; the emotion was alien to him. Danger, he soaked up like a sponge, feeding on the raw excitement as yet another source of pleasure. The fear of others sometimes amused, sometimes irritated him. Knowledge was the annihilation of fear, and Pendorran had always sought out the power of knowing. He had always known that, were some deadly

221

adversary ever to drive him to the edge of the cliffs two hundred feet above Polmadoc Cove, he would jump.

Without fear.

He closed his eyes and he could see Maria. She was pink-white and naked, soft as a thornless rose. Pendorran was not deceived; there was danger there, in that so-soft embrace, but that made her all the more desirable. They were kissing, and her tongue-tip was parting his lips with an infinite gentleness that made his whole body tremble with need.

Between his thighs, the stallion stirred, sensing his master's growing excitement. Pendorran shifted slightly in the saddle, the bare flesh of his testicles rubbing against the inside of his jodphurs as the fabric slid over the well-polished leather. He had begun to feel that the inferno of his desire would consume him if he did not have her again, soon.

The memory of her nipples, tight-puckered and hard in his cupped hands, made his cock uncoil into wakeful hardness, the constricting fabric of the jodphurs making its pierced tip press uncomfortably against the inside of the waistband. He could feel the haematite ring rotating slowly through his pierced glans, and it felt like a long, smooth caress; as though Maria's fingers were on the stone ring and she was tormenting him with it, turning it round and round with infinite slowness, forcing him to obey the pace of her need just as he had tried to force her to accept the urgency of his hunger that night when he had brought her to Polmadoc. How he longed to push his cock between those soft pink lips, framed so prettily in a smile of artless innocence.

Spurring on his horse, he galloped on across Lynmoor, Jupiter's long strides eating up the remaining miles to Polmadoc. The sky had darkened now to a dusky royal blue, and in the direction of Hilltop Tor Pendorran could make out the lights of the camp. Pendorran was not the only one who would be busy tonight.

Stabling the horse, he went into the house, brushing

aside his manservant's questions with a curt 'Later.' Joseph melted away into the discreet seclusion of the servants' quarters; he knew better than to trouble his master when he was in this single-minded mood.

Pendorran took the stairs two at a time, his long slim legs stretching the extra distance easily. Passing beneath the hanging lantern, salvaged from an eighteenth-century shipwreck, his tall figure cast a spidery grey shadow on the rough-plastered wall. At the top of the stairs he turned left, walked quickly down the corridor and pushed open the door of his bedroom, reaching inside and clicking on the light switch.

The room presented a striking contrast to the rest of Pendorran's sparsely-furnished house. Instead of bare grey stone or whitewashed plaster, the walls were decorated with rich tapestries depicting medieval and mythical scenes in vibrant splashes of colour which extreme age had done nothing to dim. To his right, hounds pursued a white hart through a forest carpeted with wild flowers; a single drop of blood falling like a pendant ruby from the arrow piercing the hart's flank. And where others had fallen, rich red flowers had sprung up in an insane profusion of colour.

On the other side of the room, near the window, stood Pendorran's bed: a magnificent Gothic creation of blackened oak, its frame carved into an intricate tracery of fruits and flowers, animals and birds. Twin ravens guarded the bed-head, their eyes fashioned from some dark-red stone that caught the light and seemed to burn with a fierce inner fire. The hand-quilted bedspread bore a scattering of embroidered flowers, points of bright colour skilfully ordered into a tumultuous harmony.

But Pendorran hardly noticed his surroundings. He paused for the briefest of moments, then moved quickly to the opposite wall, which was completely obscured by a floor-length curtain of wine-coloured velvet. Reaching up, he pulled a cord and the heavy drapery swished across.

Beyond the curtain the wall was completely bare, save

for a floor-length mirror with a plain wooden surround. Pendorran stepped closer to it. The lamplight seemed to grow dimmer as he approached, blurring the reflection.

He looked into the glass, and caught his breath. His own form was quite distinct – a tall, dark figure dressed in close-fitting black, silver rings heavy on his tanned fingers, and a knife-blade glittering at his belt. But the room behind seemed to be swimming, fading, growing less and less distinct.

He waited, and the image resolved itself, as he knew it would. Behind him now he saw not the richly-decorated bedroom in which he stood, but the huge, torchlit expanse of a great cavern, its rocky walls rough-hewn and dripping with moisture.

As he gazed deep into the glass, a woman's hand reached out, white-soft and slender. Lightly, the fingers touched his neck and a shiver ran through his body.

'Goddess,' he breathed.


The car Geraint had obtained 'from a mate in the trade' had turned out to be an elderly Volvo with a mind of its own. Still, mused Maria as she drove up the moorland track, at least it was a car. At least she no longer had any reason to feel isolated and marooned in the middle of nowhere.

It was by no means difficult to make out the lumpy, jagged outline of Hilltop Tor, even against the night sky; for Carolan had clearly prepared well for the night's ritual. A haze of whitish-yellow light surrounded the tor and even from a distance, it was possible to make out the shapes of figures, moving about among the standing stones.

She still wasn't at all sure about tonight – but then again, she'd long since ceased to be sure about anything. Visions in mirrors, melting telephones and houses that refused to let you out were enough to shake anyone's self-assurance, and Maria was simply doing the only thing she could: going back to the very roots of her faith for inspiration and empowerment. If that turned out to have been a big mistake, well, she didn't see what else she could possibly have done. It wasn't as if Pendorran was offering her any answers to her questions.

A fierce orange-yellow glare greeted her as she swung the Volvo round into the entrance of the travellers' camp. She saw that all the vans and tents had been cleared out of the stone circle to make way for a huge bonfire. Enormous flames were leaping into the air from the heap of burning brands at the centre of the tall standing stones, and as Maria opened her car door the heat hit her like a brick wall.

'Sister!' A skinny redhead in a diaphanous smock-blouse greeted Maria with an unexpected embrace. Her breath was sweet-scented with alcohol and spice. 'Carolan, Jak – Maria's come!'

Three or four other women surged forward out of the shadows and Maria saw that they were partially naked, their bodies shiny with crudely-painted magical symbols. Their hands grabbed at her, smoothing and stroking and coaxing her towards the circle. Somewhere in the distance, Maria could hear laughter and chanting as bottles clinked together. It seemed Carolan's disciples regarded this occasion less as a sacred rite, more as an opportunity for a party.

'Where are you taking me?' demanded Maria, faintly alarmed as the women took her by the shoulders and hands, pulling her forward. 'What are you doing?' These women seemed completely out of it – drunk or stoned, or perhaps both. Warning bells sounded yet again in Maria's head. This was not the dignified way taught by her coven. There might yet be reason enough to leave . . .

'We're taking you to Carolan,' laughed the first girl, her straight red hair escaping in wisps from a waist-length plait that bounced and writhed like a snake as she walked. She wheeled and danced in front of Maria, suddenly stopping to pull her blouse off over her head. Underneath, her small breasts bobbed like perfectly round apples, their nipples pierced with two tiny rings

225

joined by a thin silver chain. She threw the blouse to the ground and giggled. 'Carolan will be so pleased now that you're here. He's been in a mood all day.'

With mixed feelings, Maria followed the red-haired girl towards the standing stones, walking gradually into the dancing light that surrounded the circle. Carolan obviously had more organisational ability than good taste, for two or three of the vans had been arranged around the outside of the circle and their headlights switched on, casting their cold white beams across the trodden earth.

'Maria! Carolan said you'd come, but I wasn't so sure.'

Maria shaded her eyes, narrowing them to slits against the harsh glare. The tall, slightly gawky silhouette of a young man loomed up in front of her and she recognised the voice instantly.

'Jak?'

A hand closed about hers and steered her away from the light. She blinked in the sudden gloom.

'Carolan wants to see you. Right away.'

Maria eased her fingers out of Jak's vice-like grip. There was something slightly creepy about him, something that made her feel uneasy to be touched by him. He turned his shaven head a little to the left and light fell on the dark stain of the spider's-web tattoo, spread-eagled like a clutching hand across the side of his face and neck. His thin lips curled into a covetous smile.

'So you're taking part in the ritual, then?'

'I . . . yes, I suppose I am.' What option do I have? she was thinking. Someone has to do something. A few more weeks, and all of this will have been bulldozed into non-existence. 'It's our duty to petition the Mother-goddess in any way we can.'

'Right.' Jak's face registered tipsy incomprehension, but his body was well ahead of the game and his hand returned like a troublesome wasp, settling this time on her shoulder. It felt hot and heavy through the thin material of her dress. 'Carolan said you wouldn't let us down.'

226

She flinched as his hand slipped casually downwards to sneak a surreptitious feel of her breast. She cursed her body for its readiness to respond, even to the touch of this empty-headed gorilla. Abstinence from sex had made her hot – hotter than it was safe to be, in this highly-charged atmosphere where riotous, orgiastic sex was a hairsbreadth away. They must practise discipline; they must understand that individual appetite must come second to the demands of the ritual.

'He wants to see me, you say?' Hastily she got back to the subject, and Jak's hand returned to the pocket of his jeans. Like most of the two dozen or so travellers, he was naked from the waist up, his torso decorated with amateurish representations of circles and pentograms. A crudely-painted silver star circled his navel, out of which trickled a thin ooze of wet metallic paint.

'Yeah. It's the preparation, see.' Jak led her away from the circle, past a group of men and women who were painting each other's bodies with a dark, sticky fluid. 'That's what all this is about. Carolan's very strict about preparation.'

It seemed more like anarchy to Maria, albeit well-intentioned anarchy. It was a far cry from the discipline of her coven. A few yards away, a woman was laughing hysterically as a naked man stripped off her clothes, ripping off the fabric to reveal the pale skin beneath. Despite her disapproval, she found herself once again responding to the sight, her body's most basic instincts awakening to the call of simple, honest lust.

She tried walking a little further away from Jak, but he simply closed up the gap again, his hand and hip brushing against her at every possible opportunity. Even this unwelcome touch filtered through her clothes as a delicious warmth, and she felt her nipples stiffening slightly inside her thin cotton dress.

Carolan's huge tepee had been moved to the edge of the camp. Roughly constructed from three stout wooden poles covered with weatherproofed canvas, it was about fifteen feet in diameter and by far the tallest structure on

Hilltop Tor, towering above the gap-toothed mouth of the ancient stone circle. The light from the blazing bonfire cast dancing patterns on the plain grey canvas.

Maria paused, and Jak took the opportunity to pat her on the backside.

'Go on. He's waiting for you.' He lifted up the flap and she stooped to enter, then hesitated. 'What are you waiting for? Not scared of Carolan, are you?'

He could not have chosen a more effective incentive; Maria bent down and stepped inside.

'Welcome, Sister.'

The soft Celtic brogue was soothing and smooth, and Maria felt her tension almost instantly begin to ebb away. The interior of the tepee was in semi-darkness, lit only by a few oil-lamps which added a smoky pall to their brightness, but there was enough light for Maria to see the nine men and women sitting cross-legged around the edge of the tent. They were all naked, save for necklaces of long coloured beads, and – like the others she had seen outside – they had coloured pictograms painted on their flesh.

In the centre of the floor sat Carolan, his unruly brown hair and beard adorned with flowers and an embroidered blanket wrapped round his shoulders. The dingy half-light cast shadows that deepened the lines and hollows of his face, sculpting him into a figure of stone and bronze. He smiled at Maria as she entered and his eyes – the one remarkable feature in an unremarkable face – seemed to glitter with a triumphant recognition.

'We bid you welcome to this ancient place, Maria Treharne.'

A whisper of assent ran round the assembled travellers:

'Welcome; welcome; welcome.'

Maria took a step forward, into the smoky light from the oil-lamps, and Carolan stretched out his hand. The nails were long, yellow and tough as animal horn.

'Come and sit beside me, Maria Treharne. We must prepare for the ritual.'

Maria eased herself down onto the beaten-earth floor. Carolan at least seemed to be treating the ritual with the solemnity it deserved. And yet, with his straggling beard and craggy face, he looked for all the world like Jack-in-the-green, some timeless, capricious sprite of nature embodied in human form.

'How must I be prepared?' she asked.

Carolan's fingers entwined with hers, his grip firm, his eyes searching her face for signs of weakness.

'According to our beliefs, Maria, sex empowers us and releases the psychic energies that are within us.

Maria nodded.

'That is the Wicca belief.'

'Before the formal ritual begins, we believe that each and every one of us must be prepared, prepared to open up our bodies and souls to the Mother-goddess's all-creating, all-powerful sexual energy.' Carolan's fingers left her hand and slid lightly up her arm, making the tiny blonde hairs stand on end. 'In preparing ourselves, we shall increase the chances of success in our supplications to the Mother-goddess.'

Maria did not flinch from his touch. It was light, gentle, surprisingly pleasurable, and she felt the seeds of a familiar warmth growing, swelling, budding at the base of her belly. She sensed that all eyes were on her, watching in an expectant hush, waiting for her response. And that knowledge made her bold, excited, sensual.

'What are you asking of me?' she whispered.

Carolan's fingers caressed the abundant cascade of her chestnut hair, taking a single tress and winding it about his fingertip, then taking it to his lips and planting a kiss upon it. He took his finger from his lips and the hair uncoiled, tumbling down in a long, glossy ringlet. There was no trace of irony in his voice as he spoke.

'Tonight I shall be the god and you the goddess, my sweet Maria. I the male principle and you the female. In uniting our bodies, we shall be uniting those two principles and liberating the dormant life-force that lies within Lynmoor.'

He leaned closer, his lips almost touching hers, those clear brown eyes unfaltering as they gazed into hers:

'Will you join with me, Maria?'

Instinct ever stronger than reason, she took his hands and kissed them, one after the other.

'I will.'

Outside the tepee, Maria could hear the sound of rhythmic chanting, mingled with laughter as Carolan's less serious-minded followers welcomed the night and all that it would bring. Pleasure and worship; worship and pleasure. Which would it bring for Maria Treharne?

She watched in silence as Carolan got to his feet, swinging the embroidered blanket off his shoulders and revealing the nakedness beneath. He was not a handsome man; not well-proportioned and athletic like Jonathan, or arrogantly beautiful like Anthony Pendorran. Carolan was stocky, his broad chest tapering to powerful thighs that were white beneath a light covering of brown hair.

But if he was not beautiful, his penis was at least desirable, almost possessing a beauty of its own. It thrust stiff and menacing from the dark thicket between his thighs; a fat spike of flesh with a juicy pruple head that begged to be sucked and licked.

'And so I come to you, Maria Treharne. Naked as you see me, naked and unashamed. Will you also come to me naked?'

Maria stood to answer his challenge, reaching behind the tumbling curtain of her hair to pull down the zipper of her sleeveless cotton dress. She sensed him catching his breath, the moment suspended in time as his eyes followed her every movement, and at last anticipation became reality.

She slipped the straps of her dress down over her shoulders, and wriggled the bodice down over her breasts, their firm heaviness unfettered by any bra and their nipples already erect from gently rubbing against the inside of her dress as she walked along.

Carolan did not speak. But his eyes never left her as

230

she peeled the dress down over her hips, sliding it down over the little scrap of white lace that imperfectly covered her pubis, letting little auburn tendrils escape from the edges to curl over the white fabric like the petals of some exotic flower.

The dress slid to the ground with the faintest swish of crisp cotton, and she stepped away from it, kicking away her shoes so that she was almost naked before Carolan, her body's only ornamentation the silver amulet hanging between her bare breasts, and the lacy veil that still hid from him the most intimate secrets of her womanhood.

'Naked, Maria. Come to me naked.'

There was an urgency in Carolan's whisper, a catch in his throat as though he were fighting down some wild wave of passion that threatened to engulf him. His hands were by his side, tightly clenched; his cock glistening with wetness and the hairy purse of his scrotum tense with expectation.

Maria hooked her thumbs under the elastic of her panties. She was savouring the suspense; the sense of power that filled her as she looked Carolan straight in the eye and eased the panties down over her buttocks, stretching the elastic taut so that the scrap of white lace slipped down easily. The panties released a faint scent as she pulled them down; the sharpness of lavender mingled with the fragrant juice of her own sweet sex. She was surprised at how excited she felt.

As the lace pulled away from her belly she heard Carolan's breathing quicken. His eyes were focused on the auburn thicket of her pubic curls; the soft, springy bush that seemed to invite his kisses. Secretly pleasured by his attentive eyes, she lifted her foot and stepped out of the panties, now no more than an inconsequential ball of rumpled material. As she did so, her thighs parted and her pussy-lips opened, releasing the full potency of her secret fragrance. Like some powerful and exotic liqueur it intoxicated her, sweeping away her suspicion, her resistance, her doubt.

231

Carolan did not touch her. He was caressing her with his eyes, his gaze travelling over every inch of her exposed flesh, imagination filling in the shadowy hollows where light did not reach, his tongue savouring the imagined taste of her with all the greed of a starving man.

Suddenly he clapped his hands, and the soft, woody sound of a flute filled the air. The musician was a young man, his face painted with garish swirling patterns; he was sitting cross-legged in the corner. Maria understood at once that he was playing just for her. His eyes, like Carolan's, were fixed on her, following her, willing her to let her body move in time to the music. The formless tune swooped and trilled around her like birdsong, like the sound mountain waters make when they bubble over smooth, round stones.

'Dance for me,' said Carolan.

And she danced – not for Carolan, but for the sheer naked joy of the dance; letting the music enter her body and ripple through her soul. She was driftwood, tossed by the wild grey ocean; she was the soft, pink petal of a flower, blown on a summer breeze; she was the spirit of the earth, hungry and sensual as a rutting beast.

Maria twisted and turned, her body moving in the steps of its own instinctive choreography. She dipped and spun, her heavy breasts quivering and bouncing; her buttocks parting as her knees bent and her head swung forward and down. Her hair tumbled over her face like a cascade of autumn leaves: golds and ambers and reds that caught the light and flashed fire.

There was a liquid energy inside her, and it was boiling up, spilling out, overflowing in a superabundance of sexual desire. As she swung her head back, arching her spine, her head dizzy and her body tingling with need, she felt Carolan's hands on her. A warm, wet stickiness seemed to flow from his fingers and she saw that they were covered with a dark pigment.

He was painting her, using her as his canvas; drawing the patterns of his desire on her bare skin. Scooping up more of the warm liquid from a little earthenware dish that had been warming on a brazier of glowing charcoal, he traced the long, sinuous coils of a snake that wound its way from the centre of her back, over her shoulder to the valley of her breasts, then darted straight for the heart of her sex, its greedy head disappearing into the dense undergrowth of her pubic hair.

She could not suppress a little shiver of pleasure as his finger slipped through the springy curls and between the fleshy lips of her sex. The liquid was just hot enough to maker her clitoris throb and burn as Carolan's finger pushed back the hood and it trickled over the exposed bud. She bore down on his finger, her hips thrusting against him, moving back and forth, making him wank her. And still the music rippled and flowed around her, a never-ending stream of warmth like the hot tide of longing that seeped from the well-spring of her sex.

But Carolan withdrew his finger, and bent to scoop more of the hot dark liquid from the dish. Maria went on dancing, the dark snake seeming to coil itself about her more tightly still as her body twisted and whirled.

The warm throb of pleasure made her press her thighs tightly together as the sticky liquid anointed the crests of her nipples; spokes fanning out from the centres like stars, or the petals of a curious flower. And then Carolan was turning her round so that her back was to him. He was pushing her forward so that her back was bent and her hands were on her knees, her thighs apart and her buttocks thrust out, as though she were some shameless vixen, hot and ready for her mate.

Her breasts hung like pendulous fruit, ripe and ready to be picked; or like the full, milky dugs of some suckling beast. Maria felt her sex grow wetter as she imagined warm, wet mouths sucking eagerly at her teats, drawing their strength from her, feeding on the elixir of her sex.

The hot, slightly viscous liquid trickled down her back like molten lava, cooling only very slightly as it moved slowly downwards, but still deliciously warm as it entered the deep crevice between her buttocks. Carolan made no attempt to touch her. He was content to watch as the dark pigment flowed like warm treacle between the cheeks of her bottom; content to watch her writhe and moan as the sticky heat reached the puckered rose of her arsehole and covered it with its own uniquely warm caress.

He knelt behind her, and as Carolan's fingers gripped her buttocks, pulling them apart, Maria felt a little sigh of satisfaction shudder out of her. The music was a little faster now, its rhythm almost matching the pace of her frantic heartbeat. And then she felt Carolan's tongue-tip enter the secret world he had discovered, his face pressing against her bum-cheeks as his tongue probed and licked at the warm stickiness.

Carolan was in seventh heaven. He had designed this minor masterpiece of live theatre partly as a means of thumbing his nose at that ponce Anthony Pendorran, partly as a lesson to the delectable but haughty Ms Treharne. In the event, as he had quickly discovered, all that really mattered was the pleasure.

He'd fully intended having her, of course – getting his cock between those elegant thighs and showing her what it felt like to be fucked by a real man. But now that she was here, there was something about her that made him want to enjoy her more slowly and luxuriously; something that took his uncomplicated and rather contemptuous lust and turned it into a form of body-worship.

His tongue lapped up the sticky fluid, and the salty, coppery taste of incense and musk did not repel him; on the contrary, it served to whet his appetite for the deeper, more secret taste of her.

He licked at the sensitive flesh around Maria's bottom-hole, and she responded eagerly, thrusting out her backside so that he would lick her harder, more intimately. His tongue-tip penetrated the tight membrane, and for a moment he thought she would pull away from him, but she went on thrusting backwards so that his entire tongue slid into the welcoming hole.

234

Maria closed her eyes and let the music flow through her. She was breathing regularly and rhythmically now, moving with the pleasure instead of against it. Carolan's tongue wriggled inside her like an eel, the initial thrill of each new twist and turn sending aftershocks of pleasure right through her entire body. Her clitoris stung with frustration, and she longed to press her fingers against it, rubbing herself to a glorious climax of release; but she knew that she must not. She was not yet to be pleasured; she was to be prepared for the Goddess.

Excitement made her half delirious, and her voice rose above the music of the flute; a quavering, moaning cry of need that found its answer in the hoarse, muted rasp of Carolan's breath as he slid his tongue out of her and planted kiss after kiss on the bare, shivering flesh of her thighs.

He got to his feet and drew her up to face him; he looked wilder than ever, like some half-crazed mountain man. His cock pressed urgently against her belly, and Maria thought in that instant that he would take her – here, now, on the hard earthen floor of the tepee.

That was certainly what Carolan had intended. The preparation ritual had simply been his excuse to exercise his *droit de seigneur* on the Treharne woman before the main ceremony; which he had gauged would be bound to degenerate into a sexual free-for-all. That was what he'd intended, but the excitement was taking him almost to the point of explosion. He craved the feeling of her tight, wet womanhood sliding glove-like over the hard shaft of his penis; but something, something he didn't understand, was holding him back.

Later. He would have her later. There was all the time in the world, and besides – he still had another amusing little ceremony to perform.

'The preparation is complete,' he announced. Immediately two of the women got to their feet and put a garland of wild flowers round Maria's neck. 'But before our rite of worship to the Earth-spirit can begin, there is another ritual to perform.' He clapped his hands again,

235

and the flap of the tepee was drawn back, revealing a triangle of dark-blue sky, edged with the orange-white haze from the bonfire and the headlights of Jak's old van. 'Come, Maria.'

They stepped outside together, and Maria found herself looking at two figures. The first was a naked man, his body almost entirely covered in grotesque tattoos. In his hand he held the end of a chain. Beside him stood the naked figure of a brown-haired girl, her youthful body even younger-looking because the body hair had been shaved off, leaving her pubis as bare and innocent as a child's. The girl's anonymity was accentuated by the blindfold she wore – a black silk scarf tied tightly over her eyes. Around her neck was a heavy leather collar, from which a thick chain led to the gloved hand of the tattooed man.

Maria glanced at Carolan, uncomprehending and uneasy.

'Who . . ?'

Carolan smiled.

'This is Megan, Maria. She says she wants to join us, and help us to save Lynmoor from the developers. Isn't that so, Megan?'

The girl raised her head. Her voice was faint but steady.

'Yes. I want to join you.'

'Good.' Carolan turned back to Maria. 'What better night could there be to welcome a new member to our family? What better night could there be for an initiation?'

Megan Rothermead trembled beneath the blindfold, her whole world concentrated in the sounds she could hear around her. She was naked, alone, afraid.

But she was elated, too. Never before had Megan felt so important. Here, her body bare and her every secret open to watching eyes, she was the centre of attention for the first time in her life.

Jak had told her what to expect, but she still felt fear

236

as the chain tightened and she was led out to the tepee into the centre of the ancient stone circle. She could not see the tall standing stones, but she fancied she could feel their presence, towering over her like sentinels, each one the servant of the Goddess and each one hungry for her devotion.

She stumbled, and the chain pulled very tight, jerking the leather collar so hard that it half-choked her. But hands caught her, setting her back on her feet – though not before they had taken the opportunity to roam over the naked curves of her backside, insinuating inquisitive fingers into the deep cleft between her buttocks. She gave a gasp, half of surprise, half of pleasure, and some-one nearby – a man with a deep, gruff voice – laughed and whispered:

'Hope she's a virgin. Can't wait to get inside her.'

Another man replied, his voice a low hiss.

'Don't let Carolan hear you talking like that. You'll get your turn, don't you worry. We all will – Carolan'll see to that.'

Megan stumbled on, her unseen master leading her on the tight chain towards the fierce heat from the bonfire. She could hear it crackling and popping, and felt some-thing tickle her bare arms as tiny flakes of ash floated down through the overheated air. She felt sweat prickle her skin, beads of moisture standing out on her breasts and back, and gathering into heavy droplets which burst into long, thin, salty trickles of wetness.

Just when she thought she could bear no more, the chain fell slack and she found herself standing still and silent. She moved her head, trying to locate someone, anyone, anything with which she could connect and make contact. But no one spoke, no one communicated with her.

She felt alone – and yet she knew that she was not. She knew, from what Jak had told her, that every one of Carolan's tribe would be sitting cross-legged around the inside of the stone circle. She imagined their naked bo-dies gleaming with coloured patterns and their eyes glinting in the dancing firelight; each pair of eyes fixed on her. And her nipples stiffened to hard pink cones of need. She knew what to expect; and she welcomed it, summoned it with all the force of her impetuous young will.

'What is your name, sister?'

Carolan's disembodied voice sounded different – echoey and distant, as though it came from a very long way away. Megan turned her face towards the sound, glad of a point of reference in the prison of her blindness.

'Megan. My name is Megan.'

'And why do you come here, sister Megan? What do you wish of us?'

'To join with you.' The words thrilled through Megan as she spoke them; the most important words of her idealistic young life. At last she was doing something for herself; making choices which no one could take away from her.

There was a slight pause, and when Carolan spoke again his voice was deeper, more resonant.

'You understand that to be initiated into the ways of our people, you must make a sacrifice to the Mother of all?'

'I understand.'

'And what is that sacrifice, Megan?'

'The gift of my body.'

'You are willing?'

Megan replied without a moment's hesitation. Her whole body was singing with exultation, yearning to be admitted to the dangerous, adult world of passion from which there could be no going back. Her voice rang out, steady and clear.

'I am willing.'

For a few seconds nothing happened. The ache of disappointment began in Megan's belly, cold and hollow and lonely. The seconds passed, long and empty as years. And then she heard it; the low, keening chant of dozens of voices; a wordless ululation to the shimmer-

238

ing night sky. They were welcoming her; welcoming her to the only family she had ever truly wanted to belong to.

Fingers touched her, rough-skinned and ungentle. How many fingers; how many hands? It was impossible to tell. Above the crackling of the fire she could hear the harsh, staccato breathing of many men, perhaps many women also. They were closing in on her, the distant chanting rising to a shrill, wailing crescendo as the caresses become more brutal, more insistent.

Instinct tutored Megan's body to respond, and she greeted the caresses joyfully, kissing the hands and lips that brushed her mouth; offering herself up to each new sensation; sliding her feet wide apart on the trodden, tufted grass as fingers slid up her thighs and probed their way into the secret smile of her shaven love-lips.

Something slick and warm and heavily scented fell trickling over the flesh of her breasts, and softer hands began massaging the slippery oil in circular movements round and round the hardened crests of her areolae. Round and round went the hands, kneading and stroking, teasing and pinching so tantalisingly that Megan could feel a warm, honeysweet ooze beginning to trickle from her naked sex-lips.

She reached out her hand and met warm, smooth flesh; a hard, smooth baton so thick that her fingers barely met around its circumference. Butterfly-soft, they fluttered over the surface, toying with the domed tip that was so slippery-smooth with sex juice. She could not see it, but she knew it was the most beautiful, the most utterly seductive penis she had ever, ever touched.

Others came to touch her – more beautiful still; and she stood frozen in ecstasy, her head flung back and her lips open in a cry of joy. A slick cock-tip grazed the smoothness of her backside and then hands were pulling her down, down, down towards the waiting grass that was so soft and so welcoming to her bare skin. Hands touched her thighs, but they did not need to push or force, for already she was sliding her legs apart, opening up her entire being so that the instrument of her freedom might enter her.

'Welcome, sister,' said Carolan; and his smooth, hard penis slid into her as easily as a hot knife slicing through butter. Megan did not reply, but simply threw back her head and howled in pleasure.

Maria watched the spectacle that Carolan had prepared for her with growing cynicism. That girl was so young, so vulnerable; how could she be expected to know that she was being used? And Maria was convinced now that Carolan was using the girl for his own pleasure – her, and Maria, and every damn person here.

This was clearly no conventional Wicca gathering, dignified and disciplined. Before her, in the centre of the ancient circle, the 'rite of initiation' was rapidly developing into an orgy. Maria's lip curled in disdain as she watched Carolan cavorting around the blindfolded girl, his curly mop of brown hair topped off with a headdress made from some kind of animal pelt and a huge pair of stag's antlers. More than ever he looked like some mischievous nature-sprite, neither good nor evil but simply opportunistic.

Of course, she had never fully trusted Carolan; but for a time she had allowed herself to believe in his sincerity. Not that she had really had much choice; Lynmoor was in mortal danger, and some very strange and inexplicable things had been happening to her lately. She had believed that she could not afford to spurn any offer of help, any alliance – however unlikely.

Did Carolan really give a damn about Lynmoor? It was impossible to know the truth; but the sight of him and his followers indulging their wildest desires in a debauched parody of Wicca ritual made Maria angry and resentful. She would not stay here any longer than was absolutely necessary. She would leave this place, and she would make very sure not to get involved with Carolan ever again.

The atmosphere was becoming more and more frenzied; couples writhing on the grass as the bonfire flared higher in the night sky, and the scents of sex blended with the perfumes of incense and scented oils. A girl with spiky, punk-green hair approached Maria, her mouth red from the berry-juice she had been drinking. She handed the wooden goblet to Maria and some of the crimson juice slopped over the side onto the pale skin of her hand.

'Drink', she laughed, her eyes full of a faraway longing; and she stumbled away into the arms of her next lover.

Maria lifted the goblet to her lips. She was thirsty from the heat, and the liquid smelled of fresh berries and herbs. It seemed innocent enough. Hesitating for a brief second, she drank.

A few miles away on the other side of the valley stood Brackwater Tor, a darker, more impenetrable blackness against the dense black of the sky. The night was cloudless, and the new moon's thin, silvery light picked out the shape of the old Hall, craggy and misshapen as the rocks on which it stood.

A barn owl shrieked as it swooped into the long grass, carrying off its wriggling prey; and then all was silent, still, unmoving.

But at the very top of the empty house, just under the eaves where the slate roof met the rough, grey stone walls, something stirred. And a light clicked on behind the painted glass of an attic window, staring across the moors towards Hilltop Tor like a single bloodshot eye.

Something was happening to Maria. She felt lightheaded and directionless, like a small bird in a storm. What was causing it? Could it have been something in the berry-juice she had drunk? The more she tried to fathom it out, the less her mind responded.

Pictures were taking the place of thoughts in her head: vivid pictures that ran into each other like some crazy collage. In the primeval darkness of the waking dream

241

she could make out a line of running figures, their painted bodies weaving through the trees of an ancient forest as they raised their spears aloft to strike.

And now she could see a circle of grass-roofed huts; a stag pursued by hounds; splashes of red blood on a snow-covered hillside; a forest so dark and impenetrable that it seemed to have excluded all sunlight, and become a place of shadows within shadows.

In her dream she was running through the forest, towards a whispered voice whose words she could almost, but not quite, make out. They seemed to be summoning her and she was trying to run faster, but her legs felt like lead.

'Maria. Come to me, Maria.'

She turned her head and saw him; a familiar tall, dark figure with eyes like a stormy grey ocean. Her body filled with need. She longed for him, yearned to touch him, to hold him, to feel his body-heat pumping into her like the pulse of a mighty heart.

But she could not touch him. Stopping in her tracks, she saw that Anthony Pendorran seemed to be standing on the other side of a huge pane of glass. She touched it with her fingers, and it was cold, smooth and unyielding.

'Maria . . .' Pendorran's lips opened and his whispering voice seemed to echo through her whole body, making her tremble with a desire that only he could satisfy.

This time he reached out to her; and as she stretched out her hand their fingers met, the glass barrier between them dissolving so that flesh touched flesh; warm, living fingers entwining. A force was pulling her back; a wind gusting through the forest, trying to separate them, but she would not let go.

She tightened her grip, and felt his fingers close once more about hers.

'I want you,' she cried. 'I want you now.'

And as the dream dissolved and the chants of Carolan's men filled her dizzy head, Maria opened her eyes and saw that she was not holding Anthony Pendorran's hand at all.

Quite simply, Jak could not believe his good fortune. Here he was, playing gooseberry at Carolan's big party, and what should he land himself but the biggest prize of all?

His strong arms pulled Maria towards him and, still dazed and confused, she made no attempt to resist.

'I want you too,' he said. And his cock pressed against her belly, a mute witness to the sincerity of his desire.

# Chapter Twelve

*T*he rather elegant long-case clock in the corner of the office chimed a discreet quarter-hour, but no one was listening.

Charles Allardyce was alone with his thoughts.

Not that he was normally given to fantasising – if he wanted something he just went straight out and got it – but when he closed his eyes, it all seemed so seductively real. It was as though his imaginative powers had suddenly taken a jump into fourth gear and thrown him into a world where dreams were just another dimension of reality. It was amazing: he could feel the fingers and tongues on his skin, the kisses that tasted of dark red wine and sex. It was a virtual reality mind-trip – without the headset or the psychoactive drugs. A truly great antidote to executive stress.

He couldn't think of any reason why his sexual fantasies should suddenly have become so powerful; except maybe that he was getting a little bored with Janis and his body was telling him to get out there and find another outlet for the urge that was getting stronger by the day. In any case, why did he need a reason? It was reason enough that when he settled back into his favourite office chair and closed his eyes, the most diverting and stimulating images came flooding into his head; images so lascivious and so real that it came as no surprise that he could reach out and touch the naked bodies that surrounded him.

In his fantasy world he was naked too – lying on a soft couch in an old-fashioned room filled with ever-changing patterns of coloured light. How many women were there: three, four, more? He tried to count them but their faces kept changing, and their caresses were so exciting that it was hard to concentrate on anything but the pleasure. He felt his cock twitch into life and willed a soft hand to curl eager fingers around the hardening shaft.

To his delight, the dream-woman obeyed his will, bending over him so that the long dark sweep of her braided hair raked across the super-sensitive flesh of his lower belly. And she bent lower, opening her ruby lips so that he could discern the glistening white of her pearly teeth, and the deep pink of her tongue.

He caught his breath as she took him into her mouth, and an ocean of sensations washed over him. Other faces, beautiful faces, were bending low over his body and he reached out to touch soft-budding breasts and smooth flanks that felt like warm silk to his trembling fingers. Now his whole body was trembling, the room seeming to revolve faster and faster around him as the quest for pleasure overtook him. Lost in his own private world, he was not even aware of his own voice, whispering over and over again:

'Yes, yes, yes.'

Reaching the doorway to Allardyce's office with the morning's consignment of papers for signature, Duvitski stopped dead in his tracks. What the hell was going on?

Allardyce was lying back in his favourite black leather armchair, his eyes closed and his whole body shaking with a violence that alarmed Duvitski. Was he ill? But Allardyce was smiling, and the whispered words that escaped from his trembling lips were not the sounds of pain, but of passion.

245

Duvitski threw down the papers he was carrying and strode over to where Allardyce was lying, apparently caught in the throes of some bizarre delirium.

'Are you OK, Charles?'

He reached out his hand and touched Allardyce's hand, but he seemed totally oblivious to his colleague's presence. Alarmed now, Duvitski seized Allardyce by the shoulders and shook him.

Allardyce gave a murmur of protest, shook his head and opened his eyes. The pupils looked unnaturally large in the bright sunlight from the open window, and his voice seemed slightly slurred.

'What was that? Oh Leon, it's you.'

'I said, Charles, are you OK?'

Allardyce drew in a deep breath and let it out in a long, luxurious sigh. He smiled, but it wasn't quite like any smile Duvitski had seen before.

'Oh yes,' he said. 'I'm fine, don't you worry. Everything's going to be absolutely fine.'

It was late morning when Maria got back to the Hall, tired and dazed from the previous night's events. She still wasn't at all sure what – if anything – had really happened to her in the stone circle on Hilltop Tor, and quite frankly she didn't want to dwell on it.

She pushed open the little wicket gate and stepped onto the stone-flagged path which led around the house. Immediately she caught sight of a tall figure with tousled blond hair, stooping from the waist as his strong brown arms swung a scythe across the tangle of brambles and long grass that had once been a formal rose-garden. He had stripped off his shirt, and she feasted her eyes on the appetising caramel of his bare torso, and the pert nipples that were brown as milk chocolate – and every bit as good to eat.

Hearing her shut the gate behind her, Geraint straightened up, greeting her with a broad grin that seemed to light up his cheekily handsome face.

'Mornin', Miss T.'

'Morning, Geraint. Devotion to duty – now that's what I like to see.'

The sight of Geraint cheered Maria. He was like a rock of normality in the shifting sands that threatened to drag her down and engulf her. There was a good deal too much that was unfathomable in her life just now. But just when she thought she could no longer believe or trust anyone or anything, along came Geraint – young, strong, earthy, and dependably in lust with her.

She walked towards Geraint, wondering what he must make of her dishevelled hair and dress, and the residual smears of red and silver paint on her bare arms. Geraint leaned on his scythe and took a handkerchief out of his jeans pocket, wiping the beads of sweat from his brow. He looked at her slyly.

'Yeah, well, I bin up 'ere since seven. Didn't see nothin' of you, though.'

Maria refused to rise to the challenge of Geraint's obvious curiosity. It was none of his business where she'd been; there were no ties between them, except the ties of mutual physical gratification. Instead of answering his innuendo, she surveyed the area he had just cleared. Already it was scarcely recognisable as the impenetrable wilderness that had greeted her on her first day at Brackwater Hall.

'You're doing a good job,' she observed.

'I like to give satisfaction,' replied Geraint, with meaningful emphasis. Maria was very aware of his eyes, travelling up from her sandalled feet to the low neckline of her cotton dress. One of the straps had slipped down, baring a shoulder still decorated with a crudely-painted silver star. A line of dark-red, dried-on pigment led down from her shoulder to the deep crease between her breasts. 'Complete satisfaction – you know that.'

It was Maria's turn to smile.

'Oh, you always do that, Geraint,' she said, half-joking, half-serious. 'Perhaps I should think about giving you a bonus.' She stroked his springy blond hair and ran her fingers over the tiny hairs on the nape of his neck, rubbing them gently in the wrong direction, in the playful way that always made him go all shivery and beg for more.

He caught her hand and kissed it roughly, the bristles of his blond stubble already coming through and making his skin like scratchy sandpaper, even though he had shaved that same morning.

'Or maybe there's something I could give you?'

His saliva was wet and cool on the back of Maria's hand, and she found herself wondering what it would feel like between her thighs, cool and slippery on the hard bud of her clitoris. She was tired but not that tired; it might be fun to take him into her bed and have him suck and lick her to the first of a dozen orgasms.

'Maybe.'

'I'm hard for you, Maria.'

She licked her lips, mentally rehearsing what they would do together; the way he would taste on her tongue, the feel of him lying on top of her as she squeezed her breasts around his shaft and let the very tip of him part her lips. So many games they could play together.

'I don't doubt it.'

She let her fingers walk down the front of Geraint's jeans then cupped the swelling bulge in the palm of her hand with a cruel gentleness. She wasn't going to confess how wet she was for him; how she was squeezing the tops of her thighs very tightly together, because the very thought of his nakedness made her throb with excitement. Could I bring myself to orgasm? she wondered. Could I do it just by squeezing my legs together, so that my pussy-lips rub against my clitoris? Yes, I'm sure I could ...

Her fingers stroked the hardening pouch of Geraint's erection with a deliberate slowness.

'Mmm, yes, you *are* hard, aren't you.' Her fingers ran along the lengthening outline of the swollen flesh.

'Gawd, Maria, you're enough to drive a man crazy.' He put his hand to his fly, no doubt to slide down the zipper, but she pushed it away.

'No, not yet. Later.'

Geraint groaned, his lust taken almost to the point of no return and then . . . clicked off like a light-switch.

'Maria!'

'Later.'

Maria did not let him see her smile as she turned away. Picking up her bag, she carried on walking towards the front door of the Hall. Even though she could no longer see him, she could feel Geraint's periwinkle-blue eyes boring into the back of her, his frustrated lust stripping her naked. She swung her hips slightly as she walked, entirely for his benefit, and was shocked to realise just how much she had enjoyed teasing him. What was she doing to him, and why? Was there a latent streak of sadism in her, or did she just want to see what he would do? Poor, poor Geraint.

But she was not too worried about Geraint. She felt sure that he was enjoying it too. Geraint Morgan was used to women who were very different from Maria Treharne. From that very first time they had gone to bed together, her free-thinking, unashamed sexuality had come as quite a revelation to him. Now he couldn't get enough of it.

She turned her key in the lock and stepped inside the entrance hall. For an instant she could have sworn she sensed someone or something else in the Hall; that she caught sight of a fleeting shadow moving swiftly out of her field of vision. And then it was gone. Another chimera from the depths of her disordered subconscious? Another shadow, melting into dark corners never to be seen again?

A picture postcard lay in the wire mail-basket behind the door. Maria picked it up and scanned it, recognising the handwriting instantly:

'Car broke down in Devon, am spending a couple of days here. Tried phoning, but no luck. Finding solace with Gareth and Hans (don't ask!). With you asap, love Anthea xxx.'

Anthea! Maria had almost forgotten about the invitation,

249

and – since she hadn't heard a thing from her – had assumed she wasn't going to take it up. Now she wondered if it had been such a good idea after all. With all the bizarre things that were happening around here, perhaps it would be better if she faced up to these next few weeks on her own. On the other hand, maybe Anthea's visit would help to put things into perspective, chase away some of the hobgoblins that seemed to be waiting for her in every shadow.

She propped the postcard up on the hall table, next to her bag, and climbed the wide, winding staircase towards the first floor. A pale, gentle sunlight filtered in through the small landing windows, lightening the gloom in the dark old house and making her feel languid and just a little playful. Already last night was fading to an uneasy memory, and perhaps, after a hot shower and some sleep, it would have faded right out of her head.

Undressing as she crossed her bedroom, she left her dress, shoes and panties in a trail across the carpeted floor. It felt better, more natural, to be naked; almost as though that was how the house wanted her to be. She brushed against the drapery of the four-poster bed as she passed, and the heavy velvet seemed to linger, seemed to curl around her body like a caress, unwilling to let her go.

She paused for a moment, unwelcome thoughts hemming her in. Was she really 'tuning in' to something in this house, or was she putting her own psychic interpretation on events that – however bizarre – might have some other, far more rational explanation?

Understanding would not come. Questions tumbled one after the other in Maria's mind, but there were no answers. She unhooked the silver pendant from her neck and laid it carefully on the shelf over the sink. As she looked up, she caught sight of herself in the mirror, and scarcely recognised the face that looked back at her.

Her hair was a mass of knots and tangles, a wild bush of chestnut waves with long tendrils that snaked down over her bare shoulders and breasts; her mouth was a dark smudge of red, still stained from the berry juice she had drunk at the ceremony; and her skin still bore vivid traces of the scarlet and silver patterns which Carolan had painted on it. In the clear light of morning, they seemed childish rather than mystical and – not for the first time – she cursed her own idiocy in ever giving Carolan the benefit of the doubt.

How could she have been taken in by that two-bit con-man: a man whose ideas of paganism amounted to the sort of sexual free-for-all you might find in the more sensational Sunday tabloids? What sort of good did he think that was going to do for the movement to save Lynmoor? Or did Carolan really care about anything but his own sexual gratification?

As she turned on the water and stepped under the steaming-hot shower jet, Maria smelt the potent fragrance of her own body; a memory too indelible simply to be washed away. Indeed, as the warm water trickled down over her stomach and divided into little runnels as it coursed over her pubic hair, the scent seemed to become even stronger. It was the scent of rutting beasts, the blended perfumes of sweat and incense, and something indefinable but undeniably the elixir of pure, unfettered sexual desire.

Guilty memories of her own gratification flooded back as she basked in the scent of her own lustful hunger. There was no denying the feelings within her. With hindsight, last night had been a dreadful mistake, and yet she had found pleasure in the arms of Carolan's shaven-headed bodyguard; falling laughing into his embrace as his stumpy, thick penis sought out the soft, wet heart of her.

There had been others too – many others, so many that she could not remember their names or even their faces. Even the sensations had blurred together into a single memory of pleasure that had been renewed again and again and again.

She lifted her face to the shower-head and the powerful

251

surge of water massaged her skin with its thin, insistent fingers; each little needle-sharp jet rebounding into a fine stream which joined the coursing water as it dripped down her face onto her body. Reaching out blindly, she took a fresh bar of soap from the shelf and began running it over her body, working it up to a rich, creamy lather. Thick gobbets of white foam dripped down over her shoulders and breasts, joining the steaming-hot water as it ran down her belly to the russet triangle at the apex of her thighs.

Slowly and luxuriously she ran the bar of soap down the slight curve of her belly and into the wiry curls that straggled over her pubis. It felt springy-soft to the touch. She slid her feet slightly apart on the floor of the shower cubicle, and her strong, spicy scent wafted up as the hot, soapy water trickled between her thighs. The soap slipped easily between the plump lips of her pussy, distending the flesh, filling up the slippery wetness with a new slipperiness and a new, sweet scent. A second later and it was right inside her, sliding up into the tight, wet love-sheath of her vagina so easily that it seemed to move effortlessly, with a will of its own.

Her thighs and pussy-lips tingled with excitement as the harsh, scented soap pushed into her again and again, filling her up with creamy-white lather whose perfume added to, but in no way diminished, the potent, almost fishy scent of her sex. Each breath of that mingled perfume, each stroke of the bar of soap across her inner sex-lips, made her more excited, and readier for pleasure.

She was so lost in her own dreamworld of desire that she did not hear footsteps coming across the floor of her bedroom towards the bathroom, did not see the mud-spattered jeans and the white briefs joining the jumble of her clothes on the carpet.

The first she knew was the touch of a hand on her backside – a firm, determined touch that made her cry out in surprise and wheel round, shaking the water from her eyes.

Geraint was behind her, his naked body and hers sharing the rush of hot, steamy water. She giggled, wriggling herself round to face him and pressing her backside into the cupping caress of his hand.

'You frightened me! I mean, you could have been anybody.'

Geraint tightened the grip of his fingers on Maria's backside. His voice was husky and, thought Maria, curiously humourless.

'Little tease.'

She pressed her wet belly against his, and he responded by pulling her towards him, suddenly and savagely crushing his mouth against hers. His rough stubble scraped painfully across her sensitive skin again and again, and she pulled away gasping, her wet hair plastered to her face in long, dark rat-tails.

'Ouch!' she protested, rubbing her hand over her abraded chin. Geraint wasn't normally this rough, even in love-play.

Looking up at him, she noticed that Geraint's bright blue eyes were fixed on hers, but they seemed not so much to be looking at her, as through her.

'Little tease,' he repeated, and he gripped her round the waist, so tightly that he squashed all the breath out of her and the soap fell from her hand; a thin spiral of white lather mingling with the water as it drained away.

His hands moved slowly over the hot, wet, expanse of her backside, which was now very pink from the heat of the water. The callouses on his hands felt rough and arousing on her already excited flesh. He breathed in deeply, taking in the scent of her, and his cock-tip danced on her belly, adding its own wetness to the rivulets of water coursing down into the deep valley between her thighs.

This was a new and diverting variation on their usual games, and Maria responded to him hungrily, moving her hips slowly back and forth as his right hand darted between her legs, and hard, unforgiving fingers cupped the pouting mouth of her womanhood. There was no hiding her desire now. She could feel her own wetness welling up inside, oozing out and forming a warm pool in the palm of Geraint's hand. If he were to take his hand away, that pent-up wetness would come cascading out of her, running in tell-tale rivulets down the inside of her thighs.

'Playin' games with me. Teasin' me.' His fingers tensed again, and this time Maria felt the sharpness of jagged fingernails, digging into the soft, painfully-sensitive flesh of her vulva.

'Gently, Geraint, please. You're hurting me.'

There was something mechanical in Geraint's voice, and despite her excitement Maria felt suddenly uneasy. She tried wriggling out of his grasp, but he had her fast, his fingers unyielding as iron and the muscles of his forearms bulging with the slight effort of holding her still.

'Please, Geraint. Let go of me.'

He took not the least bit of notice. It was as though the Geraint Morgan she knew had been stolen away from her, and in his place nothing remained but the shell of him, a shell animated by a dark and primitive need for the most intense, the most violent of sensations. His eyes were cold as stone and his voice atonal, flat; the voice of an automaton.

'It ain't right. Playin' games. Makin' a man want you like that.'

Maria's mind was in a turmoil. Her body was crying out for the brutal sensations that Geraint's lust promised, her hunger reaching out to answer his. Her clitoris throbbed as his fingers rubbed harder and harder against her burgeoning bud. She wanted him with a powerful, gnawing hunger that made her yearn to abandon herself to his need; but fear was crying out inside her.

Fear of the darkness.

She could feel it building up around her, a thick, swirling fog that blotted out the light; a choking, whirling darkness that filtered into the brain like an insidious

254

whisper, urging still more and greater excess. And the darkness was engulfing her as it had already engulfed Geraint, suffocating her resistance, making her hunger rage like a forest fire. She wanted it, she wanted it; but she also wanted it to stop.

'You tease a man, you got to pay. It's only right. Teasin' little bitch.'

With all the strength she could muster, she pushed him away. She was in luck; taking him by surprise, she made him stumble and slip on the wet floor of the shower cubicle. That was all the chance Maria needed, and she leapt past him, running with all her might out of the bathroom, across the bedroom and onto the landing, slamming the door behind her and turning the heavy brass key in the lock.

In the eerie silence that followed, the watery-pale sunshine seemed to waver and then fade, as though all the light was being sucked out of Brackwater Hall by some unseen force.

Water dripped from Maria's body onto the polished linoleum, marking the seconds with a halting rhythm like the ticking of an unruly clock. She gasped, trying to get her breath back, trying to make sense of the great swirling mass of blackness that had tried to overwhelm her. The waiting seemed endless, the fear immense.

It was the last straw; the one thing Maria had needed to make her change her mind. She would go to Pendorran – now, this very moment – and she would ask him for help. If need be, she would beg. The time for pride had long passed.

Anthea looked up at the sky. That morning it had started off as a deep and flawless blue, but now it was turning a dirty grey and there were little fluffy clouds, like pink-edged marshmallows, threatening to ruin the day. That was a pity; she'd been looking forward to a little more afternoon delight.

She glanced across at Hans. He was fast asleep, stretched out on the grass beside the picnic hamper and the two – no three – empty bottles of sparkling wine. She giggled, ever so slightly tipsy herself, and walked unsteadily across the road to the telephone box.

Putting her money in the slot, she hesitated, trying to work out what she was going to say to Maria. 'Sorry, but I won't be there until goodness knows when; I got distracted by a Welsh poet and a gorgeous German waiter called Hans' didn't really sound like a very plausible excuse; but it was the truth, and she felt sure Maria of all people would understand. Maria had had her share of gorgeous hunks, and perhaps her difficulty in getting through to Brackwater Hall had something to do with another passionate liaison. Anthea fervently hoped it had: Maria was not going to be very pleased when she heard what her precious Jonathan had been up to in her absence.

She fished the letter out of her pocket, and dialled up Maria's number, tapping her fingers on the telephone console as she waited impatiently for the ringing to begin.

A long silence, punctuated by the odd electrical crackle, ended in a long, unbroken tone which Anthea recognised only too well. It was the same tone she'd been getting every time she tried phoning Maria: number unobtainable. But that was silly! She was sure it was the right number – why, she'd even checked it through Directory Enquiries. Lynmoor 53129. And all she kept getting was this long, low drone.

Glancing over her shoulder, she saw that Hans had woken up, rolling onto his side to make faces at her through the glass of the telephone booth. Still holding the receiver to her ear, she opened the door a little, propped it open with her foot and peeped out at him, trying her best not to laugh.

'If the wind changes you'll stay like that,' she said.

'Then come and make love with me again, *liebchen*. I am getting so lonely here without you!'

'And what if I don't?' she demanded.

'If you don't, I shall shout so loudly that the old woman in that cottage over there will hear, and when she comes out I shall tell her how you took advantage of me, you English hussy!'

In fits of giggles now, Anthea jammed the receiver back onto its hook. There were some things that just wouldn't wait. And in any case, she'd be seeing Maria very soon. What possible difference could a few more days make?

Maria drove like a maniac across the moors to Polmadoc, her hair still hanging in damp disarray and her only clothing the huge and very flimsy raincoat she had snatched from the coat stand in her headlong rush to get away from Geraint.

Even in the warmth of a July day she was shivering, perhaps more with fear than with cold. She still couldn't believe what had happened back there at the Hall, and more particularly what had happened to Geraint – happy-go-lucky Geraint who was always ready for fun, always ready to play some innocent game of lust. There, as the soul-black darkness had swirled about them, shutting out the light, she had felt all the innocence recoil and flee like a frightened animal, driven out by some great black beast with teeth as sharp as razors.

What on earth had she got herself into? What malign fate had brought her here, cunningly binding up her life with the fate of this beautiful, frightening place where nothing was quite as it seemed?

The battered Volvo bumped over the crest of the hill and Polmadoc lay before her: a few scattered, stone-built cottages and beyond them, almost at the very edge of the vertiginous cliffs, Pendorran's house.

It was the first time she had seen it in daylight, and even with the sun on it, the dark grey stone looked cold and rather forbidding, as though it were the guardian of some great secret that it was loath to share with anyone. The three-storey building had all the appearance of a castle, with its thick, heavy walls and tiny windows; an impregnable fortress built to withstand centuries of storm and siege. As she wound the car window down and breathed in the tangy salt air, she heard the tumultuous crash and roar of surf as breakers battered and tumbled against the cliffs, so very far below.

She drove up towards the house, towards a brass plaque which read 'Pendorran Estates', and the electronic gates opened with an almost inaudible whirr; an incongruous touch of the modern in this otherworldly place. The car slid forward, down the driveway and through a second gateway, into the inner courtyard around which the main body of the house was built.

A man in a dull grey suit was waiting for her as she steered into the cobbled court, parking the rusting heap with an acute awareness of how out of place it looked next to the immaculate black lacquer and brass carriage lamps of the antique landau, and the gaily-painted donkey cart with its shiny harness.

'Miss Treharne?'

Maria got out of the car, pulling the raincoat more closely around her as she did so. More than ever, she felt like a complete fool. She could hardly be unaware of Joseph's studiedly impartial gaze, travelling down from the auburn straggle of her still-damp hair to the oversized raincoat and the bare feet; so white against the age-smoothened cobbles on which they stood.

'Yes, Joseph . . . I'm terribly sorry to intrude like this, but I really must see Anthony.'

'I'm afraid Mr Pendorran is very busy this afternoon. He has given strictest instructions that he is not to be disturbed, under any circumstances.'

Maria's heart sank. A sixth sense told her that Pendorran's sudden desire to be alone might have more than a little to do with the awkwardness of their last meeting. But she wasn't giving up that easily.

'It's very urgent, Joseph.'

'Yes, I'm sure it is, Miss Treharne; only Mr Pendorran did give the strictest instructions. Perhaps if you were to leave me with a message for him I could . . .'

'No, Joseph. You don't understand. This is urgent, really urgent, you have to believe me.'

'Well, Miss Treharne, I really don't know.'

She took Joseph's hands between hers, and his eyes widened in surprise.

'Please.'

Joseph sighed. He was an elderly man; it had been many years since a young woman had taken him by the hand and gazed imploringly into his eyes. He was well aware of the penalties for disobeying his master's strict instructions, but after all he was only flesh and blood.

'You will find Mr Pendorran in the stables. That's the block of outbuildings over there, towards the sea.'

He was quite unprepared for the kiss of gratitude which Maria planted on his cheek. His face reddened in embarrassed surprise, and as his fingers moved absent-mindedly to the place where her lips had touched, he remembered younger, lustier days when he would have extorted a higher price than a simple kiss.

Maria ran across the cobbled yard and round the corner of the house towards the cluster of single-storey out-buildings which Joseph had pointed out to her. Everything seemed very quiet, very deserted, with no-thing at all stirring. Above in the clear sky a couple of seagulls swooped and soared, their unearthly wailing cry doing absolutely nothing to chase away the black mood that had overtaken her.

Beyond the stable blocks she could see rough grass-land sloping gently down towards the perilous cliff edge; it ran for a few hundred yards at most, no more. Anthony Pendorran's ancestors had certainly liked liv-ing dangerously; or perhaps Polmadoc had been further from the sea in those days, and the sea was encroaching, slowly but hungrily, on the prey that had escaped it for so many centuries.

Before and all around her, the endless vista of the ocean filled the horizon. Sunlight glittered on the turbu-lent grey waters, and it seemed to Maria that all the power in the whole world was contained within those rolling, crashing, foam-crested breakers. What power could be greater than the elemental force of the ocean?

Her bare feet soaked up the stored heat from the dry grass as she walked quickly towards the stable buildings, hardly able to keep her eyes from the rolling, tumbling sea-swell. There was something magnetic about it, something very like the look in Anthony Pendorran's eyes.

She reached the outbuildings, and walked through a passageway into another cobbled courtyard, this one lined with stable doors. The long, aristocratic head of a fine chestnut horse peered at her over the top of one, its liquorice-black lips curled back with all the appearance of a sneer. The name-plate above the door read 'Asphodel'.

The cobbles were uncomfortably hot underfoot, and Maria walked quickly round the stable-yard, her bare feet making no sound on the smooth stones. The place seemed deserted. Perhaps Joseph had been mistaken. Mercury, Demeter, Lysander, Croesus: the name-plates led her round the yard, peering into stables at horses who stared back at her with a studied lack of interest.

'Anthony? Are you here, Anthony?'

Her words echoed round the weathered stone walls, but there was no reply. She walked on, pushing open the door of a stable marked with the name 'Jupiter'. It was dark inside, the windowless stable so gloomy that for the first few moments she could see nothing but the retinal after-image of the sun reflecting off polished brass. She could hear nothing but the sound of breathing, somewhere close by; and the gentle, rhythmic jingle of harness.

Then a pale shape loomed up out of the blackness, and something massive lumbered against her in a sudden rush. Caught off balance she stumbled, crying out more in surprise than fear.

'Jupiter, no!'

As she fell a hand caught her in a vice-like grip, pushing her towards the side of the stall and holding her there, forbidding all movement. In the gloom nearby, she heard the white stallion's heavy body thud into the wooden wall, its hooves clattering on the stone floor.

'You're a bloody fool, Maria Treharne. He could kill you with one kick, do you realise that?'

It was Anthony's voice, unmistakeably smooth and unmistakeably annoyed. As light filtered into the gloom from the half-open stable door, she made out the tall shape of him, towering over her like a great black bird of prey.

'I . . . I'm sorry, I didn't think.'

Pendorran let out a sigh that was not quite exasperation, and not quite relief. As her eyes grew more accustomed to the half-light, Maria saw to her surprise that his face was ashen-white and drawn, his eyes bright wells of light that contrasted sharply with his haggard expression.

'I gave strictest instructions,' he snapped. His hand was still on Maria's shoulder and she could feel the fingers tightening. 'And I expect those instructions to be obeyed.'

'It was my fault. I told Joseph I had to see you urgently.'

'Joseph is old enough to know better. And he knows what it means to wilfully disobey me.'

All Maria had longed for was to feel the strength and security of Pendorran's embrace, but now she shrank from his touch. She had never heard him so angry before. Or was there more to it than that? There was something else in his voice, certainly; something that sounded more like fear than anger.

She took hold of his fingers and prised them away from her shoulder.

'Look, I need your help. I'm not too proud to beg you for it. Are you too proud to give it to me?'

For long, breathless seconds Pendorran did not reply. Nothing moved. The only sounds were the rustlings of dry straw, and the slide and grate of iron-shod hooves on stone. He was still standing very close to her, his tall frame covering her so completely that it almost blocked out the light. She could smell the tang of his sweat, taste the hint of fine Armagnac on his breath; she could so nearly touch him.

When he spoke again, his voice was calmer, cooler, as though he had finally managed to master his emotions.

'Come outside. We will talk.'

Pendorran turned on his heel and walked out of the stable into the sunlit yard. Maria followed behind, a little nervous that Jupiter would charge at her again, but he seemed quiet now, almost placid.

In the harsher daylight, Pendorran's face looked paler still beneath his tan, but his grey eyes were eagle-bright.

'Is there something wrong?' asked Maria.

'Wrong? Why should there be?'

'I have no idea. But you seem ... well, distracted somehow.'

Pendorran laughed, and the laughter seemed to bring colour to his handsome face. He was magnificent, thought Maria; as magnificent as the pale stallion that only he could tame, and perhaps as dangerous too. But here, in the sunlight, any danger from Pendorran seemed insignificant, and not worth considering. Once again she craved that touch, that kiss, the warm strength of that embrace.

'There is absolutely nothing wrong with me, Maria, but you ... What on earth happened to you?' He surveyed his dishevelled visitor with obvious amusement. In his open-necked shirt and fawn riding-breeches, Pendorran was the very embodiment of casual chic, whilst Maria ...

Still hugging the enormous raincoat over her nakedness, Maria glanced down at herself: two thin white legs emerging from the expanse of grey material; long damp rat-tails of dark red hair snaking down over her shoulders; bare feet shifting uneasily on the hot cobblestones. She must look an absolute mess – hardly the snake-hipped temptress who would seduce Anthony Pendorran into giving up all his secrets.

'I left in a hurry.'

'So I see,' observed Pendorran with good humour. He let his eyes rest briefly on Maria's hands, tightly bunching up the fabric of the raincoat over the rosy swell of her breasts – not entirely concealed from his view, since the wide-open neck of the coat had slipped a little sideways. 'Are you going to tell me about it, or do I have to guess?' He paused, running his hand lightly over Maria's bare shoulder, and his lips twitched into a smile. 'Guessing might be fun.'

Maria felt the tension in her relax, making her feel suddenly exhausted, weepy, exhilarated, relieved, all at once. Her fingers unclenched and the raincoat fell open, revealing the fleshy dome of her left breast, and the smooth curves of belly and thigh. She ran her fingers through the damp tangle of her hair, pushing it off her face.

'You were right about Carolan. He's just a grasping bastard, out for what he can get. Kinky sex mostly.'

Pendorran shrugged.

'You went to the ritual, of course.' It was a statement of fact, as though he already new – or guessed – what was in Maria's head.

'I had to.' Annoyance flared briefly in Maria, then died down as instantaneously as it had begun. She could not look into Pendorran's wild grey eyes and not feel strangely troubled. 'What choice did I have? You refused to help me. Will you help me now?'

Pendorran put his arms round her, drawing her close to him, burying his face in her hair; feeling her body offering itself up to his embrace. In that moment one facet of her personality struck him more forcefully than it had ever done before: her essential vulnerability.

'What I can, I will do. But you overestimate my power to help you.'

Maria raised her face to his, anguished, her eyes searching for some truth that she could hold on to. Could she trust him? Could she really trust him now, with the incredible tale of all that had happened to her at the Hall, and last night at the ritual? She wanted to tell him about the vision, the waking-dream she had had; she yearned to ask him what it had all meant, and why he had seemed to be standing on the other side of a mirror. But she could not. Something held her back, locking away the deeper, stranger secrets in her heart.

'I still don't understand, Anthony. You can help me by making me understand.'

His fingers slid underneath her hair, stroking and massaging the tense muscles at the back of her neck with an intensely erotic skill. Gratified and aroused, Maria pressed her face against him and kissed his chest through the soft white cotton of his shirt. She could feel the wiry, dark hairs through the thin material, and wanted to unbutton his shirt and taste them with the very tip of her tongue, worshipping his magnificent, vibrant flesh with her kisses.

'I cannot make you understand, Maria. I, of all men, cannot make you do anything. Showing is the best that I can do. The rest, my sweet, is for you to discover for yourself.' He kissed her again, and it was as if he were forcing his breath, his very soul into her with the welcome invasion of his tongue. 'And you *must* discover it soon, Maria; for the sake of Lynmoor it must be soon.'

'Then show me. Show me now.'

Maria returned his kiss with all the force of her passion; willing him to answer her need. Her hands slipped round his waist, feeling the hard, sinewy strength of the muscular torso beneath the thin cotton shirt; her body remembering how good it had felt to be flesh against flesh, burning up in the body-heat of their coupling.

She let her hands slip downwards and savoured the firmness of Pendorran's taut backside, so wonderfully smooth beneath the skin-tight fabric of his riding-breeches. How she longed to touch bare skin, to cup his buttocks in her two hands as she knelt before him and took the arrow of his desire into her eager mouth. She knew that he wanted her, could feel him hard and swollen in his breeches as he pulled her closer and the rough fabric rubbed against her bare belly.

'You don't need this.' Pendorran gently slid the raincoat over her arms, freeing her from the last impediment to her desire. Warm sunshine baked down on her bare skin and she basked like a lizard, greedy for the comfort of pleasure. He kissed the tips of her breasts very lightly, and they puckered at the touch of his lips, drawing themselves up into shameless little cones of pleasure-hungry flesh. 'Your body should hold no more secrets from me.'

The feel of his fully-dressed body pressing against her nakedness was uniquely exciting, and Maria rubbed herself against him harder, relishing the stimulation of her nipples sliding over the smooth fabric of his shirt. Her clitoris throbbed yearningly as she ground her pubis against Pendorran's belly, causing the little fleshy hood to cover and uncover the pink bud by turns. Its head felt swollen to the point of bursting, and little by little her thighs parted instinctively, so that Pendorran's thigh slid between her legs and she was able to rub her pubic bone against the hardness of his muscular flesh.

Somewhere in the distance – Maria had lost all sense of time and place – a horse whinnied. Above in the steel-blue sky a single gull wheeled and banked, riding the thermals, soaring and swooping in a silent celebration of its own power. Far below surf crashed on the shore, its thundering no more immense than the pounding of Maria's heart. The wanting was intense and unstoppable now.

She put her hand on the waistband of his breeches, meaning to undo the buttons and release him to share the same freedom that she enjoyed. But Pendorran caught her hand and lifted it away.

'No. Not here. Come with me.'

To Maria's intense disappointment, Pendorran took her hand and led her back towards the house. Frustration ached inside her like an old wound, freshly opened.

'Where are we going?'

'To the house. I having something to show you.'

He led her out of the stable-yard and towards one of the back entrances to the house. Maria saw a curtain twitch in one of the downstairs rooms and guessed that

Joseph must be watching the picturesque little scene as his master led a naked woman across the driveway and into the house. She no longer cared who saw her. Her body had taken over from her mind, her instincts from her reason; all she cared about now was the desire that was coursing through her, the need that must and would be satisfied.

Deep in her heart, she knew that she still could not quite trust Anthony Pendorran. There was a danger within him, and yet the fear of that danger only served to make her want him all the more. And there was another need in her – the need to know, to understand. For all her fear of him, she knew that Anthony Pendorran was the only person who could explain to her what was happening, and what she must do to make it stop.

They passed through the kitchens of the old house, redolent with the aromas of cinnamon and lemon verbena, and out into a corridor which Maria did not recognise. Lined with dark wood panelling, it was windowless but lit by a row of small wall-lights with green glass shades. At the end of the corridor Pendorran picked up an electric storm-lantern from a small table, and they turned right through a sliding door into a narrow, dark passageway which seemed to follow the outside wall of the house. The rough stone outer wall was damp to the touch, and there was a sound of dripping water.

Pendorran clicked on the lantern and lifted it up, revealing the walls of a rough-hewn cavern and a tunnel which seemed to lead downwards into the body of the cliffs.

'Where are you taking me . . ?'

Pendorran's face looked a touch satanic in the orange beam from the lantern.

'I fear the activities of the Pendorran family have not always been entirely legal and above board,' he explained. 'In the eighteenth century, this passageway was used to transport smuggled goods between Polmadoc Cove and the house.' He took a few steps forward then turned back towards Maria. 'There is a long flight of stone steps – watch your footing.'

He took Maria's hand once again and helped her down the first of the steps. They felt slimy and cold under her bare feet, and she began shivering. Pendorran gripped her hand more tightly, as though willing her not to give in.

The lantern's beam lit up wet stone covered with orange and grey lichen as they descended the winding steps towards a distant pinprick of light. The air was chill and Maria felt the tiny hairs on her arms erecting the skin into gooseflesh. But Pendorran's hand felt hot as a furnace around hers, the pulse of his desire steady as the lantern's beam in the lightening darkness.

As they walked gradually downwards, the pinprick of light became larger, expanding to a jagged mouth that yawned wider and wider; and the sound of roaring, rushing wind and water grew thunderous and immense, echoing round the high-roofed, rocky chamber. Pendorran pulled her along with him, half-dragging her across the slippery-wet stones and scree towards the cave mouth, where sunlight and thundering, glittering water seemed to fill the whole world.

And at the mouth of the cave they stood together, gasping for breath, their bodies pressed close as they blinked in the sudden explosion of light.

'Power, Maria. Can't you feel it?' Pendorran's hand caressed her backside, the fingers teasing and smoothing the cold, shivering flesh.

Maria took a step forward, into sunlight and wild sea-spray. The sudden warmth of the sun on her bare skin made her shudder with delight as her body awoke once more to the overwhelming need for pleasure.

The sand was soft and squishy between her toes, and she felt the grittiness of pebbles and crushed shells beneath the soles of her feet. Around her were the tall, encircling cliffs, soaring grey and forbidding into the blue dome of the sky. And ahead of her stretched the ridged expanse of flat brown sand, the surface deeply corrugated like the ribs of some slumbering beast, spreadeagled between land and sea.

And at the far margin of the sand crashed the foam-crested breakers of the ocean, grey-green and blue, with fronds of brown and orange weed tumbling in the surf; long, watery fingers clawing at the sand as the sea began its long, slow inward journey towards high tide.

She lifted her face to the sun and let it warm her, delighting in the contrast of hot sun and cold spray, the tiny droplets spangling her skin like crushed diamonds. The air smelt fresh, clean, exhilarating; a capricious breeze tugging at her hair and making the long, damp tendrils dance like serpents around her face.

'Feel the power, Maria. Let it enter you.' Anthony was right behind her, his arms about her waist, his hands moving steadily upward towards the heavy globes of her breasts. His palms closed over them, and Maria thrilled to his touch, instinctively pushing backwards into the warmth of his embrace. 'Can you feel it?'

'I feel it. It's like . . . like electricity, it makes me feel so alive and so excited.'

'That power is a thousand times smaller than the power that is within you.'

She wheeled round to face Pendorran, the red banner of her hair aflame in the sparkling air.

'More riddles! You're lying to me, Anthony. You're hiding the truth from me. You promised to *help* me!'

He held her fast, his strong arms mocking her struggles to push him away.

'I promised to *show* you. I am showing you a tiny fragment of the power that is within you, if you will only stop suppressing it.' He forced a kiss onto her throat, then let his lips travel down towards her breasts. She groaned in unwilling desire as his mouth engulfed the pink muzzle of her nipple, biting and sucking her to a crescendo of need.

'Please, Anthony, please.' She hardly knew what she was begging from him, only that little by little, she was losing her mind. The pleasure was too brutal, too extreme, the sound of the crashing surf echoing the pounding of the blood in her veins. 'No, please . . .'

He let her go, his chest heaving as he panted for breath.

'Your flesh is sweeter than honey. Have you any idea how much I want you?'

A tear escaped from Maria's eye and trickled down her cheek, its salty stream mingling with the dry saltiness of her lips. Why could he not understand? Why would he not release her from this torment? Her words were a shuddering, sobbing cry of need.

'Anthony. Help me. Show me how to understand.'

He seized her by the wrist with such sudden violence that she gave a gasp of discomfort. And then he was running, running with her towards the ocean, his riding-boots sinking into the soft sand as they ran together into the sea.

The water was jarringly cold, splashing bare calves and thighs in an icy tide that made Maria's head spin. And still he dragged her further into the water, until the waves were crashing about her waist and she could hardly stand in the swirling foam.

'Open your eyes, Maria – the power is all around you! It is within you and it is everywhere . . . in the hunger I feel for you, and the hunger you feel for me.'

Anthony's dark hair was dripping water, his shirt soaking wet and plastered to his skin, and the dark circles of his nipples were clearly visible, puckered with cold and with desire. Foam-flecked water was swirling around the tops of his thighs, soaking his riding-breeches so that the fabric betrayed the slanting outline of his thickening penis. Maria could even make out the line of the stone ring that pierced his glans, its dark shape both menacing and inviting through the semi-transparent material.

His eyes were as wild as the sea; and as Maria gazed into them they seemed no longer a pure, plain grey, but a multicoloured, ever-changing kaleidoscope of greys and greens and blues, like the tumbling ocean they mirrored. Those eyes were the mirror and the wellspring of her desire, an ocean of sex in which she would willingly drown. Waves crashed around their bodies, but as they kissed a white-hot flame seemed to sear through them, making the ocean boil and bubble in the heat of their desire.

Maria fumbled at the fly-buttons of Anthony's riding-breeches, cursing the age it took her to release his member from the imprisoning fabric. At last it sprang into her hand, and she felt the power arcing between them, rising in her like sap, surging out of her like purest electricity.

And at last, she began to understand.

His fingers touched her hungrily, opening up the flower of her sex so that the cold water splashed up into the intimate heart of her, the saltiness stinging and arousing the delicate, rose-pink flesh of her vulva. She was slippery-wet and welcoming, and his fingertips slipped easily inside her, stretching and coaxing her flesh until her sweet sex-juices ran in rivulets over her petal-soft sex, coursing down her legs to join the ocean-swell whose cold, lascivious tongue lapped at the honeypot between her thighs.

The tip of his manhood nudged blindly against her pubis, seeking out the heart of her need; the black stone ring hard against the fragile softness of her outer pussy-lips. She slid her feet a little further apart on the yielding sand of the sea-bed, and he pressed his cock-tip between her thighs once again.

'Now, Anthony. Now.'

Like a well-greased piston he entered her, the engine of his desire hot and urgent as it drove between the lips of her hungry sex. Half-laughing, half-crying, Maria received him, her pelvis driving against his as he thrust deeper into her; the power of their lust filling the air with a crackling, burning energy. And slowly, their bodies locked together, they sank into the waters that surrounded them.

Rolling and tumbling with the waves that crashed

onto the beach, they abandoned themselves to the ocean shallows; their hunger as wild as the sea that swirled about them as they moved in synchronicity. Their bodies were now neither of the sea nor of the land, but coupled to form a creature of the margin between land and sea, earth and sky; a creature of pure energy, and pure power.

The lovers lay face to face on the sand as the cold waves bubbled and splashed over their bodies, oblivious to the cold or the sea-water washing over them as they coupled. Their only consciousness was of the urgent quest for more and greater pleasure.

Maria felt her whole body begin to shake as Pendorran's cock-ring sought out the spongy g-spot, high on the inside of her vagina, and drove hard against it, again and again. The need was mounting, the anticipation rippling through her, and she thrust against his prick with all her strength, willing the ecstasy to come and free her from the tyranny of pleasure.

And at last it came, the world turning to a spinning web of many-coloured light as Maria rolled on top of her lover and rode him the last few, delicious strokes to the summit of pure delight. It began with a burning warmth in her belly, a tingling that spread through her entire body until at last she heard him cry out in his joy and her vulva contracted in the first, breathtaking spasm of orgasm.

It seemed to last for ever, the pleasure tumbling and spinning and floating down from its peak to a residual warmth that went on and on and on. At last, drowsy and breathless, Maria rolled off Pendorran and he propped himself up on one elbow, icy ocean water washing around his still-clad body as he gazed down at her.

'You ask me to help you, Maria, and yet it is you who should be helping me.'

She searched his face, looking for more answers, but there were none.

'It is time for honesty,' continued Pendorran, running his fingers over Maria's body, flecked with sand and fronds of vivid green weed. 'Because now, Maria, I believe you are truly beginning to understand.'

The empty house waited patiently in the gathering dusk. Over the many long centuries, it had grown accustomed to waiting.

In the bluish twilight something moved. Something – or someone.

Charles Allardyce pushed open the gate nervously, but with firm resolve. There could be no question of going back. He had left reason far behind; thinking only caused pain and uncertainty, whilst blind instinct led him forward with a sense of purpose which astounded him. And it had brought him to Brackwater Hall.

He ignored the driveway which led to the front door of the Hall, and instead opted for the stone-flagged path, which skirted the old house, leading through the knot-garden, past the sunken lily-pond and towards the remnants of the kitchen garden, which was still overgrown with ground elder and bramble.

But he did not get as far as the kitchen garden. Just before he reached the archway to the rose-garden he turned his head to the left and noticed a small red door, set in the ancient stonework of the house. Odd, he was sure he would have noticed it if it had been there before; but that seemed not to matter somehow.

Without a moment's indecision he crossed to the door and took hold of the round bronze handle. It turned easily, and the door opened with a faint click. The warm, dancing light within seemed to call to him, and he smiled as he stepped inside.

It seemed almost as though the Hall was glad to see him.

# Chapter Thirteen

$P$atsy put two slices of white bread on the grill pan and slid it under the flame.

'Toast'll be ready in a few minutes,' she called.

Geraint did not reply, but a few seconds later he came into the kitchen and she felt his arms close round her, his bear's-paw hands cupping and squeezing her breasts. She tried craning her head back to look at him, but he caught the tender skin of her earlobe in his mouth and began licking and biting it.

'I see the parish council's goin' to let the developers build on the land behind the old church,' she observed, trying her best not to give in to Geraint's single-minded pursuit of her body. She was always giving in to him, and she felt annoyed with herself for not leading him more of a dance – like the one he was constantly leading her. 'Don't squeeze so hard – you're hurting.'

'Don't tease. I want you.' Geraint tried to slip his hand under the bottom of Patsy's summer blouse, but she wriggled out of his grasp.

'What the hell's got into you?' she demanded tetchily, stalking over to the pantry and taking out a jar of home-made gooseberry jam. 'You're wearing me out, honest you are.'

He followed her back to the stove, and watched her

flip the slices of toast over and slide them back under the grill.

'I told you – I want you.'

She turned to face him, her back up against the work surface.

'Again? That's three times already this mornin'.' Geraint had always been lusty, but his sudden single-mindedness made Patsy feel uneasy. It had been like this since he came back from his last shift at the Hall, and to Patsy it seemed as if his sexual desire wasn't a natural exuberance any more – instead there was some sort of burning, clawing need in him, an obsession that had somehow got inside Geraint's head and wouldn't let him go. And now the exorcism of that need had become an imperative rather than a pleasure, so he'd become like a hardened addict looking for his next fix.

'So they're rationin' it now, are they?' He stood uncomfortably close, so that she could hardly focus on his face. 'You're my woman, Patsy – I got rights.'

She laughed in his face.

'Rights? You ain't got no rights, Geraint Morgan. Why don't you try askin' your fancy-woman up at the Hall if you got rights over her!'

Her mocking anger only served to rekindle the flame of lust that was burning in Geraint's belly. Slow and deliberate as an automaton, he took hold of the neckline of Patsy's blouse, scrunching up the material in his fist.

'Get off, Geraint!' Patsy's eyes flashed a warning. 'And for Pete's sake go away, the toast's startin' to burn.' An acrid trickle of greyish smoke was filtering out from under the grill-hood. Patsy tried to turn away, but Geraint wasn't letting her go that easily. His hand clenched tighter, and suddenly he jerked it downwards, ripping the flimsy material and exposing the bulge of her full breasts, spilling over the top of her too-tight bra.

'You want it. Prick-tease. You want it, I know you do.'

Patsy's breathing quickened, her body beginning to be aroused in spite of herself. This was a new side to Geraint, one that she had scarcely glimpsed before. Despite her unease, despite the twinge of fear she felt when she caught the glance from those stony blue eyes, Patsy felt sexual hunger lapping like a warm tongue at the edges of her resolve. Behind her, the steady heat from the gas-stove warmed her back like a lover's embrace, and she felt her clothes sticking to her as beads of sweat formed on the overheated flesh.

'Don't you bet on it, Geraint Morgan. You think I'll do anythin' to have your dick in me, don't you? Well I hope you ain't holdin' your breath.'

Ignoring the black smoke now pouring out from under the grill, Geraint seized Patsy in his arms. His work shirt was grimy and smelly from the milking parlour at Lamorna Farm, but Patsy hardly noticed it. His arms were steel-hard with muscle, his whole body tensed against hers in one great spasm of desire.

'You want me. Tell me how much you want me.'

'No!'

He pushed her back against the work surface, his breath hot and sour on her cheek.

'So that's how you want to play it, is it? Let's *see* how much you want it.'

His work-roughened hand slid into the tight, white cotton cup of Patsy's bra, seized her left breast and lifted it out. The nipple was hard and pink and juicy as a rosebud, and he laughed at this betrayal of her true feelings. The second soft, white globe he pulled out with no pretence at gentleness, and his calloused fingers pinched the nipple into even greater hardness. She winced, and he pinched still harder. Instantly a hot trickle of scented juice ran out of her vulva, soaking the gusset of her panties with a telltale, fragrant wetness.

'No, don't.' Patsy knew her words would not deceive him. The hard, rubbery teat between his teeth was sufficient proof of her desire for him to continue. Warm wetness was spreading between her thighs, and her whole body was responding to the crude hunger of his caress. 'I don't want you to.'

Geraint released her nipple as suddenly and as brutally

275

as he had taken it into his mouth. He was panting slightly, and his eyes were narrow blue slits in his tanned face.

'Please,' whimpered Patsy; but she had quite forgotten what she was pleading for. Did she want him to stop, or was she really begging him to keep on doing it to her, taking more and wilder liberties with her helpless desire? 'Please, Geraint . . .'

'Bitch.' Oddly, the word was softly spoken; a low, urgent whisper that was almost a caress. Geraint took Patsy's breasts in his hands, gripping them tightly at their base so that the flesh bulged out into two perfect spheres, the nipples standing proud, blushing a deeper pink from the sudden rush of blood. His pelvis pressed hard against her belly, and for the first time she felt the full extent of his lust. His message was clear: he would allow no going back.

With his face pressed between the two globes of her breasts, Geraint began licking and biting her flesh. The sharp blond stubble on his chin scratched and abraded her like glasspaper, but she could no longer conceal her pleasure. Her moans of pretended protest were an instinctive cry of mingled fear and joy.

When he rolled her onto her belly, bending her forward over the worksurface so that the Formica-covered top almost cut her in two, she made no protest. She willingly allowed Geraint to unbutton her jeans and wrench them down to her knees, baring the tiny triangle of flowered cotton stretched across her backside. Geraint's fingers slid between her legs, exploring the wetness that had soaked right through her panties to the denim and moistened the tops of her thighs with a pale blue stain. And then his hands were on the sides of her panties and they were being pulled down, exposing the white full-moons of her buttocks, round and inviting.

She heard his zipper slide down, and guessed that he was going to take her from behind. The thought excited her, and she lay docile and still where he had positioned her, her bare breasts squashed against the cold, smooth surface and her clitoris tingling with its own, shameless need.

When Geraint's fingers touched her again, she felt surprise. They no longer felt calloused and dry, but seemed to be covered in something warm and oily, something that slipped and smoothed easily as it was rubbed into her skin. What was it? What could it be that was so warm and slippery, that slid so easily over her buttocks and into the deep, dusky crease between?

Geraint scooped up a second handful of butter from the dish. In the summer sunlight it had grown warm and oily, soft but not quite liquid – exactly right for what he had in mind. Without any pretence at gentleness he spread his lover's buttocks, and was delighted to feel her thrusting backwards at his touch, opening herself more fully to his will. His heart was pounding now, his hunger gnawing and urgent.

Patsy felt the butter sliding between her buttocks like some exotic skin-cream, its warm runniness deliciously sensual as it trickled down from the base of her spine to the deep amber of her anal ring. But it was not until Geraint pressed the tip of his erect phallus against the entrance to her most secret intimacy that she realised what he intended to do.

'Please, Geraint,' she moaned. But again, she no longer knew what she was begging for. In the secret, shameless depths of her heart she knew that what she really longed for was for him to show her no mercy, to thrust into her like the wild, unthinking beast he had become. That alone would bring her the raw, rough pleasure she truly craved.

The smooth, purple head of his penis nudged against her puckered sphincter a second time and she recoiled from the touch, suddenly afraid of this most intimate of caresses. But Geraint held her fast and thrust a third time. This time he entered her in a single stroke, his dick sliding with well-greased ease into the sweet kiss of Patsy's tight-lipped nether mouth. And Patsy Polgarrow shivered with the fear of her own hunger, its strength suddenly more immense and more terrible than she could ever have imagined.

Black smoke curled around them as they coupled, the charred toast forgotten and unnoticed under the grill, its last remnants carbonising in a low orange flame.

As Geraint took his pleasure, he dreamed of other, more savage pleasures to come. Soon, he would lead Patsy up to the Hall, taking her a dozen different ways whilst the sun moved slowly towards the western horizon and Brackwater Hall waited, watched.

And lusted.

It was morning and Maria was once again sitting at Anthony Pendorran's table, hearing that sonorous voice. Even after a night away from the Hall she felt shaken and confused by all that had happened to her; and this time, she had made up her mind to listen to whatever Pendorran had to say. But the 'truths' he insisted on telling her stretched even her ability to believe.

She set down her glass on the bare, age-smoothed oak of the long dining table. Her voice was steady, but her eyes betrayed her incredulity.

'You are telling me that my house is a temple?'

Pendorran sat back in the old carved chair. With his elegant ringed hands placed neatly one on either arm, he looked like some ancient enthroned British king. Everything about him was calm, authoritative, almost impassive; with that unruffable quality that both irritated and excited Maria.

'Brackwater Hall has existed – in one form or another – since before the dawn of recorded history. But in all its many incarnations, the Hall has been a most sacred temple dedicated to the Goddess. And of course in each age, the temple must have its priestess.' He paused, as though uncertain whether or not to continue, perhaps weighing up Maria's likely reaction. 'In this present age, Maria, you are that priestess.'

Maria felt the blood drain from her face, and when she looked down at her hand, its fingers wrapped around the stem of the crystal glass, it was trembling, making the foot of the glass dance on the polished wood. Something inside her had long since anticipated Pendorran's words, and now she was struggling against acceptance with all her might. She fought to regain control.

'You're joking of course.'

'Believe me, Maria, I wish I were. The burden which my words are placing upon you is an intolerable one, I know that. But that does not alter the facts – that you are the priestess, the Mistress, the Queen; and that you and you alone can save Lynmoor.'

Maria put her hands to her throbbing temples, as though trying to reach inside her head and pluck out the unwelcome thoughts that were tormenting her.

'Explain this to me properly, Anthony; you owe me that at least. I'm not really taking any of this in. You have to realise ... this isn't an easy thing for me to accept.'

Pendorran got up from his chair and walked over to the window, his long, black-clad limbs moving with an easy grace that, even in her confusion, Maria found herself admiring. Shifting patterns of sunlight were reflected into the room from the sea, picking out his strong, aristocratic profile, and the sheen of glossy black leather, tight about his long, slim thighs.

'Since time immemorial, there has been a Priestess at Brackwater Hall. The Hall – the Goddess's own temple – has provided a vital link of communication between the Goddess and her Priestess, a channel through which her will may be expressed and fulfilled. As long as this sacrament of wholeness continued, Lynmoor had nothing to fear; through the sensual joining with Temple and Priestess, the Goddess's protection was assured over all things.

'Some years ago, Maria, Clara Megawne came to Brackwater Hall as its new Mistress, the heir to its hereditary priesthood. But Clara was not of the faith, she was not even a native of Lynmoor. She had no understanding of what lay ahead of her, and the power that was within and around her proved much too great for her. Over the centuries, the Hall itself had developed and nurtured a power; a lawless, selfish power which required great strength to control it – the strength of the enduring link between Goddess, Temple and Priestess. But Clara Megawne was too weak, Maria. She could not but fail in her duty.'

Pendorran turned and looked directly at Maria.

'Clara Megawne went quietly insane.'

Maria drained her glass, filled with the sudden conviction that she needed something much stronger than orange juice to help her cope with all this; something to warm her chilled blood.

'My . . . my aunt went mad? Are you trying to tell me she was driven mad by a *house*?'

'Of course, strictly she was not your aunt. She was, as I understand it, a quite distant cousin – but yes; she lost her mind. In time the power of the Hall overwhelmed her, and as she lost contact with reality, so the sacred link with the Goddess was weakened and fragmented. Without that link, the Goddess's power within Brackwater Tor began to decline, and her protection over Lynmoor was lost. At which point, as you will no doubt have surmised, CA Developments started taking an unhealthy interest in the area.'

'So . . . so you're telling me that the Hall has a power of its own? A power separate from the power of the Goddess?'

'Certainly it does. It has grown wily and resourceful in the long centuries of its existence, and it has absorbed great strength from the sexual energies of those who have lived at the Hall. Unfortunately,' Pendorran turned to face her, one side of his face picked out by the sunlight and the other in shadow, 'the will of the Goddess and the will of her Temple are no longer in harmony. You have been brought here, Maria, to ensure that the link is restored, the power brought back to its natural wholeness.'

Pendorran strode towards her across the bare stone

floor, and perched himself on the edge of the table, looking down at her with those intense, grey eyes. The eyes of some beautiful bird of prey.

'Do you understand Maria? Do you understand the power that is within *you*? The sensuality that flows out of you like energy from a white-hot sun?' He took her hand, as though willing his own understanding to flow into her through his slender fingers.

'I think I understand that there is something ... a force. Or at least ...'

'Then understand this, Maria: that you can make things happen just by *wanting* them to happen.'

'No. Surely not ...'

'Surely. As surely as the sun rises; as surely as Charles Allardyce and his minions will destroy this place, and me and you together, if you do not oppose him with all your strength.'

Maria's confusion deepened. What was happening to her? Would she wake up in her rooms at St Alcuin's, and realise that the whole thing had been a bizarre dream? Or had she walked into the middle of a living, breathing nightmare? She pinched herself, and the pain was real. There would be no waking up.

Maria met Pendorran's gaze.

'What must I do?'

'You must restore the oneness of the Goddess's power. You must challenge and overcome the will of the Temple. Because I very much fear, Maria, that Brackwater Hall may have developed an appetite for destruction.'

'I still don't see,' began Maria, withdrawing her hand from Anthony's. 'I still don't see how I can do these things. I understand the basics of magical ritual, I understand about the power of the Goddess; but how can I make something happen just by wanting it? That's something that I really can't believe.'

Anthony's face tensed, a dark shadow passing over his bright grey eyes.

'You have to believe it, Maria. If you don't believe it, Lynmoor will die.'

'I'm trying, Anthony. Truly I am, but . . .'

Anthony thumped the table with his fist, and Maria's glass overturned, the last remaining drops of orange-juice spattering the table-top.

'No buts, Maria. If you will not believe, you know that I cannot make you. But this afternoon you shall come with me to the moors beyond Hilltop Tor. I have something that I must show you. If I cannot convince you, perhaps the evidence of your own eyes will.'

Time had passed. Allardyce knew that time must have passed, but he had long ceased to understand the measure of it. Minutes, hours, perhaps even days . . . how long? Here, in the warm red belly of Brackwater Hall, time had no meaning. The only thing that mattered was pleasure.

The woman with the soft, red-blonde hair smiled at him from the landing at the top of the winding staircase, her body lithe and tempting in a long white gown that clung to her curves and moved with her as she walked.

'Grace?'

She did not speak, but beckoned to him, her eyes bright with mirth and her lips pouting a welcome. And then she turned away from him, climbing further up the stairs until all he could see were her little white feet, and the hem of the swishing white gown.

'Wait for me. Grace, don't go.'

It mattered not at all that none of this made sense; that he had entered the Hall through a door that wasn't there, and that he was now being greeted by one of his own employees – a woman who had disappeared off the face of the earth, weeks ago.

He had always desired her, always craved the touch of those full red lips; but Grace Harmer had made it abundantly clear that she wasn't interested in him. And now she was here and she was warm and inviting, the sleek curves of her body calling to him like a seductive whisper that drew him on up the staircase, into the red luminescence that surrounded her.

Gripping the wrought-iron balustrade he followed her, his body tense with expectation, his mouth dry with excitement. Before him Grace's form moved slowly and silently, save for the soft swish of her white robe as it moved in a liquid swirl about her feet. She did not turn round, but he sensed that she knew he was following her. Her long back moved sinuously under the thin fabric, her wide, firm hips swaying smoothly as she climbed the stairs in front of him. His eyes followed her greedily, his head growing dizzy as the staircase wound round and round inside the grey stone turret.

At the top of the stairs she paused and half-turned, glancing at him over her shoulder so that he saw her large, lustrous eyes, dark and velvety in the whiteness of her face. He could not see her lips but he knew that she was smiling. Smiling just for him.

She waited for him and he joined her on the landing. Before them stood a door. The dark wood was polished and gleaming and there, in the very centre, was a plain brass ring. Grace's hand turned the ring and the door opened, swinging away from them with a creak of ancient hinges.

Beyond lay a windowless room furnished in a sumptuous modern style which surprised Allardyce. Somehow he had expected something more archaic, more antique. The walls were papered in a Liberty print of flowers and grapes, the pattern echoed in the purple and green and orange of the Chesterfield sofa and the deep-pile carpet. On a low marble table stood a lamp in the shape of a globe, its soft white light mellowing the darkness, lightening the shadows.

No words were exchanged between them, but it was as though he could see her thoughts, forming word-patterns in his head:

*Come. Pleasure awaits.*

As she stepped through the door, an amazing transformation took place. As Allardyce looked on, Grace's white robes seemed to melt away and were replaced by the same chic outfit she had been wearing on the last day he saw her, the day of the briefing at CA Developments' London HQ.

He remembered how much he had wanted her then; and how she had scorned his advances. How much more beautiful and radiant she looked here and now: her collar-length red-blonde hair falling in soft waves around her face, her breasts pert and mobile beneath her smart green suit. He looked into the depths of her dark eyes and felt the vibrations of her thoughts.

*Touch. You want to touch. Do you dare?*

He dared. His fingers stretched out, meeting hers with a jolt of electricity that set his mind reeling. And then he was holding her against him, kissing her, feeling the ripe swell of her buttocks beneath the tight sage crêpe de Chine. Would she let him? Would she let him go further, let him touch the flesh beneath? He sensed instinctively that she would, that all that he dared would be permitted. And his fingers slid down towards the hem of her tight skirt, sliding it up so that he made contact with the margin of bare thigh between her stocking-top and her panties.

He burned for her, yearned to lower her onto the sofa and have her right there, not even stopping to slide her panties down over her slim tanned thighs. He'd waited so long for this moment; why should he let it pass?

Her eyes gazed into his, in no way cowed by the ferocity of his desire. They seemed to lure him on to greater audacities, daring him to turn his dreams into reality. And here, in this warm, irresistible dream-world, it seemed that all things could be made possible.

Allardyce's fingers travelled upwards, searching out the heart of Grace's sex, the secret land where he had for so long yearned to travel. His fingertips met the slipperiness of moist satin, and he gave a groan of triumphant lust, the object of his quest so close, so tantalisingly close.

To his chagrin, Grace pulled away, greeting his look of pained surprise with a sultry smile which melted his disappointment, adding fuel to his already all-consuming lust.

*Come. I have other things to show you. Don't be afraid.*

Afraid? Allardyce was anything but afraid. He was hot, hungry, ravenous as a starving wolf for the sweetness of her sex. Willingly he followed her towards a door in the far wall of the room and in his eagerness preceded her through it into a second chamber.

This was much the same in shape as the first, but instead of being decorated in a modern style, it was furnished with the dark wood and picturesque clutter of a Victorian drawing-room. A fire burned in the hearth beneath an ornate mahogany fireplace, above which a huge arched mirror hung, its vast smooth surface reflecting the light from three hissing gas-lamps. The walls were lined with bookshelves filled with leather-bound volumes, and on the circular polished table stood a collection of Indian brass and ivory ornaments.

Turning questioningly to Grace, he saw that a second transformation had taken place. Her red-blonde hair seemed much longer, and was piled into a loose knot on top of her head, whilst her slender form was dressed in a full-skirted, tight-waisted gown of pale blue muslin, her shoulders bare and a pendant of carved jet swinging between the small, ripe hillocks of her breasts.

*All things to all men, Charles. All things to you.*

If anything, Grace was even more ravishingly desirable in her coquettish Victorian ballgown, and he gathered her up into his arms, an urgency of need swelling his manhood to a painful hardness. The crackle and rustle of crisp white petticoats thrilled him with a joy that was almost the joy of violation, the sweet rage of defiling a pure, helpless, innocent creature – a joy that Charles Allardyce knew very well indeed.

There was such a contrast of softness and strength within her; her soft, almost fragile body imprisoned in the hard outer casing of her whaleboned stays. How he longed for a knife to slit her stay-laces and release those juicy, bobbing breasts into the welcoming haven of his mouth.

She sank back onto the polished table, and a few of

the ornaments slid across the surface, falling almost soundlessly onto the intricately-woven Afghan carpet. He was on top of her in an instant, lifting up her petti-coats to discover the knee-length, lace-trimmed panta-loons beneath; and oh, the blissful discovery of the long split between pubis and arse, so that when she spread her thighs she displayed the red-blonde fringe of her plump sex-lips.

Her pussy-lips parted and he smelled her; the musky scent filling his nose, his head, his whole being, until sex was the only thought, the only imperative within him. Her wetness was dribbling out of her, more abundant than any other woman's. He wanted to feel it, taste it, savour its warmth as her sex-lips closed about him in that most intimate of kisses.

'Grace. Grace, for pity's sake. I must have you.'

*Here, you have only to take. Take whatever you dream of. The dream will never disappoint you.*

He opened his pants and felt for the long, hot stalk of his phallus. Curved as a sabre, it sought out its target with an instinctive ease, sliding smoothly between Grace's sex-lips. Clutching at his hips to pull him further into her, she arched her back. As her mouth opened in a silent cry of pleasure, he saw the pinkness of her tongue, and the whiteness of her little sharp teeth.

They moved together smoothly, Grace's thighs wrap-ped round his hips so that he was as much a prisoner of her lust as she was of his. And he had never wanted to escape less in his entire life. He welcomed her hungry pelvic thrusts, closing his eyes tightly, the better to sa-vour the delicious feeling of her silky vulva caressing his penis. It felt as though his whole body was being stroked, caressed, teased to the point of no return and then far, far beyond.

Desire was simmering, bubbling, boiling inside him; the tip of his sex tingling and burning as he made the final few thrusts that would bring him to the peak of ecstasy. Already he could feel her muscles clenching around him as she abandoned herself to the pleasure.

And at last he reached the dazzling summit and let go, falling and tumbling through space like a snowflake melting in the sun.

In the dizzy, dancing dream of his ecstasy, he was scarcely aware that Grace was getting down from the table, leading him towards another door, another room . . .

Opening his eyes, he saw a very different room from the first two. The walls were of rough, irregularly-shaped stones, and the air smelt of smoke and a sweet, musky dampness. Burning torches made from bundles of sticks hung on the walls, the flames casting weird shadows as they flickered and flared. On the floor lay a scattering of reeds, and the only furniture: a table and rough stool. On the opposite wall, however, hung a tapestry of exquisite beauty; depicting the naked figure of a man surrounded by many beautiful women, their flesh white against the green of the forest floor as they danced for his pleasure.

By his side stood Grace, her tall, slender frame more irresistible than ever in her black gown, covered with intricate embroideries in gold thread. Cut low at the neck, it bared a creamy swell of neck and bosom, and at her throat she wore a band of purest gold. Her red-blonde hair seemed even longer now, and more luxuriant; and it was hanging down her back in a single braid, wound in and out with black and gold ribbon.

Allardyce felt dizzy and disorientated. But the desire was stronger in him than he could ever remember. Grace was pressing her red lips together in a coy pout, her dark eyes urging him on, her fingers fluttering with butterfly softness as they touched his face, his torso, the sap-filled bough of his cock.

Slowly she turned away from him, swinging the long red-gold plait over her shoulder so that he could see the whole long sweep of her slender back. The dress was held together with a lacing of gold thread, stretching from neck to backside. It would be so easy, so delicious, to unfasten those laces, and touch the bare skin beneath . . .

He turned his head and saw the knife gleaming on the table. Its blade of beaten iron was pitted with rust, but its edge was wickedly sharp.

*Anything you want, Charles. Anything. For you.*

He seized the knife, testing its sharpness with his fingers, then slid the point of the blade under the laces running down the back of the gown. They gave way without the slightest difficulty, and with a savage joy Allardyce slit them from bottom to top, watching with a raw ache of hunger as the heavy fabric of the gown peeled away, baring Grace's pure white skin and the tiniest rose-tattoo on her right shoulder-blade.

The dress slipped from her shoulders with consummate ease, its own heaviness pulling it to the ground and displaying the nakedness beneath. A low growl escaped from Allardyce's lips and he spun her round, pressing her to him, covering her neck and breasts with kisses as his cock-tip sought out the entrance to her womanhood.

*There are other ways. If you let me, I'll show you.*

He did not resist. By now, he was beginning to understand. Grace was his guide in the pathways of this new and sensual world of delicious fantasy. She would lead him unerringly towards pleasure. She took his hand and drew him towards the tapestry, leaning her back against it; and then, to his astonishment, lifted her leg with the supple agility of a ballerina, resting her bare foot on his shoulder. Her eyes were smiling into his, the message clear:

*Take me. Take me now.*

He needed no second bidding, entering her with a smooth thrust that left him gasping. And as they made long, smooth, slow love, Grace began to whisper secrets in his ear.

'You recognise it, of course.'

Anthony Pendorran looked towards the long lines of trees, his hands thrust into the pockets of his black jeans, his dark hair ruffled slightly by the afternoon breeze.

Maria looked about her. She was standing in the middle of two parallel avenues of hawthorn trees. Ahead of her, the trees were bisected by two further parallel groves, forming the shape of a cross. And surrounding the point where the four avenues of trees met was a wide circle of thorn-bushes. Yes, she recognised it, though she had never encountered anything quite like it in her own form of paganism. She nodded.

'It's a Celtic cross.'

'Meaning.'

'Meaning that this used to be a pagan place of worship – a pagan church, if you like.' She looked up at the trees; some were stunted, and many were withering. 'It's seen better days, though.'

Anthony came to stand beside her. His head bowed in reverence, he laid a sprig of mistletoe on the ground.

'This is still a place of worship, Maria,' he said, his voice very still, very quiet. 'But you are right to see the change and decay that has been wrought here. In years gone by, this was no mere church; it was a cathedral of trees, a most sacred place. But Clara Megawne's hold on her power was too weak; she could not maintain the link between Goddess and Temple which had safeguarded Lynmoor for so long.'

He cast a long, slow gaze around the groves of trees, their dried-up leaves shaking in the breeze with a sound uncomfortably like a death-rattle. Sorrow and anger filled his heart.

'It is only in the last few days that this has begun to happen,' he said, stroking the withering branch of an ancient hawthorn. 'But it is a beginning, and if it is not halted the process will continue until nothing, *nothing* is left. Lynmoor is slowly dying, Maria. Only one person can save it, save us all. And that is you.'

There was a flame of pain and rage behind those grey eyes, and Maria backed away in alarm.

'Don't run away from me, Maria. Listen!'

'Anthony, I'm trying to listen. I'm trying to believe. Give me time.'

'There is no time left.'

'This power. This power I'm supposed to have.'

'It is yours. Yours alone.'

'But Anthony, surely someone, someone else . . .'

'No one but you.'

She turned away, and as she did she stumbled. Reaching out to stop herself from falling, she caught the dried-up branch of a withered tree, and used it to lever herself upright.

When Pendorran spoke again, his voice was quietly triumphant.

'Now do you believe me, Maria?'

She followed his gaze to her hand, still grasping the branch of the tree, and saw that even as she watched, something wonderful and unbelievable was happening. Where dead leaves had hung, lifeless and dry, succulent green buds were springing, uncurling, their leaves unfolding into vibrant colour in the deep yellow of the afternoon sunshine.

Maria stood and stared, hardly daring to take her hand away. And when she did, the miracle did not stop. The leaves were still there, still uncurling, still awakening to life in the midst of this desert of death and decay.

'I did that?'

'You don't need me to answer that. I've told you before, you don't need me for anything.'

'No. No, that's not true.' She took halting steps towards Pendorran and put her arms round his neck. Her kiss was a shivering, quivering breath on his cheek, her lips still chilled with fear. 'I need you more than ever I knew. Now I'm beginning to understand, but only beginning.'

His hands smoothed the long waves of her hair as she pressed against him, hungry for the warmth and the certainty of his embrace. How could he tell her that he could offer her no assurances, save the assurance of mortal danger? He answered her kiss with an unaccustomed gentleness, no longer angry with her for her reluctance to believe. How could he blame her for not wanting the burden he had placed upon her? His own burden was heavy enough to bear.

Passion began as a subtle warmth in Maria's belly, then spread to a sultry heat that flooded through her whole body, awakening the purest, the warmest of lusts. Her fingers plucked urgently at the buttons of Pendorran's shirt, clumsy and fumbling in their need to touch flesh. And he helped her to her goal, unbuttoning his shirt and throwing it to the ground. His belt-buckle yielded with a flash of the raven's crystal eye. Maria unzipped his jeans, and cried out with pleasure as she peeled them down over his hips to reveal the upraised tribute of his hunger-stiffened phallus.

Maria remembered that first time, in the stone circle behind Brackwater Hall, where Pendorran had found her naked and they had performed the ritual together. And now the roles were reversed, and here he was, naked and vulnerable as she had been, his body and his desire her playthings ... if she wanted it so. But Maria wanted only the pleasure of his touch, the ecstasy of their coupling.

'Undress me,' she breathed, her voice a hoarse whisper of need. 'I want to feel your hands on me again.'

The oversized shirt and jeans she had borrowed from Pendorran slipped off easily, and she was naked underneath. Now, at last, they were equals.

His hands gripped hers and he knelt on the ground, pulling her slowly down until she was facing him, face to face, breast to breast. And he took her face in his hands, and kissed her with a tenderness that sent shockwaves of longing through Maria's body.

'Are you ready for the sacrament of joining?'

She did not reply at once, but ran her fingers down his body, savouring the firmness of his torso; skimming the flesh of his belly and letting her hand slide between his parted thighs, to cup the sublime heaviness of his balls. There seemed no need for words, but she smiled and nodded.

'I am ready.'

Pendorran released himself from her embrace and lay down on the ground, his cock pointing heavenward as though forming a spire for the cathedral in which he lay; the silvery-black of the cock-ring glinting at its very apex.

'And I am ready for you, Mistress.'

Maria needed no prompting. She was already wet for him, and as she straddled his slim, tanned thighs, her sex-lips parted instinctively, welcoming the intrusion of this beautiful invader. It took all her self-control to hold herself over him. She allowed the very tip of his phallus to touch the sensitive flesh of her vulva, but would not yet admit him to the inner sanctum of her womanhood. She savoured the moment; feeling how good it was to have the sun on her back and the beautiful body of Anthony Pendorran clasped tight between her thighs. A long, slow trickle of clear fluid emerged from her vulva, anointing Pendorran's cock-tip with the sweetest, the gentlest of kisses.

But the moment could not last for ever. With a sigh of satisfied desire, she sank down onto the impaling spike, letting it run her through in a single deft stroke. The thick, curving shaft of Pendorran's penis stretched her to capacity, sliding further and further in until the glans was driving against her hidden pleasure spot. It felt like heaven. And still he was not all inside her, not quite. She bore down harder, and the last centimetre of flesh disappeared between her love-lips, the delicious pressure bordering on pain as she began flexing her knees and hips, releasing him a few inches, only to swallow him up again and again.

As they moved slowly together, their bodies fused into a single, ecstatic whole. Maria was too lost in desire to notice the miracle happening around them: the riot of flowers budding in the greening grass; the red and white blossom on the hawthorn boughs; the blaze of sunlight in the perfect summer sky as lark and curlew and lapwing melded in a harmony of birdsong.

But Anthony knew. He had always known. And when

pleasure had faded and reality laid its cold hand on their shoulders once again, Maria would have to believe.

Because now, she had no choice.

Two bright blue butterflies danced across the knot-garden, delirious with sunlight and fragrance on this, the most perfect July day that Lynmoor could remember.

Brackwater Hall seemed quite alone today; the gardens deserted, no tell-tale movement behind the brocade-curtained windows to indicate that anyone was at home.

When the front door opened, the muted click sounded across the gardens like a rifle-shot, as though even the Hall itself was surprised to learn that it had had a visitor.

Charles Allardyce stepped out onto the front steps, closing the door behind him with a decisive thud. How long had he been inside the Hall – a day, two days, three? He could not remember and he no longer cared. He was calm, relaxed, in control; and his broad smile revealed a flash of perfect white teeth.

But his eyes glittered with a strange and secret light; and thoughts were tumbling pell-mell in his head. His new idea was his best yet. He really didn't know why he hadn't thought of it before.

# Chapter Fourteen

*T*he lipstick was a deep, shameless crimson, and Kirin ran the tip of it over and over her lips as though it were the tip of a glossy red dick which she was teasing, before plunging it into the full, red O of her mouth.

She put it down on the bathroom shelf, picked up a tissue and closed her lips together onto the soft white paper, leaving the bright red imprint of a kiss. The first of many kisses . . .

Tonight was going to be a special night for Kirin Johanssen. Not only was she celebrating her appointment as a Fellow of St Alcuin's; she was also fêting the departure of the much-loathed Terry Kestelman. Not that she was immodest enough to suggest that she had been the sole reason for his sudden resignation, but once he had succeeded in getting her the Fellowship she didn't want him sniffing around her any more. Terry's boasts and vulgarities had made it so easy to get him thrown out of St Alcuin's, out of Cambridge, and right out of her life.

She glanced at the clock as she dressed. Only seven-thirty. There was plenty of time. But she wanted to be sure that when her new lover arrived, she made a *really* good impression on him. Of course, Jonathan didn't know he was her new lover, not yet; but it was just a matter of time. She'd seen the look in his eyes, the indiscreet swell of his long, thick penis beneath the loose drape of his cricket flannels. No doubt Jonathan Gresham thought he was about to seduce *her*. But Kirin Johanssen knew different.

Her dress was chic rather than overtly seductive, but Kirin did not make mistakes; her judgement in matters of the flesh, as in all things, was impeccable. The ice-blue dress was made of a soft, silky fabric which clung to her curves as she moved. The looseness of the wrap-over style was deceptively modest since every curve and hollow was thrown into relief by the thin, almost transparent material. The two sides of the dress crossed over between her breasts, the plunging V just low enough to hint and tantalise, but not sufficiently deep to be revealing.

Kirin admired herself in the full-length mirror on the back of the bathroom door. She looked cool as Alaska, hot as a sleeping volcano. How could Jonathan possibly resist her? And once she had hooked him with a hundred different, fleeting glimpses of her body, she would unveil the bounty beneath. He might think he was clever enough to get the better of her, but Kirin Johanssen was nobody's victim, nobody's one-night stand, taken, enjoyed and then forgotten.

The dress swirled around her legs as she walked downstairs to the living-room. She wouldn't normally dream of wearing stockings and suspenders, but on a night like this she would use all the weapons in her armoury. Besides, she liked the feel of a seven-denier whisper of nylon on her athletic legs, and the way cool currents of air caressed the bare inches of skin between stocking-top and panties.

As she moved, she felt another caress – something secret and shameless, pressing itself into the deep valley between her thighs. She flushed with excitement, knowing that this was her secret and hers alone. Jonathan would not share it until his sex was hers to command.

The pleasure was inescapable, a waking torment that

dared her to deny it. With each small movement, the butterfly massager rubbed against her pussy-lips, its ridged disc fixed between her thighs with tight, unyielding straps, so that she could not have escaped it, even if she had wanted to. And escape was the last thing on her mind. The pink plastic butterfly might look harmless enough, but its ridges and flexible spikes were utterly ruthless, tickling and tormenting the exposed head of her clitoris like a battalion of spiny tongues.

No matter what she did – twisting, turning, sitting, standing – the butterfly's very special kiss was still on her love-lips, caressing her in a thousand different ways, making her wetness well up in a sweet, cascading tribute. Few women, and fewer men had pleasured Kirin with such unfailing skill; she wondered with amusement if Jonathan Gresham would turn out to be as skilful as he clearly thought he was.

The doorbell rang, and she swept into the hall, her ice-blue skirts swishing, opening at the side to reveal a long, slim expanse of smooth white thigh, encased in pale seamed stockings that clung like a lover's hands. She glanced at herself in the mirror and saw glossy, crimson lips smiling under cool blue eyes, her long, straight hair white-gold as flax about her shoulders. She was ready for anything.

Outside on the landing stood Jonathan, holding a bunch of freesias and a bottle of champagne, wrapped in tissue paper. His smile switched on like a blaze of electric light.

'Hi, Kirin. Missed me?'

She leaned on the door frame, in no hurry to let him think she was desperate for him.

'Now, how could I possibly have missed you, Jon? I saw you this afternoon at the SCR meeting, remember?'

His smile dimmed a few watts, then flickered on again.

'I brought some Bollinger with me. Thought we could have a little drink together before we go for dinner.'

'Bollinger, huh? And it's ice-cold too.' She took the

bottle from him and stripped off the paper. 'But you know I only drink Krug.' She paused for a moment, letting him suffer, then stood back to let him pass. 'Still, you'd better come in.'

Jonathan preceded her down the hall and into the living room. Kirin scorned College rooms, but then she could afford to: Daddy was something big at the Embassy, and had never left his daughter short of money. The flat was tastefully furnished in a spare, Scandinavian style, all clean lines and bright, fresh pine with the odd touch here and there of expensive elegance: a Tiffany lamp, a Susie Cooper tea-set, a pair of alabaster figurines.

'Hmm. Nice place you've got here.' Without waiting for an invitation, Jonathan sat down on the blue and cream sofa-bed, his long legs crossed at the ankle and his hands clasped behind his head. Kirin looked at him approvingly, hoping he had not noticed the look of pure lust in her eyes as she took in the muscular, Greek-god beauty of his lithe young frame. 'When I finish college I'll get somewhere like this. And of course, there's the family pile up in Norfolk.'

'Drink?' Kirin unwound the little wire cage from the top of the champagne bottle. Jonathan nodded, a little smile turning up the corners of his perfect mouth.

'Thought you only drank Krug,' he observed.

'I'm prepared to make an exception,' replied Kirin. 'Just for you.' As she crouched with the bottle between her knees, she eased the cork slightly and felt it move under her fingers, the pressure building up like the passion in her belly. The warm plastic of the butterfly flattened itself over her parted pussy-lips and she felt the spikes rubbing, grating on her clitoris as her body tensed itself for the explosion.

The cork burst out of the bottle in a starburst of white foam, falling in creamy, fizzing gouts of wetness onto the eggshell-blue carpet. And Kirin found herself laughing, licking the delicious wetness from her fingers as though it were a lover's seed.

297

'Not bad,' she conceded, drawing her finger out between her crimson lips. 'For Bollinger.'

Filling two tulip glasses, she sat down – not next to Jonathan, as he had expected, but in the armchair opposite. As she did so she crossed her legs, and the silky fabric of her wrapover dress slid open, revealing one sleek knee and the creamy slope of her inner thigh. What it did not reveal made her giggle with secret pleasure, her other lover's caress firm and unyielding between her love-lips.

She raised her glass and drank deeply, aware of Jonathan's eyes following her every movement, watching the muscles of her throat contract as the chilled liquid slid down into her stomach.

'I hear Terry Kestelman's left Cambridge,' hazarded Jonathan, his eyes watchful and bright with longing as he sipped his champagne. Kirin could feel his need, and rejoiced in the waves of longing radiating out of him.

'So I believe,' she replied. 'But I wouldn't really know.'

'But I thought you and he . . .'

Kirin threw back her white-blonde head and shook with a laughter that made her small, pretty breasts bounce and quiver under her silky dress.

'Do you really think I'd look twice at that creep?' Her lips glistened in the light from the Tiffany lamp. 'I mean, he's hardly my type, is he?'

Jonathan leaned forward to pour himself a second glass of champagne from the bottle on the table.

'Ah, but who *is* your type?'

She looked at him. He was so full of certainty; so arrogantly sure that he was exactly what she wanted, and that all he had to do was get her drunk and buy her dinner, and she would let him put his cock inside her. He wanted her for his plaything, something tight and warm and welcoming; another conquest to boast about, another fantasy brought to life and relived again and again in his wet dreams. He wanted to use her, that much was obvious. He was hard already and fully expected this evening to go exactly as he had planned. Obviously Jonathan Gresham didn't quite understand that there could be two sides to these little games.

Kirin did not take her eyes from his face, but her fingers were working at the three little fabric bows that held her wrap-dress together. They yielded easily, silently, and Jonathan's eyes grew round as saucers as he watched the silky, slinky material slip away, the two sides of the dress parting to reveal the white lace and satin teddy beneath; long white suspenders stretching down over her thighs to the tops of her pale stockings.

She stood up, and the ice-blue dress floated off her skin like a cloud, sliding down over her arms and falling across the armchair. Jonathan gazed up at her, towering above him on her white stilettos, her small breasts squeezed into the teddy which hugged her athletic figure in the tightest of embraces.

'I thought we might skip dinner,' she said coolly, as if she were proposing a quiet night in front of the television. 'What do you say?'

Inside she was feeling anything but cool. The warm plastic ridges of the butterfly were wet with her secretions, the little spikes digging unforgivingly into the flesh of her vulva, tormenting the hard wet bud of her clitoris. But then Jonathan couldn't know that. All he could see was the confection of white satin and lace, the opaque gusset hiding the irresistible truth: that she didn't need a man to give her pleasure.

Jonathan gave a sigh of disbelief as Kirin straddled him, her long white thighs encasing his, her breasts within kissing distance of his hungry lips. He had expected dinner, a little moonlight, a little smooth seduction; but Kirin was offering him a very different meal – the feast of her flesh. The succulent flesh of a maneater.

Slowly Kirin slipped one thigh between Jonathan's, so that his thigh was between her legs. As she bore down on him the little pink butterfly that was her own precious secret ground more and more insistently against the fulcrum of her pleasure. She began moaning, very quietly, very rhythmically, as she brought herself towards the most brutal and the most satisfying of orgasms.

And all the time she never took her eyes from Jonathan's. He returned her gaze, not daring to look away. He was breathing heavily, moving his thigh slightly in time to her thrusts, his body instinctively understanding her needs. They had not even kissed, yet Kirin was taking her pleasure from him – using him to give her what she needed, the satisfaction of the climax that she saw as her right, and his humiliation.

He burned for her. He could not understand what was happening to her, but his cock throbbed and burned with a fierce energy. If his hard-muscled thigh could give her so much pleasure, how much more would she derive from the merciless thrust of his cock? He longed to touch himself, to take out his shaft and play with himself. His fingers moved towards the zipper of his pants.

'No. I forbid it.' Kirin's voice had a terrible, exquisite majesty. Her command could not and must not be disobeyed. And the knowledge of her power made Jonathan hotter for her than ever. He did not even question her, enchanted by the audacity of her lust.

She rode him as she would ride a steed, using him as the instrument of her physical satisfaction. Moving rhythmically back and forth on his thigh, feeling the hard plastic bite again and again into her soft flesh, she remembered all the times she had ridden her father's horses bareback and without panties, simply for the unrivalled sensation of warm, rough horsehair rubbing against the inner surface of her vulva.

In her mind she was galloping again over the English downlands, her thighs wide and the horse's bare back hot and scratchy between her parted sex-lips; her love-juices mingling with the horse's sweat as the pace quickened and the familiar fire flared up in her belly, making her sex-muscles tighten and her ecstasy judder out of her in a great, long cry of satisfaction.

Her expression betrayed no trace of her inner turmoil as pleasure flooded out of her and her love-lips opened and closed over the hard, pink shell of the butterfly massager. But Jonathan felt her come; he saw the skin of her breasts mottle pink and white as the climax shook her body and the love-juice trickled onto the tops of her thighs, moistening the thick cotton of his trouser-leg.

His eyes gazed deep into hers, his lips forming the silent question he dared not even breathe:

'Please?'

She would make him beg before the night was out; would make him cry out in a great, agonising scream of need. And then, maybe, but not before, she would let him take out his dick and press it between her thighs.

Kirin's fingers slipped between her thighs and released the hooks which held the white gusset taut across her pubis. The fabric sprang back and for the first time, Jonathan glimpsed his rival. She spread her thighs still wider, so that he could see the curious pink shield more clearly, the little straps that held it flat across her pussy-lips. Already its secret fingers were working her up into another frenzy of animal lust.

She smiled as she showed him how little she needed him. Smiled, not simply because she had Jonathan Gresham to satisfy her every need, but because she had won. Terry Kestelman had been banished and forgotten; the hated Treharne woman had lost her job and was hiding herself away in some unspeakable corner of nowhere; and now Kirin Johanssen, clever, flax-haired Kirin, was about to screw Maria's ex-lover until he begged for mercy.

It was all most satisfactory. Perhaps Maria Treharne would realise now that she should have been more careful whose thesis she rejected; and whose feelings she trampled upon.

Leon Duvitski didn't like the way things were turning out at all. Allardyce hadn't been himself since the day they'd gone up to see Maria Treharne at the Hall. Mind you, Duvitski had felt a bit wobbly himself. Even now he could still see that kitchen table dancing on the stone floor, that glass jug flying through the air and missing his head by inches. That was the sort of thing you laughed at when you saw it at the movies; but when it happened to you, it suddenly felt uncomfortably close to home.

But Charles didn't seem to have been frightened by the Hall. Quite the reverse. For the last couple of days he'd been walking round with a great big beatific smile on his face. Now, Allardyce's usual insincere smile was one thing – Duvitski was used to that. But this smile radiated a slimy sincerity, an evangelical fervour that made Duvitski's flesh creep. It was spookier than any dancing table.

And now all this talk of a 'bold new clean sweep'. It wasn't right. It wasn't like Allardyce in the least.

Duvitski surveyed the wreckage of what had been Allardyce's prized scale-model of the Lynmoor Development. First thing that morning, Allardyce had breezed in to the marketing suite, and ripped out all the models of the planned buildings: leisure dome, international conference centre, the exclusive shopping mall, the lot. The village, too: all those rows of picturesque stone cottages arranged so prettily along ancient winding cobbled streets – the very thing that gave Lynmoor its unique, and very marketable, character.

And what had Allardyce left in their place? Nothing but a great big grey, circular, lumpy thing which looked like a blow-up Stonehenge and formed a ring around Brackwater Tor, with the Hall at its very centre.

'This *is* a joke,' he'd said hopefully, staring aghast at the devastation.

'Joke? My dear Leon, I've never been more serious in my life, believe me.' Allardyce's smile had far too many teeth in it for Duvitski's liking. He shrank away slightly, uncomfortable in the presence of such overpowering fervour.

'But ... you can't *do* this. What about the backers? They'll never let this happen.'

'Leon.' Allardyce placed his hand on Duvitski's. It felt hot, almost feverish. Perhaps Charles was ill. 'It may have been their money to start with but it's mine now. It's my name on all the papers. I can do whatever I like.'

As Duvitski stood staring down at the new model, wondering what the hell was going on, Allardyce appeared in the doorway behind him.

'Ah, Leon. Admiring the new development I see. Beautiful, isn't it? I don't know why I didn't plan it that way in the first place.'

'Yes, but . . . what *is* it?'

'What do you mean "what is it?" It's my creation, Leon. No, it's *our* creation, that's what it is. Now get your coat and come with me. I'm taking you into the village for lunch.'

'I don't know, Charles. I've got a lot of work to catch up with,' Duvitski demurred.

'I said now, Duvitski.' Allardyce's voice darkened and Duvitski sensed that refusal was no longer an option. 'And I mean now. So get a move on. I want to get these new plans underway as soon as possible.'

Jak glanced towards Carolan's tepee, his face a scowling mask of resentment.

'Something the matter, Jak?'

Jennah laid the distaff across her knees, a lumpy string of off-white spun wool trailing down from the spindle. A handsome woman of around thirty, she had been a New Age traveller before the New Age had even begun. She had seen just about everything; and she had certainly seen Jak's moods blacken over the last couple of weeks.

Jak hunched his shoulders, his hands in the pockets of his battered combat trousers.

'Thinks he's bloody God, doesn't he?'

'Ah.' Jennah sat back against the side of the van, tucking a hank of her wispy brown hair behind her ear. Her long Indian silver earrings jingled as she slowly shook her head. 'Carolan again, is it?'

Jak lowered his voice. They weren't that far from the rest of the group, and you could never be sure who was listening – though, to judge from the sounds of music and laughter emanating from Carolan's tepee, his own attentions were fully occupied for the time being.

'How come he gets everything and we get nothing?'

'Got the girl again, has he?' Jenna picked absent-mindedly at a tuft of creamy-white fleece. When she first came to the camp on Hilltop Tor she had been one of Carolan's first disciples – one of his first concubines, too. But recently Carolan had had other, prettier and younger women to divert him and he had called less and less often on the services of his original followers. It didn't seem right somehow.

'It's not just that,' protested Jak, but it was. He couldn't stand the way Carolan took all the best of the women for himself. Any new followers – and there had been quite a few recently, what with the publicity over the Lynmoor Development – had to be initiated by Carolan personally. If Jak was lucky, he might just get Carolan's leavings. His lucky strike with the Treharne woman at the ceremony had just been a fluke, and if anything it had made things with Carolan even worse. The trouble was, their beloved leader just couldn't stand to see anyone else having any of the fun. 'It's just ... well, he treats me like dirt.'

'You and everyone else,' replied Jennah. She'd always liked Jak, though he was rough and ready and had none of Carolan's roguish Celtic charm. 'He bowled me over at first, really convinced me he could get things done, but now ... I suppose it's worn a bit thin.'

Jak stretched himself out on the ground beside Jennah. He'd had her a couple of times, but he'd been pretty much out of his head and she'd just been one of a string of Carolan's leftovers. But now he was beginning to see her in a new light.

'He's still trying to convince me I'm the reincarnation of some Celtic warrior,' he commented, pulling up a few blades of grass and rolling them between his fingers. He pulled an angry face that dissolved into a wry smile. 'He must think I'm a bloody moron. He's only doing it so as he can get me to stand around looking noble while he gets his end away with anyone he fancies.'

Jennah made a little chuckling sound in the back of her throat. She reached out her hand and stroked Jak's cheek.

'Poor Jak,' she murmured. Poor all of us, she told herself as she thought what would happen if Carolan failed to save this place from the developers and it disappeared under an impenetrable concrete tomb. And they would be moved on again, a sorry caravan of broken-down old vans winding its way through the countryside in search of another temporary home, another place to live life the way they wanted to.

'Do you think he really cares any more?' said Jak suddenly, his eyes flicking up to meet Jennah's.

She avoided his gaze as she answered.

'Yeah. Of course he does. He's our leader, isn't he? Whatever he says goes.'

'Yeah.'

They stayed like that, in thoughtful silence, for several minutes, Jennah's smooth hand stroking the spider tattoo on the side of Jak's neck. It was as though a simple truth had just flashed into their minds at the very same moment; a truth which neither of them particularly wanted to face up to.

In the beginning, Carolan had seemed indisputably genuine, a man with the fire of righteousness in his belly and a love of live in his heart. But at the ceremony, he had cavorted like a pantomime villain whilst Maria – the woman Carolan derided at every opportunity – had seemed like something very close to the real thing.

The question was: who was right?

Maria kept as near as she could to Pendorran as they walked down the hillside towards the village. She craved the security of knowing he was close by, his hand almost touching hers as they walked in step down the winding cobbled lane.

'*More* things to show me, Anthony?'

He ignored the gentle irony in her voice. Pendorran seemed very serious again, almost as distant as when she had first known him, and little crackles of irritation flashed through Maria from time to time. She wanted him, yes; but she wanted him to stop being unfathomable, to open up and let her see into his heart.

But then again . . . If she could see the wholeness that was Anthony Pendorran, could see into every patch of light and shadow in his heart, would the mystery be gone forever? Would she still desire him with the same unquenchable thirst?

He turned his grey eyes on her.

'Many things. There is a great deal for you to learn and understand, and very little time.'

He paused outside the empty, boarded-up shell of what had once been a pretty cottage.

'Here, Maria, was the cottage where the wise woman lived. Touch the stones that she touched. Feel what she felt.'

Maria laid her hand on the weathered stone, and instantly her mind filled with pictures: an old woman dressed in a long black dress and headscarf, picking herbs in a cottage garden filled with flowers that waved their heads in the sunshine. When she took her hand away, the pictures vanished, but her fingers tingled as though she had just had an electric shock.

'That . . . that was a picture of something that really happened?'

Pendorran's slender fingers traced the line of Maria's cheek.

'The past is in this place, sunk deep into stone and wood. And the past is in you too, Maria. You are as much a part of this place as the cottages and the cobbled streets.'

Walking on together, they passed the old chapel, now used as a storehouse for animal feed.

'Touch the walls, Maria.'

She obeyed, laying the flats of her hands against the

stones so that their warmth flowed into her and the pictures surrounded her again. She half-expected to see women in long dresses and poke bonnets, their heads modestly bowed as they filed into some Victorian Sunday service. But this time she did not see the chapel as it was, or as it had been; she saw instead a low structure of rough-hewn logs, and around it, the dancing, painted bodies of naked women, long necklaces of animal teeth swinging between their breasts.

She drew back, startled, and felt Pendorran's hand on her shoulder.

'Our discovery of the past is not always as we expect it to be,' he said quietly. 'Your power is such that you have the ability to tap into much deeper levels of history, past ages so long ago that they predate the village of Lynmoor itself.'

'They were ... worshippers of the ancient path?'

'The old ways have been practised in Lynmoor since the dawn of time. Come with me – I have more to show you.'

Maria followed him down the lane and into the bustle of the village high street, silent and deep in thought. Could Pendorran see and feel what she had seen and felt? And if so, what strange power lurked deep within him? Not for the first time, she had the uneasy feeling that Anthony Pendorran was by no means an ordinary man.

'You see, Maria,' continued Pendorran, 'I have to show you these things. It is vital that ...'

He froze in mid-sentence, and Maria followed his gaze to a familiar figure. There, standing outside the Rowan Tree Restaurant, was Charles Allardyce, a broad and rather fixed smile illuminating his face. Maria was so taken aback that she hardly noticed Leon Duvitski, standing a little way behind, as though a somewhat reluctant companion on Allardyce's expedition.

'Well, well, if it isn't sweet Maria. What a pleasure it is to see you again.' Allardyce's voice was smooth as double cream.

'Er ... Mr Allardyce.'

'Call me Charles. Please.'

'I'm in rather a hurry, Mr Allardyce.' She didn't like the slimy, ingratiating way he was smiling at her one little bit. It reminded her of something she couldn't quite recall. Something that frightened and ... no, it couldn't be. Something that attracted a deep, dark, shadowy part of her that she had no desire to acknowledge.

Maria turned to Pendorran for help but to her astonishment and annoyance he had gone; melted away into the lunchtime bustle as if he had never been there at all. She turned back to Allardyce, impatient to get away.

'Yes of course,' butted in Duvitski, his manner hurried and – to Maria's eyes – slightly agitated. 'We mustn't keep Miss Treharne from her business, Charles.'

'Business. Ah yes.' A light seemed to flicker on behind Allardyce's stony eyes. 'I'd like to talk business with you, Miss Treharne. Sweet Maria.'

Allardyce reached out and touched her but she drew away instantly, snatching her hand from the grasp of his hot, sweaty fingers. At his touch something had flashed into her mind, something scary, something with the teeth of a demon and the caress of an angel. Something dangerous.

'Some other time, perhaps,' she said, smartly side-stepping Allardyce's clumsy attempt at an embrace. Was he ill? Drunk? Half-mad? Judging by the look in Duvitski's eyes he wasn't very happy with his colleague's behaviour, either.

'I must apologise, Miss Treharne ...,' he began, a faint note of desperation in his voice.

'No apology is necessary, Mr Duvitski,' she replied curtly. 'But I really must be going.'

She pushed past Allardyce, deliberately ignoring his hungry eyes and the words he called after her as she hurried away down the street:

'I shall see you again soon, Maria. Very soon.'

Maria shook off the encounter with a businesslike determination, telling herself that this was just another of

Allardyce's ploys to get her to sell the Hall. His greasy charm hadn't worked the first time, and it certainly wasn't going to work now.

She wondered where Pendorran had got to. Typical, unfathomable, unreliable Pendorran – getting the hell out of it just when she needed him most. He'd looked rattled, though; really unsettled, in a way she'd never seen him before. She had seen his jaw muscles contract with tension, had almost felt the hairs standing up on the back of his neck.

The Glovers' health-food shop was the natural next stop on her excursion; after all, there might as well be some purpose to her visit. The doorbell jangled as she slipped into the shop, past a couple of villagers who – as usual – studiously ignored her. Obviously things hadn't changed. What did it take to get these people to realise that their whole way of life was under threat?

Emily Glover greeted her warmly.

'Well, Miss Treharne. We haven't seen you for ages. Been busy have you?'

'Sort of.' Maria set her basket down on the counter and surveyed the shelves. 'I'll have a jar of that heather honey, please; oh, and some more of that wonderful wholemeal bread.' She searched her purse for the right change. 'To be honest, I've been a bit of a fool.'

Ben Glover stopped bagging flour and looked up.

'How do you mean?'

'Oh, I let Carolan spin me a line. I went up to that so-called ritual at Hilltop Tor, a few nights back. It turned out to be a complete charade, of course. The man's nothing but a cheap con-merchant.'

She looked up, holding out the change, and saw Ben and Emily staring at her, their whole bodies stiff with indignation.

'I'll thank you not to talk like that in this shop,' said Emily, her voice very quiet and quavery. 'Carolan's a good man. He's done a lot for us.'

Ben laid his hand on his wife's shoulder.

'She's right, Miss Treharne. Without him, paganism would be dead in this place, dead and buried.'

'If you ask me, he's doing his best to kill it off,' retorted Maria, instantly regretting her inability to keep her big mouth shut. It was obvious that Ben and Emily didn't share her views – why antagonise them? But the truth was bubbling out of her, refusing to be suppressed. 'All he wants is sex – cheap sex and power. A man like that does nothing for pagans – just makes us a laughing stock.'

Emily's fingers were clutching the edge of the counter, her eyes filled with fury now.

'How dare you!' she snarled.

'I'm sorry,' said Maria. 'Truly I am. I didn't mean to upset you.'

'Then take back what you said.'

'I can't.' Maria held out her money, but Emily ignored it. 'I wish I could, but believe me, Carolan's just a liar and a cheat. He's trying to use me, you, all of us.'

'Get out.' Ben's anger escaped from him in an angry hiss.

'But I haven't paid for . . .'

He swung his fist at her, knocking the coins out of Maria's hand so that they fell to the floor with a clatter, rolling away across the bare wooden floorboards.

'We don't want your money. We don't want anything from people like you.'

'Carolan's a good man.' Emily was gripping her husband's sleeve, as though trying to hold him back, suppressing the sudden and inexplicable violence that was welling up inside him. But there was rage in her eyes too as she flashed a gaze of pure loathing at Maria. 'He may not have your education, and he may not have your airs and graces, but he's going to be the saviour of this place. Carolan's done a lot for Lynmoor, Miss Treharne. More than your sort will ever do.'

At the camp on Hilltop Tor, Megan Rothermeade was discovering a whole new world of duty and desire that she had never imagined in her wildest dreams. Her young body, its needs and pleasures neglected for so long, was gradually awakening to the fullness of sensation under Carolan's expert tutelage.

She had not thought it would be like this. In all honesty, she had not really thought about it very much at all. She was young, she was hungry for excitement; she needed something to rebel against, a cause to fight for so that she could find out who she really was. Running away from boarding school and joining the travellers' camp had been ambition enough, in the beginning. If she had ever tried to picture how life would be, she had perhaps imagined that she would spend her days helping her new friends in their protest campaign, performing heroic acts that would save these wild moors from desecration.

Certainly she hadn't pictured how it would be to become Carolan's special, personal slave. He had explained to her what a great honour it was, how in becoming his slave and concubine she was serving the will of the Mother-spirit. Although no longer a virgin she was pure in heart and sexually inexperienced; she would make a fitting consort for the man who was the very embodiment of the Earth-Mother's strength and will. Perhaps in time, he told her, she would bear him strong sons and daughters; giving him her fertility as a sacred offering.

There were some who whispered treason against their leader, but Megan knew better than to listen to them. With all the fervour of a zealot, she longed to be virginal again, so that she would bleed as Carolan wounded her with his lance of proud flesh, her maiden-blood drenching the barren earth and making it fertile and strong. And since that could not be, she would serve her new master in any way he demanded, giving him her young and tender flesh to be the vessel of his will.

All was darkness behind the blindfold: a thick strap of leather bound tightly over her eyes so that it shut out every last chink of daylight. Megan had lost track of how long she had been wearing it. It was tight and uncomfortable, the rough edges of the strap chafing the fragile skin of her cheeks and the bridge of her nose, but she knew she must not protest. This was a discipline, and she must abide it with patience, welcoming it as the next step in her schooling. When she had been fully broken to the will of her master, her mind and body trained to obey him without question or delay, she would cease to be Carolan's slave and would become his concubine. He had promised that it would be so.

How many long hours had she been sitting here, cross-legged and naked on the grass? Around her were the familiar sounds of camp-life – laughing, talking, the clatter of pots and pans – but it never came any nearer and no one ever touched or spoke to her. This was her ordeal, her test of strength, and she must bear it alone. She had lost all sense of time and place, did not even know where she was, except that she was outside and that at first the air had felt very cold and damp on her bare skin. Now it was warmer; she could feel a big patch of warmth, like the heat from a fire, on her back, and she sensed that they must have passed from night into the warmth of noon.

Megan shifted slightly on the hard grass, and the blood began flooding back into her numbed limbs, making them tingle painfully. Her bladder felt uncomfortably full, the urgency to pee increasing with every tiny movement. Oddly enough, the discomfort felt vaguely pleasurable; a feeling on the borders of pleasure and pain, which she wanted to stop right now and yet to go on for ever, giving her that distinctive, seductive throb between her swollen pussy-lips.

'Time for your next act of service, Megan.'

Although Megan could not see the woman's face, she recognised the voice as that of Ceridwen, the thin Welsh girl who, with Delma, had prepared her for the first night of initiation. Ceridwen was one of Carolan's favourite concubines and Megan could not suppress a pang of jealousy as she thought of the Welsh girl sharing Carolan's bed, taking his penis between her thighs, laughing as she brought him to pleasure. Why, Ceridwen wasn't even pretty. What had she got that Carolan found so desirable?

She allowed Ceridwen to help her to her feet. Her bladder felt even fuller now that she was standing.

'Please . . . I need to go to the toilet.'

Ceridwen laughed, her voice as high and musical as rushing water in a mountain stream.

'Bladder a bit full, is it? Want to pee, do you?'

Megan felt herself colouring up, her cheeks burning under the leather blindfold.

'Yes. Please could you take the blindfold off, so that I can . . ?'

She felt Ceridwen's palm tracing the swollen curve of her stomach, her fingers pressing hard on the bulge of her distended bladder so that she winced with discomfort.

'No, please!'

'This is all part of your discpline, Megan. You have to learn to control your desires – *all* of your desires. Do you understand?'

'I . . . yes. I suppose so.'

'Now come with me. Carolan is waiting for you to serve and entertain him.'

Ceridwen led Megan across the grass, her bare feet stumbling occasionally on the hard, stony ground. Her bladder shifted painfully in her lower belly with each step forward, and she felt sure that if she did not find release, she would disgrace herself.

'Please, Ceridwen. I really do need to . . .'

'No. I absolutely forbid it, do you understand?'

'I . . . yes.'

Megan realised that everything had gone very quiet, and that all she could hear was the sound of her own feet on the ground, and the swish of the wind in the stumpy, twisted trees that surrounded the summit of Hilltop Tor. It was as though the whole world was watching and waiting. Suddenly she felt very important, like she had felt on that first night, at the ritual of initiation.

'Your slave, Carolan.'

313

Carolan's voice was rich and syrupy, the Celtic lilt more pronounced as it always was when he was aroused. Already, in her short time at the encampment, Megan had learned to recognise Carolan's moods merely from the tone of his voice.

'And has she behaved herself.'

'Apart from some slight show of defiance.'

'I see. Tell me about this defiance.'

'She keeps asking me if she can empty her bladder.'

There was a long pause. Megan could hear the sound of her own heart thumping madly in her chest. Had she done something terrible? Had she made Carolan angry with her? The thought of his displeasure made her feel as tearful as the naïve schoolgirl she had been, not so very long ago.

'Well, I see no reason why she should not . . .'

Megan's heart soared. He wasn't angry with her after all.

'Thank you,' she gasped. 'May I take off the blindfold now?'

'No, Megan, you may not. This need of yours could be useful in getting rid of your inhibitions. Squat down and do it here for me, Megan. I want to see you pee.'

'What – here! No, no, I couldn't . . .' The blood surged in her veins, her mind in a turmoil. Surely he couldn't be asking her to do *that*, not here, where everyone could see her.

'Do you want to be my slave, Megan?'

'Yes of course, but . . .'

'Are you defying me?'

'No, of course not . . .'

'Then do as I say. Or would you rather leave the camp? No one will stop you. But once you leave here, you can never come back. Is that what you want?'

'No!'

That self-same, watchful silence was all around her. Her belly ached; her bladder yearned for release; her clitoris throbbed from the pressure and the sudden excitement of being here, naked, and robbed of all her most intimate secrets.

She squatted down on the ground, feet apart. She wanted desperately to let go, but it was so difficult. Some deep-seated inhibition was holding her back.

'I can't,' she sobbed. 'I just can't.'

Carolan's voice sounded husky when he next spoke.

'Help her, Ceridwen. Help her, Eden. *Make* her do it.'

To Megan's shame and astonishment, she felt hands – soft, feminine hands – begin to touch her all over. Hands on her breasts, stroking and exploring; hands on her belly, working their way down towards the parted lips of her bare sex. She tried to fight the desire, but instead of going away it got stronger, making her whole body throb with the pain and pleasure of her need.

'Relax, Megan.' Ceridwen's voice was soft and sweet, yet commanding. 'Relax and do exactly as you are told.' A warm, wet tongue ran down the crease between Megan's breasts, and lips fastened on her left nipple, sucking and teasing the flesh into a hard, puckered cone of pleasure. 'You know you want to.'

Fingers; soft, knowing fingers slid down over the stubbly, shaven triangle of Megan's pubis and dived into the hot, wet furrow between her pussy-lips. And all the time the lips were sucking and the tongue licking away her resistance. She began to moan softly, a low keening sound that signalled the torment of her distress and her desire. She couldn't; she couldn't let go of the last traces of her modesty, the last vestiges of the prim sixth-former she had been, a thousand years ago in another world.

'So that's the way you want it, is it?' Eden's voice was sly and smooth, and Megan felt fear; fear that Eden knew her body and its needs better than she did. And a moment later she knew that her fears had been well-founded, for Eden's fingers pressed hard on the swollen button of her clitoris, its fat round head bulging shamelessly out of its fleshy pink hood.

'Please, please,' she moaned. Her thighs ached from squatting, and her belly was throbbing in long spasms that threatened to overwhelm her. But she knew Eden and Ceridwen had no intention of stopping, and was no longer even sure that she wanted them to.

Eden's fingers made slow, circular movements around the head of Megan's clitoris, caressing her with a ruthless accuracy that brought her steadily towards the point of no return.

'No, no, no,' whimpered Megan, but her body was screaming yes! Make me do it, make me abandon myself to you utterly, make me wild and unashamed and a plaything of your will.

With a well-judged skill that made Megan scream with pleasure and shame, Eden pinched the head of her clitoris between finger and thumb. The orgasm was a shattering, juddering climax that made her head reel and her whole body go into a wrenching spasm. At the very moment of climax, she felt her sphincter relax, and a flood of warm wetness gushed out of her bladder, the ecstasy of release adding hugely to the pleasure of orgasm.

'Good girl.' Carolan's voice echoed through the haze of her need as her warm, golden rain fell onto the ground. He sounded mellow and satisfied, like he did when he had just had sex with her. 'Now, let's see what reward we can give you for your obedience.'

Megan waited in a delirium of triumph and shame, her world turned upside down by the abandonment of everything she had ever held onto. Now there was nothing to guide her – nothing but Carolan's voice and the power of Carolan's will.

'Onto your knees,' he ordered. His voice sounded closer, as though he had approached to get a better view of the proceedings.

Slowly and mechanically, she let herself sink down onto her knees, the ground damp, fragrant and cooling beneath her bare skin. Silent in the darkness behind her leather blindfold, she waited for Carolan's next command.

'Show her the beads,' he said. 'Let her touch them. I want her to know exactly what's happening to her.'

Something touched her hands and she reached out for it, a dangling, elusive heaviness that kept swinging away as she tried to catch it. At last she succeeded in getting hold of the thing and it fell into her palm. What could it possibly be? Her fingers explored it, her heart thumping with fear and desire of the unknown.

'It's your reward, Megan.'

'But what . . ?'

'You'll know soon enough. Touch it. Feel it.'

She ran her fingers along the length of the snaky, rubbery thing in her hand. It felt like a long, flexible string with five, no six smooth beads the size of large marbles strung along it at regular intervals. But what was it? What on earth could it be for?

Hands took it from her again before she had time to explore it further.

'Onto your hands and knees, Megan. It's time for you to have your reward.'

An inexpressible excitement coursed through Megan's body as she crouched on the ground, propping herself up on hands and knees, the hot sun raising beads of sweat on her back.

Soft hands touched her again, this time more firmly. They were pulling apart the cheeks of her backside. No, not that! She wriggled but the fingers were inexorable, their caresses too insistent to escape. Then something hard and cold and smooth touched the puckered mouth of her anus, making it contract instinctively against the would-be invader.

'Oh! Please . . .'

'Remember: you can submit, or you can leave this camp for ever,' said Carolan, his voice a seductive purr.

She submitted, tears sparkling behind the blindfold as she gave herself up to the wild, forbidden desires she had never even guessed existed within her until this moment. The cold, hard, smooth thing touched her again, only pressing harder; and this time she felt herself open up like the hungry mouth of a sea-anemone to swallow it up, the hard, round bead disappearing swiftly and smoothly into the tightness of her rectum. Another followed, the invader dilating her flesh as it entered, stretching the inner membrane as it slipped further up inside her, pushed by the momentum of the third bead, the fourth, and the fifth.

No more. She could take no more. It felt as though her whole body was filled up with the bead-string, her rectal muscles fighting to expel it and her clitoris throbbing a reluctant welcome. It was a sweet torment, a blissful agony she could hardly bear, and yet it racked her body with the most exquisite pleasure.

The sixth bead remained outside her body, teasing the flesh between her buttocks as it danced on the end of the long, flexible rubber string.

'I think she's ready,' announced Ceridwen. 'Just look at the way she's swallowed it all up – the horny little bitch.'

'Excellent.' Carolan's speech was less a word than a sigh – a long, slurred sigh of sexual excess.

A finger sneaked between Megan's thighs, sliding into the slippery wetness of her vulva and scooping some of the juice over the head of her burstingly-hard clitoris. Megan groaned with delight, unable to fight the overwhelming waves of pleasure that washed over her with each skilful stroke. Then something warm and fragrant brushed against her lips – something soft and fleshy, that carried the familiar spicy aroma of desire.

'I want you to eat it all up, Megan. Put out your tongue and taste.'

The questing tip of her tongue explored the warm softness, the springiness of wiry pubic hair that curled over the flesh of the juicy split peach beneath.

'Oh no, I can't. I can't.'

'Of course you can, Megan. You're my slave. You can do anything I tell you to do. And you will, won't you?'

The finger on her clitoris pressed harder, and she gave a yelp of discomfort as the too-sensitive flesh burned and throbbed, and the muscles of her rectum contracted around the string of beads that still distended her flesh.

The cruelty of the pleasure made tears spring once again to her eyes, moistening the underside of the leather blindfold.

She put out her tongue again, and tasted the tang of another woman's sex for the first time in her life. A large drop of a slippery liquid fell onto her tongue and she savoured its sweetness.

'More, Megan. Don't stop.'

A curious delight stole over her as she wriggled her tongue-tip deeper into the soft folds of the unseen woman's sex. The finger on her clitoris tormented her with a demonic skill, refusing either to release her from the captivity of her need for gratification, or to bring her quickly to the summit of pleasure. Realising that the only way to escape from her torment was through obedience, she lapped up the wetness. The taste was so like the taste of her own desire, and her tongue-tip quickly discovered a round, hard button of flesh that quivered at her touch.

'Good girl. Good, obedient slave. The Mother-spirit will be well-pleased.'

It was all like some crazy dream. Here, in the darkness, her senses were reduced to touch and taste, hearing and smell. But pictures whirled in her mind: wild, phantasmagorical pictures of naked women; of sex-lips that opened like the mouths of strange sea-creatures; of clitorises like long, wriggling tongues spangled with sweet, slow-dropping dew.

'Please, please. Carolan – I can't take any more.'

'You'll take anything I tell you to.'

The beads inside her belly felt hard as iron; they were shifting about, jiggling and sliding inside her rectum, making her whole body tremble and ache. Why did pleasure have to be so cruel? Why was he doing this to her? If she begged him, would he be gentle and soft with her again? In the tumult of her warring emotions, she forgot all that she had been taught about obedience.

'Please. I want it to stop.'

'You want to leave me already, Megan? Just when

319

your pussy's getting really hot for me and I'm teaching you all these wonderful new pleasure-games? I really can't believe that. You want me to throw you out? I'll never take you back if you go now, you know that.'

'No. No, that's not what I want. I want . . .' She hardly knew what any more. 'I want you. I want to please you. It's just that . . .'

'Then do it. Do it for me, Megan. I want to watch you doing it.'

Wetness flooded her tongue and her vulva; a river that seemed to begin at her tongue and flow right through her to the broad, fertile delta of her sex. She was that river, a rushing, surging expanse of liquid desire. And suddenly desire sparkled inside her head, like an explosion of white-water spray caught in sunlight. Rainbows burst and fragmented; pleasure shattering into tiny, jagged pieces of coloured light that fell with her through the warm air as pleasure took her in the first massive spasm of her orgasm.

It seemed to go on for ever, shaking and twisting her helpless body like a leaf caught in a waterfall. Hands were pulling the hard round beads out of her arse, slowly and deliberately, with a knowing skill that made the feeling go on and on and on . . .

'Yes, yes; oh, you sweet little bitch.'

Something warm and wet fell onto her skin, and she arched her back to receive the burning rain of Carolan's desire. Somewhere, very far away or so it seemed, she could hear him laughing, and crying out:

'The king of Lynmoor. That's what I am. The king of Lynmoor.'

She wanted to believe him, truly she did. Hadn't she accepted him as her master? But even in the sweet haze of her pleasure a tiny voice kept whispering its treason in her ear. Whispering that maybe, just maybe, Jennah and Jak might be right.

# Chapter Fifteen

*A* slight breeze flapped the curtains, and fingers of early-morning sunshine filtered in through the small-paned windows, filling the kitchen with a mellow golden light.

Little trickles of sweat ran down Patsy's bare back, the beads of moisture so heavy that they burst as she moved, covering her skin with a filmy sheen of moisture. Her breath came in short, rasping gasps, and her eyes were half-closed; her gaze unfocused and her pupils dilated by unspoken pleasure.

Geraint's strong hands were under her buttocks, holding her up as she tightened her thighs about his waist and levered herself up, savouring the silky-wet pleasure of their coupling as she sank back down, with luxurious slowness, onto her lover's erect phallus.

Her mouth opened in a smile, and she laughed silently, drunkenly, the laughter making the flesh of her ample breasts ripple and quiver like warm, pink jelly. Now she was beginning to understand why Geraint had kept going on and on about bringing her up here, to Brackwater Hall. She'd been reluctant, certain that they would run into *her*; and that there would be some tremendous cat-fight over Geraint. Patsy had long been tolerant of her lover's peccadillos, but if she met one face to face .. well, that would be something quite different. Then, it would become a matter of honour.

It wasn't until Geraint told her that Maria wasn't at the Hall – that she'd gone rushing off to Polmadoc a few days earlier and hadn't been back since – that Patsy had agreed to come up to Brackwater Hall. It had been easy to get in, much easier than she'd expected. They'd got in through a little red door that they'd found unlocked, at the side of the house.

And Patsy hadn't regretted her spur-of-the-moment decision either, not for one second. Geraint was right. There really was something special about the place, something that made you feel incredibly horny, just being there. Or was it more to do with the excitement of the forbidden, the exultation of doing it right here, so that their juices dripped down onto the floor of Maria Treharne's precious kitchen?

Silent laughter shook her again, and she threw her head back, her hair tumbling down in a shower of per-oxide curls. Her neck stretched back in a creamy-white arc, and Geraint couldn't resist kissing it, his teeth nibbling hungrily at the taut flesh as he ground his penis hard into the tight wet tunnel of his lover's sex. She answered with a wiggle of her hips that made his glans flip back and forth in a tantalising caress.

'You're enough to drive a man mad, Patsy Polgarrow.'

Geraint clutched harder at her buttocks, the memory of that mad morning at Hawthorn Cottage still fresh and arousing in his mind. He was strong, and it was easy – ridiculously easy – to support Patsy's slight weight with one hand. The fingertips of his other hand touched her anus and she squirmed and gave a little giggle of excite-ment, suddenly lunging forward to grab him tightly round the neck and plant greedy kisses all over his face. He growled with delight, his fingernail testing the recep-tiveness of her tight little hole, remembering how good it had felt to have his well-greased dick slip inside her in a single sabre-thrust.

Suddenly he wanted to do it all over again – and to

do everything else to her, too. Every damn thing he could think of. He wanted four cocks – one for her mouth and one for her pussy and one for her arse, and another one to rub long and slow over her fat, jiggling breasts. He wanted a hundred mouths to kiss her and bite her and suck her, tongues to wriggle into her wet, secret places and lick them out, scooping out great gobbets of honeysweet nectar and letting it drip stickily down his chin.

He put his fingertip into her, trying her out, seeing how far she would let him go. It was incredible, wonderful; she seemed drunk on her own desire, not angry at all with him for all the imperious demands he had been making on her body. On the contrary, her body seemed to be begging him to go further, do more, do it all . . .

Patsy danced on his prick like a ballerina, her whole body shaking with the need to bring herself to orgasm. Sweat was pouring off her now, coursing over her back and breasts as she levered herself up and down on her lover's erection, rubbing her nipples against the wiry blond hairs on his chest as she paced herself. Long and slow, long and slow; take your time, don't rush it, let it build up in you like rising flood-water, waiting to force its way out in a damburst of ecstasy.

With painful, delicious slowness she rubbed herself up and down the length of Geraint's hardened shaft, her slick wet vulva caressing him like a knowing mouth.

'Patsy, Patsy,' groaned Geraint. 'Do it to me, do it to me harder. Harder.'

She wanted to speed up the pace, to race him to orgasm; but why hurry? The pleasure would be all the greater if she kept it slow, made it last. She gasped out her need:

'Touch me, Geraint. Touch me like that . . . again.'

He lifted her up and pulled her down hard on his cock, making her cry out with helpless delight.

'Touch you, eh? Where d'you want me to touch you?' He liked this game, it made him feel even hornier than ever. The sun was on his back, the heat magnified by the glass of the kitchen windowpane, and this place had really got under his skin, put him in the mood for long and wicked sex. 'Go on then – tell me. Where?'

'On my . . . on my . . .'

'Yeah? Go on.'

'On my . . . arse. Put your finger up my arse,' gasped Patsy, her yellow-gold curls bobbing as she slid up and down on Geraint's prick. She was hot now, really hot for him. She couldn't remember ever having felt quite this way before, and as for asking any man to do *that* . . .

Geraint was only too happy to oblige. His calloused finger jabbed into her without gentleness, his hunger as sharp as hers and his mind filled with images of what they might . . . no, what they would . . . do together.

'Like this?' He wriggled his fingertip a little further inside Patsy's arsehole, and wound it round in a circular motion, feeling the stretchy, slippery membranes yield at his touch.

'Oh yes. Yes! In and out, push it in and out.'

He drove his finger into her, right up to the knuckle, and she stiffened in his embrace, her whole body going rigid with pleasure at this new and exciting sensation. His finger was wriggling like a fat electric eel, its tip twisting and pressing on the sensitive flesh so that her sphincter kept dilating and contracting, gripping the base of his finger like a tight little mouth.

It was just as good for him as it was for her; the feeling of power this was giving him was pumping so much blood into Geraint's already-swollen cock that he wondered how much longer he could possibly last. He was like tempered steel between her pussy-lips, and she was dripping a waterfall of sex-juice that left a cool, shivery slick of wetness over his balls and pubic hair. His cock-tip was tingling, and that old familiar urgency was in him, making him want to drive those last few strokes into her, hard and fast and unforgiving as a steam-hammer, until at last they would come together and his head would spin as the spunk drained out of him, leaving him hungry for more.

Patsy felt her belly-muscles tense as Geraint's second finger entered her, and then a third, so that her sphincter seemed stretched so tight that she lost all control and felt she could take no more.

'Oh. Oh no, no, no! You can't, Geraint! No more, you can't!'

His fingers began moving in and out of her, and with each inward thrust, he moved deeper, stretching her further, making her moans of pleasure rise to a crescendo of blind, screaming delight.

At first neither of them noticed the shadows moving in front of the sunlit window; they were too lost in their own private world of lust. The first Geraint knew of the new presence was the gossamer-light touch of a hand on his shoulder, breaking the spell, making him open his eyes and look round.

There were two of them there by the kitchen window – a man and a girl; both naked. Good-looking girl too, not really that tall but sort of willowy so she looked much taller; reddish-blonde hair and velvety eyes, and lips continually moistened by the flick of that bright pink tongue.

The man by her side had tousled sandy hair and a roguish smile. Geraint thought he vaguely recognised the two strangers. Weren't they those townies he'd seen weeks ago, drinking at the Duke of Gloucester? He'd only seen them the once, and he couldn't recall their names. Then, they'd been smartly-dressed and the girl had been kind of snooty, not warm and welcoming like she was now. Come to think of it, they both seemed very different here and now, like they were figures out of a dream.

The girl's hand was on his shoulder and she was looking straight into his eyes. Her lips were moving, but no sound was coming out; and then Geraint realised that he was hearing her words – or were they her thoughts? – in his head. He did not think for a moment that this was odd; here, in Brackwater Hall, all seemed as it should be. The only thing that mattered was the gratification of lust.

*We're glad you came, Geraint. Both of you. We've been waiting for you for such a long time.*

He felt the woman's hand on his, drawing his fingers gently out of Patsy's arse; and Patsy looked up at them both, her eyes filled with regret and incomprehension, her breath halting and hoarse.

'But why? Why!'

The woman with red-blonde hair put her finger to her lips, commanding silence, and turned to look at her companion.

The guy with the tousled sandy hair and the chocolate-brown eyes was not bad-looking, thought Patsy to herself. His body was firm and smooth; slender hips throwing into relief the generous spike of his penis, the loose pouch of his balls, hanging heavy with the abundance of his seed. He was smiling, and in her head she could hear him speaking to her:

*Don't be afraid, Patsy. We only want to give you pleasure.*

Patsy wasn't at all afraid. She was surprised to find that the only emotion within her now was excitement; a roaring, surging readiness to accept anything and everything. And when the girl's hands touched her, cool and smooth and so skilful, she felt her whole body relax in a great sigh of contentment, opening itself to the next great spasm of desire, the next sensual adventure.

His dick still firmly embedded to the hilt in Patsy's welcoming vagina, Geraint began thrusting again, strangely untroubled by the new visitors. He did not question their presence, did not think even for a moment about why they were here, naked, their hands exploring him, their warm wet tongues running over his bare skin, awakening him to new heights of carnal lust.

In the midst of his raging, burning desire, Geraint felt curiously at peace, his mind undisturbed by thoughts of the world outside. Indeed, he had almost forgotten that it had ever existed. This was his world now – his world and Patsy's; a world of raw sexual energy where the sun would always be golden and warm and only pleasure mattered.

Hands touched his backside, and instinctively he slid his feet apart, unafraid of what was coming next, though he sensed it even before it happened. The man's cock slipped easily between his buttocks, its glistening tip spreading its own lubrication over Geraint's amber furrow. He was not afraid; he was happy, excited, hungry for sex. And as the cock-tip sword-thrust knifed into him he made no sound but a low groan of pleasure, experiencing the pain as a warm ocean deep within his belly, intensifying his longing.

They thrust together, the nameless man holding him by the hips as he buggered Geraint, and Geraint moving Patsy up and down on his straining cock, exulting in the wondrous knowledge that, if he wished, this could go on for ever.

Patsy felt the woman's butterfly fingers fluttering down her back, her kisses soft and light as a baby's breath on her skin. She opened herself up to the new sensations like a revelation of some truth that had been hidden from her and was now revealed in the full majesty of its glory. She had never been touched by a woman before. Geraint had suggested it once, lewd and half-joking, and she had called him dirty, perverted, unnatural.

She knew now that she'd been wrong. How wrong, she was only just discovering. The woman was touching her more beautifully even than she could touch herself, her fingers and tongue searching out all the most secret places and arousing a whole symphony of sensation. One finger, two fingers, three; and now a whole curled fist, forcing its way into the secret heart of her, opening up the soft, frail tissues of her anus with such gentle cruelty that her sobs were all of pleasure.

As her climax came – a great shuddering spasm that answered the jerk of Geraint's turgid prick – Patsy thought she caught sight of a dark shadow; the shape of a fifth figure, silhouetted against the sunlight; watching them.

But what did it matter? What did anything matter, as

long as the pleasure kept on getting stronger and the cock and the fingers kept moving in and out of her helpless, pleasure-drunk body, in delicious complicity? She was glad; glad with all her heart that she and Geraint had come to Brackwater Hall.

And Brackwater Hall was glad, too.

'And as soon as I give you the go-ahead, I shall want this done in seven days. Is that quite clear?'

Allardyce moved his arms across the top of the scale model in a broad, sweeping gesture that reminded Rokeby of a windmill. The contractor exchanged nervous glances with his two colleagues.

'If I could just go over this one more time, Mr Allardyce, just so that I've got it straight in my own mind – you understand?'

'Get on with it,' snapped Allardyce irritably. He was tired of delays and impatient for his brilliant new plan to be put into operation.

'You want the area above the village cleared within one week of instigation?'

'Correct. And the rest of the upland site within a further two weeks from the date of commencement. You can leave Hilltop Tor for the time being.' Allardyce returned the contractor's uneasy blink with a calm stare. 'Is there a problem with that, Mr Rokeby? Because if there is, I have only to pick up the phone and get someone else in. There are plenty of building contractors begging for work.'

'No, sir. There's no problem.' Rokeby scratched his ear with his pencil. 'But planning permission for these new works . . .'

'Will be no problem. I have some most obliging contacts in the DOE and the local planning department. All is completely in order, I can assure you. Just one or two minor loose ends to tie up. I should be able to give you the go-ahead soon, very soon. If all goes well – and I assure you it will – you should be able to begin work within the next few days.'

Allardyce laid his hands on the top of the glass case and stared down at the model beneath, as though willing his creation to become reality. The circle of grey monoliths seemed to stretch upward, trying to touch his fingers; at their very centre, the great brooding shape of Brackwater Hall. His heart started beating faster, the adrenalin pumping through his veins damn-near giving him a hard-on.

'And if work begins within, say, the next seven days?' began Rokeby tentatively. He really didn't know what to make of all this at all, but in his mind he was already working out the fat profit his company would get for supplying the fleet of diggers, all that structural steel, all those tonnes of concrete.

'Yes?' Allardyce's brown eyes interrogated his for signs of weakness.

'What sort of completion date would you be looking at?'

'The end of September.'

Rokeby drew in breath.

'But Mr Allardyce . . . that only gives us just over two months to do the whole job. And there's the village . . .'

'What about the village?' Allardyce looked at him sharply, drawing his fingers, claw-like across the surface of the glass, so that the sweat-moistened fingertips produced an eerie squealing sound. 'I have bought it up – lock, stock and barrel.'

'Yes, but . . . you're absolutely sure you want the demolition to go ahead?'

'Do you think I'm a fool, Rokeby? Do you think I don't know my own mind?' Allardyce did not wait for a reply, but continued, his eyes fixed once again on the scale model and his voice slow and emphatic. 'I want it destroyed – all of it, do you understand?'

'Yes, Mr Allardyce. You want the village destroyed.'

'Bulldoze it, raze it to the ground, every bit of it, every last stone. I don't want there to be any sign that the village of Lynmoor ever existed.'

There was a long pause. In the corner, the local girl

329

who had been recruited to take the minutes of the meeting broke down into quiet, shuddering sobs. Leon Duvitski turned to look at her, and saw that her eyes were pleading with his: don't let it happen, don't let this thing happen to my home. He wanted to help her, really he did, but he just didn't know how he could.

And there was something else he wanted, too. Not for the first time, Leon Duvitski felt really, *really* uneasy. Incredibly horny, too, so much so that his erect cock was rubbing painfully against the inside of his pants. None of this made sense. He was beginning to wish he'd never set eyes on Charles Allardyce.

Maria walked through the stable-yard of Polmadoc and out across the gently-sloping grass towards the point where grassy cliff-top met sky. She could hear the surf crashing on the jagged rocks, many feet below. She tasted the salt in the air and heard the high, wailing cries of the gulls as they wheeled through the clear blue sky. It all seemed so peaceful and so normal, as if nothing untoward had ever happened or could ever happen in this wild and forgotten place.

'Anthony? Where are you, Anthony?'

Her voice was carried away on the strong sea-breeze that buffeted her face. Even on the hottest summer day, with the blinding-white circle of the sun at its zenith, Polmadoc Point was filled with a sense of elemental power. Its energy was all around her; in the breeze that tugged and twisted her hair, in the crackle and spring of the grass beneath her feet, in the roar and crash of tumbling, ice-cold ocean waters.

Where had Pendorran got to? Joseph had told her that he was out here somewhere, but there had been no sign of him at the stables. She had to see him, but as usual when she most needed him he was nowhere to be found. Her growing dependence on him both irritated and frightened her. She desperately needed his help, and sensed that he knew far more than he was telling her; but still he persisted in his assertion that she must ultimately help herself, and that he could do no more than be her guide. She must see him, and talk things through with him. Perhaps then he would drop the protective shield that she sensed around him, meet her on her own ground, and tell her what was really in his heart.

As she got nearer to the cliff-edge and the ground sloped downwards at a slightly more acute angle, she saw him: a lean, dark figure silhouetted between earth and sky, his face turned towards the rolling grey mass of the Atlantic.

Stripped to the waist, he was sitting cross-legged on the ground, his tanned torso gleaming in the wind and his shoulder-length dark hair whipped about his face in long black tendrils. His hands were outstretched in meditation or worship, the thumb and index finger of each hand forming a perfect O. Without turning to face Maria, he greeted her.

'It took you a long time to find me, Maria.'

She took one more step forward then paused, faintly antagonised by his calm, unruffled tone.

'I wouldn't have had to find you if you hadn't deserted me in the village,' she pointed out, coming up alongside him. For the first time, she realised just how very close to the edge of the cliff he was. She hardly dared look down in case the sight gave her vertigo. 'Why did you leave me like that?'

Pendorran did not answer for a long, tense moment, but kept staring towards the middle distance, his eyes half closed.

'I had to.'

'But why?' Maria sat down on the grass beside him, and touched his hair with her hand. Immediately his eyes opened, and he half-turned his head to look at her.

'Because of Allardyce.'

'Charles Allardyce? I don't understand.'

Pendorran slewed his long legs round so that he was facing Maria. There was nothing of calmness in his expression now. His grey eyes seemed as wild and

331

troubled as the ocean; deep wells of sorrow and anger that almost frightened Maria.

'I have been a fool, Maria. I did not fully comprehend what had happened until I saw Allardyce, and then I was sure. I should perhaps have warned you, but if I had been mistaken . . .'

'Warn me of what?' Maria was caught between annoyance and curiosity.

'He belongs to the Hall now. Somehow, Allardyce has become a creature of its own twisted will. As soon as I looked into his eyes I saw that it was true. And now, with such cold, deeply sexual evil as its servant, I fear Brackwater Hall cannot be opposed.'

Maria felt a half-smile rise unbidden to her lips.

'Not even by me?'

Pendorran did not return the smile. His eyes seemed to radiate a fierce white light; the twin reflections of the sun's molten heat.

'Not even by you, Maria. Though you are the chosen one and the power of oneness is within you, it may even now be too late.' He scooped up a handful of dry dirt from the cliff edge and ran it through his fingers. 'You have heard what he intends to do? He wants to destroy the entire village.'

'But it's not that simple, surely . . .'

'It is as simple as he wants it to be. It is the Hall's doing, Maria. The Hall has his mind; it will not let him go now.'

'And the Goddess?'

Anthony turned his head and looked out to sea, as if all the answers lay there, in the tumbling swell of grey-green water.

'I have been praying for strength. Strength and knowledge.'

'And what about me, Anthony?' Maria knelt before him, taking his hands in hers. 'Do you pray for me?'

Pendorran did not reply, but Maria thought she saw a shadow of pain pass across his grey eyes as he held her close, his lips brushing hers, his breathing hot and regular on her cheek.

'You're holding back on me, aren't you?,' she said. 'Just like you always have done. Well, you keep telling me that I have to help myself – and so I shall. If you won't help me, I shall have to fight this battle on my own.'

He caught her hand and kissed it, his passion suddenly bursting out, his lips hot as a furnace; and she knew that he had guessed her intentions even before she had voiced them.

'The danger is too great now, Maria. You must not go back.'

'On the contrary, Anthony,' she replied. 'I must. If I really am the chosen one, the Priestess, then surely it's my duty to go back. If I don't do something to save Lynmoor, who will?'

Pendorran's grey eyes did not flicker, but his hand closed more tightly about her fingers.

'The power may destroy you. You realise that.'

'Of course.'

He was still gripping her hand tightly as he spoke.

'Look down, Maria; over the edge. What can you see?'

She looked down over the cliff-edge, and vertigo churned her stomach.

'I see waves crashing on a rocky shore. I see ... danger. Great danger.'

'And are you afraid?'

She answered him with a kiss, her lips pressing hard against his and her tongue forcing its way into the cavern of his mouth. Their tongues jousted for supremacy, and when Maria had savoured the taste of his passion, she withdrew. Looking into his face, she lied.

'No, I'm not afraid.'

'Then join me on the edge, Maria. Join me on the very edge of the world.'

His challenge made her heart skip a beat, but she could not back down now. Her pride would not let her. And besides, the sensual urge was burning in her belly, the voice whispering in her head of the sublime gift of pleasure that she could only share with Anthony Pendorran.

Pendorran's arms enfolded her, pulling her down onto the hard ground, the dry grass yellowing and brittle on the thin soil. Sharp stones pressed into her back and her legs, but Maria scarcely noticed them. She was gazing up at Pendorran's face, feeling his hands working at the buttons of her blouse, freeing her body from its imprisoning cocoon of fabric.

In the distance, but not so very far away, she could hear the rhythmic to-ing and fro-ing of the ocean, and above it, the louder roar of the breakers as they rolled towards the base of the cliffs. Far enough away to seem like part of some other world, but near enough to be mortally dangerous. Never before had she felt the danger so clearly, or felt so very much alive because of it.

She stretched out her hand and touched Pendorran's thigh. He was kneeling astride her, the thick cotton of his black trousers pulled tight at the crotch, pushing forward the heavy bulge of his testicles and throwing into relief the uncurling snake of his penis. She ran her fingers along it, feeling its heat pulsing through the fabric, gripping the thickening shaft as it stiffened, echoing her own hunger.

The blouse fell open and she felt the cool breeze waft across her bare breasts, erecting the nipples and raising goose-bumps on her skin. The mingling of sensations was intoxicating: the cold of the sea-breeze all around her, and the steady, baking heat of the sun, beating down on her out of a clear blue sky.

Pendorran unbuttoned her skirt and eased it down over her hips as she lifted her backside slightly to help him. Her panties yielded effortlessly, the silky black fabric sliding down over her smooth thighs. The ground felt hard and scratchy underneath her bare buttocks, but Maria's only thoughts were for the pleasure that was to come.

She watched Pendorran unbuttoning his trousers, standing up to pull them off, and her hunger intensified to fever pitch. His manhood stood erect now, the black stone ring that passed through its head glittering like precious metal in the fierce sunlight. And beneath, between the parted thighs that so loved to straddle her like a steed, hung the downy purse of his seed, the twin fruits that seemed to have an inexhaustible supply of pearly-white juice.

As he lay down beside her, and began stroking her flesh with his sensitive, ringed fingers, she felt a great sob of longing escape from her. How far from the edge were they – only inches, perhaps? The danger of their embrace sent the blood coursing faster through her body, plumping her pussy-lips and making them throb with need.

Pendorran's fingers described a slow-narrowing spiral around the base of her breast, flattened slightly now that she was lying on her back, but still heavy with promise. Each new caress of his fingertip, light and playful, made her shiver with renewed lust.

'Kiss me,' she gasped; and he lowered his face to hers, suddenly grabbing hold of her with both hands and rolling onto his back so that he was the steed and she the rider. As she looked down, dizzy from his game, she saw how perilously close they were to the edge; how easily he might have misjudged that distance and sent them plunging over the edge into oblivion.

Strangely, the thought excited rather than angered her. She found herself wondering how it would be to plunge together through empty space, her body and Pendorran's one glittering, living entity; their fall endless and breathtaking, so that no matter how long or how far they fell, they would never ever reach the needle-sharp rocks below.

With her thighs on either side of Pendorran's hips, it would have been so easy for Maria to take him there and then into the soft wet heart of her, swallowing him up. But she did not want the game to be over so quickly. His cock-tip looked so appetising, like a glistening purple plum, and she longed to savour its unique taste.

As she slid slowly and sinuously down his body, her heavy breasts hung low over his chest and belly. The puckered nipples trailed lightly and deliberately across his skin whilst her long, wavy hair teased and swirled as the breeze caught it and turned it into a floating chestnut cloud.

'If you only knew what you do to me,' Pendorran murmured softly as her tongue trailed up the inner surface of his thigh. His flesh tasted salty, his sweat crystallising on her tongue as she lapped at him, eager and passionate.

She did not reply, but wondered if Pendorran had any idea what he did to her, with his beautiful body and those sea-grey eyes that seemed to gaze into the very depths of her soul. Did he realise how it felt to have his hands on her breasts, his fingers smoothing her bare backside, his smooth, handsome phallus diving deep into the epicentre of her sex?

Her tongue moved up to the margin of his pubic hair and he gave a gasp of astonished pleasure as suddenly and wickedly she opened her mouth to take his right testicle into her mouth.

It seemed huge and fragile, the wiry black hair like a protective net about this most precious jewel, this pleasure-egg, this fruit so juicy that it seemed to melt on her greedy tongue. She let the wetness of her saliva moisten it, making it slippery and mobile in its loose purse of skin; then applied just the faintest pressure to it with her mouth. Pendorran let out a long, shuddering sigh.

'Sorceress . . .'

Her fingers fluttered to his left testicle, gently stroking and cradling it like a lost child; lavishing caresses on it so skilfully that she saw a huge, clear droplet of sexfluid appear at the eye of his cock. His lips parted and he mouthed wordless sounds of torment, the ache of need so painfully strong that he seemed to have lost all power to express the depth of it. His fingers clawed at the ground and he arched his back slightly, as though willing her to take all of him inside that knowing mouth.

Maria closed her lips more tightly on his flesh and felt his trust, his utter abandonment to the pleasure she was giving him. Here, at the edge of the world, if they did not trust each other, each would surely drag the other to destruction. Gently she released him from her kiss, the ripe plum dropping from her mouth, heavy with juice.

Astride him again she slid up his body, carefully not touching the bursting branch of his prick, but planting dozens of tiny kisses up the long, smooth curve of his torso; nipping and biting lightly at his nipples, erected now into small, dark crests that seemed made for kissing. She suckled him like a baby, her lips working at his right nipple whilst at the left, her fingers were pinching and rolling the flesh into even greater hardness.

Behind her warm, soft backside, Pendorran's cock jerked repeatedly upward in search of its elusive goal, its domed head trickling with pure, clear lust. And still she did not touch it or kiss it or caress it. She was making him wait; playing with his need as he had played with hers, building it up like a head of scalding steam that would soon burst out in an irrepressible orgy of hunger.

As Maria bent low to kiss his nipples, her backside thrust out and her love-lips parted wide, she felt the bitter sea-breeze on her delicate flesh, its stinging salt tongue darting between the outer lips of her vulva and into the very softest depths of her womanhood. It felt like a little lash of punishment, a little whip flicking onto her vulva again and again as the breeze gusted around the cliff-top, capricious and lewd.

The wind's cold kisses met the fire in her belly and sparked a need that snarled and roared for gratification. Passion twisted and turned her body, rubbing and grinding against Pendorran's belly, and she felt the strength in him grow, his hands clutching at her back, the nails raising red welts as he clawed at her flesh. The wanting was too great, too all-consuming to resist any longer. His voice rose above the roar of the surf, the buffeting of the sea-breeze. It was clear, resonant, exultant; not a question but an affirmation:

'Do you dare, Maria? Do you dare join with me at the edge of the world?'

They clutched at each other, no longer aware of where they were or what they were doing, only that the need in them must be satisfied. And Maria felt herself rolling over and over along the cliff-edge as Pendorran's strength overwhelmed and yet melded with hers; and suddenly he was on top of her, his body pressing down on her and his sweat mingling with her sweat.

She could not see his face. His whole body was a black silhouette against the clear blue sky, whilst above him the sun's white-hot disc framed a bright halo around his dark head. She could not see his lips, but she knew that they were parted, glossy with moisture from their kisses, glossy as the purple head of his phallus, which even now was pressing itself between her willing sex-lips.

Her hips thrust upwards to meet him and their flesh met, the contact thrilling with an electric joy that sent ripples through Maria's body; ripples that began at the rosebud of her clitoris but extended their delicious tingling to belly and breasts and thighs and fingers and toes. Even her lips seemed hyper-sensitive, so that when Pendorran pulled her towards him and kissed her, it felt as though he were kissing her whole body, each nerve-ending quivering with the overload of pleasure.

Their love was animal now, their passion taking over, annihilating all reason. Maria opened her eyes and saw the sky whirling, kittiwakes crying as they described widening circles in the painfully bright blue above her. The roof of the world was shifting, spinning, severing her grip on reality. The delicious heaviness of Pendorran's body felt like the only solid thing in the whole, wide world; the only thing anchoring her to existence. She could hear his voice, crying out to her: 'Come, Maria; come with me; come ...', and felt her body answering his call, the muscles of her belly tensing as they awaited that final, decisive caress: the one that would push her over the edge of pleasure into the oblivion of ecstasy.

In the violence of their passion, their bodies writhed and danced on the cliff-top, their bare flesh abraded by sandy soil and stones. Maria felt something move beneath her and she put out her hand to steady herself. But shifting scree rolled away in a hail of tiny stones, and suddenly her fingers were clutching at nothing but empty air.

The pure exhilaration of terror overwhelmed her and for a split second she turned her head. Mere inches to her left, the cliff fell away in a sheer drop to the razor-sharp rocks, two hundred feet below. There was nothing; nothing but empty sky and hissing, spitting salt water between them and extinction. Nothing but the embrace which through its very passion threatened to destroy them both.

She clutched at Pendorran's hips, pulling him deeper inside her, and feeling his hands tighten around her.

'Now, Maria. Can't you feel it? Now, Maria – jump with me . . .'

And she jumped; her body anchored to the cliff-top, her spirit leaping with Anthony's into the dazzling spectrum of ecstasy as they met in orgasm. Spasm after spasm racked their bodies, so tightly locked now that they seemed truly one flesh, one spirit.

As the pleasure ebbed away, Anthony rolled onto his back, pulling her on top of him, and she saw his face. His skin seemed pale beneath the golden tan, his eyes unnaturally bright.

'So close, Maria,' he whispered, holding her tight. 'Almost on the very edge.'

A sudden calmness overwhelmed her, and she smiled as she stroked his face.

'Sometimes the edge is the only sensible place to be,' she replied.


Anthea wondered what Maria would have to say when she finally made it to Brackwater Hall – not days, but whole weeks late. But Gareth and Hans had been so absorbing, and let's face it, Anthea wasn't really a middle-of-nowhere person. Maria would understand. Maria always did.

She'd been looking forward to seeing Maria much more than seeing Lynmoor, but as she drove down the valley and into the outskirts of the village, she had to admit that she was beginning to feel quite intrigued. Something very major, even cataclysmic, seemed to be going on around here. High up on the hillside, directly above the village, half a dozen bright yellow diggers were parked, silent and frozen in postures reminiscent of skeletal dinosaurs; and here and there the earth had been gashed into several deep trenches that looked very much like the beginnings of foundations.

Everywhere she looked she could see red and white stakes and lines of plastic tape, marking out land which had been surveyed . . . but for what? Maria hadn't said a word about any of this in her letter; but then again, Anthea hadn't had any contact with her since she'd received Maria's invitation, several weeks ago. She'd tried phoning numerous times, but each time she'd been thwarted by that irritating unobtainable tone, and the operators she'd spoken to had been totally unhelpful. There was something distinctly odd about a place where the telephones never worked, and Anthea wondered what a sophisticated woman like Maria Treharne saw in it.

Still, no doubt Maria would soon be selling up and using the cash to live on until she got another lecturing post. The thought brought with it an unwelcome pang of guilt. Maria probably knew by now that she'd lost her lectureship at St Alcuin's, and Anthea hadn't been there to tell her that everything was all right and they'd fight that bastard Armstrong-Baker together. What's more, there was still the sticky subject of Jonathan Gresham's treachery to broach; and what on earth would Maria say when she heard what Anthea had been getting up to with Tony Fitzhardinge? Ah well, time enough once she got to Brackwater Hall. This was one scene she'd have to play by ear.

The Fiat drove past a painted wooden sign that said 'Welcome to Lynmoor', and almost at once Anthea felt the engine cough, splutter and die.

'Damn you!' Anthea thumped the dashboard and twiddled the ignition key in the lock, but the Fiat did not respond. Not a cough; not a wheeze. Perhaps she was out of petrol? No, of course she wasn't. She'd filled up only fifty miles back. Oil? She'd had that checked, too. Yet the car was suddenly and inexplicably dead.

She got out and swung a poorly-aimed kick at the front bumper.

'Bloody useless, you are.' She heartily wished now that she'd taken Maria's advice and bought a better car, instead of penny-pinching and spending the rest on that holiday in Bali. What now? She supposed she'd have to walk. What a horrible thought. Maybe someone in that pub across the way would be able to give her a lift.

She took the smallest suitcase out of the car and locked the rest in the boot. They'd have to stay there until she got herself a lift or managed to get the car fixed. Feeling a little more optimistic, she checked her make-up in the wing-mirror and crossed the road to the Duke of Gloucester.

She lifted a hand to push the door open but to her surprise it refused to yield. Locked and bolted? But surely these country pubs stayed open at all hours of the day and night, especially in the summer months.

And then she caught sight of the notice: a yellow piece of paper, covered with a sheet of plastic and nailed to the door. Now she had spotted it she wondered how she could ever have overlooked it. The words 'Notice of Demolition' shouted out from the paper in two-inch red capitals.

Demolition? Anthea stood back and surveyed the building with a practised eye. This place must be three, maybe four hundred years old, and at the very least a Grade Two listed building. Demolition? Half the valley covered in theodolites and diggers? It just plain didn't make sense. Something very cock-eyed was going on around here.

Seeing no one else around to help, Anthea picked up her suitcase and consulted her map. That must be

341

Brackwater Hall – that oddly-shaped building silhouetted against the sky, high on the moors. If she took the right-hand fork up the side of the valley, it should only take her a couple of hours. A couple of hours! She groaned inwardly and looked down at her unsuitable, high-heeled shoes. Obviously she should have known better than to break her unwritten rule *never* to visit the country.

Picking up her suitcase, she began the long, weary trek. She cursed silently as she imagined superfit Maria striding up the hill like a mountain goat – that's what came of being in the SCR women's rowing eight. Anthea had always preferred to take all her exercise in the bedroom.

The sun was hot and getting hotter, the road ahead hardly more than a blur beneath the rippling heat-haze. The tarmac felt warm and squidgy beneath her feet, and she could feel her spiky heels digging in. That's another pair ruined, she thought, mentally counting the cost of a return visit to Harvey Nicholls.

At first she didn't notice the sound of the engine behind her; in fact, she didn't notice the car at all until it drew level with her, and rattled to a halt.

'Anthea? It is you, isn't it?'

Anthea turned in amazement, to see Maria Treharne sitting at the wheel of the most ancient, battered, disreputable orange Volvo she had ever seen.

'Maria! Am I glad to see you. My car broke down way back there, and I had to leave it in the village. What the hell is that you're driving?'

'Don't ask.' Maria's lips twisted into a crooked smile. 'And what are you doing here? When I didn't hear from you, I thought you weren't coming.'

Anthea wrenched open the rusty passenger door and got inside, throwing her case into the back. Her bare thighs stuck instantly to the hot plastic seats.

'Your phone's been out of order for weeks. Don't tell me you didn't know.'

'Yes, of course. I'd forgotten.' Maria's initial pleasure at seeing Anthea was rapidly turning to a cloud of anxiety. So many things had happened – things that Anthea wouldn't understand in a month of Sundays. How could she possibly explain what was going on? Anthea would think she'd finally gone loopy.

'There's loads to talk about,' said Anthea, wriggling her bottom uncomfortably on the burning-hot seat. 'Terry, for instance – last thing I heard, they were thinking of giving him the sack. Can you imagine that?'

'Really?' Maria tried to sound interested, but these days Cambridge seemed like somewhere out of another universe. 'Well, it's no more than he deserves.'

Anthea glanced sideways at Maria, trying to fathom out what it was that seemed different about her. She looked the same, sure, but there was something about her manner – an anxiety perhaps; a maturity . . ?

'You OK?' she said suspiciously. 'Only you look a bit . . . tired.'

'Of course I am. I'm fine.'

Anthea was baffled. There was obviously something bothering Maria, but what? They'd always shared things – all things. They simply didn't have secrets from each other. Well, maybe just one or two, she thought as she remembered Tony. But she was going to come clean about that anyway.

'It's not . . . the job, is it? You're not worrying about St Alcuin's?'

Maria laughed, and for the first time her face relaxed into a proper smile.

'Believe me, Anthea, that place is the least of my worries. I've had a lot more to think about since I came to Lynmoor. You've no idea . . .'

'Look, Maria, what are we waiting for? Aren't you going to take me home to this amazing mansion of yours?'

'Well, I . . .' How was Maria going to explain that she didn't much fancy going to Brackwater Hall herself, let alone taking Anthea along with her? 'Er . . . I'm not sure how to put this, but I'd rather not take you there, if you don't mind.'

'You're joking! I've come all the way from Cambridge to see the damn thing, and you don't want to show it to me? I mean, if you didn't want me to come you shouldn't have invited me. Or have you got some gorgeous yokel stashed away up there, and you're afraid I'll steal him from you?'

'Oh no, no, it's nothing like that. But if I told you, you wouldn't believe me.'

'Try me.'

Maria started up the engine again, easing the car into gear. The power to explain was beyond her. Maybe if she took Anthea up there and they just had a quick look round, everything would be OK. Maybe Pendorran's tales of gloom and doom were out of all proportion to the real danger.

'It's OK, take no notice of me. We'll go up there now and I'll give you a quick Cook's tour.' Maria steered up the steep, winding road, concentrating on her driving to keep her mind off the nagging fear that was plaguing her. Overhead, a single fluffy grey cloud was creeping stealthily towards the sun. 'It's just . . . well, one or two peculiar things have been happening lately, and I'd rather not discuss them until they're properly sorted out.'

'Looks like somebody's giving Lynmoor a pretty comprehensive sorting out,' observed Anthea, looking back down at the valley floor, its entire surface divided into sections like the pieces of a jigsaw puzzle. It all seemed unnaturally quiet, with hardly anyone around, hardly anything moving.

'That's one of the things that have been happening,' replied Maria grimly. 'Some crazy firm of developers wants to bulldoze Lynmoor into the ground, build all over it. Do you know, they even want me to sell them Brackwater Hall.'

'Well, if it's a good offer and they're going to ruin the place anyway, why not? I mean, you've got no ties to the place, have you? Take the money and run, that's what I say.'

344

Maria felt a shadow fall over the car and looked up. Where, only minutes before, there had been a flawless vault of blue sky, there was now a gathering cluster of heavy grey-brown clouds, their dark fluffiness almost entirely obscuring the sun. The air felt tense and heavy, almost unbreathable. And the nearer they got to the dark house on the horizon, the more uneasy she felt. She kept her eyes on the road, trying to ignore the stuffy, choking heat.

'Weather's gone off a bit,' remarked Anthea, winding down the window.

'It can change very suddenly round here,' replied Maria dismissively. But not this suddenly, she was thinking; not so suddenly that in the space of a few minutes the whole vast sky can turn from blue to steel grey, almost entirely covered with thunder-clouds. Up ahead, very close now, the dark shape of Brackwater Hall loomed over them; and for the first time Maria felt its sensual lure turning to menace.

'Do you think we're in for a storm?' Anthea wiped beads of sweat off her forehead.

'Could be.' Maria slowed the car almost to a stop. She didn't want to go on. Her whole body was trembling and her bare arms were covered in a cold sweat. 'Look – would you mind if we turned back? I know this really nice hotel . . .'

Anthea laughed.

'Hotel? What do I want a hotel for? They're all the bloody same, every one of them. I want to see the house, Maria – I want to see what it is that's been keeping you incommunicado down here for all these weeks.' She shut up abruptly and stared at Maria. 'What's the matter? You're trembling all over.'

'Nothing. Nothing's the matter.'

'Are you ill? Do you want me to drive?'

'No!' Maria's knuckles clenched the wheel tightly, whitening with the tension. She fought down the rising tide of panic. 'No, I'm fine. We'll be there in a couple of minutes.'

There in a couple of minutes. A couple of minutes in which they would eat up the welcome, protective distance between them and Brackwater Hall. Was Maria imagining it, or could she hear distant mocking laughter, daring her to come closer, daring her to pit her own power against the power of Brackwater Hall?

Lightning flashed; thunder rumbled above them and the sky grew darker still. The light was dwindling to a thick, heavy dusk that turned the stunted trees to gnarled black bodies with twisted fingers that beckoned them on. Seconds later, a jagged blade of lightning ripped through the thunder-grey sky, picking out the façade of the Hall in Gothic chiaroscuro.

In that split second, Maria froze in terror. For she was quite certain of what she had seen, and equally certain that it had not been there before. It was a small red door, set into the front of the house, right next to the porch; a little red arched door fresh with bright new paint; red as blood, red as flesh; beckoning her in.

Into the silken cage.

The next bolt of lightning struck the hollow trunk of a dead tree, igniting the dry timber like kindling and sending flaming branches cascading around the car.

Maria was not waiting for more – and worse – to happen. She gripped the wheel of the Volvo and swung it round, its ancient chassis squealing and grating in protest.

'What are you doing?' demanded Anthea.

'Turning the car round – what does it look like?' snapped Maria, her eyes blazing.

'But surely ... surely we should press on and take shelter in the Hall?'

'Listen Anthea.' Maria pointed the car away from the Hall, refusing to look back in case its seductive power proved too great for her. Huge, fat drops of rain were falling now, fizzing and crackling on the burning branches of the stricken tree. 'If you know what's good for you, you'll shut up and let me drive you back to the village. And another thing.'

346

'What?'

'You'll thank your lucky stars that you've never set foot in Brackwater Hall.'

Leon Duvitski stood on the moors near Hilltop Tor, looking down at the village. The storm had faded away as swiftly as it had come, and Lynmoor was once again a soft huddle of golden and grey stone, nestling in the bosom of a deep green valley. He was by no means a sentimental man – hell, his business adversaries called him hard, ruthless, amoral – but quite unexpectedly, unforgivably, he had grown to love this place. And the pain of that love was perhaps his punishment for having ever got involved with Charles Allardyce.

Had he completely taken leave of his senses? He must have been out of his mind to think that Allardyce's audacious plan would be the salvation of Lynmoor. Had he really imagined that building hypermarkets, conference centres and all-weather Olympic leisure domes would give the village a new lease of life? Or had he just convinced himself that it was all a good idea because Allardyce was paying him a great deal of money – and besides, he had never been wrong before?

He realised now that both of them had made a horrible mistake. The Lynmoor Development wouldn't give Lynmoor new life – it would kill it stone dead. And now, with the sudden and horrific unveiling of Allardyce's grotesque new plans, that death was going to happen more quickly than Duvitski had ever imagined. He knew now that he had had just about all that he could take.

As he got back into the car and drove across the moors, he cursed himself for his naïvety in thinking he could ever influence Charles Allardyce in any way. That had just been an illusion – one of the ones that Allardyce created so convincingly, to promote loyalty among his staff and business associates. Duvitski saw clearly now that Allardyce had never been anything other than a one-man-band. Allardyce only recognised two positions:

347

for and against him. And those who were against, he routinely destroyed.

Feeling more helpless than he had ever done in his life before, Duvitski parked the car and got out. The Lotus Elan was his pride and joy, but he didn't even bother to lock it. Somehow the minutiae of daily living didn't seem that important any more.

Slowly and determinedly, he walked towards the house, crunching his way up the driveway towards the imposing front door. He raised his hand, hesitated for a split second, then rang the bell.

A few moments later the door opened and he was greeted by an elderly man, formal as an undertaker in his dark grey suit.

'Do come in, sir,' smiled Joseph. 'We've been expecting you.'

# Chapter Sixteen

*L* eon followed Joseph into Pendorran's mansion. Normally he would have been fascinated by the raw grandeur of the place, the craggy splendour of grey stone walls and high ceilings where grotesquely-hewn faces peered down through a fine tracery of carved fruit and flowers. But today his preoccupation was not with any place; unless that place was the threatened village of Lynmoor.

A massive oak door creaked inward on its hinges, revealing a huge vaulted chamber and within it, three silent, unmoving figures. The tension was palpable, almost breathable in the hot, stuffy air. Leaning with his elbow on the mantelpiece stood Anthony Pendorran, darkly sardonic as ever in fine linen and black leather; and in front of him, her body pressed lightly against his, stood Maria Treharne.

By her side sat a woman Leon had never seen before. Dark-eyed, petite and fiery, with bobbed hair dyed a glossy burgundy, Anthea turned her head towards him as he entered the room, and he felt sexual electricity crackle between them. Who *was* she? For the first time that day he felt his black mood lift for a second. Whoever she was, this was a woman you couldn't fail to notice.

'What the hell are you doing here?' demanded Maria, moving slightly towards him as though to confront him. 'Haven't you done enough damage already?'

'I had to come,' replied Leon quietly. His mouth and throat were suddenly as dry as sandpaper. It felt like walking into a courtroom scene, with himself cast in the role of defendant. 'I had to, it's all gone horribly wrong.'

'And whose fault is that?' enquired Maria. Her lips were pale and trembling, whether through fear or anger, Duvitski could not tell. He'd never been a very good judge of people. Perhaps that had been his problem all along.

'Mine,' he replied, shortly and simply. 'I've been a bloody fool.'

'Who is this?' Anthea's voice broke in, cutting through the tense atmosphere. 'And will somebody please explain to me what's going on?'

Maria laid a hand on Anthea's shoulder.

'This is Mr Duvitski,' she said. 'Leon Duvitski – close friend and colleague of Mr Charles Allardyce.'

'Allardyce? Isn't that the one you told me . . ?'

'That's right,' snapped Duvitski, preferring to damn himself rather than let others do it for him. 'I'm employed by Allardyce to . . . facilitate his development plans in various parts of the country. Or rather, I was. I've decided I don't want anything more to do with him.'

Maria's face betrayed the merest flicker of interest. She'd sensed, that day at the Hall, that Duvitski did not quite mirror his master's concentrated ruthlessness. Perhaps her first instincts had been right after all.

'So what's brought on this sudden change of heart?'

'Look, would it help if I told you everything from the beginning?'

'It might. It couldn't hurt.' Maria perched herself on the padded arm of Anthea's chair, the soft drape of her flimsy skirts outlining the graceful curve of her long limbs.

'I've worked for Allardyce for several years now.'

Duvitski wanted to sit down too, but he couldn't. Three pairs of eyes were fixed on him and he squirmed like an insect about to be impaled on a pin. It was just like being a schoolboy again, standing in front of the headmaster's desk. 'At first, he impressed me. He's a very ... charismatic man.'

'He's a scumbag,' muttered Maria.

'When he first showed me the plans for the Lynmoor Development, I thought they were wonderful – just what Lynmoor needed to bring it up to date, get more tourists in, create more jobs. Of course I was wrong. It was just a licence for Charles to print money, but if I've been naïve I'm not the only one. Two hundred private and corporate investors have sunk all they have into this development, and now the money's all Charles's. Every damn penny of it.

'But I didn't know that at the time. I thought it was all financially sound, so when Charles suggested helping things along a little, I thought it was a great idea. A few sweeteners for the District Council and the DOE, handouts for the villagers – why not? But the New Agers were creating all sorts of trouble and refusing to move from Hilltop Tor, so Charles suggested we got ourselves a fifth columnist ...'

'Carolan,' interjected Pendorran, in a matter-of-fact voice. 'Or should I say, Benjamin Arthur Tarrant, late of Foleshill Open Prison?'

Maria's jaw dropped.

'Carolan ..?'

Pendorran stroked Maria's russet hair with a long sweep of his slender hand.

'He took a lot of people in,' he commented. 'His sort always do.'

Duvitski was aware of Anthea's eyes on him; not so much watching him as scrutinising him intently, her gaze laser-sharp on his face and body, travelling slowly over every inch of his skin as though she were mentally undressing him. Despite his agitation, it was all he could do to keep himself from returning the compliment. He

351

ran his finger round the inside of his collar, easing it away from his constricted throat.

'The next thing is, Allardyce has decided he wants to buy Brackwater Hall and he's sure he can intimidate the owner into parting with it.'

'By the owner, I assume you mean me?' enquired Maria bitterly. 'Or don't I count as a person? No, of course I don't. I'm just an impediment in the way of your Mr Allardyce's precious development.'

'I'm sorry,' said Duvitski. 'But at the time it seemed like an OK thing to be doing – standard practice, in fact. It's a cut-throat business, civil engineering. But when that weird stuff started up at the Hall, the day we came to visit you, well ... I have to admit, I began to have doubts. And then Allardyce started to change, became sort of ... wild-eyed and evangelical; started talking about a clean sweep and a whole new beginning.

'And that's when he showed me his new plans.' With a groan of recollection, Duvitski sank down into a chair, head in hands. His next words sounded half-stifled in his throat. 'I just couldn't believe it. I was sure he'd gone crazy.'

'Believe what?' Anthea's voice made Duvitski look up, and this time their eyes met. He couldn't help thinking what a wonderful mixture of colours they were: a rim of dove-grey surrounding a pale green that graduated to warm chestnut-brown around the pupil.

'That he wanted to destroy Lynmoor. Everything – not just the menhirs on Hilltop Tor, not just the stony upland sites where you can't farm anyway; the village. He wants to destroy the entire village!'

'Yes, we know that,' replied Pendorran. Moving away from the fireplace, he walked slowly and thoughtfully around the room, the steel toe-caps of his boots tip-tapping on the bare stone floor. 'I should think everyone in Lynmoor knows by now – there are demolition notices all over the place. But the question is, *why* does he want to destroy the village? Tell us that, Mr Duvitski.'

Duvitski followed Pendorran around the room with his eyes. He didn't even want to say it. Saying it might make it real, and at the moment it was just a nasty dream in the back of his head; the image of a mad-eyed man gloating over a papier-mâché model in a glass case.

'He wants to build this . . . thing,' he blurted out, embarrassed by his own inarticulacy.

Pendorran stopped by the window and stared out, his hands resting on the windowsill.

'Thing? Do please try to be more specific. What does it look like?'

'I dunno . . . Like a sort of huge Stonehenge – you know, immense grey blocks in a circle around Brackwater Tor, with the Hall in the middle. I don't understand it . . . Do you?'

'Goddess!' The word exploded from Pendorran's lips in a gasp of horror, his breath misting the windowpane as he gripped the cold stone sill with both hands. 'No, not that.'

Anthea was staring at the scene in a sort of half-amused horror, her eyes flickering between Pendorran, Duvitski and Maria as though watching some stage-managed conjuring trick and trying to work out how it was done.

'Will somebody please explain . . .'

Maria ignored her, leaping to her feet and going across to Pendorran. His body relaxed slightly at the touch of her hands, but she could feel a violent trembling, very deep in the heart of him.

'What's the matter, Anthony? Tell me.'

He spun round slowly to face into the room, his hands behind him to support himself on the windowsill. His eyes blazed, unseeing; and Duvitski froze, suddenly very afraid.

'Yes, Mr Duvitski; I do understand it. I wish I did not. This is the Hall's doing. It has become a dangerous and unstable force, and now it is seeking to grow still stronger, creeping across the face of Lynmoor until its power is over everything. And now it has been unleashed, Mr

353

Duvitski, it will not stop until it has created its own empire of darkness and lust.'

Jennah did not want to give in to the pleasure, but there was so much to feel, to touch, to taste.

At the centre of the ancient circle on Hilltop Tor a fire burned, its embers red and glowing like the fire in Jennah's belly. The decoction of herbs, steeped in wine, that Carolan had given them all to drink had made the travellers mellow and receptive to pleasure. She could read lust on their faces, in their eyes, in the sly and sinuous movements of their naked bodies as they pranced and writhed in the firelight.

The ritual of conjuration was a vitally important one, or at least that was what Carolan had told them. But he had announced it rather as a parent announces a treat, not as a holy man announces a sacrament. Out of the corner of her eye she could see him, a crown of myrtle on his tousled brown locks and the blindfolded slave Megan at his feet, her lips fastened around the head of his swollen penis. He was laughing – laughing like a maniac.

For a moment – a brief moment only – Jennah felt anger. How dare he demean his followers like this, using their simple pagan faith and their love of pleasure to enslave them to his perverted will? The mistrust and the resentment were building up inside her, and she knew that they must surely burst forth soon. Already she had lost the childlike faith that she had once had in their leader, her fervour swiftly turning to bitterness. Soon, very soon, she knew that she must denounce him for what he was.

But not tonight. The drink had made her feel too joyous and lustful for that. Her body felt as though it were light as a feather, her bare feet scarcely touching the ground as she leapt and chanted with the rest.

They were dancing in a ring now, hands tight-clasped as the flute and the bodhran set the beat and they mouthed the words of the conjuration. The drumbeats entered her brain, setting the pace of her heart, the rhythm of her breathing. She was becoming the drumbeat, the pulse of the music that seemed to echo the eternal song of the spheres.

The travellers wove in and out of each other, describing circles within circles, winding silky, coloured ribbons about each other's naked bodies. She wanted to touch them all, kiss them all, slake her thirst with their sweat.

And as she twisted and whirled, she felt another's hand close about her fingers, making her pause and stand still. Her body was no longer moving but her head was spinning, her head full of the fragrance of the sweet woods and oils Carolan had thrown on the ceremonial bonfire.

Jak was looking at her; very intent, eyes very bright and unblinking. She could see reflections of the dancing flames in his eyes, their flickering brilliance mirroring the lightness of her soul. She wanted to laugh, and cry, and fuck.

As she looked back at him her world contracted; growing smaller and smaller until it contained only two people: Jennah and Jak. The music was still playing, the chanting rising above the steady thump of the bodhran, but inside Jennah's head all was silence. She was living in slow motion, her desire unrolling like the frames of a silent film, stylised yet compelling.

Deep orange firelight illuminated one side of Jak's face; the other side was masked in shadow save for the flickering, glassy brightness of his right eye. The spider tattoo was like a black hand with long, thin, fingers, across one side of his neck and the bottom half of his cheek. She wanted to kiss it, trace the imprint of those inky fingers, find out how it tasted and felt to run her tongue over the contours of Jak's high-cheekboned face.

She let out a little sigh of contentment as Jak's fingers released her hand and moved to the soft curve of her bare shoulder. As he touched her, she noticed for the first time that there was something slippery and warm on his fingers, something fragrant like a musky rose-water. The thick, sweet scent made her head reel even more but she welcomed the sensation, her whole body quivering with anticipation as Jak began rubbing the scented ointment over her shoulder and throat; working his fingers down into the shallow depression between her collarbones.

He grew more audacious, scooping up more of the fire-warmed ointment from a little copper dish on the ground and placing a thick blob at the base of her neck, watching for a few moments as the warm, viscous, semi-liquid ointment dripped down in a long, shiny stream between her breasts.

It felt like a caress, like a long and lascivious tongue teasing her very slowly and knowingly, and she closed her eyes and let the sensation take hold of her. Without even realising it she was holding her breath, waiting for the warm wetness to trickle still lower to her belly, wondering in her sensual dream if the wetness between her breasts would finally join up with the wetness between her thighs and form one continuous, surging river of lust.

Lust beat like a drum inside her, and her whole body tensed. Her flesh became as taut as the goatskin bodhran and more full of music than the wooden flute whose liquid tune swooped and bubbled around them. She arched her back, flinging back her head as Jak filled the palms of his two hands with the scented cream and cupped them over the plump hillocks of her breasts. He moved them in a slow, circular motion, the cream oozing between his fingers as he massaged it in, erecting the nipples with his caresses.

Never had his lovemaking known such skill, such gentleness. Jennah had certainly never thought of Jak as a sensitive man; he had never shown anything more than a passing animal interest in her. But tonight he was all she had ever dreamed of, and so much more. He was every inch the reborn Celtic warrior, his body filled with an ancient spirit of sorcery and strength. His hands seemed to hold true magic, a magic that soaked into her from his fingertips, making her ache to be embraced, kissed, and taken in innocence like a virgin.

And tonight she truly was that virgin; that timorous yet sensual creature blending wide-eyed wonderment and knowing lust. Her body felt as it had never felt before, not even on that first night of passion, so many years ago. She felt renewed, aroused, excited as she had not been since the dawn of adolescence.

She opened her arms and Jak came to her, his hot, strong body melting against hers, making the warm ointment slip and slide between their bodies. His kiss both answered and intensified her hunger. They made no sound; communicating only by kiss and caress, their bodies moved together in an instinctive harmony.

The world danced in the firelight as the lovers sank to the ground, oblivious to the pounding of the dance around them. The fire was hot on Jennah's face; Jak's belly and chest were a furnace of desire against her back. Fire and flesh had become her twin lovers, each caressing her in his own way, pleasuring her with an almost spiritual skill.

Jak's hands slipped round to her belly as he pressed up against her, the shaft of his cock hard as a steel rod against her buttocks. His fingers began at her breasts, tweaking and pinching until Jennah was gasping and writhing, her buttocks pushing back again and again against his pelvis, willing him to enter her, begging him to impale her on his prick. But tonight Jak wanted to make it last. For the first time ever, he was deriving pleasure simply from pleasuring his lady; and he rejoiced in the way she drove her body against his, hungry for him in a way that excited him beyond belief.

With his right hand still on Jennah's breast, Jak let his left slip deftly and smoothly down her belly and onto the stubbly gooseflesh of her shaven pubis. He had had women with shaven sex-lips before, but it had never been so exciting, never felt so gloriously, wickedly arousing. He ran his finger against the grain of the sprouting hairs and felt Jennah give a little squirm of approval. The second time he did it, he felt her whole body tense and relax, as though she were experiencing a mini-orgasm.

The flesh of his hand was almost burning from the heat of the fire, and the furnace of Jennah's desire, her pubis scorching-hot with the force of her need. Eagerly he let his fingers explore her further down, and met the round hardness of the three silver rings she wore piercing the left side of her outer sex-lips. As he touched them he felt her writhe, and a little surge of sex-fluid oozed out of her, moistening his fingers. He took them to his mouth and tasted her juice; it was sweet as berry-juice, yet every bit as bitter and potent as the magical herbs steeped in Carolan's ritual wine. He trembled at the taste; and emboldened, moved on.

As his fingertips touched Jennah's clitoris, Jak sensed that the magical circuit was almost complete. Her whole body was vibrating to the rhythm of their mutual need; his cock was throbbing with the insistent message of its own imperative urge.

Take her. Take her now. Give yourself up to the pleasure.

This was an entirely novel experience for Jak. Never before had he understood that pleasure could be a sacrifice, a complete abandonment of the self. But tonight, nothing seemed to exist but the need to worship that pleasure, to abandon himself to it utterly. With an almost religious fervour, he sought out the welcoming hole and sank into it, her wetness inundating both cock and finger as he entered her.

He felt the power in his own body, and knew he must not abuse it. With one brutal stroke of his fingertip he could bring Jennah to a painful, shattering orgasm that would leave her sobbing and unsatisfied. But if he teased and caressed her with featherlight gentleness, her pleasure – and his – would be intensified a thousand-fold. He let his fingertip brush against the head of her clitoris, very gently, as lightly as a summer breeze, and she rewarded him with a powerful backward thrust of her hips, swallowing him up to the hilt in her beautifully tight pussy.

Her pleasure bud felt huge and swollen, her richly oozing wetness lubricating it constantly so that it felt like slippery-wet glass beneath his fingertip. Gently, tormentingly, he eased the fleshy hood back and forth across the rounded head, at the same time sliding in and out of Jennah's vulva with an easy rhythm: not too fast, not too slow; building up the pleasure to exploding point by almost imperceptible degrees.

Jennah felt the heat of the fire on her breasts and belly. Sweat was coursing down her face and body, and her fine brown hair felt damp and matted, but she did not care. She hardly noticed the scorching flames, so very close to her. The heat of her lover's body felt much greater and more compelling; a seductive, addictive heat that made her want to stay like this for ever.

But a delicious warmth began to assert itself, above and within the burning of the fire and Jak's desire. It was a warmth that came from within her own body; a tingling, spreading warmth that tensed every muscle in readiness for the fulfilment of pleasure.

There was an endless moment of anticipation; a moment held suspended in time as both Jak and Jennah realised that they had reached the point of no return. And then it came, with a whirling cascade of colours and sensations; sending them tumbling and drowning in white-water rapids of purest delight until at last they emerged on the other side, half-dead with ecstasy.

The senses of time and hearing returned slowly – a distant cacophony that grew louder and more raucous; and Jak and Jennah moaned their distress at the imperfection of reality, embracing more tightly as Carolan's exultant voice rose above the discordant chanting.

'Come to us, O spirits of earth and sky. Answer our prayers.'

'Answer our prayers,' echoed the chanting voices. 'Our wishes, our dreams.'

Carolan lifted his hand and threw a handful of powder onto the fire. It was nothing special – just common salt, mixed with a rather ingenious little cocktail of flammable chemicals he'd devised on a laboratory workplacement whilst out on parole. But it had always produced reliably spectacular results in the past, and he had no reason to think it was going to let him down this time.

'Come to us!' he cried as he threw the powder into the flames. A few seconds, he thought, and it will be all pretty colours, and these half-stoned, half-witted nohopers will think I'm God again. It can't fail.

But as the powder hit the flames, something rather different happened: something Carolan hadn't bargained for at all. Instead of turning the flames into a predictable kaleidoscope of pretty greens and reds, the powder hit home with an immense explosion which threw him to the ground. Raising his head in dizzy disbelief, he saw the bonfire flare up into an immense wall of flame, so high that he could not see the top of it and so wide that it extended from one side of the stone circle to the other. The revellers staggered back from it, suddenly astonished and afraid.

Carolan too looked on, open-mouthed. Shielding his face from the scorching heat with one hand, he watched in fright as the figure of a man stepped slowly and menacingly out of the flames.

A thin, high, keening of terror and amazement ran round the assembled throng. Naked figures moved back, scuttling away from the impossible apparition of a tall man in a grey suit, stepping unscathed out of the middle of an immense inferno.

Jak was first to marshal his thoughts, gasping his disbelief.

'Allardyce? Charles Allardyce? No, that's crazy, it can't be. Pinch me, Jennah. I'm dreaming, I must be.'

Allardyce surveyed the scene with a supreme and joyous disdain. His eyes were like burning coals in his ghost-pale face, the flames behind him licking about him like the tongues of fawning pet dogs.

'My dear Carolan,' he said, his voice a sneer of contemptuous amusement. 'You really ought not to play games with forces you do not understand. The strangest things can happen.'

'Allardyce? No, it can't be you.' Carolan was transformed to a picture of quivering, cringing terror. 'Those flames, like a furnace they are ...'

Allardyce laughed drily.

'Such an ignorant little peasant, aren't you, Carolan – or should I say Mr Tarrant?'

He stepped a little further away from the flames, and his fire-bright eyes swept the huddle of naked figures around the edge of the circle; thin white bodies crouching in the lee of the ancient stones, as if they could offer some protection. Pathetic, all of them. Pathetic like children, helpless and wide-eyed and stupid. He noted a shadow of confused disbelief, then anger move across their frightened faces as he began to tell them a few home-truths about their precious leader.

'Of course, your dear leader's name isn't really Carolan – or did he forget to tell you that? Mr Benjamin Tarrant isn't quite all that he seems, as I am sure the East Midlands Constabulary would be happy to attest. What was your last conviction for again, Carolan – criminal damage, petty theft and deception, wasn't it? Oh, and by the way, he isn't much of a shaman either; and he certainly isn't as clever as he thought he was; are you, *King of Lynmoor*?'

The words were spoken with a vehement sarcasm that cut Carolan to the quick and made rage burn in his cowardly belly. Emboldened for a moment, he raised his head and turned his gaze on the travellers, trying desperately to reimpose his will upon them. They were watching him, but their expressions were changing, darkening, the last vestiges of their belief and trust ebbing rapidly away.

'Don't believe Allardyce!' he snarled. 'He's lying to you.'

Carolan screamed in sudden, vicious pain as Allardyce

361

seized him by the brown mop of his hair, jerking his head back so that he was looking up at Allardyce, towering above him.

'Please, please . . . don't do that.' His fingers scrabbled to free himself, but Allardyce had him fast, twisting and pulling his hair and beard until the pain was so terrible that he was forced to stop struggling.

'I shall do whatever I like, Carolan. The power is mine now. Isn't that right, Mr Tarrant?' As Carolan did not respond, Allardyce twisted the hair a little tighter. '*Isn't it?*'

'It . . . it is,' yelped Carolan, pain searing through him, almost robbing him of speech.

'You see how magnificent your king is?'

Spitting out the words with venomous contempt, Allardyce let go of Carolan's hair and pushed him violently away. He fell to the ground, a crumpled, sobbing heap of defeat and despair.

Walking back towards the bonfire, Allardyce stretched out his hand and thrust it into the heart of the inferno. The multicoloured flames lapped at his flesh obsequiously, and he laughed with delight, feeling neither heat nor pain. All eyes were staring at him, fixed on this thing that could not be true, this hellish apparition of dark power.

Lying on the ground at Allardyce's feet was a naked girl, blindfolded and unable to run away. He stooped to touch her and she squirmed with fear, unsure of what was about to happen to her and instinctively afraid. He pulled her on to her knees and saw that she was very young and rather pretty; pretty enough to satisfy even his hunger – for a while. There was a sheen of still-wet semen on her lips, and he anticipated the pleasure of filling her mouth with his own burning-white tide of lust.

Raising his arms to the black arch of the night sky, Allardyce summoned up the new and exhilarating power that was within and around him. A subtle change began to creep over the encampment, as fear ebbed away to be replaced by the throbbing need to couple.

Jennah felt Jak's arms tighten about her, his penis hardening once again in the small of her back; and in spite of her fear the warmth of desire returned. But it was no longer a pleasant sensation; this time it was a raw need, shaking her like a puppet, stealing away her will and making her the servant of some dark, unwelcome hunger.

'You have a new king now,' laughed Allardyce, his eyes mad with the lusts of power and sex, his fingers unbuttoning his pants and taking out the stiff, menacing shaft of his cock. 'Dance for your king! All of you, dance! I command it.'

And as desire stole over the encampment like a hungry wolf, the orgy began again.

At dead of night, in the valley that lay between Hilltop Tor and Brackwater Hall, the doomed village was emerging from sleep. Figures were moving in the shadows, voices whispering and calling in the darkness.

The villagers were gathering in ones and twos, in mating pairs like wild beasts. They were rutting, coupling; neighbours and bitter enemies alike forcing pleasure from each other's bodies as heedlessly as if they were mere machines of blood and sinew. They had no real consciousness of what they were doing, only a vague understanding that this must happen, that as they obeyed the silent command, the power of the desire within them would in some way become part of the much greater, much wilder power that was growing all around them.

Old and young, beautiful and ugly; all heard the silk-smooth voice within them, calling up lewd pictures that forced their bodies to respond. Some wept as they walked naked into the darkness; some half-lost recollection made the tears course down their expressionless cheeks, though their bodies were exulting in the raw pleasure of this new and compelling passion. Others laughed to themselves in the madness of their lust, their voices the voices of excited children, full of the expectation of forbidden joy.

The Hall laughed too. And its laughter was like a dark mist that crept down over the moors and into the valley, enveloping it in a soft, impenetrable cloak of night.

'More wine?'

Anthea held out her glass and Leon filled it, the cold yellowish liquid forming a mist of condensation on the outside of the glass. Anthea put it to her lips and ran her tongue-tip over it, lapping the distilled wetness with enjoyment. That done, she took a sip of the wine, letting it roll slowly back over her tongue in a starburst of flavour.

'Thank you,' she said, searching Duvitski's dark face for clues that would show he understood, that he was experiencing the same emotions and sensations. 'I don't normally get plastered this early in the afternoon, but in the circumstances, I think we could both do with a drink.'

She wondered if he could feel it too – the great throbbing intensity of attraction she had felt the very first moment their eyes had met. Since then, the feeling had not abated but grown palpably stronger; and not for the first time, Anthea caught herself fantasising about what it would be like to make love with him – not gently or playfully, as she usually liked to do, but with a wild savagery, as if they were two animals.

The thought both amused and perplexed Anthea as she sipped her wine and edged a little closer to Duvitski on the sofa. It wasn't as if this man was even her type. She liked them younger, boyish even; not intense and brooding like Duvitski. But right here and now, on the sofa in Pendorran's drawing room, he seemed to her to be the most attractive man in the whole wide world.

Her thigh brushed his and he looked up, his dark eyes questioning and deeply sensual.

'Is this real?' Duvitski replaced his glass on the small side-table. 'I need to know. Is it really happening, or am I just going quietly mad?'

He ran his fingers through his shock of short, dark

hair, and Anthea thought that she too would like to do that – would like to savour the sensuality of the touch. She breathed in the faint but lingering scent of his cologne, and the feeling grew and blossomed within her as she listened to his voice.

'Hearing Pendorran talk, I think I must be insane – I mean, it's obvious that Allardyce wants to take over the world, but – a house?' He looked her straight in the eye. 'Can you believe that?'

Almost independent of her will, Anthea's fingers reached out and touched Duvitski's thigh. To her immense satisfaction he did not flinch from the touch, and she spread her fingers over the smooth fabric of his trousers, feeling the slight hint of steel in his strong, muscular leg.

'*This* is real,' she replied. And she leaned over him, her small breasts brushing lightly against his shirt-front as she kissed him full on the lips. 'You could start by believing that.'

She withdrew, her heart thumping, almost shocked by her own audacity. Not that she had ever been reticent when it came to getting what she wanted; but this felt different. This felt disturbingly like flirting with danger.

'Do that again,' murmured Duvitski, his hands roaming over Anthea's back, surprisingly sensitive fingers seeking out the zipper of her dress and easing it down a fraction of an inch. The message was clear, and Anthea took it to heart instantly, forcing her lips against his in a message of pure lust.

'I could do more,' she said, letting her fingers graze the long line of swollen flesh beneath Duvitski's pants.

'I wish you would.' Duvitski hesitated. 'But what if Pendorran comes back?'

'Then he'll just have to stand and watch, won't he? Maybe he'll even learn a thing or two.' She giggled.

What had got into her this afternoon? Anthea hardly recognised herself. It was as though there was something special about Lynmoor – something that made you want to forget all your inhibitions and simply let go. She could feel her clitoris swelling so hard that it seemed to fill the entire space between her love-lips, becoming the very centre of her universe.

Duvitski pulled her onto his lap and she knelt astride him as he slid the zipper down to the small of her back. Her fingers loosened his too-formal tie, eased it off and threw it to the floor, a coiled and disarmed snake. The top button of his shirt was stiff and her scarlet nails were too long to be practical, but he helped her, releasing the button with one hand whilst the other smoothed up and down over the long, silky V of bare back between the gaping teeth of her zipper.

She stripped him of his shirt greedily, tugging the sleeves over his hands without even bothering to remove the monogrammed cufflinks. His bare torso invited kisses, and she ran her lips over the broad expanse of his chest, tweaking the nipples with her teeth.

'Now you,' smiled Duvitski as she sat up, breathing heavily.

Anthea slid off his lap and wriggled the tight white dress down over her shoulders. Her body emerged from the stretchy material like a butterfly from a chrysalis, her bright red lacy bra and panties as insolent and daring as lipstick on a harlot's mouth. She basked in the heat of Duvitski's gaze, his eyes devouring her as she stepped out of the dress and threw it aside.

'So – do you like what you see?' she teased. She posed provocatively for him, her skin deeply tanned from the bohemian lifestyle she had enjoyed in Devon with Hans and Gareth. She felt elated, tremendously aware of how good her body must look; a morsel easily delicious enough to eat.

Duvitski gave a low, throaty growl.

'Come here, and don't tease.'

'Why not? You know you like it.'

Anthea was intoxicated with lust. She thrust out her breasts, making the small but juicy mounds seem huge and inviting in their tiny bra. Her thumbs were hooked under the strip of elastic which ran along the underside of her bra cups, and she was dancing, just for him.

'Want to see some more?'

'Of course I do. Can't you see how much?' Duvitski's cock twitched convulsively in his pants, its swollen head fighting for release from its prison.

'Then show me some more of *you*. Take off your trousers. I want to see what sort of present you've got for me. Then maybe – just maybe – I'll let you see . . .'

Duvitski fiddled with the buckle of his belt, cursing quietly to himself as the metal pin refused to budge. At last it yielded and he swiftly unbuttoned his trousers, sliding them down over his hips and kicking off his shoes as he pulled them off. The white briefs beneath moulded the contours of his body like a second skin, the fabric distended by the insolent thrust of his swollen prick. An ooze of wetness had already made the thin cotton almost transparent, so that the purple plum of his glans was clearly visible.

The sight excited Anthea to new heights of appetite. In a swift, triumphant move, she flicked up the elastic under her bra-cups, so that the red lace bra lifted in a single movement over the small hillocks of her pert breasts.

It lay now in a tight red band across the tops of her breasts, the scarlet of the lace complementing the deep rose-pink of her nipples, engorged with blood. The elastic was stretched very taut, making the flesh bulge out, and the areolae were swollen with need, the blue veins standing out against the tanned golden flesh. She was so hungry, so famished for sex, that she almost threw herself upon Duvitski there and then.

But she hung back, wanting to tantalise him still further, wanting to make the anticipation last before finally giving in to this raging, surging passion within her.

Duvitski's thighs were parted, forcing the fabric of his briefs even more tightly across the head of his penis; and his hand moved to his balls, cradling their aching weight through the material. He fondled them gently, lovingly, making love to himself as he watched Anthea strip for him, the power of her lust guiding his caresses.

'If you want more,' she said, bending over Duvitski so that her breasts stood out on her chest, the nipples swollen and proud, 'you'll have to show *me* more.' Her fingers slipped down Duvitski's torso to the waistband of his briefs. 'Much more.'

He put his hand on the waistband, as though to slide off the pants, then stopped. He smiled.

'Well, maybe I will and maybe I won't.'

'You don't want me to strip for you?'

Duvitski reached up and took the juicy fruits of Anthea's breasts into his cupped hands, rejoicing in the feel of the flesh firming at his touch, the nipples growing erect and rubbery in the palms of his hands. Slowly and deliberately he let his fingers slide to her back, feeling for the catch of her bra and releasing it, making the elasticated fabric spring away from her flesh. Gently he slipped the bra over her arms and threw it away.

'Of course I want you to strip for me.'

He began massaging her breasts again, freed now from the impediment of the bra. Anthea's eyes were half-closed in pleasure, her breathing synchronising instinctively to the rhythm of Duvitski's caresses.

'But Leon, I'm not going to take off my panties unless you take off yours,' she pouted teasingly.

'Why don't *you* take mine off, then?' Duvitski took hold of Anthea's hand and guided it to the sap-filled branch of his prick, still veiled by the thin cotton briefs. 'Go on – undress me. I want to feel you doing it to me.'

Feeling utterly wicked, Anthea let her fingers enclose the stiff rod, moving it gently up and down so that she could feel fabric moving over flesh, and beneath it, flesh on flesh as Duvitski's foreskin slid back and forth over the glans. She knew how it must torment him, to feel her caressing him through his pants; knew how he must yearn to have fingers on his shaft, skin against skin. But she would torment him a little longer – with her caresses and her scent.

As she bent over him, one knee resting on the sofa, one foot on the floor, her thighs parted and a cloud of musky fragrance wafted up from the soaked gusset of her red panties. She could feel Duvitski's chest rising and falling as he breathed it in deeply, filling his lungs with the sweet intoxication of her sex; and his excitement communicated itself to her, renewing the eternal spring of passion between her moist, warm thighs. She couldn't believe how hungry for sex she was, how carried away with the sheer wickedness of unbridled lust.

At last she peeled down the briefs, sliding them down in a single movement so that Duvitski's cock sprang out, its twin-lobed, purple fruit glossy with juice and beneath the thick, smooth shaft, the heaviness of his scrotal sac, his balls large and mobile beneath the velvety purse.

She stepped back, not taking her eyes off Duvitski's sex as she stripped down her own red panties, stepping out of them with a lascivious daintiness which drove Duvitski to distraction.

'For pity's sake come here.'

Anthea shook her head.

'Come and get me.' She took a couple of steps back, so that she was just out of range.

'Don't play games with me, Anthea.' Duvitski's eyes were half-laughing, half-pleading.

'I told you – if you want me you'll have to come and get me.'

Anthea darted behind a chair and Duvitski leapt after her, shaking with laughter as he made grab after grab for her, and each time his quarry succeeded in escaping his clutches. It was a game – a glorious, sensual game of kiss-chase; and they were children again. Strangely knowing children in grown-up bodies, discovering a teasing, tormenting, exhilarating pleasure.

At last she let herself be caught, surrendering herself to him and letting him trap her between his hungry body and the age-blackened doors of a carved oak cupboard. She couldn't wait any longer, couldn't resist the thunderous beating of her heart, or the crazy surging blood in her veins; or the soft caress of a hand on the very margin of her pouting sex-lips.

369

'At last,' panted Duvitski. 'But now I've caught you, whatever shall I do next?'

Anthea pressed herself against him, nipple to nipple, hip to hip, and whispered:

'I'm yours, Leon. Yours to do whatever you want with.'

He kissed her, and she felt the hard ridges of the oak cupboard digging into her back and backside. Duvitski's desire was no less unyielding. It felt to him as though the tension and anxiety of the last few days were suddenly escaping from him in a great explosion of pent-up excitement. He couldn't work any of it out, but what he did know was that he was here, alive, hungry; and now he had the most amazing woman, naked in his arms. What's more, he also had the most terrible feeling that the world might come to an end before he had made love to her even once. How could he possibly let that happen?

He flexed his hips to and fro a few times, letting Anthea feel the extent of what she had done to him. There was cool wetness all over the head of his cock, smearing and dripping over Anthea's belly. And he could feel dewdrops of her own sex-juice transfer themselves to his skin as she rubbed her triangle of brown maidenhair against the base of his cock.

'What's the matter – don't you know what to do?' teased Anthea, grinding her pubis hard against the root of his shaft.

'Oh, I know exactly what I'm going to do,' he replied. And he placed his hands under Anthea's backside, clutching the cheeks, opening them up with his hands as he lifted her up and sat her on top of the oak cupboard.

It was at exactly the right height. With her thighs outspread and her pussy-lips parted, Duvitski could see right into the very heart of Anthea's sex. It glistened a deep, moist pink between fringed lips of a plump, paler pink flesh which framed it like some precious treasure in a fur-trimmed casket. And at the very centre, running with moisture, gleamed the round pink pearl of Anthea's desire: the fat tip of her engorged clitoris.

He bent to kiss it. It tasted of all the desire in the world. Urgency drove him and he lapped hungrily at the round bead, savouring the juice that trickled and ran around it. He took the shaft of her clitoris between his lips and Anthea started making little animal cries of pleasure, shuffling her backside on the cupboard top so that her bum-cheeks parted and the roughly carved top began to rub the delicate flesh between.

'Leon, oh, oh, please . . .'

Anthea's words came in staccato gasps as he licked her out, driving her to unimagined transports of delight. It was odd if he thought about it, very odd. Duvitski had never experienced any special pleasure in tonguing a woman's clitoris. In fact, his enthusiasm for oral sex had been almost entirely confined to getting his girlfriends to do it to him. But here and now, the rules had changed. He didn't have to prove anything any more. The only thing that mattered was to obey the driving impulse within him, the voice that whispered to him to do it, do it, do it . . .

It felt like heaven, having her clitoris on his tongue. As his tongue-tip caressed her, Leon felt as if his whole body was being stroked and kissed. Miraculously, the more he pleasured Anthea, the more he felt that pleasure himself, swelling his cock almost to the point of explosion. Her juice was spicy-sweet in his mouth, filling his whole being with the delicious flavours of sex: dozens of little taste-bombs bursting on his tongue as he sucked and licked her to the brink of orgasm. And when he had brought her there a second time – and only then – he decided that he would allow himself the luxury of sliding his aching dick between those beautiful silky thighs.

Anthea arched her back as she felt it begin to happen – the calm before the storm, the unnatural silence in her head as simple pleasure gave way to the first paroxysms of ecstasy. Her breasts stood out on her chest, the nipples hard and red and succulent as fresh strawberries, and her whole body tensed as the spreading

371

warmth began to localise, focusing at last on the hardened bud between her thighs.

Duvitski received the tribute of Anthea's orgasm joyfully, her wetness running in rivulets over his lips and tongue as her pleasure-muscles contracted again and again and again. His penis strained for release and suddenly, overwhelmed by the sight and the taste and the feel of his lover's come, he felt his balls tense and his shaft stiffen. His mind whirled and his body refused to obey him; he could not hold himself back any longer. A moment later, his seed was spurting out in hot, thick jets that dripped down the front of the cupboard and onto the bare stone floor.

In the doorway to the drawing room, Joseph coughed discreetly – as ever unruffled by even the most curious goings-on in his master's house. If he had learned anything in his long years of service, it was never to question anything.

'Pardon me sir, madam,' he began. 'Mr Pendorran feels you may wish to join him and Miss Treharne in the study. A number of people from Hilltop Tor have arrived to see him.'

Jennah brought her fist down on the desk with unaccustomed force.

'You have to do something!'

Pendorran sat back in the bosun's chair that had been salvaged from a tea-clipper wrecked on the rocks at Polmadoc Point, a good two centuries ago. His face betrayed no emotion, but Maria thought she detected a note of despair in his voice.

'Indeed; but what would you have me do?'

'Something – anything. Anything to stop him before he destroys us all.'

At that point Anthea and Duvitski entered the room, and Jennah spun round to face them, spitting fury.

'You! It's as much your fault as his, you bastard. You're evil. That's what you are, evil.'

She lunged at Duvitski, but he parried, catching her

wrists. His face was a pale mask of horrified realisation. He had never quite understood before just how much he was hated in Lynmoor; or was it just that it had never really mattered to him before?

'I'm sorry, miss, I . . .'

Maria interrupted, keen to defuse this potentially explosive situation.

'Strange as it may seem, Mr Duvitski is helping us, Jennah. Now, if you could just try and explain exactly what's been happening.'

Jennah sank down onto the window seat, suddenly very tired. Jak was standing by her side, stony-faced and silent. Duvitski felt even more intimidated by his silence than by Jennah's overt rage.

'OK, I'll try,' began Jennah. 'Last night, at Hilltop Tor, we had a ritual. Carolan said he wanted to conjure earth-spirits to help us fight the developers.'

'Ignorant fool,' muttered Pendorran, stabbing the point of a fountain pen into his blotting paper.

'He gave us stuff to drink – stuff that made us light-headed. But we weren't out of our heads, Mr Pendorran, you've got to believe that. Me and Jak and the others, we know what we saw.'

'And what was that?' Maria sat down on the window seat next to Jennah and took hold of her hand. It felt very cold, and despite the summer heat Jennah was shivering.

'In the middle of the ritual, the fire blazed up into a raging inferno and – you won't believe this, I know you won't; I can hardly believe it myself . . . Charles Allardyce walked right out of the middle of that damn fire! I swear it, Miss Treharne, I saw it clear as day. The flames were all round him but they weren't even touching him. And he just kept on laughing.'

'What *is* she talking about?' hissed Anthea.

Duvitski gripped the top of a bookcase to steady himself.

'I don't think I want to know,' he replied.

'Go on,' said Maria, silencing Duvitski with a glare. 'We believe you, I promise you we do.'

'He frightened the living daylights out of us, and as for Carolan, well . . .' Jennah gave a grunt of disgust that was almost a sob. 'Well, Allardyce told us all about what Carolan really was, and then he did something . . . I can't explain what it was . . . but he started shouting "I have the power now – dance for your king", and the next thing we knew, we couldn't stop ourselves. It was like this tremendous heat flaring up inside; we had to have sex, couldn't get enough of it.'

Jak laid a hand on Jennah's shoulder, and she looked up at him questioningly.

'Of course,' Jak said bitterly, 'when it was all over we found out our so-called leader Carolan had pissed off with what little money we had and most of our food. And there have been some very strange things happening in the village, too, Mr Pendorran. Orgies in the middle of the night, some say. We daren't go near – it's like a madness, you can't stop it.'

'Even up here I can feel it,' whispered Jennah, all her self-possession evaporating now that the story had been told. 'Can't you? It's like the air is full of . . . full of sex.'

Maria looked at Pendorran. His eyes seemed clouded, as though he were gazing into the far distance, at something inexorable and dark. His voice was leaden with despair:

'It has begun, and it is worse even than I had foreseen. In the days to come, the power of the Hall will grow and spread across Lynmoor, awakening lust and ruin as it creeps across the moors to the sea. And when it has sated its lust, Brackwater Hall will sit atop the dead and violated body of the one true Goddess.'

'No!' Jennah let out a gasp of disbelief, and her fingers clutched at Maria's as she drowned in fear and incomprehension. 'You can't let that happen.'

'It will happen,' replied Pendorran. He hesitated, and turned to focus his sea-grey eyes on Maria. 'But you can stop it, Maria. You know you can.'

'Me?' Maria felt the colour drain from her face. 'But how? What can I do?' She looked around the room, at the ashen faces and the empty, despairing eyes. She pleaded silently for their understanding, but she could feel the weight of their expectation on her. 'Look, I can't just walk in through the front door of Brackwater Hall and . . .'

She turned back to Pendorran, but he was gone. They were all gone: Anthea and Duvitski, Jennah and Jak and Pendorran. Even the study at Polmadoc was gone.

'What . . ? How . . ?'

A moment ago it had been broad sunlight, but now she found herself in semi-darkness, relieved by a blaze of flickering candlelight. This was not a summer's afternoon; it was not even Polmadoc.

With a shock she realised that she was standing in the great dining hall at Brackwater Hall. But it was not as she had left it, a few days ago. In place of the electric lights there were candelabra and a vast chandelier blazing with hundreds of tiny candles, illuminating the oval mahogany dining-table beneath. Was she dreaming, or was this really happening? Could she really have travelled here in the space of a thought, or was this all just some crazy hallucination which would end in a moment?

Maria tried to move, but her clothes felt heavy and restricting. Looking down, she saw that she was dressed not in the light blouse and skirt she had been wearing at Polmadoc, but in an elaborate hooped creation of dark-red watered silk and Brussels lace with a low, square neckline and a bodice so tight that it pushed her breasts up into two round, white globes.

The dress was so closely fitted that she could hardly breathe, and as dozens of petticoats swirled about her legs she realised that she was completely naked underneath. Reaching up, she touched her hair and found that it, too, had changed. Instead of falling in a loose cascade of unruly waves, it was piled up in a tall confection of tight coils, with a few small, springy ringlets that bounced and bobbed around her cheeks as she moved.

As Maria's eyes grew more accustomed to the gloom

beyond the blaze of candlelight, she saw shadowy figures gliding silently towards her out of the gloom. Two maids and two footmen, dressed in a livery of crimson and white; a livery that would not have been out of place in the eighteenth century . . .

The tall, sandy-haired man and the red-blonde girl Maria did not recognise, though they smiled at her as if they knew her well. But the young footman and the maid with the curly bleached-blonde hair, she knew instantly; covering her mouth with her hands, she gasped and took a step backwards in astonishment.

Here, in this surreal world of period fantasy? Surely it could not be.

'Patsy? Geraint – it is you, isn't it? What are you doing here? What am I doing here?'

They did not speak, but bowed their heads respectfully and offered her silver salvers filled with brightly-coloured sweetmeats.

'Maria?'

The familiar voice made her blood freeze and she turned slowly round to face the long, polished dining table. Beyond the glare of the chandelier, beyond the cluster of cut-glass wine goblets and the decanter of ruby wine, she saw a figure, seated at the distant end of the table.

Because of the blaze of candle-light he was little more than an indistinct silhouette, and she walked towards him along the curving rim of the table until the glare of the chandelier was behind her. But even before she glimpsed his face, she knew who he was. An aristocratic Englishman with cold eyes and an insatiable lust for power.

Fear gripped her heart like a freezing hand as he raised his glass to toast her, and smiled.

'Hello, Maria,' said Allardyce. 'I've been waiting for you. Won't you join me?'

# Chapter Seventeen

*P*endorran's study was strangely hot and humid, and Anthea could feel little trickles of sweat pooling in the small of her back, soaking into the already-moist fabric of her white summer dress. Despite the heat, ice-cold shivers were running over her skin, erecting all the tiny hairs on the backs of her hands, and making her teeth chatter with fright.

No one spoke. What could they possible say? Jak and Jennah were wide-eyed and pale, and by her side Anthea could feel the rigid terror in Duvitski's body. Not one of them could believe the evidence of their own eyes.

The figure glittered in the afternoon sunlight, its stillness both beautiful and terrifying: a perfectly transparent, perfectly remembered image of Maria Treharne, frozen in time, like a coloured photograph reflected on glass.

Pendorran extended the index finger of his right hand to touch the image; and at the first contact it burst like an iridescent soap bubble, leaving not the slightest evidence that it had ever existed.

Curling his fingers into the palm of his hand, as though trying to recapture the invisible, Pendorran announced to the empty air:

'She has gone beyond our reach. The Hall has her now.'

Seated at her own table in the immense dining room at Brackwater Hall, Maria ate as though in a dream. The food was brightly-coloured and tasted like nothing she had ever eaten before, but she continued eating because it was part of Allardyce's game.

The house's game?

At the opposite end of the table Allardyce helped himself to another glass of the dark-red wine. She watched him drink deeply, and in spite of her loathing of the man, she could feel her resistance weakening. Now that she was back here at Brackwater Hall, she could no longer maintain any semblance of detachment from the darkly-sensual power that was all around her. It was like a narcotic drug, seeping into her through every pore of her skin, awakening her slowly but steadily to a sensual hunger that was as much spiritual as physical.

'Why have you brought me here?' she demanded. The red wine tasted coppery, almost like blood, but her thirst was insatiable and she drank again, feeling the treacherous heat spreading from her lips to her throat and belly.

'My dear Maria, I did not bring you here,' protested Allardyce, all injured innocence and charm. 'You came here of your own accord. Your own desire has brought you to me.'

'I have no desire for you,' countered Maria, the spoon in her hand shaking so much that the candlelight struck repeated flashes of light from the polished silver bowl.

'There is no purpose in deceiving yourself,' said Allardyce. He looked handsomer than Maria remembered him. The richly-embroidered brocade frock-coat and frilled shirt suited him, as though his brand of elegant arrogance had at last found its ideal decor. 'I can feel how much you desire me.' He leaned slightly forward, and the candlelight lent his features a satanic charm. 'In fact, Maria, I can *taste* your desire. It is sweet and spicy, and it makes me hungry for much, much more.'

Maria avoided his gaze, but as she looked eyes met Geraint's. They were fixed on her, alm. blinking in their steadiness, blue and clear and co lapis lazuli. They seemed to be looking right into he. heart, reading the truth of a desire so dark that she dared not admit to it, even to herself.

'I have wanted you since the very first time I saw you,' continued Allardyce, ignoring or perhaps savouring her confusion. 'But no, that is not quite true.' He paused. 'I wanted to conquer you even before then; the thought of you intrigued and amused me. I thought even then of all the pretty games that you and I could play together. And I know how much you love to play, Maria.'

'I am not your plaything and I never shall be,' snapped Maria, her anger surfacing through the red mist of desire. 'I do not have to do anything that you want me to do.'

'No, of course not.' Allardyce sipped wine and held the glass up to the light. A swirling, coiling redness seemed to fill the glass, something that seethed and swam and lived. 'Only what you want to do. But you *do* want to, don't you Maria?'

She did not reply. Her treacherous body was betraying her, the tight-laced dress and the crisp, starched petticoats stimulating her mercilessly whenever she made the slightest movement, or breathed in the shallowest breath. She fought down the tide of sensations, but it was rising up her body, threatening to engulf her. This was a test, a trial of her endurance, she knew that; but knowing that did not make it any easier to bear. All the caution and the fear that she had mustered in her defence were ebbing away, and the empty void within her was filling up like a glass vial, replenished with the golden honeydew of desire.

Allardyce watched her, following her every tiny movement with the arrogance of certainty. She was compellingly attractive, even beautiful; and he craved the touch and taste of her flesh with an obsessive need that contained every fertile seed of madness. Maria Treharne was not as clever as she had imagined she was – or as powerful. How could she possibly have thought she could resist him? He could just take her here and now, if he chose; force himself on her, but that was not what the Hall wanted. It hungered to break and possess her spirit, so that she would come crawling and pleading to him, begging him to take the sweet gifts she offered. He saw into her mind and felt her resistance melting, crumbling away. Soon, she would give herself to him.

He dabbed the corners of his mouth with a napkin and clicked his fingers. Silent figures loomed up out of the shadows, ready and willing to do his bidding.

'Grace, Benedict – take Miss Treharne to the robing room.'

Hands touched Maria, sliding under her arms and lifting her to her feet. The touch was gentle but firm, and when she tried to resist she discovered a steely strength in the hands that held her, guiding her away from the table, and towards the door. She looked back, and saw Allardyce standing by the table, flanked by Patsy and Geraint. All their eyes were on her; watching, waiting, following her greedily into the unknown.

Unsteady and disorientated, she allowed herself to be led out through the door and into the corridor, lined with burning candles that cast an eerie, flicking glow. It was not at all as she remembered it. In the Brackwater Hall she knew, this corridor – or one very like it – ran for perhaps five or six yards, then was cut off short by a blank wall. But this corridor seemed to go on for ever, its far-distant end curving away to the right and then disappearing into fathomless shadows.

The whole shape of the place seemed wrong, too – the floor seemed to slope away from her at a crazy angle, all the door frames seemed gnarled and crooked and when she looked at them a second time, she saw that they were made not from dead, painted wood but from the trunks of living trees, hacked into rough pillars yet defiantly sprouting with green-leaved twigs.

Her dress swished around her legs as she walked, the many layers of starched petticoat rubbing and tickling her thighs and bare backside. The tight-laced bodice kept shifting slightly from side to side, producing a slow rubbing sensation on her belly and breasts. The neckline of the bodice was so low, and her breasts pushed up so high, that her sensitive nipples rested on the very margin of the fabric, its scratchy lace edging producing the most irresistable and lascivious frottage.

Already excited beyond the limit of mortal endurance, Maria felt her body yielding to these secret, unseen caresses; and cool, sweet juice moistened her thighs in the fear and hope of some dark and dangerous pleasure.

A shrill, piercing cry rent the air. As she turned her head, her eyes were dazzled by a sudden sunburst of colour, and seconds later a flock of brightly-coloured parakeets flashed overhead, screeching as they flapped their green and scarlet wings. Moments later they were gone, becoming once again one with the darkness of the Hall.

No one spoke. Grace and Benedict seemed able to communicate with each other by look and touch, but they made no attempt to speak to her. She could only guess at their intentions from the touch of their soft, smooth hands. As they reached an archway leading into another room, they paused. Maria saw that the rounded frame of the arch seemed to be made of carved grey stone, smooth like slate but radiating a curious warmth. When she touched it, she recoiled in horror; for it was warm and soft and yielding as living flesh.

She made some small attempt to resist, but Grace and Benedict easily succeeded in making her enter the room. And as she stepped inside, she realised with a shock that she recognised it – it was her bedroom, but changed in ways that she was afraid to comprehend.

Instead of pale peach-coloured wallpaper, exposed stone met her eyes: huge, rough lumps of grey rock held together with a coarse, gravelly mortar. And between the stones grew crazy clumps of garishly-coloured flowers and moss, their roots seemingly embedded in the fabric of the house, as though they drew their life from the very soul of Brackwater Hall.

The dressing-table and chair were still there, and the washstand with the bronze-framed mirror above it – tokens of a seeming normality long since passed. But where Maria's bed had once been there stood a great square block of granite, its polished surface carved with pagan symbols, a cloth of white embroidered linen half covering the pinkish-grey stone. This was no longer a bed; it was an altar.

Beside it stood a white enamel bath, filled with a clear, rich red liquid that had the sweet, yeasty smell of summer fruit, mingled with the deep, rich spiciness of mulled wine. A warm steam rose from it, clouding the mirror, sending a waft of fragrance into the bedroom, making Maria feel dizzy and light-headed.

Her dress felt suddenly very tight and restricting – no longer offering the savoured caress of pleasure but a jealous lover's imprisoning embrace, something that she longed to be rid of.

It was as though Grace had read her thoughts. In a moment she was behind Maria, her white fingers fluttering at the base of the bodice as she released its tight-bound laces. And Maria gave a deep sigh of pleasure as the tightness was released and the sides of the dress moved apart, revealing the bare flesh beneath.

Benedict slid the puffed sleeves of the gown down over Maria's arms, and the crimson silk bodice slipped down until it was hanging down from her waist, her pink-nippled breasts naked and lonely for caresses. Maria had ceased to question whether or not this was what she wanted; it was something that she must endure. Would she be strong enough to resist the need for sex that burned within her?

Fear gripped her again, but it was weaker than the desire – the insidious, unwelcome desire that filled her head with wild imaginings. She tried to fill her mind with thoughts of Anthony, but he was far away; how could he help her here? He had warned her, and now she knew that it had all been true. She was the one; the only one who could help them all now. And she feared that, like Clara Megawne, she would prove unequal to the task.

The dress was stripped from her with a teasing sensuality that made her fear fade to a dull ache. The petticoats that hung from her waist yielded one by one to Benedict's practised fingers, while Grace ran her hands over Maria's shoulders and back, thrilling her with the lightest, the softest of caresses.

Maria let out a sigh as Benedict unfastened the tape holding the last of the white cotton petticoats tight about her waist, sliding the starched cotton down over her thighs and making her step out of it. The air felt cool on her overheated flesh, and she let her feet slide very slightly apart, so that a cool draught could tease the curly russet fringe at the top of her thighs.

Distant music filled her head; a rippling, coursing sound that bubbled like the dark, deep waters of an underground stream. It seemed to rise up out of the very earth itself, the music of the Tor, dark and sensual and compelling. Benedict led her across to the altar and she made no attempt to resist, the music mesmerising her, sapping her of her will. She was scarcely aware of climbing up, lying down on the white cloth and feeling the sinister warmth of the stone beneath her.

As she lay on her back, looking up at the twisted beams of the high ceiling, they seemed to swim in and out of focus, resolving from time to time into half-recognised images: faces, flowers, trees, rushing water, the outline of an erect penis that seemed both threatening and alluring.

She was vaguely aware of Grace and Benedict moving silently about the room, their feet seeming to glide over rather than touch the carpeted floor. And moments later Benedict was at Maria's head, rolling her onto her belly, stroking her hair back from her face, strong fingers kneading the muscles of her neck and shoulders as his caresses urged her to relax and submit.

And Maria's whole body began to relax instinctively as she felt Grace's fingers moving over her back, loaded with some creamy, scented unguent that slid cool and smooth across her bare skin in wide, circular movements all the way from shoulders to sacrum. A shifting fragrance hung and drifted in the air – the balance of scents changing, but always carrying the sweetness of rosewater, the exotic spiciness of sandalwood and the sacred, heavy muskiness of myrrh.

As Grace smoothed and kneaded the muscles at the base of her spine, Maria felt a wonderful sensation of warmth spreading downwards from her back to her belly, making her move her pelvis automatically back and forth, rubbing her pubic bone against the warm, living stone. It was as though the stone altar was becoming her lover, its hardness pressing again and again against her soft sex-lips, so that the pink fleshy cowl slid back and forth over the head of her erect clitoris.

Grace's hands moved downwards to the ample swell of Maria's backside, smoothing more of the cool, scented cream into the flesh of her buttocks, teasing away the tension and the fear. Maria wanted to resist. She tried with all her strength, but she could not. It was too blissful, too skilful a massage, and her whole body was crying out to be satisfied. Grace's thumbs moved gradually downwards, working their way into the deep crease between Maria's buttocks, making the eye of her anus dilate and contract in rapid succession as the tip of her long, scarlet thumbnail grazed the sensitive flesh.

The two thumbs met between her arse-cheeks, the nails pressed together, forming a perfect instrument of tormenting pleasure. Maria anticipated their next move, but she had lost her fear of it and welcomed the sudden, smooth knife-thrust as the dagger-point of the two thumbs entered her together, distending the tight sphincter in a single, efficient stroke.

It felt like a fiery blade plunging into her, making the desire within her flare up, the flame white-hot as phosphorus. But even this pain was pleasure – pleasure in a new and wonderful disguise. Her whole body began to abandon itself to the delight of these new sensations, aided by Benedict's gentle massage of her neck and shoulders. Maria was not fighting any more; she was letting the intruders have their will with her, slipping in and out of her in well-greased smoothness. The thumb-nails scratched the walls of her rectum, but the sensation delighted her, making her twist and moan on the altar of her pleasure's sacrifice. Her breasts rubbed against the white linen cloth, the hypersensitive buds of her nipples buffed by the rough fabric; but this served only to intensify her agony of delight.

Pictures came and went in the dark palace of her mind; images of shadowy figures half-remembered, their eyes wide with fear, their lips parted in a warning she could not hear. They were too far away to reach her, their faces slipping in and out of focus; and the call to pleasure rose high above all other sounds, filling her head with the rush and roar and scream of her own blood boiling in her veins.

When Grace withdrew her thumbs, Maria gave a little sob of emptiness, the pain of loss biting into her more keenly than any physical hurt. But already Benedict was helping her to roll onto her back, soothing her with new and ingenious caresses that covered her throat and belly and the proud crests of her nipples, deep rosy-pink with the urgency of her desire.

Grace expertly parted Maria's thighs, making her draw up her knees so that her sex opened in a moist, full-lipped kiss of welcome. Her fingers wound about the tight chestnut curls that adorned Maria's pubis, pro-voking little gasps and moans. The wetness was pouring out of her now, moistening the white linen beneath her, and running in glistening rivulets over the coral-pink inner lips of her womanhood.

Overwhelmed with shameful desire, Maria gazed up at the ceiling; it seemed to smile back at her, and music filled her head again as something cold and smooth and ruthless pushed its way between her love-lips. How much longer could she hold out against this overwhelming pleasure . . ?

Once more seated at the oval table in the dining hall, Allardyce gazed into its polished surface and saw reflected there the patterns of Maria Treharne's seduction – soon to become her degradation and submission. The yellowed ivory of the ancient dildo was slipping in between Maria's sex-lips with ease, and she was twisting and turning on the altar as she floundered helplessly in the deepening tide of pleasure. Lost, lost, almost lost for ever.

He would not have to wait very much longer. Soon she would be begging him to accept her surrender, crawling on her belly to him, pleading with him to take the gift of her body and her soul and force her into delicious subjugation.

With a malicious delight, he selected a fine, ripe peach from the glass bowl before him and held it up to the light. As his hand tightened around it, crushing the downy-skinned flesh, its thick, syrupy juice dripped between his fingers and onto the table-top, and he smiled to himself at the expectation of greater pleasures, yet to come.


'Can't we help her? Is there nothing we can do?'

Anthea was slowly coming to realise that this was neither a dream nor an elaborate deception; that the paganism which she had always scoffed at was not a pretty, middle-class game. If it was a game at all, it was a very dangerous one indeed.

Jennah stood up, putting her arm round Jak's waist.

'Yes, surely – surely there's something we can do. We can't just sit here and let this happen to her!'

'Well, I say we should go there – to the Hall,' announced Duvitski. He was not a patient man, infinitely preferring action to sitting around waiting for the worst to happen – whatever the worst might turn out to be. 'Surely that way we could stop Allardyce.'

Pendorran silenced him with an exasperated sigh.

'You don't understand,' he said. 'None of you have the faintest idea, do you? Maria is not at Brackwater Hall.'

'But you told us . . .', protested Anthea.

'Yes, the Hall has her; she is its captive. But she is not there within our own conception of time and space. Her soul has been taken into the very fabric of the house, too deep for us to reach her. Unless . . .'

'Unless what?' Fear and frustration had rendered the normally monosyllabic Jak unusually talkative. 'If there's something, whatever it is, the least you can do is tell us. Are you hiding something from us, or what?'

Pendorran shook his head.

'Not hiding, no. But considerable danger would be involved – perhaps a level of danger that you would find unacceptable. Mortal danger for every one of us.'

'Tell us,' insisted Anthea.

'We would need to perform a sexual ritual.'

Jennah let out a gasp of disbelief.

'Sexual ritual – like that mumbo-jumbo Carolan tried to con us with? Just when I was beginning to think you were genuine . . .'

'A sexual ritual, Jennah, yes.' Pendorran's steady tone did not waver. 'Needless to say I would not normally even consider it, but the only way for us to have a slight chance of reaching Maria is for us to create as much sexual energy as we can. We must try to match the dark energy of the Hall with light, do you understand?'

There was a long silence as cautious glances were exchanged. And then Anthea spoke.

'Look, Pendorran, I don't trust you but it looks like I'm going to have to. Maria's my friend and I'm damned if I'm going to leave her to the tender mercies of that mad bastard at Brackwater Hall. I'll do it.'

'Yeah. OK.' Jennah and Jak exchanged nods, and Jennah spoke. 'It's not as if there's any choice really, is there?'

Duvitski hesitated, then nodded wearily.

'Yeah, OK, OK. Count me in. I won't pretend to

understand what this is all about, but I've seen enough to know that there's something scary going on around here. And seeing as most of this is my fault, I guess it's the least I can do.'

'So be it.' Pendorran sounded genuinely relieved. 'Then you must all undress – quickly now, there is no time to lose. The longer we leave her, the further her spirit drifts away from us.'

Turning his back on them for a moment, he opened a wall-cupboard and took out a three-branched candle-stick with tall, white candles. Placing it in the middle of his desk, he lit the candles in turn, murmuring a chant as he did so. Then he took a piece of chalk from his desk drawer, and crouched down, filling the stone floor with a roughly-drawn pentacle whose five points almost touched the walls of the room.

'You must all be within the pentacle,' he said. 'The magical figure is your only protection against the dark-ness that will seek to engulf and destroy us.'

Naked now, they moved within the chalk lines, self-conscious and secretly afraid. No one spoke. Her heart thumping, Anthea felt Duvitski's fingers close around hers, warm and reassuring.

Pendorran took a jug of iced water from his desk and poured a little into a shallow glass dish, together with a pinch of red powder. Then he took the dish in both hands and lifted it chest-high. The water lapped at the edges of the dish, casting patches of liquid sunlight on the stone walls and floor of the room.

'This water is desire,' he intoned. 'This water is life itself. As it touches the sacred earth and refreshes it, so you will feel your bodies refreshed and filled with de-sire.'

And he tilted the dish with infinite slowness, so that the water first bulged then spilled over the edge.

As the first fat droplets touched the floor, it seemed to Anthea that the room began spinning crazily like some mad roundabout, everything around her blurring to an indistinct haze, so that all she could see was Duvitski, his eyes aflame with need as he drew her towards him in a kiss of searing passion.

Anthony waited at the centre of the pentacle for a few moments, letting the energy of their coupling flow into him like warm blood, strengthening him for what must come. Jennah and Jak, and Anthea and Leon, moved like silent automata before him, their bodies jerking and thrusting in a ritual of mute, unseeing ecstasy. He felt terrible doubt, and an agony of guilt for the grave danger he had placed them in; but there must be no going back now. There must be no trace of fear.

He stepped out of the pentacle, beyond the flimsy wall of protection that he had built for his companions. That much at least he owed them; but he could do no more. Only the Goddess could protect them now; and if he failed ... Now he could only see their faces and bodies as though through a mist, a veil that seemed to grow thicker and darker even as he looked at it. He felt himself being pulled away, the first greedy tongues licking at his flesh as they sought to suck him down into their dark vortex.

Swiftly he slipped the hunting knife from his belt and looked at it as if he were perceiving it for the very first time. The silver blade was delicately engraved, but the elaborate decoration concealed the vicious sharpness of a razor.

Ripping open his shirt, he ran the very tip of the knife lightly over his skin from throat to navel. A thin trail of deep red blood sprang up where the blade had touched, but he felt no pain. He had travelled far beyond the realm of physical sensation.

With a whispered supplication, Pendorran seized the knife in both hands and plunged it deep into his own heart.

The room was like a tropical lagoon; moist and hot and steamy. Maria's body felt supple and relaxed in the silky white shift in which Grace and Benedict had dressed her. Her skin was smooth and fragrant with oil, and she

389

could still recall with agonising clarity how good it had felt to have the ivory dildo inside her, thrusting in and out of her vagina, pressing hard against the neck of her womb as it drove her to new heights of sensual need.

Grace's skills had aroused her without satisfying; they had taken Maria almost to the very brink of orgasm a dozen times, each time denying her the final, supreme pleasure she so craved. And the pleasure-craving had dulled her brain as it had sharpened her senses. At the back of her mind, Maria knew that there had to be a purpose in this ritualistic deprivation, that she was being saved for something else . . . something she did not want to happen.

What could it be? Her memory seemed to have faded almost entirely away. She remembered that she was Maria, and that she had been brought to the Hall to fulfil a purpose; but she could no longer recall what that purpose was. It was as though some dark and sensual power had soaked into her skin along with the scented massage oils, making her drowsy and forgetful. All she could remember was that, for some unaccountable reason, she must not give in to the pleasure. She must resist the overwhelming desire to abandon herself to orgasm. But why? If only she could remember . . .

Allardyce seemed to emerge from the ruby-red dusk, as though he were a creation of the shadows. He was naked but for a long robe of white silk loosely belted at the waist. He said not a word, but Maria's eyes were drawn to him, unbidden excitement bubbling up inside her. The sheer white silk was so thin that it moulded itself to his body as he walked, and the mid-brown tangle of hair at the base of his belly appeared as a dusky shadow through the fabric, framing the long, thick, mobile appendage of his manhood.

When she first glimpsed it, it was in repose; but as she watched, it seemed to take on a new and vibrant life of its own, growing and swelling like a juicy sapling, full of fresh, hungry life. She wanted to touch it, but she was too fascinated to move. Rooted to the spot, mesmerised

390

by the power of some huge sensual will, Maria began to sway to the rhythm of distant music.

Like breath it was: as soft and fleeting, as deep and passionate. She could not discern the tune, and yet she knew what it was. It was the music of her own soul's desire, amplified into a symphony of sound and sense that wove its silken coils around her, imprisoning her in a cage of infinite sensual pleasure.

She felt Allardyce's arms close about her waist, and suddenly they were dancing together, their bodies moving instinctively to the rhythm as the spring tide of yearning rose within them. Allardyce's eyes were shining; shining with a deep red glow that reflected the flames burning in the fire-grate with a low, yet intense heat. And their heat seemed to melt her as she looked into them, making her laugh and throw back her head as Allardyce held her and they spun slowly round on the warm stone floor.

As she lent back in his arms, her pelvis was thrust forward against Allardyce's lower belly, and she felt the throbbing power of his manhood – growing, swelling, budding into an instrument of the sweetest torture. Her oiled and scented body began to run with tiny trickles of sweat as the heat of the room met the heat of her own inner desire. She was burning up; caught in a fever of such intensity that it could only be assuaged by the taste of Allardyce's seed on her parched tongue.

Allardyce's eyes narrowed as he tightened his embrace, forcing Maria to dance closer, to spin and whirl faster until her eyes grew quite unfocused with dizziness. He remained silent but inside he was laughing like a madman; he could feel her submitting to him with each new second that passed. He could sense that she had almost forgotten who she was – she had obviously long since ceased to understand why she was here.

And now she was putty in his hands, her strength ebbing away and her frail softness sinking lower and lower into his arms. Allardyce's whole body ached for her, for the triumph that would very shortly be his. The white silk robe skimmed the wet, hypersensitive head of his phallus again and again, and he ground his belly against Maria's, knowing that if he chose he could bring himself in seconds to the crisis-point, soaking her with the flood-tide of his come.

She was his; he could feel it. Her breasts were pillow-soft but iron-tipped beneath her robe, the nipples huge and rose-pink through the thin veiling of pale silk. She was lying back in his arms and he was supporting her as she danced with him, his thigh between hers, the flesh hot and wet with the sweet ooze of her intimate juice. What a little fool she was – to think that she could overcome this power, so much greater than the puny flickering within herself. In a few moments, she would become for ever a part of that power.

Slowly, making the moment of his triumph last, Allardyce began undressing Maria, unfastening the series of tiny bows that ran down the front of the robe one by one, then at last slipping the swishing, whispering silk down over her shoulders in a billowing cascade whose sheer white surface reflected a million shades of scarlet and crimson.

He slipped the robe from his own body and they were at last naked together, his sap-filled cock seeking out the succulent blossom of her sex with a hungry urgency. As he picked her up in his arms and laid her down on the deep, soft rug, a distant rumble of thunder cut through the thick, heavy air and she opened her eyes for a moment – as though, fleetingly, she had remembered. But the memory faded as quickly as it had come, and he knelt astride her, his manhood casting a dark shadow across the flesh of her belly as he prepared to take her.

The candles guttered for a moment as lightning flashed through the room, and a sudden hot, wild wind caught the heavy drapes at the windows, making them billow and writhe like the embodiment of souls in torment. Locked in an hermetic world of forbidden sensuality, Maria thought she heard Anthony's voice crying out to her; crying in agony: Maria, Maria, Maria. But his voice sounded so faint and far away, so very difficult to hear . . .

Allardyce raised his clenched fist and instantly the world seemed to stop on its axis: the music, the wind, the thunder and lightning, the voices, all faded to nothing, leaving silken, expectant silence.

The Hall was waiting.

Eyes flashing triumph, Allardyce placed the tip of his penis at the entrance to Maria's haven, and her hands moved to his hips. At last she was welcoming him in, inviting him to dive deep into the heart of her. He closed his eyes and prepared for the final sword-thrust of victory.

'No!' Maria's voice was a snarl of defiance, and Allardyce was so astonished that he did not even attempt to resist as she threw him violently onto his back. 'You may have your tricks, but the Goddess knows many more . . .'

He tried to move, to push her off him, but it was no use. Even if he had succeeded in struggling free, he knew that she would pursue him and capture him again. He was her victim now. She had him securely in her grip, her strength no longer merely human but the strength of something far greater that had flowered within her. Her vulval lips felt hot as molten lava as they closed about his upraised prick, and as she began to ride him he gave a thin scream of agonised, unwilling pleasure.

Little by little, the room began to change. The shadows seemed to lighten, the darkness lifting, the thunderous, unbreathable air cooling to the freshness of a summer night, fragrant with sleeping flowers. Allardyce had never felt such brutal, unforgiving pleasure before; Maria's sex had him in an iron grip and she was sucking the pleasure out of him, siphoning it out of him with such violence that he began to sob and plead for mercy – a mercy that he knew she would never give.

Suddenly the dark, heavy curtains were rent from top to bottom as a mighty wind rushed through the room, whirling and buffeting everything in its path, catching Maria's long russet hair and blowing it into a fiery banner. And after the wind came the light; not the gentle warmth of a summer sun, but a blinding whiteness whose purity made Allardyce cry out in sweet, unbearable agony. The room became a spinning, tumbling ball of light and at its centre two bodies coupled, the woman's head thrown back in triumph as she rode her victim to the summit of ecstasy.

Once again, as Maria's pleasure-juices welled up from the perpetual spring of her sex, she heard Anthony's voice calling to her – still very far away, but more clearly now. And now his distant soul was exulting with hers as the power within her drove away the darkness, letting in the light.

'Submit to me,' she cried, as her sex-muscles clenched in victorious ecstasy. 'Submit to your Mistress!'

Allardyce fought her will, but it was a thousand times too strong for him. And it was no longer simply the will of Maria Treharne. It was the will of a power that transcended his human understanding. He did not reply, but wept in anguish as his body betrayed the depth of his submission.

'Submit to your Mistress!' repeated Maria, and she ran her fingernails over Allardyce's flesh with a savage, cat-like pleasure. 'Submit to the one true Goddess.'

# Chapter Eighteen

The high moors were awash with August sunshine; great yellow pools of warmth that spilled down the hillsides and into the deep, lush valley where the village lay, its grey slate roofs shimmering in the heat-haze. It was the very image of rustic tranquillity.

Duvitski got out of his car and breathed in the warm, heather-scented air. A fat, furry bumble-bee droned by, laden with pollen and drowsy with nectar. It sounded immensely loud in the stillness, with only the faintest of gentle breezes to disturb the long, soft blades of grass about his feet.

Some nameless authority had spirited away the regiment of yellow diggers that had perched like birds of prey on the hillside above the village. Duvitski asked himself again and again: how could a village which, days ago, had been a ghost-town of churned-up turf and demolition notices be so silently, so miraculously restored to its former tranquil perfection? He could get no answers to his questions. If it weren't for Hawthorn Cottage, lying silent and empty, it would be almost as if nothing untoward had ever happened.

But there were other mysteries, equally baffling and infinitely more disturbing. What had really happened to Charles Allardyce and Anthony Pendorran? Not a sign had been seen of them since that day, a week ago, when the whole world had been turned upside-down. Each had disappeared as completely as if he had never existed.

What would Duvitski do next? He would stay. That much, he had decided. After all these years in the cut-and-thrust world of business, unquestioning acceptance did not come easy to him, yet the decision to stay in Lynmoor had been the easiest one of his life. Of course, he was crazy about Anthea, but even if she decided to go back to Cambridge in September, he knew he would remain here. For the first time ever, he had come to understand that some things could be more important than individuals and their desires.

Someone had to make sure it never happened again.

Unshed tears clouded Maria's eyes as she walked slowly through the stable yard at Polmadoc. Without Pendorran the whole house felt desolate and abandoned; she had to get out into the fresh air, take a walk along the cliff-top between earth and sky, where she could almost imagine she heard her lost lover calling to her in the wind-song, in the crashing of waves on the beach far below.

Jupiter, Anthony's pale stallion, whinnied in recognition as she passed his stall, but she turned away. Her own sense of loss was too great, her own pain still too acute to pay him much attention.

It had been a full week now, since the day when she had returned to Polmadoc and found the silver hunting-knife lying on the study floor, its ornately-engraved blade obscured by a thick, rusty-brown smearing of dried blood. Anthony Pendorran's blood. But still she could not accept what he had done for her; and in her pain and desire she felt angry with Pendorran – angry that he had left her when she needed him most.

Maria clenched her fingers into fists, so tightly that the nails dug into the flesh of her palms. What if she should leave this place? But of course, she never could, not now; she must find a way of coping. She had tried to drive away the memories, but the impression of his presence was so overwhelmingly strong. It seemed all around her, as though the warm wind and the sun and the fragrance of wild flowers were all part of his spirit, combining into a single, sensual caress that awoke a terrible yearning within her.

She emerged from between the stable buildings and the sea-breeze caught her hair, tossing and twirling it into copper-gold, glittering ringlets, as though the wind and the sun were her lovers. Her only lovers now. How she yearned for Pendorran's touch. She imagined she could feel his fingers stroking her face, his lips pressing into the nape of her neck as he bent to kiss her and his dark, swept-back hair fell forwards, lightly brushing her bare shoulder.

And then, in the distance, she saw him. A tall, dark figure framed against the flawless blue of the sky, his raven-black hair streaming out behind him as he stood on the cliff-top, gazing out to sea. But no; she must surely be mistaken. Anthony was dead, gone, lost to her forever; this could be no more than some crazy phantasm of her deluded desire.

'Anthony?'

Maria half-walked, half-ran the next few yards, then stopped in her tracks, his name tearing out of her in a great sob of joy and disbelief. Even before he turned to face her, she knew that he was smiling; and as he turned he beckoned to her to join him.

She ran to him and he took her in his arms, kissing her with a force that left her gasping for breath.

'But Anthony, how? I thought . . . I was afraid . . .'

'I've been waiting a long time for you,' he smiled, silencing her questions with a second kiss. 'My only Mistress.'

And as they stood together, feeling the power of their desire surging through them, elemental as the crashing waves below, and the burning sun above, Maria knew that they would be together for ever.

For ever at the very edge of the world.

\* \* \*

High on Brackwater Tor, the ancient Hall basked beneath the china-blue dome of the August sky. Tortoiseshell and scarlet butterflies fluttered and danced about the gardens, like stray blossoms blown from the laden bushes and trees. In the well-tended orchard, fruits swelled, bending the branches of the ancient trees with a bounty of red, green and gold; and the crystal-clear waters of the sunken pond glittered and shimmered with the moving shapes of a hundred tiny fish.

The promise and the prophecy had been fulfilled. The Mistress had returned to Brackwater Hall, and at last all was as it had been ordained. From now on, all would be harmony, life would be vibrant, and the certain expectation of eternal joy would prevail. Unless . . .

Somewhere in the core of the house's lost understanding, sunk into the stones so deep that it was almost forgotten, lay the small seed of a memory that had not quite been destroyed. A seed of power and purpose that might one day swell and grow again.

And as the Hall waited for evening to fall and Maria to come back from Polmadoc, it yearned also for its memories to return; patiently hoping that one day – sooner or later – some other prey would stray through the red door into its hungry mouth.

Into the silken cage.

B L A C K
*lace*

## NO LADY
### Saskia Hope

30 year-old Kate dumps her boyfriend, walks out of her job and sets off in search of sexual adventure. Set against the rugged terrain of the Pyrenees, the love-making is as rough as the landscape. Only a sense of danger can satisfy her longing for erotic encounters beyond the boundaries of ordinary experience.

ISBN 0 352 32857 6

## WEB OF DESIRE
### Sophie Danson

High-flying executive Marcie is gradually drawn away from the normality of her married life. Strange messages begin to appear on her computer, summoning her to sinister and fetishistic sexual liaisons with strangers whose identity remains secret. She's given glimpses of the world of The Omega Network, where her every desire is known and fulfilled.

ISBN 0 352 32856 8

## BLUE HOTEL
### Cherri Pickford

Hotelier Ramon can't understand why best-selling author Floy Pennington has come to stay at his quiet hotel in the rural idyll of the English countryside. Her exhibitionist tendencies are driving him crazy, as are her increasingly wanton encounters with the hotel's other guests.

ISBN 0 352 32858 4

## CASSANDRA'S CONFLICT
### Fredrica Alleyn

Behind the respectable facade of a house in present-day Hampstead lies a world of decadent indulgence and darkly bizarre eroticism. The sternly attractive Baron and his beautiful but cruel wife are playing games with the young Cassandra, employed as a nanny in their sumptuous household. Games where only the Baron knows the rules, and where there can only be one winner.

ISBN 0 352 32859 2

## THE CAPTIVE FLESH
### Cleo Cordell

Marietta and Claudine, French aristocrats saved from pirates, learn their invitation to stay at the opulent Algerian mansion of their rescuer, Kasim, requires something in return; their complete surrender to the ecstasy of pleasure in pain. Kasim's decadent orgies also require the services of the handsome blonde slave, Gabriel – perfect in his male beauty. Together in their slavery, they savour delights at the depths of shame.

ISBN 0 352 32872 X

## PLEASURE HUNT
### Sophie Danson

Sexual adventurer Olympia Deschamps is determined to become a member of the Legion D'Amour – the most exclusive society of French libertines who pride themselves on their capacity for limitless erotic pleasure. Set in Paris – Europe's most romantic city – Olympia's sense of unbridled hedonism finds release in an extraordinary variety of libidinous challenges.

ISBN 0 352 32880 0

## ODALISQUE
### Fleur Reynolds

A tale of family intrigue and depravity set against the glittering backdrop of the designer set. Auralie and Jeanine are cousins, both young, glamorous and wealthy. Catering to the business classes with their design consultancy and exclusive hotel, this facade of respectability conceals a reality of bitter rivalry and unnatural love.

ISBN 0 352 32887 8

## OUTLAW LOVER
### Saskia Hope

Fee Cambridge lives in an upper level deluxe pleasuredome of technologically advanced comfort. The pirates live in the harsh outer reaches of the decaying 21st century city where lawlessness abounds in a sexual underworld. Bored with her predictable husband and pampered lifestyle, Fee ventures into the wild side of town, finding an urban outlaw who becomes her lover. Leading a double life of piracy and privilege, will her taste for adventure get her too deep into danger?

ISBN 0 352 32909 2

# AVALON NIGHTS
## Sophie Danson

On a stormy night in Camelot, a shape-shifting sorceress weaves a potent spell. Enthralled by her magical powers, each knight of the Round Table – King Arthur included – must tell the tale of his most lustful conquest. Virtuous knights, brave and true, recount before the gathering ribald deeds more befitting licentious knaves. Before the evening is done, the sorceress must complete a mystic quest for the grail of ultimate pleasure.

ISBN 0 352 32910 6

# THE SENSES BEJEWELLED
## Cleo Cordell

Willing captives Marietta and Claudine are settling into an opulent life at Kasim's harem. But 18th century Algeria can be a hostile place. When the women are kidnapped by Kasim's sworn enemy, they face indignities that will test the boundaries of erotic experience. Marietta is reunited with her slave lover Gabriel, whose heart she previously broke. Will Kasim win back his cherished concubines? This is the sequel to *The Captive Flesh*.

ISBN 0 352 32904 1

# GEMINI HEAT
## Portia Da Costa

As the metropolis sizzles in freak early summer temperatures, twin sisters Deana and Delia find themselves cooking up a heatwave of their own. Jackson de Guile, master of power dynamics and wealthy connoisseur of fine things, draws them both into a web of luxuriously decadent debauchery. Sooner or later, one of them has to make a life-changing decision.

ISBN 0 352 32912 2

# VIRTUOSO
## Katrina Vincenzi

Mika and Serena, darlings of classical music's jet-set, inhabit a world of secluded passion. The reason? Since Mika's tragic accident which put a stop to his meteoric rise to fame as a solo violinist, he cannot face the world, and together they lead a decadent, reclusive existence. But Serena is determined to change things. The potent force of her ravenous sensuality cannot be ignored, as she rekindles Mika's zest for love and life through unexpected means. But together they share a dark secret.

ISBN 0 352 32912 2

## MOON OF DESIRE
### Sophie Danson

When Soraya Chilton is posted to the ancient and mysterious city of Ragzburg on a mission for the Foreign Office, strange things begin to happen to her. Wild, sexual urges overwhelm her at the coming of each full moon. Will her boyfriend, Anton, be her saviour – or her victim? What price will she have to pay to lift the curse of unquenchable lust that courses through her veins?

ISBN 0 352 32911 4

## FIONA'S FATE
### Fredrica Alleyn

When Fiona Sheldon is kidnapped by the infamous Trimarchi brothers, along with her friend Bethany, she finds herself acting in ways her husband Duncan would be shocked by. For it is he who owes the brothers money and is more concerned to free his voluptuous mistress than his shy and quiet wife. Alessandro Trimarchi makes full use of this opportunity to discover the true extent of Fiona's suppressed, but powerful, sexuality.

ISBN 0 352 32913 0

## HANDMAIDEN OF PALMYRA
### Fleur Reynolds

3rd century Palmyra: a lush oasis in the Syrian desert. The beautiful and fiercely independent Samoya takes her place in the temple of Antioch as an apprentice priestess. Decadent bachelor Prince Alif has other plans for her and sends his scheming sister to bring her to his Bacchanalian wedding feast. Embarking on a journey across the desert, Samoya encounters Marcus, the battle-hardened centurion who will unearth the core of her desires and change the course of her destiny.

ISBN 0 352 32919 X

## OUTLAW FANTASY
### Saskia Hope

For Fee Cambridge, playing with fire had become a full time job. Helping her pirate lover to escape his lawless lifestyle had its rewards as well as its drawbacks. On the outer reaches of the 21st century metropolis the Amazenes are on the prowl; fierce warrior women who have some unfinished business with Fee's lover. Will she be able to stop him straying back to the wrong side of the tracks? This is the sequel to *Outlaw Lover*.

ISBN 0 352 32920 3

*Three special, longer length Black Lace summer sizzlers published in June 1994.*

## THE SILKEN CAGE
### Sophie Danson

When University lecturer, Maria Treharne, inherits her aunt's mansion in Cornwall, she finds herself the subject of strange and unexpected attention. Her new dwelling resides on much-prized land; sacred, some would say. Anthony Pendorran has waited a long time for the mistress to arrive at Brackwater Tor. Now she's here, his lust can be quenched as their longing for each other has a hunger beyond the realm of the physical. Using the craft of goddess worship and sexual magnetism, Maria finds allies and foes in this savage and beautiful landscape.

ISBN 0 352 32928 9

## RIVER OF SECRETS
### Saskia Hope & Georgia Angelis

When intrepid female reporter Sydney Johnson takes over someone else's assignment up the Amazon river, the planned exploration seems straightforward enough. But the crew's photographer seems to be keeping some very shady company and the handsome botanist is proving to be a distraction with a difference. Sydney soon realises this mission to find a lost Inca city has a hidden agenda. Everyone is behaving so strangely, so sexually, and the tropical humidity is reaching fever pitch as if a mysterious force is working its magic over the expedition. Echoing with primeval sounds, the jungle holds both dangers and delights for Sydney in this Indiana Jones-esque story of lust and adventure.

ISBN 0 352 32925 4

## VELVET CLAWS
### Cleo Cordell

It's the 19th century; a time of exploration and discovery and young, spirited Gwendoline Farnshawe is determined not to be left behind in the parlour when the handsome and celebrated anthropologist, Jonathan Kimberton, is planning his latest expedition to Africa. Rebelling against Victorian society's expectation of a young woman and lured by the mystery and exotic climate of this exciting continent, Gwendoline sets sail with her entourage bound for a land of unknown pleasures.

ISBN 0 352 32926 2

BLACK
*lace*

# WE NEED YOUR HELP . . .
*to plan the future of women's erotic fiction –*

## – and no stamp required!

Yours are the only opinions that matter.

Black Lace is the first series of books devoted to erotic fiction by women for women.

We intend to keep providing the best-written, sexiest books you can buy. And we'd appreciate your help and valued opinion of the books so far. Tell us what you want to read.

---

# THE BLACK LACE QUESTIONNAIRE

## SECTION ONE: ABOUT YOU

1.1  Sex (*we presume you are female, but so as not to discriminate*)
Are you?

Male ☐
Female ☐

1.2  Age

under 21 ☐          21–30 ☐
31–40 ☐          41–50 ☐
51–60 ☐          over 60 ☐

1.3  At what age did you leave full-time education?

still in education ☐          16 or younger ☐
17–19 ☐          20 or older ☐

1.4  Occupation _____

1.5 Annual household income
  under £10,000 ☐    £10–£20,000 ☐
  £20–£30,000 ☐    £30–£40,000 ☐
  over £40,000 ☐

1.6 We are perfectly happy for you to remain anonymous; but if you would like to receive information on other publications available, please insert your name and address

_____

_____

_____

_____

## SECTION TWO: ABOUT BUYING BLACK LACE BOOKS

2.1 How did you acquire this copy of *The Silken Cage*?
  I bought it myself ☐    My partner bought it ☐
  I borrowed/found it ☐

2.2 How did you find out about Black Lace books?
  I saw them in a shop ☐
  I saw them advertised in a magazine ☐
  I saw the London Underground posters ☐
  I read about them in _____
  Other _____

2.3 Please tick the following statements you agree with:
  I would be less embarrassed about buying Black Lace books if the cover pictures were less explicit ☐
  I think that in general the pictures on Black Lace books are about right ☐
  I think Black Lace cover pictures should be as explicit as possible ☐

2.4 Would you read a Black Lace book in a public place – on a train for instance?
  Yes ☐    No ☐

## SECTION THREE: ABOUT THIS BLACK LACE BOOK

3.1  Do you think the sex content in this book is:
        Too much      □     About right      □
        Not enough    □

3.2  Do you think the writing style in this book is:
        Too unreal/escapist  □    About right      □
        Too down to earth  □

3.3  Do you think the story in this book is:
        Too complicated    □    About right      □
        Too boring/simple  □

3.4  Do you think the cover of this book is:
        Too explicit      □    About right      □
        Not explicit enough  □

Here's a space for any other comments:

## SECTION FOUR: ABOUT OTHER BLACK LACE BOOKS

4.1  How many Black Lace books have you read?      □

4.2  If more than one, which one did you prefer?

4.3  Why?

## SECTION FIVE: ABOUT YOUR IDEAL EROTIC NOVEL

We want to publish the books you want to read – so this is your chance to tell us exactly what your ideal erotic novel would be like.

5.1 Using a scale of 1 to 5 (1 = no interest at all, 5 = your ideal), please rate the following possible settings for an erotic novel:

Medieval/barbarian/sword 'n' sorcery ☐
Renaissance/Elizabethan/Restoration ☐
Victorian/Edwardian ☐
1920s & 1930s – the Jazz Age ☐
Present day ☐
Future/Science Fiction ☐

5.2 Using the same scale of 1 to 5, please rate the following themes you may find in an erotic novel:

Submissive male/dominant female ☐
Submissive female/dominant male ☐
Lesbianism ☐
Bondage/fetishism ☐
Romantic love ☐
Experimental sex e.g. anal/watersports/sex toys ☐
Gay male sex ☐
Group sex ☐

Using the same scale of 1 to 5, please rate the following styles in which an erotic novel could be written:

Realistic, down to earth, set in real life ☐
Escapist fantasy, but just about believable ☐
Completely unreal, impressionistic, dreamlike ☐

5.3 Would you prefer your ideal erotic novel to be written from the viewpoint of the main male characters or the main female characters?

Male ☐ Female ☐
Both ☐

5.4 What would your ideal Black Lace heroine be like? Tick
as many as you like:

| | | | |
|---|---|---|---|
| Dominant | ☐ | Glamorous | ☐ |
| Extroverted | ☐ | Contemporary | ☐ |
| Independent | ☐ | Bisexual | ☐ |
| Adventurous | ☐ | Naive | ☐ |
| Intellectual | ☐ | Introverted | ☐ |
| Professional | ☐ | Kinky | ☐ |
| Submissive | ☐ | Anything else? | ☐ |
| Ordinary | ☐ | _____ | |

5.5 What would your ideal male lead character be like?
Again, tick as many as you like:

| | | | |
|---|---|---|---|
| Rugged | ☐ | | |
| Athletic | ☐ | Caring | ☐ |
| Sophisticated | ☐ | Cruel | ☐ |
| Retiring | ☐ | Debonair | ☐ |
| Outdoor-type | ☐ | Naive | ☐ |
| Executive-type | ☐ | Intellectual | ☐ |
| Ordinary | ☐ | Professional | ☐ |
| Kinky | ☐ | Romantic | ☐ |
| Hunky | ☐ | | |
| Sexually dominant | ☐ | Anything else? | ☐ |
| Sexually submissive | ☐ | _____ | |

5.6 Is there one particular setting or subject matter that your
ideal erotic novel would contain?

_____

## SECTION SIX: LAST WORDS

6.1 What do you like best about Black Lace books?

_____

6.2 What do you most dislike about Black Lace books?

_____

6.3 In what way, if any, would you like to change Black
Lace covers?

_____

6.4   Here's a space for any other comments:

_____
_____
_____
_____

*Thank you for completing this questionnaire. Now tear it out of the book – carefully! – put it in an envelope and send it to:*

**Black Lace**
**FREEPOST**
**London**
**W10 5BR**

*No stamp is required if you are resident in the U.K.*